A FATE SO COLD

Also by Amanda Foody and C. L. Herman

ALL OF US VILLAINS DUOLOGY
All of Us Villains
All of Our Demise

A Fate So Cold

Amanda Foody
and
C. L. Herman

First published in Great Britain in 2025 by Gollancz
an imprint of The Orion Publishing Group Ltd
Carmelite House, 50 Victoria Embankment
London EC4Y 0DZ

An Hachette UK Company

The authorised representative in the EEA is Hachette Ireland,
8 Castlecourt Centre, Castleknock Road, Castleknock, Dublin 15, D15 XTP3,
Republic of Ireland (email: info@hbgi.ie)

1 3 5 7 9 10 8 6 4 2

Copyright © Amanda Foody and C. L. Herman 2025

The moral rights of Amanda Foody and C. L. Herman to be
identified as the authors of this work have been asserted in
accordance with the Copyright, Designs and Patents Act of 1988.

All rights reserved. No part of this publication may be reproduced,
stored in a retrieval system, or transmitted in any form or by any means,
electronic, mechanical, photocopying, recording, or otherwise,
without the prior permission of both the copyright owner and
the above publisher of this book.

All the characters in this book are fictitious, and any resemblance
to actual persons, living or dead, is purely coincidental.

A CIP catalogue record for this book is
available from the British Library.

ISBN (Hardback) 978 1 399 61215 9
ISBN (Trade Paperback) 978 1 399 61216 6
ISBN (eBook) 978 1 399 61218 0
ISBN (Audio) 978 1 399 61219 7

Printed in Great Britain by Clays Ltd, Elcograph S.p.A

www.gollancz.co.uk

to twenty-two-year-old us:
we're glad you chose each other

A FATE SO COLD

Domenic

SUMMER

Domenic Barrow didn't know if he loved magic enough to die for it.

He trudged through the forest, the glow of his wand so feeble he didn't catch the puddle ahead until his loafer sank deep into mud. But he didn't risk feeding the wand more magic. Already its cheap plywood had begun to splinter, and the grit of its sawdust caked between his fingers, flaking like dead skin. If he'd known the night would require an expedition, he would've packed a spare.

"Would you *please* just tell me where we're going?" he asked.

"You promised to keep an open mind," Hanna said, several paces ahead of him.

"That was before I started to wonder if by 'intervention' you meant dragging me out here to murder me."

"Oh, don't be so dramatic."

"To kidnap me, then?"

"If I'd fancied kidnapping you, you'd already be in the trunk of my car."

Domenic huffed but didn't dispute it. After all, nothing about his flimsy training wand resembled the one she carried. Its pale aspen shaft curled underneath itself like an overgrown fingernail, and the dark knots in the handle looked uncannily like eyes, squinting into the golden radiance of Hanna's enchantment. Whereas his wand's romantic origins began on a conveyor belt, destined only to be drained and discarded—about the furthest thing from real magic, Domenic had always felt—Hanna's was so ancient to be called an artifact, so powerful to be called notorious, so singular that it even bore a name.

Syarthis.

Syarthis was a Living Wand, an everlasting instrument that bonded to a sole wielder until their death, then passed onto successor after successor—an honor students such as Domenic devoted their lives to attaining.

Of the 536 Living Wands in Alderland, only forty-two did not currently bear a wielder. And, so Domenic suspected, those forty-two wands were the subject of his intervention tonight.

"So," Hanna drawled, "how's school going?"

"Spectacular, as always." For the fifth year running, Domenic had clinched the title of dead bottom of his class.

"Mhm. You still holding your breath for that random old magician to keel over?"

"I wouldn't—" He cursed as he stumbled over a tree root. "I wouldn't put it like *that*."

"Well, how would you put it?"

Domenic had never been good at phrasing his thoughts into words. He settled with: "I think Octorion would suit me, is all."

"Then kill him." After a pause, Hanna chuckled. "*Kidding.* Kidding."

Domenic wanted to believe her. And he did—he *did*. But Hanna had changed in the five years since she'd bonded with Syarthis and joined the Magicians Order. Gone was the girl who'd used a faded postcard of Gallamere as a bookmark, who'd insisted their first task upon arrival was hiking up the city's mountainside to compare the sepia skyline to the real view. Now Hanna didn't stop to admire much of anything. Redness tinged her brown eyes from nights spent poring over moldy parchment. Her fair skin had gone ashen. Her nails were bitten to their beds, her lips perpetually scabbed, as if she chewed on them past the point of drawing blood.

Of course, wielding Syarthis would change anyone.

"So is that really your plan, to wait for him to die, then wait another year after that?" Hanna asked. A magician could only bond with a Living Wand on the death day of its previous wielder. So unless a student was present for that wielder's final breath—as Hanna had been—another year needed to lapse before testing whether they were a match.

Domenic cringed as he sank into another puddle. His socks were soaked. "There are worse plans."

"What about Ravfiri? Its vigil is on the twenty-eighth, isn't it?"

"Ravfiri is volatile."

"No, Ravfiri is powerful. Those words don't mean the same thing."

This wasn't the first time Hanna had suggested Ravfiri to Domenic—or Pyrrinisus, or Ulthrax, or Quellbarrow. They were all incredible wands, ones many of his peers dreamed of wielding.

But Domenic wasn't like his peers.

To the young magicians of the Order's academy, Hanna Mayes was the prodigy and Domenic Barrow the enigma. His sightings in class were few and far between, but what he did with his spare time, no one could say. Many considered him lazy. Even more assumed him troubled—not that anyone blamed him for it, of course. And though his disheveled russet hair and exceptionally freckled fair skin weren't handsome in the conventional sense, amid a school obsessed with prestige, he had the unique allure of a bad decision—one that, if you believed the gossip, a great many had made.

Before Domenic could muster a response, the forest ended at a cement tunnel in the base of a cliffside. Ropes crisscrossed its entrance, hung with a sign that warned DANGER–KEEP OUT.

While Hanna ducked beneath it, Domenic asked, "What is this place?"

"You'll see."

"But the sign . . . Are we gonna get in trouble for this?"

"Careful. You wouldn't want to ruin that whole bad-boy thing you've got going on."

"I'm being serious, Hanna."

"So am I. Do you know how hard it is to keep a straight face when I hear what they say about you? The boy who always carried flowers in his pocket, now apparently arguing with his teachers? Sleeping with half his class? Your reputation suits you less than Octorion."

Even if Domenic's persona was exaggerated, he didn't care. Anything was better than the alternative. "Whatever. First you drag me into the woods in the middle of the night. Then you won't tell me anything. And now we're, what, trespassing? Well, I'm done. I only agreed to this because I never see you anymore. And if you *were* ever around, you'd know I'm fine! I don't need your help. I don't need anyone's help."

As he spun to storm off, Hanna seized his wrist and twisted him back around to face her.

"I'm sorry I'm never home anymore," she rasped. "But I worry about you, and—"

"I told you. I'm fine."

"I know you better than that."

He wrenched his hand away. "It's late. I'm going home."

"Wait. *Please*, Dom? For me?"

Domenic's indignation withered, but it didn't die. He leaned against a tree, pressed his head against it until the bark bit into the vulnerable meeting point between neck and skull. It smelled like Summer out here. Real Summer. Like mountain moss and honeysuckle and whispered secrets that misted the humid air. Not at all like the sweating asphalt and exhaust fumes he'd grown used to.

"The City of Magic" was Gallamere's nickname. It didn't live up to it.

"I swear this will all make sense if you just come with me. If you trust me." When Domenic still didn't respond, Hanna rummaged through her pockets until she procured a packet of bubble gum. She slid out two foiled sticks, opening the first for herself and offering the second to him. "Are you really gonna make me kidnap you?"

He snatched it and ripped off the wrapper. He chewed unhappily. "Fine."

They started into the tunnel, the light from their wands shimmering off the damp floor—Syarthis's a blazing gold, Domenic's an artificial, almost fluorescent white. Domenic guessed the tunnel burrowed beneath the city, deep within the mountain. And indeed, within minutes, a passing subway rumbled overhead, like the tossing and turning of a sleeping giant.

Unable to bear the silence, he asked, "How's Pritha?"

Hanna glowered.

"What? You mock my love life and I can't ask about yours?"

"We're not seeing each other anymore," she replied curtly. Domenic was disappointed but not surprised. It wasn't like he was the only one who rarely got to spend time with Hanna.

"I'm sorry."

"Don't be. She made this weird squeaky sound whenever she sneezed. I hated it."

"When did you break up?"

"Oh, about six hours ago. It was mutual. Or, it wasn't at the time, but I'm pissed now, so it feels mutual."

"Hm. Are you sure this is *my* intervention?"

At last, the passage concluded at a metal door. With a flick of Syarthis, mechanisms churned within its lock. It creaked open, revealing a corridor of vaulted ceilings and timeworn stone. Iron sconces burned along the walls with motionless flame—enchantments.

Domenic stifled a noise of alarm as he realized their destination:

the Vault, the very heart of the Magicians Order, housing all Living Wands without a wielder. Never had Domenic known anyone to successfully breach it. After all, it was located thirty floors beneath the Citadel, the Order's headquarters, which itself was a fortress of towers and wrought iron and over four thousand steps. And if physical obstacles weren't enough, the Citadel crawled with magicians at all hours. Magicians who carried wands that could dismantle a pistol faster than it could fire. That could summon a lightning strike on a cloudless day, could disintegrate a person into dust.

Not that Hanna, one of the Order's most influential members, worried about petty things like danger or laws.

I promised her, Domenic reminded himself. *I promised her. I promised—*

"Halt!" a voice called from ahead. "How did you get in here? This area is off-limits!"

Hanna stiffened—she clearly hadn't expected company. Yet as she whirled around, readying Syarthis, it was Domenic who reacted first. He grasped the steady warmth of power in his rib cage, then channeled it into one of the three classes of magic: corporeal magic. A stunning spell blasted out of his wand in a flash of white. The guard cried out as it struck him in the chest, and his unconscious body crumpled to the floor.

Domenic paced wildly, stricken by the guard's appearance, at his own lack of hesitation. "Shit," he gasped. Gravely, he took in the guard's wand fallen at his side. Its elm shaft was contorted and grayed like a sliver of driftwood, striped with saltwater stains. That was no training wand. "I just attacked an Order magician."

Hanna cursed as well, clutching Syarthis against her heart. "Sorry, I didn't think we'd run into . . . It's fine. It'll all be fine. I'll take care of him."

As she started forward, this time, it was Domenic who seized *her* wrist. "'Take care of him'? Are you serious?"

"You got a better idea?"

He didn't.

Muttering under her breath, she shrugged him away and strode toward the guard's body. She crouched, cupping his jaw and resting Syarthis at the corner of his eye. A lone teardrop spilled out, shimmering like a bead of glass—his memory of this encounter. The wand's curved tip unraveled and snatched it faster than a serpent's tongue. When the guard woke, he'd have a new memory of the night entirely.

Though Living Wands could perform all classes of magic, each bore a specialty. Syarthis was the most powerful corporeal wand, famous for its ability to devour and alter even a person's most precious memories. According to Hanna, Syarthis possessed an archive of a thousand years' worth of recollections. And so, while other newly fledged members of the Order maintained the nation's infrastructure or joined the unceasing war against Alderland's deadly winters, Hanna worked as a uniquely specialized historian, exploring Syarthis's hoard the way archeologists might excavate ruins that had gone centuries without human touch. However, she did so under intense supervision. Many of her predecessors had broken their own minds under the immensity of Syarthis's power.

Domenic never doubted that Hanna was brilliant, that she knew her limits.

But she wasn't the only one who worried.

Hanna kicked at the air. "I had it all figured out, I swear. I made arrangements with the guards and everything—the guards who were *supposed* to be here tonight. They promised me they'd—"

"I don't care about them, Hanna. I care about you. My skipping class is one thing, but *you*—sneaking into the Citadel? Bribing guards? Wiping someone's memory like it's nothing? You're so . . . You're so . . ."

"So what, Dom?" Hanna glared up at him. Their shared fame

aside, they'd always made a distinctive pair: Domenic measuring far above six feet even when he slouched, Hanna not close to gracing five even in her bulky boots. Domenic so slender his suspenders were never optional, Hanna soft everywhere but the razored points of her smile. Yet they did have one trait in common—that same fierce, haunted stare. A stare that had seen each other through the worst but refused to see the worst in each other.

"So . . ." His voice caught in his throat.

"No, I want to hear you say it. So *what*?"

He swallowed, wondering if he could finally bring himself to say all the things he buried deep.

"Look," he spoke instead, "I don't care what happens to me. If the Order had the balls to expel me, they would've done it years ago. But if we get caught, what happens to you? What happens to Iseul?"

"We won't get caught," she answered, so cavalierly, so infuriatingly matter-of-fact. But she was probably right. Hanna was a stronger magician than anyone relegated to the Citadel's night shift. And even without a Living Wand, Domenic probably was too. "And Iseul wanted me to talk to you. She—"

"I doubt *this* is what Iseul had in mind."

"All right. Coming here was my idea. But we're both worried about you. Sometimes we wonder . . ."

"Wonder *what*?"

Hanna's tone went hushed and careful. "Wonder if you even want to be a magician."

Domenic flinched. Magic might've nearly killed him once, but he *loved* magic. He'd always loved magic.

"What? Of course I do," he choked. "How could you think that?"

"Because you're eighteen, Dom. You still have time, but if you keep waiting for whatever you deem the perfect wand, you'll miss your window entirely. Is that what you want? To never join the Order? To be a hedge magician for the rest of your life?"

"*No*, obviously. But I'm not like you. I don't want a powerful wand."

"All Living Wands are powerful."

"You know what I mean. I want a Living Wand. I just don't want one like . . ."

He stared at Syarthis.

And, so it always seemed, even clutched in Hanna's hand, Syarthis stared back.

A reel of emotions flickered across Hanna's face. She reluctantly slid her wand into the sheath clipped to her trousers, and the radiating, humid heat of its power diminished. "I get it. Really, I do. But can't you see you're lying to yourself? You're one of the most extraordinary students in your class, even if you've convinced everyone otherwise. You can barely cast a single spell without obliterating your training wands. *Look*."

In the shock of the guard's appearance, Domenic hadn't noticed that his training wand had snapped clean in half, its tip on the ground beside Hanna's boots. He hastily scooped it up and stowed the broken scraps in his pocket. His fingers grazed flowers, still fresh.

"Stop and *listen* to me," Hanna pleaded, making him still. "Winter keeps getting worse year after year. All your classmates, they might be—I don't know—clinging to some delusional sense of security, but *I'm* there in the Council meetings. *I've* seen history firsthand in Syarthis's Archives. And I know what's coming."

There was nothing Alderland feared more than Winter.

Though Summer reigned most of the year, for six brutal weeks, Winter raged, razing towns and claiming hundreds of lives. Even after it ended, to open a window at night was to invite its monsters. To shiver was a sign of bad luck.

It was the duty of magicians to protect the nation. But every century or so, the Winters worsened beyond the capabilities of the Order, triggering a singular existential disaster—a cataclysm. And thus the greatest of the Living Wands would thaw from its icy slumber to Choose a champion to subdue Winter once more.

"Valmordion," Domenic croaked. "You really . . . You really think it'll wake soon?"

A faraway look shrouded Hanna's eyes. She was here and yet she wasn't, reliving some memory that had never been hers.

"Given every cataclysm Syarthis and I have seen," she murmured, "I'm surprised Valmordion hasn't awoken already."

Chills swept down Domenic's spine. "And what does that have to do with me?"

"With the power of a Living Wand, you'd be safe—as safe as any of us can hope to be, at least. But Iseul and I, we also want you to be *happy*. Because the boy I knew in Danmere? He never shut up about all the amazing things he was going to do. He wanted to be a great magician. He wanted to be a hero."

That was a long time ago, Domenic wanted to say, but couldn't. *That was before.*

"I'll admit coming here was drastic," she continued, "but I'm not just doing this for you. The two of us—we promised to join the Order together. And yeah, I bonded with Syarthis young, but it's been *five years*. I didn't think I'd have to wait for you this long. I thought if you saw the wands . . . If you really let yourself imagine what you could have . . . Maybe I wouldn't have to do this all alone." Tears shone in her eyes as she nodded down the hallway. Domenic couldn't remember the last time he'd seen her cry. "The Vault is right around the corner. So will you go with me? Please?"

Domenic grappled with the impossible decision: to disappoint her now, or later. Because even if Hanna's words were true, deep down, he knew nothing would come of tonight. He was broken in a way that couldn't be fixed.

"Sure," he said weakly. "I'll go."

This way, when she realized he'd failed her again, he wouldn't have to see it.

They stepped over the incapacitated guard and rounded the corner, where an archway opened into a silent, vast chamber.

Even peering in, Domenic sensed something ancient about this place, so different from the flashing lights and bustle of the outside world. Sinewy branches had wheedled between the grooves of the stone walls. What few buds sprouted from them, so distant from the surface, reached toward the wands like paupers' hands.

Warmth seeped across Domenic's skin as though cast by sunlight. Living Wands were regarded as instruments of Summer, yet in all his years at the Citadel, never had he felt as much magic as he did in this room.

Hanna held out her hand. An invitation. A plea.

He grasped it.

Together, they wove through the aisles, each labeled with a golden plaque and sheathed in glass. Every Living Wand in Alderland had a place here. And though, as Hanna said, no Living Wand was truly weak, the lesser wands were kept to the front. Domenic's gaze skimmed across empty shelves and locked on a candle several paces ahead, marking an occupied case.

Etheralis, a wand of enchantment, the most common class of magic. Its previous wielder had died only a few months back, so it had yet to develop any signs of neglect. Among the Order, it was considered a personable wand with a flair for whimsy and wonder; its poplar shaft even coiled like a corkscrew. With a pang, Domenic wondered if Etheralis might've once suited him. It certainly didn't now.

In the next row was Praxis, a low-grade corporeal wand. Domenic had tried and failed to bond with it last term. Only two years had passed since its previous wielder had died, and already its unique signs of neglect had begun to show; its normally beige cedar wood had yellowed, and a single leaf had sprouted from its dagger-sharp tip. Practical and reliable, it favored magicians with a proclivity toward discipline, so Domenic wasn't surprised it thought little of him, even if the rejection had stung.

"What are you thinking?" Hanna whispered.

That this isn't helping, he thought. *It hurts.*

"I'm rehearsing my testimony for when we get caught."

She sighed and dropped his hand. "How about I give you a few minutes to yourself? Would that help?"

"Sure."

While she slipped off, Domenic roamed the aisles. The warmth he'd noticed earlier had strengthened into a smothering heat, and he forced down slow, deep breaths. He wasn't in danger, even if his body swore otherwise. And if he had a breakdown here, Hanna would blame herself.

He passed more wands: Firaxi, nicknamed the "Daughter of Sunshine"; Lorth, another nature wand, which was the third and final class of magic; Guinvallah, a defensive asset on a battlefield. Then Domenic began to slow. Deeper within the Vault were the most powerful Living Wands, many of which had gone years, even decades, without a magician to wield them. Ulthrax, which could fell a monster from a hundred yards away. Iberiad, the wand that had single-handedly constructed a town. And in the farthest depths of the chamber, Valmordion. During its last historical appearance, it had dispelled a winterscurge that would've annihilated Alderland's entire eastern coast, sacrificing the life of its magician in the process.

After three more paces, Domenic froze altogether, staring at the few remaining candles that shined ahead.

He'd been wrong—this didn't hurt. This was agony.

This, *this* was the life he was supposed to have. If he could only get over what had happened, he could stop playing this senseless game of waiting for a wand strong enough to satisfy him but weak enough not to terrify him. He could stop disappointing everyone he cared about. He could, maybe, go back to the person he used to be.

But he couldn't. He could only stare at the wands and *want,* want so badly he ached.

"Dom?" He jolted, Hanna's call rousing him as if from a trance. "Come here."

He wiped his eyes and followed her voice into the bowels of the Vault.

With irritation, Domenic realized she stood in front of Ravfiri, the very wand she'd suggested to him outside. The famous enchantment wand was curved like a crescent moon, its rowan wood coated in amber, its magic radiating an immense, ardent warmth. Ravfiri was a wand of spectacle, of heroes.

In its forty-seven years of slumber, tendrils of ivy had woven over it in a stranglehold.

Domenic squeezed his eyes shut. "I already told you no."

Drip.

Drip.

"You're too good for Octorion. Or Welk, or Dyad, or any of the other wands near it."

"I mean, I already knew I was better than Welk. I've got *some* standards, you know."

"Don't be an ass. You *want* Ravfiri. You want it so badly you can't even look at it."

"That doesn't matter."

"Why?"

"Because . . ."

Because it didn't matter what he used to want—what part of him would always want.

He'd already proven he was no hero.

She groaned. "I know how strong Ravfiri is—its wielders were some of the best enchantment magicians the Order ever had. And sure, it's a stubborn wand. It's picky. And it has its dangers, just like all Living Wands. But I looked through Syarthis's memories about it. It's never had an unbonding, and each of its old wielders, they were so . . . *bright*. When they held Ravfiri, its amber lit up, and it was like once you saw them, you couldn't look away. And you . . . I'm not going to give you some bullshit about duty, and I know you hate that everyone knows what happened. But if you just let people look at you, *really* look at you . . ."

Drip.

Drip.

"Do you hear that?" he asked, opening his eyes.

"*Seriously?* I'm begging you to listen to me, and you're not even—"

"No, I mean it. I hear something. It sounds like . . . water."

Domenic couldn't explain why he turned away. Maybe he wasn't brave enough to face her desperation. Or maybe it was the sudden, insistent pain in his chest, like roots squeezing his rib cage. Ignoring Hanna's gawking, he treaded deeper into the Vault. Here, so few lights shined that he couldn't even see where his steps fell.

Drip.

Drip.

When Domenic's pace finally slowed, he wasn't sure if he was breathing, if his heart was beating. For once, his panic was absent. He felt nothing but the heat, as hot as a wildfire.

On the final cabinet against the farthest wall, a puddle pooled. The twin set of torches burning above it rendered Domenic's lanky reflection in a halo of gold.

His gaze dragged up the case to the wand within. Vines twisted around the gnarled white shaft and bristled with thorns, a weapon designed to harm even those who wielded it. At the base of its handle, those vines splayed out as if freshly ripped from the earth, and at its other end, blackness singed its tip. The faint lines that patterned it first appeared like the natural grain of the alban wood, but upon closer inspection, they were fingerprints, documentation of every great magician the wand had ever Chosen.

Encasing it was a hazy sheath of ice.

Melting ice.

Domenic's heartbeat returned painful and all at once.

Valmordion was awakening.

ELLERY

SUMMER

Ellery Caldwell was utterly devastated—not that she ever would've admitted it.

On the surface, she was every inch the model young magician. Her navy uniform blazer and skirt were perfectly pressed, her patent-leather shoes gleamed black, and her training wand peeked out from her satchel, stowed sensibly in its sheath. She tipped her head back, ash-blond waves swinging, and studied the massive calendar in the students' lounge.

The enchantment was gorgeously done, a twenty-foot-high stone wall subdivided into carved panels, one for each day of the year. Each square denoted academy events and future wand vigils in a tidy, businesslike script. At the top fluttered an illusion of the green-and-white Aldrish flag.

Ellery withdrew her training wand and aimed it at Alcoria's sign-up list.

"What are you doing?" Julian Norwood asked.

"What does it look like I'm doing? I'm registering for the next wand vigil."

"But Iberiad's is a week later. And it's much more powerful." Julian cracked his knuckles. "You should wait for it."

"Power isn't everything," Ellery countered. "Alcoria's wielders have consistently made a bigger impact on Aldrish history."

"Yeah, well, either would suit you better than *Welk*." He gestured at today's date on the calendar. A congratulations message flashed alongside it, proclaiming the name of the wand paired with its wielder—some fifth-year Ellery barely knew. For the rest of the month, the message would serve as inspiration for younger students, pressure for older ones, and a constant reminder that by bonding with Welk, the wand's new wielder had officially graduated from the academy to the Magicians Order.

Ellery had tried to bond with it—and failed.

Normal students expected to test several wands before finding a match. But today was the eleventh time she'd failed. And it wasn't normal for Ellery Caldwell, top of her class, to fail at anything.

"Don't spare my feelings," Ellery said.

"I'm not," said Julian. "I'm glad you failed that vigil. You can do better. We both can."

Ellery's hand twinged with phantom pain. She clenched it into a fist. "Careful. Talk too loud and people will say you're cocky."

"People have said that for years. Also, being cocky implies I'm overestimating my abilities. It's not bravado if I can back it up."

"Little do they know, you're so much more arrogant than the rumors suggest," she said affectionately.

He shot her a grin. "Somehow it hasn't stopped you from hanging out with me."

"Well, what would I even do without you?"

"Die of boredom, probably."

"Make better choices, maybe."

"What, like going to bed at eight instead of nine?" Julian nudged her with his elbow. "Someone has to stop you from being so ruthlessly sensible."

"And someone has to stop *you* before your ego makes your head explode."

The child of a brilliant doctor and a prestigious lawyer, Julian Norwood had never doubted his fate was anything less than grand. His lean, muscular frame contained an almost electric energy, his elegant, light brown hands constantly in motion, his eyes dark and glimmering with intensity. He was the last to leave a party and the first to answer a question in class. He liked his coffee boiling hot and his showers freezing cold. Once, he'd broken his own arm just to see if he could heal it correctly.

He hated nothing more than failure. And he wanted nothing more than a Living Wand.

But Ellery didn't just want a Living Wand. She *needed* one. And after so many disappointments, she could no longer afford to let any remotely suitable wand pass her by.

"Iberiad built Portmere," Julian pressed. "It constructed the Gallamere subway."

"Yeah, and the Red Line's been closed for 'construction' since I moved here."

"El, I get why you'd be nervous to wait for a wand. Half our class has either graduated or had their window close. But every wand in the Vault is waiting for a magician like *you*. Someone powerful, someone disciplined, someone well-rounded. You've got your pick, so why pick something mediocre?"

Ellery chewed on her lower lip. She hated letting people down, especially him.

"I suppose the subway could use my help." She slid her training wand from its sheath and focused on the panel for Iberiad's vigil. The panel glowed, indicating that her submission had been received. Vigil sign-ups were anonymous; none of her classmates, not even Julian, knew how many she'd attended. Ellery was determined to keep it that way.

"You think you can single-handedly fix the subway?" he teased. "So you *do* have an ego."

Ellery snorted, tucked her wand away, then strode alongside Julian through the recently renovated students' lounge.

To be accepted at the Order's academy was an incredible honor. The Living Wands, unique to any other country in the world, represented Alderland's greatest source of national pride.

The magicians who wielded them had penned a long history of Aldrish prosperity and independence.

Although the Order didn't actually govern the country, it was a public institution, and it collaborated closely with Parliament while maintaining its own autonomy and traditions. And those traditions held strong. While the rest of the world embraced technological innovation, Alderland still idolized magic, still ardently harbored old superstitions. Only in recent years had that finally begun to change.

Even the Citadel, the very heart of the Order, had begun to modernize. Old wooden tables now stood interspersed with fresh furniture, the crumbling ceiling replaced by a giant skylight. Intricate panes of glass crisscrossed by metal beams allowed sunlight to flood the space.

Some at the Order derided the break from tradition. For a thousand years, Alderland had shaped itself around magicians, not the other way around. But the trappings of modern life thrilled Ellery, the convenience of automobiles and telephones, the spectacles of skyscrapers and movies.

In the lounge's corner, a small alcove made the perfect spot for the Order's favorite prospective magicians to hold court. Ellery sank into an upholstered chair whose feet periodically tapped against the floor, as if impatient. Its plush blue cushions never ripped or sagged, despite its frequent usage. Julian flicked his training wand, and another chair skidded over to join Ellery's. His student lapel pin of the Order insignia, an alban tree, glowed gold at the use of magic.

"I just wish I didn't have to wait so long," he complained as he sat beside her. "Belixor's vigil isn't until halfway through next Summer."

"*You* could go for Iberiad," Ellery pointed out.

"No, I can't." Before Julian had ever held a wand, he'd dreamed of wielding a scalpel. Now his heart was set on both.

His mother was a surgeon whose operation techniques had saved thousands of lives. If he bonded with Belixor and gained access to its corporeal magic, he could expand her work, training as both a healer and a doctor.

"You're really not worried about your window closing?" Ellery asked.

Magicians had a short period of time to pair with a Living Wand, a few precious years when they were strong enough to wield such a powerful instrument, but young enough that their magic could still adapt to bond to it. By twenty-one, that window was almost always closed. Ellery, at nearly nineteen, already felt the pressure. If she failed to secure a Living Wand, she'd spend the rest of her life as a hedge magician, only able to use training wands and ineligible for Order membership.

She touched the pin on her own lapel. If it stopped glowing when she used magic, her window would be shut, her chance at a Living Wand gone.

"It won't happen," Julian said. "And I know how I sound. I really do. I just . . . I know I'm meant for a powerful corporeal wand."

"Julian. Are you seriously about to invoke *destiny*?" Ellery failed to say the word lightheartedly.

Julian leaned forward, his voice fervent, his gaze distant, as though fixed on something she couldn't see. "So what if I am? You're telling me you never think about yours?"

Only one out of every hundred people in Alderland had magic. Science claimed their occurrence to be random, with no correlation to region, family, or circumstance. But Aldrish culture believed otherwise—that to bond with a Living Wand was to assume a destiny.

She shrugged. "All the Wands ultimately have the same destiny, don't they? A duty to serve the country."

Julian examined her carefully. "Sure, but some destinies are still greater than others. And everyone else thinks your destiny must be—"

"Everyone else doesn't know me. Everyone else is convinced I'm . . ." *Perfect.* The word wrapped around her throat like a vise.

By any measure, Ellery Caldwell *was* perfect. A Councilor's protégée, magically gifted, with a rags-to-riches origin story that rivaled any movie heroine. Her beauty, too, seemed conjured straight from the silver screen. Blond finger waves accentuated each delicate feature on her fair, heart-shaped face, her large eyes a distinctive pale blue, her high cheekbones often flushed a rosy pink. She had no shortage of admirers, although if the rumors were to be believed, she'd politely turned each of them down aside from the occasional clandestine kiss.

She was polished to a sheen, poised for a bright future.

What no one seemed to realize was that she'd sculpted herself that way.

Five years prior, an awkward, unqualified girl had arrived at the academy on a wave of unexpected fame. She shouldn't have lasted a month. But she had no home to return to. No other choice. So instead, she became a diligent student, not just of magic but of Aldrish culture. She styled her frizzy hair and invested in an eyeliner pencil. She eradicated all traces of her Northern accent. She absorbed the media her classmates consumed, the jokes they told, the accolades they bragged about. Until at last, Ellery was ready to play her part.

She hadn't known all these years later it would still feel like a performance. Or that the Order would insist she forever play the role that had splashed her name across headlines: a hero.

"What's going on?" Julian asked gently. "Is this still about Welk—"

"It isn't," she said. "I'm fine."

"In the long and storied history of people who've claimed to be fine, not a single one has ever meant it."

"Well, maybe I'm the first."

Julian reached across the space between them, those long, elegant fingers a hair's breadth from hers. He waited for her, a vestigial instinct, a habit Ellery thought they'd broken.

"It doesn't have to be like this," he said seriously. "You can still talk to me. I promise."

Julian was Ellery's closest friend, but the echoes of their romance still lingered. Despite her ending it months ago, despite her wishing it had never happened at all, she still ached to confide in him.

"I-I . . ."

She remembered Welk recoiling from her, splitting open her palm. As though the Living Wand wasn't just wrong for her—it despised her.

She clamped her mouth shut.

Julian tried to hide his hurt, but his gaze dampened, as though something within him had flickered out. Sometimes Ellery forgot that beneath all the bravado and boasting was a boy who just wanted to fix things.

But some things couldn't be fixed.

"There you are!"

Ellery yanked her hand back, relieved, as Demelza Turner hurried toward them.

"I've been looking everywhere for you both." Demelza rummaged in her designer bag, then brandished a packet of paper triumphantly. "I passed!"

To test for each type of wand, a student had to score highly on a corresponding exam. Ellery had aced all three, not that it was helping much.

"Congratulations," Ellery told her.

"Which one?" asked Julian, although his focus hadn't left Ellery.

"Nature magic. I'm throwing a party to celebrate, obviously." Demelza beamed, her hazel eyes aglow. Although exams started early in the morning, her pale cheeks were pink with blush, her lips glossed. Her coiffed curls, dyed a trendy platinum blond even lighter than Ellery's, tumbled down her shoulders as she leaned to put her exam away. "I've already invited everyone else, but you two *must* come along. I won't take no for an answer."

"Of course I'll be there," Ellery said. Like Ellery, Demelza loved the modern trappings of Gallamere life. But unlike Ellery, she'd been born into it. Her parents, a movie star and a producer, were behind some of Ellery's favorite blockbusters. Once this would've left Ellery starstruck, but such prestige was par for the course among the Order's favorite magicians-in-training. They impressed in class and dazzled outside it. They were the children of politicians and celebrities and industry titans. They dreamed of their names on billboards and screens and headlines, and for many, those dreams became reality. The academy's average graduation rate was 40 percent, but for the favorites it was significantly higher.

And Ellery walked among them. For now, anyway.

"Who's everyone else?" Julian asked.

Demelza gestured around the alcove. "My sixth-year study group, the magical design club, that cute boy in Advanced Enchantment Theory . . ."

"So, half the academy," Ellery teased. "Who else passed?"

Before Demelza could answer, the nearest doors slammed open and a group of mostly boys burst in, hollering. They waved their papers in the air, jostling each other hard enough that one slammed into a wall. He bounced off, still grinning.

"Oh, great," Julian muttered. "The NDC groupies finally have their tickets north."

Magicians played numerous roles in Aldrish society, each role influenced by which of the three types of wands they wielded. Enchantment wands were the most common and the most varied, their wielders contributing to everything from infrastructure to art to administration.

Corporeal wands were rare, making the discipline the most

competitive amidst the academy's already brutal culture of competition. Those who did bond with a corporeal wand continued on to specialized healing training.

Last were the nature wands. Half managed Alderland's agricultural production, ensuring endless bountiful harvests.

But of all the roles a magician could play, no profession was more heroic than enlisting in the Nature Defense Corps. Each year, the NDC protected Alderland from winterghasts—mindless, vicious monsters of ice. They were dangerous enough alone, but when they appeared—randomly, without warning—they summoned terrible storms. If left unchecked, winterscurges could freeze rivers in minutes, could entomb entire towns in snow. Although ghasts could show up anywhere, they disproportionately terrorized the colder North. Thankfully, they only spawned during Winter. But those six weeks often seemed more like six months. Alderland feared ghasts nearly as much as they loved Living Wands.

Ellery tensed as the students rushed past, whooping and cheering.

"How many of them do you think have actually been up past Undermere?" Julian asked skeptically.

"Probably none," Ellery muttered.

"Oh, come on now. The NDC's a noble pursuit," Demelza said. "They're so dedicated to keeping us safe."

Julian frowned. "Yeah, or they've got a death wish. There's a reason so many nature wands are in the Vault."

"You want to be great, don't you?" Demelza jabbed at him. "Are you really so different?"

"Oh, I'm different," Julian said. "If I was called to fight for Alderland, I'd do it right. They don't take it seriously."

The NDC attracted a specific type of magician, drawn to glory and adrenaline. Muscles wouldn't do anything to winterghasts—neither would guns, or bombs, or anything that wasn't nature magic. Yet an intense dedication to the gym seemed to be a prerequisite for trying to fight them.

Ellery was pretty sure that if any of them saw an actual winterghast in the flesh, they'd piss themselves.

Demelza sighed. "What about you, Ellery? I mean, you'd obviously suit a nature wand. Don't you ever think about going back up north?"

Julian stiffened. Ellery didn't. She'd been asked repeatedly why she didn't want a nature wand; she was used to answering.

"I think I've fought enough monsters for a lifetime," she said.

Demelza gulped. "Of course. I totally understand."

Ellery didn't dream of glory. Her ambitions were sensible: a predictable enchantment wand that would let her stay in Gallamere, a safe, steady administrative career.

All she had to do was pass a single wand vigil.

An enchanted loudspeaker crackled to life, and a voice rang out through the student lounge.

"Councilor Glynn's called for an assembly. We expect every student to gather in the grove, immediately."

* * *

The Citadel was the oldest district in Gallamere, a fortress perched on the city's mountain like the jewel atop its crown. The grove hid within its labyrinthine stone walls, a small forest at the edge of the cliffs that overlooked the iconic skyline. But today there was no time to admire the view. Ellery hurried to the clearing at the center, already packed with people.

Academy classes averaged fifty students per year, and all of them were here, from the Citadel's newest recruits, barely twelve, to those like Ellery and Julian, who'd passed their qualification exams and were stuck in continued studies until they found Living Wands. Most crammed closely beneath the cloudless Summer sky, but the Order's favorites were a bubble unto themselves. Ellery, Julian, and Demelza joined the rest of them below a juniper tree, murmuring pleasantries to their classmates.

Standing in the sun, surrounded by lush nature, it seemed

impossible Summer could ever fade. Yet when the scythe of Winter fell, it would all wither in an instant, leaves rotten, the earth frozen and dead.

"Did Glynn tell you about this?" Julian asked Ellery, while Demelza slid on a pair of trendy sunglasses.

"No," Ellery whispered. "I would've said."

"Thank you for arriving on such a short notice." As though she'd summoned him, Edgar Glynn appeared before the crowd. He was in his late thirties with prematurely gray hair, fair skin prone to sunburn, and a thinning mustache. Thick spectacles hid his watery brown eyes. His wand, Aetherium, was plain, a simple branch of oak perpetually coated in dust.

But despite Glynn's unassuming demeanor, the respect he carried within the student body silenced everyone immediately. As the Order's Director of Education and Recruitment, he oversaw admissions for the academy and engineered its curriculum. He held the entire grove's future in his hands.

Nerves fluttered in Ellery's stomach as a second figure joined him: Alexander Sharpe. As President of the Magicians Order and the Director of Infrastructure and Administration, he was one of the most influential people in the country. Despite being twice Glynn's age, he towered over him, his imposing frame topped with a shock of white hair, his fair skin carved with deep frown lines. His own wand, Ballathim, was formidable to behold even from a distance, made of gnarled blackthorn and famous for once constructing the Citadel.

"What we're about to tell you is of the utmost importance." As Sharpe spoke, Demelza adjusted her sunglasses. Julian straightened his crooked tie, smoothed back an errant brown coil.

The two men had chosen to stand beneath the massive alban tree in the grove's center, with a trunk so wide Ellery couldn't have wrapped her arms around it. Its wood was stark ivory, its branches tall and twisted. Thin golden leaves spidered between the twigs, so delicate the sun shone through them like windowpanes.

Alban trees only grew in Alderland. They were so rare and revered that most towns and cities had been built around them, keeping them at the heart of Aldrish life. They were radiant beacons of Summer, the only foliage that stayed in bloom year-round, impervious to the change of seasons. The mere sight of one left an ache in Ellery's chest, so she avoided them. She couldn't remember the last time she'd come to the grove on purpose.

"At the Order, we strive to instill in you an understanding of your magic and your potential," said Glynn. "We do our best to prepare you for the responsibilities of a Living Wand and joining in our ancient, proud tradition. *You* are the next generation of magicians, each with a crucial role to play in service of Alderland."

Glynn scanned the crowd. Although Ellery knew he couldn't possibly pick her out from the masses, she felt the force of his gaze anyway. He wanted her to be part of that future almost as much as she did.

"With that in mind, our announcement," Glynn continued. "Valmordion has awoken once more."

Valmordion. *Valmordion.*

The name scorched through Ellery as the crowd broke into gasps and chatter. Julian swore softly, while Demelza let out an awed exhale. Now Ellery understood why they'd made this announcement in the grove. Valmordion was the only wand crafted of alban wood.

In fact, Valmordion had been born from this very alban tree.

"Winter cannot be destroyed, but it *can* be defeated," boomed Sharpe. "In a thousand years, time and again, Valmordion has quelled Winter's storms and annihilated its monsters."

Sharpe left out the darker footnote: although most of

Valmordion's past wielders had survived their cataclysm, its previous Chosen One had died in the process of saving the country, burned alive by the wand's own flames.

"Valmordion is the greatest wand of Summer. Thus, its wielder bears a destiny greater than any other," said Glynn. "They alone have been foretold from birth to thwart Winter's cataclysm. They alone will fulfill the prophecy that will save Alderland. They are our Chosen One, our nation's savior. And they will forever be remembered as a hero."

Hero.

The crowd whispered the word, fervent, nearly reverent.

"Under such extraordinary circumstances," Glynn continued, "we've elected to create an application process for the wand's vigil. Anyone who wishes to submit their candidacy for Valmordion may do so in the next week."

"And for any of you thinking of signing up as a stunt or out of empty arrogance, consider this," Sharpe warned. "While all wand vigils bear a risk of injury, laying a hand on Valmordion poses true danger to those not meant to wield it. Examine your potential, your capabilities, your past. And ask yourself if you truly believe *this* is the path destiny has designed for you."

Hunger gleamed in Julian's eyes, a hunger reflected in Demelza, in every other favorite standing shoulder to shoulder with Ellery.

Yet when Ellery dared peer at the rest of the crowd, their gazes locked on one magician and one magician alone.

Her.

Years of practice kept Ellery's expression unchanged. But deep within her, a secret unfurled, a long-dormant dread rooted in her rib cage. And although it was still Summer, she could've sworn she felt a foreboding chill in her bones.

Alderland needed a hero. But it didn't matter what the rest of the Order believed.

That hero wouldn't—couldn't—be her.

III

Domenic

SUMMER

Domenic slumped into a seat in the back row of a movie theater.

In the four days since sneaking into the Vault, he hadn't attended school. He couldn't bring himself to face his classmates, who were no doubt hedging bets on which of them was the Chosen savior of Alderland.

Meanwhile, the *drip drip* of Valmordion thawing haunted Domenic's every moment of silence. The chills on his arms wouldn't disappear even when he rubbed his skin raw, as if his body was already braced for Winter, a Winter worse than any he'd lived through. In the few hours Hanna or Iseul ever *were* home, their worried stares followed him—and they both had far more important things to worry about.

He could feel himself unraveling.

And so he'd taken himself to the movies.

Despite the theater's location in Gallamere's tourist-clogged downtown, few others had ventured out for the weeknight show. As the lights dimmed and the opening credits rolled, Domenic kicked his loafers up on an empty chair, sipped his cherry soda, and willed himself to relax.

Until a cool draft kissed his neck, and someone claimed the spot several seats to his right.

Domenic startled at the latecomer, one of his own classmates.

Ellery Caldwell.

He sat up abruptly and smoothed his rumpled shirt. Yet Caldwell hadn't noticed him, her gaze fixed on the screen. And despite all his efforts to avoid his classmates, Domenic grasped desperately for something to say. He could nearly hear Hanna's howl of laughter, that he should find himself alone with the very girl he'd been infatuated with for five straight years.

But he was hardly the only student infatuated with Ellery Caldwell. When she entered a room, everyone craned for a glimpse of her, hushed so they could hear her. It wasn't just that she was beautiful, an arresting, dizzying sort of beautiful that made everything around her seem lackluster in comparison. And it wasn't just that she was famous—at thirteen years old, during the fall of Nordmere, she'd slain a winterghast with only a training wand. It was that, from a feeling that ran deeper than gossip or reputation or the insufferable politics of Order favorites, everyone knew that to be in the presence of Ellery Caldwell was to behold someone extraordinary.

From her first day at the academy, Domenic had been enamored by her. She was everything he'd proven not to be.

But before he could conceive of anything remotely clever, the credits ended, and he gave up and turned his attention to the film. Within minutes, he was enthralled. The movie featured his favorite premise: a smalltown boy discovers he has magic. A heroic quest. A femme fatale. A triumphant finale. It was predictable in exactly the way he adored, grand in a way that had always thrilled him, ever since he was a child. Because it didn't matter if the whole country associated his name with tragedy: Domenic Barrow would always crave a happy ending.

Once the movie finished, he rose and stretched. Subtly, he glanced at Caldwell, who stood clutching an empty bag of popcorn and a well-loved purse, its leather crinkled with smile lines.

Now or never, he heard Hanna goad.

"Um, extraordinary times we're living in," he blurted, then immediately cursed himself. Nothing set the mood better than the nation's impending doom.

It took Caldwell longer than he would've liked to place him. "Barrow? What are you doing here?"

"Where would you have expected to find me? The library?"

She peered at the empty chair beside him, as if skeptical of finding him alone. Although the gossip about Domenic might've been exaggerated, it was true he didn't always attend the movies by himself. On several occasions, he and his date had claimed seats in this very row, where no one would notice how little attention they paid to the screen.

Not that such experience proved any help now. He resisted the urge to fiddle with the flowers in his pocket, just to have something to do with his hands.

Caldwell slung her purse over her shoulder. "Sorry . . . What was it you said before?"

Domenic's ego shriveled more by the second. "The times," he repeated weakly.

"Oh. Yeah, history's really in the making, I guess."

Domenic might've known Caldwell's seat in their shared lecture, the names of her friends, the people she'd reportedly kissed at parties. But he didn't *know* her, not really. Yet he was still stunned at her stilted tone. Domenic didn't buy into that destiny bullshit, that the magicians who'd bonded with Valmordion were predetermined from diaperdom. But in his mind, the Chosen One ought to be valiant. Someone with the strength to wield Summer's fire, the selflessness to suit a hero.

If he were a betting man, he would've staked everything on her.

But maybe she, like him, had come to the movies seeking escape.

He changed course. "I mean, a movie about a blandly likable kid who goes from humble schoolboy to the greatest magician in the world? That's unprecedented all right."

Her mouth tilted into something awfully close to a smile.

"Yeah, what a bold new perspective. And the magic—completely accurate. You can really tell how painstakingly they researched."

"I'm floored, actually. Who knew our Order education was so flawed?"

Now she laughed, exposing the gap between her front teeth. It was wider than he'd ever realized, up close. "My favorite part was when the main character used his friend's wand. Can you imagine touching a Living Wand bonded to someone else?"

"How about when he found out both his father and sister were magicians?"

"Right? What family has two magicians in it, let alone three?"

"A surprisingly functional one, considering." Domenic shuddered to imagine either of his parents or older brothers wielding magic. "Actually, *my* favorite part was how he didn't realize he had magic until he was sixteen. I mean, come on. I know the average age is seven, but even before I knew—"

"I knew."

Domenic had never heard anyone echo that before, and he could tell from the curious tilt of her head that she hadn't either.

He warned himself to be careful. Hope was such a painful thing to prune.

"Well, at least this was only a waste of a few dollars," she declared.

"Waste? Now hold on a second. I never said the movie wasn't a masterpiece."

"You're . . . you're serious?"

He deployed one of his rare but effective smiles. "'Course I am. Why bother with the boring details of logic and magical theory when stories like this are so much more—"

"Melodramatic?" She smirked. "Cliché?"

He clutched at his heart. "You're killing me, you know."

"Well, what were you going to say?"

"No, no. It's fine, Caldwell. I'll just spend the rest of tonight licking my wounds."

Tossing up his hands, he spun and stalked down the row. And though she had no choice but to follow—he was closest to the exit—his stomach fluttered as she quickened her pace to catch up to him. Side by side, they exited the theater into the assault of lights and cacophony and crush of bodies that was Mercester Square.

"I have to ask," he said. "If you didn't come to this movie for its *brave* and *groundbreaking* cinematography, why trek all the way out here? There are theaters closer to campus."

"I like Mercester Square."

Domenic swore she was joking. She must be. No Gallamere resident would dare admit such a thing. But whereas he squinted into the glare of the electronic billboards, she seemed to marvel at them, their flashes gleaming across the blue backdrop of her eyes.

"You really mean that, don't you?"

"Huh. Terrible taste in movies but a classic Gallamere snob. I'm not sure you get to be both."

"Oh, it isn't snobbery. I hate all of Gallamere. I just hate Mercester Square the most." Hastily, he added, "Not that I'm trying to be an asshole. But you did just pan my new favorite movie. I've earned a right to fight back."

Caldwell raised a brow coyly. "You won't win."

"Against you? I wouldn't dream of it. But it doesn't mean I'll surrender." He stood needlessly on his tiptoes, making a show of scoping the crowds. "So let me guess . . . Is it the trash? The pigeons? No, wait—it's the traffic, isn't it?"

"No," she said, with an amused sort of exasperation. "It's . . . Look at those storefronts." In a nearby department store window, mannequins waved and curtsied at passersby. Domenic swore one even winked at him. "Or the street performers. How many of our classmates could enchant a whole band?" A musician swished her training wand to and fro like an orchestra conductor, while a hovering violin, flute, and accordion obediently played. Caldwell tossed a few coins into her violin case. Domenic joined her. "Or the subtler enchantments. Signs of every magician who's come to make their mark on the City of Magic."

Domenic still wasn't sure he saw its charm, but he could almost hear it, in the wistful cadence of her voice. "Subtle? I'm gonna need evidence. Because so far as I can tell, nothing about Mercester Square is subtle."

The words were a risk. Certainly, Ellery Caldwell had better things to do on a school night than play tour guide. But if she'd come here for distraction, then she knew his reputation, knew he could give her exactly that. He'd probably give her anything, if she asked.

"I actually spotted one earlier," Caldwell said. "Come on."

She led him to a bus stop across the square. They stepped over the trodden litter to the corner, and it felt tantalizingly private despite being anything but.

Caldwell pointed to a faded piece of graffiti.

Welcome to Gallamere.

A moment later, the words rippled and changed, like a coin plunking into a fountain.

The city is enchanted to meet you.

"I know it's corny," Caldwell said. "But considering how much you loved that movie, I figured—"

"I never said it was corny."

He touched the metal wall, just barely tingling with magic. The enchantment would fade soon, but that only added to its charm. A stand against the inevitable.

"I've never noticed anything like this here before, which is impressive. Mercester Square *is* my closest theater, so I'm here a lot. But I've spotted other enchantments throughout the city. There's this one I sometimes run into on my commute to the Citadel. It's a butterfly, all golden and glittery. It flutters around inside a particular train car on the Gold Line. Sometimes it lands on your fingertip if you hold it out." Technically, Domenic didn't know that to be true, as he'd never seen the butterfly interact with anyone but him. He liked to think it was fond of him. "I'm pretty sure it's permanent, so I've always wondered which Living Wand cast it. Then I wonder why Order magicians aren't leaving enchantments like that all over the city. That's what I'd do, if I had an enchantment wand."

"Pretty sure it's because of, you know, these little things called 'laws.' You can't just go around enchanting public property."

"I'd start with the Citadel," he crusaded on. "Leave my name scrawled in a bathroom stall. *D.B.—Even better than advertised.* Forever immortalized."

Caldwell's laugh escaped with a snort. She covered it with a hasty cough.

"Sorry," Domenic said, though he wasn't. "I shouldn't have said anything. Does that implicate you? Are you my coconspirator now? Damn. All that potential. All those accomplishments. That's a real shame."

She chewed on her lower lip—a gesture Domenic tried not to stare at, especially as he worried he'd committed a fatal error in reminding her of just how little they had in common. But then she declared, "Well, if my fate's already sealed . . . There's a very boring theory book Professor Clark read from every day last semester. What if whenever he opened it, it swore?"

He feigned clutching at pearls. "Caldwell, I am *scandalized*."

"Then I'd do something about those run-down buildings in the back of campus. The ones people only visit to drink or hook up in. You're familiar."

"Hey now." He laughed.

"I'd clear away all the weeds and ivy. Strip the beer-stained floors. Replace the creepy tapestries, the grimy windows—"

"You'd destroy them?" Domenic didn't even need to feign his horror.

"Well, they're not exactly in their prime anymore, are they? Those tapestries are beyond warped. And there's always some enchantment on them so that all the magicians and knights and kings are either flipping people off or mooning—"

"The Hook Up Halls are *historic*."

"They're probably full of mold."

"They have *character*."

"They smell like must and despair."

"Hey now."

Again, Caldwell smirked. And though it might've been his imagination, he swore she inched closer to him.

Their conversation wandered on. Toward every other neglected spot on campus needing a little imagination. Through places in Gallamere that deserved the same. To enchantments of every variety, letter boxes that belched as you fed them envelopes, mirrors that reflected you trying on any possible outfit, cobblestones that squirmed if you stepped on them, streetlamps like lighthouse beacons leading the lost home. As minutes bled into hours, as even Mercester Square's tumult grew drowsy, Domenic learned a lot about Ellery Caldwell he'd never realized. The traces of her Northern accent when she swore. Her encyclopedic knowledge of fashion trends. (The mirror was her idea.) Her uncanny sense of direction. (The lamps were very much his.)

After so long casting Ellery Caldwell as the perfect hero, Domenic was struck by the revelation that Caldwell was, in fact, simply human.

It did nothing to dull his fantasies of her. If anything, they sharpened, like a far-off sight coming into focus.

"So I know I interrupted you earlier, but I can't stop wondering," Caldwell said, now beside him on the grated bench. Though several others had come and gone from the bus stop, Domenic had stopped noticing them. He and Caldwell could be sitting amidst a crowd and he'd still feel they were alone. "How can you, a magician, love a movie with such an unrealistic depiction of magic?"

Domenic warred with himself. Not just because he'd never been good at explaining how he felt. But because if he was honest, she might look at him like all his other classmates—with pity. Or even like his parents—with bewilderment. He'd be devastated to a mortifying degree, if so.

But he never dared fantasize himself in this position, so close to Ellery Caldwell that he could smell her: like crisp air and evergreen. The stakes felt astronomical. Worth risking it all for.

"All right. Honestly?" His leg jittered. "I don't think the movie was that unrealistic. Sure, it made a mess of the details, but it made magic *feel* like magic always has to me. Like something more than any textbook could describe or exam could measure. And I'm not just saying that because I'm no honor student. I know my magic, and it's not rules or theories. It feels deeper than that. It's . . ."

Domenic stopped himself. He was rambling toward nowhere, as always.

"It's instinct," Caldwell finished softly.

"Y-yes." His voice cracked. He was pretty sure he heard his reputation crack along with it.

Her throat bobbed. "My magic feels that way, too."

Then her gaze slipped away, wistful, and Domenic followed it toward the bus stop's corner, where the enchantment had since faded.

Domenic stalked toward the transit map against the far wall and made a show of examining it.

"This is it," he declared. "This is what we'll enchant. This is what we'll start with."

"What, right now? There are still people around."

"Oh, no one's looking. And think about it. Tomorrow, maybe someone will notice it. Some tourist who just got to Gallamere. We can mark all your favorite places. Mine too, even if I haven't got many of them. A guide to the City of Magic, made by two very different magicians."

Domenic waited, wilting. He squeezed the flowers in his pocket.

Finally, he said, "Never mind. I shouldn't have—"

"No. Let's do it."

Caldwell joined him, pressing close—to obscure what they were doing, Domenic reminded himself. They rested the tips of their training wands against the glass. Together, their enchantments flooded the city. Domenic contributed few: a light blinking fervently over the Gallamere Gardens, a butterfly fluttering up and down the Gold Line, a beer bottle tipping over the far corner of the Citadel. Caldwell decorated the map all over: a neon storefront on Chestnut Avenue, arrows pointing out favorite restaurants, a shimmer in the windows of the Gallamere Grand Hotel. At the end, she lit the entire Citadel until it sparkled like a diamond.

It was impressive magic, intricate and dazzlingly—even brazenly—bright. Caldwell admired it breathlessly, the gap in her teeth bared. Domenic was far more captivated staring at her.

He was no longer infatuated with Ellery Caldwell—he was hopelessly smitten.

Mustering his nerve to ask her out to another cinematographic masterpiece—or more daringly, if it was too late to make tonight a double feature—Domenic exited the bus stop and squinted at the movie posters displayed outside the theater. His focus glazed over a comedy, a horror, then snagged onto *Foretold*, the highly anticipated biopic of Valmordion's previous wielder, Alice Rhodes. The poster depicted the leading actress clasping Valmordion before an ominous backdrop of smoke. It was due for release this very Winter.

A coincidence of timing, Domenic was sure.

But Alderland didn't believe in coincidence.

Drip.

Drip.

A question weeded inside him. It escaped before he could pluck it.

"Are you trying for it?"

"What?" Caldwell asked from across the bus stop, still tracing the enchantments with her finger.

"Valmordion."

Immediately, her shoulders stiffened. "No."

"Really? You're not?"

"I'm really not." Then, after a pause: "Are you?"

He bit out a mirthless laugh. "I'm not in search of a grand destiny."

Again, she appraised him. The something dark in her eyes didn't look like pity. At least, that was what he told himself. But his story was every bit as famous as hers—if for opposite reasons. Just because he didn't want to see the truth didn't mean it wasn't there, that it wouldn't always be there. That she was extraordinary.

And he was nothing.

Reflexively, Domenic looked away.

Drip.

Drip.

"It's late. I should get going," he heard himself say. He spun around, frustrated. Not only had he spoiled an opportunity he'd likely never have again, but his mind now strayed back to the exact thoughts he'd fled here to avoid.

Yet as he strode down the sidewalk, a sudden wind tore across the square, so fierce that Domenic grasped onto a trash bin to keep his balance. A shiver coursed through him, violent and bone-deep.

Overhead, the traffic lights flickered.

Domenic whipped around, scanning every shape and shadow for a monster. But that was only his panic fooling him. Unseasonable or not, it was still Summer.

Again, a wind blustered, and its cold seared through the flimsy cotton of his button-up. As other pedestrians ducked toward the buildings for cover, Domenic shielded his eyes with his hand and twisted around to where Caldwell still hovered by the stop, her hair whipping across her face. They locked gazes. Their shock mirrored each other. Their breaths fogged in the air.

Between them, flurries of snow whirled, glittering in the many lights of Mercester Square.

Until, with great groans of failing generators, the bright storefronts blackened. The traffic lights cut out. The headlights of cars sputtered and died.

Domenic staggered toward Caldwell, only a silhouette in the dark.

"Th-this doesn't make sense," he gasped through chattering teeth. "It can't be."

And yet Caldwell looked away from him and followed the direction of the wind. In the lane ahead of them, the snowflakes coalesced into a vortex. Into a form.

"You know what this is, right?" Caldwell whispered. And while Domenic couldn't bring himself to answer, she drew her training wand from her purse. Domenic recognized her expression well, so grim and resolute. He'd seen Hanna wear it once before. "This is a winterghast."

 IV

Ellery

SUMMER

Freezing wind stung Ellery's bare arms and face, threatening to wrench her training wand from her grasp. Cold seeped through her, and a disarming power tugged deep in her chest, faint yet oddly familiar.

Around the square, people bolted from the Winter magic whirling in the street. The ghast within was still half-formed, hunched low and curled in on itself. Fractals of ice circled it in a deadly, impenetrable vortex, snapping into place atop jagged limbs and a crudely arched spine. Its silhouette grew with every heartbeat. They had a minute, maybe less, before the monster finished spawning.

Ellery swore and glanced around. Cars skidded to a halt as their passengers joined the fleeing crowds, leaving behind stagnant vehicles belching exhaust. For seemingly the first time in history, Mercester Square had gone dark. Ellery cast a light and shouldered against the tide of people as she rushed not away from danger, but toward it.

"Wh-what are you doing?" Barrow gasped, stumbling after her. His freckled cheeks and nose already gleamed with frost.

"We have to kill this monster as soon as it wakes. Before it can summon a winterscurge."

"But Gallamere's NDC patrols—"

"Are on leave for Summer. By the time they show up, we'll all be dead."

Winterghasts slaughtered with impunity, not for sustenance, but with a cruel, unceasing violence that could only be stopped by violence in return. And their storms could annihilate countless lives if left unchecked.

Barrow's eyes bulged. "You mean it's up to—to us."

Ellery recognized his fear. After the fall of Nordmere, she knew it well. But when she'd arrived in Gallamere after losing everything, the Order had promised it was safe. No winterghast had breached the city limits in centuries, not since the Thirty Years' Chill.

Until now.

Ellery's own fear crept up inside her, as brutal and paralyzing as the cold. But she'd faced a winterghast before. She could face one again. And based on Barrow's reputation, she'd likely be facing it alone.

No sooner had she pointed her wand at the maelstrom than it burst apart. The fully formed winterghast rose onto its hind legs until it loomed above them, then unsheathed twin sets of claws.

All ghosts bore different animalistic appearances, and this one resembled a mutated bear carved of ice, with a narrow, hideous face and shards bristling like fur down its back. Blue eyes beamed at them like floodlights, and silver Winter magic emanated from its body, casting the abandoned cars and blacked-out buildings in an eerie glow.

Bile rose in Ellery's throat as its jaw unhinged, wide, too wide, revealing rows and rows of razor-sharp teeth.

She readied an attack, but before she could cast it, a powerful burst of nature magic shot at the creature's chest.

Stunned, Ellery twisted around to glimpse Barrow clasping his wand with two hands. Again and again, his spells blasted at the beast, glittering white. The gusts tore a hole through its stomach and the monster roared, flailing back.

Maybe Barrow had more skill than she'd given him credit for. But he'd clearly still skipped some crucial classes.

"Wind will only delay it," she called out. The winterghast

hunched over the curb, its wound already sealing. "Use heat. Light. Fight Winter with Summer, yeah?"

At first, Ellery wasn't sure he'd heard. He only stared, stricken, at the monster. Then Barrow nodded and widened his stance. "Got it."

Together, they pointed their wands at the beast. Ellery thought of warmth and light, sun and flame. But as their fire spells flickered to life, the ghost tipped back its head and let out a deafening howl.

A winterscurge descended.

The snow thickened, and the wind accelerated as the temperature plummeted. Across the square, the neon movie theater marquee groaned and crashed to the ground. Two billboards followed it, while a nearby newsstand blew over, its contents flying into the air. A claustrophobic darkness prickled against Ellery's skin like a tangible force. Streetlights and starlight vanished, smothered by the storm.

Ellery's spell winked out. Something else stirred inside her again, something terribly familiar.

It couldn't be real. It couldn't be.

Beside her, Barrow launched a torrent of flame at the ghost, far larger than hers, but it snuffed out, too.

"It's not working," Barrow croaked. White blisters of frostbite already swelled across his knuckles, and as he gasped, a frozen sheath netted across his lips.

"I know!" Ellery tasted ice with every breath, yet her own skin bore no marks of frostbite. Magic surged in her veins, pushing toward the surface, as though trying to rupture her skin from the inside out. The winterghast roared again, and for a moment, its cry sounded not horrifying, but hypnotic, like a song she'd heard before.

The creature lunged for them.

Ellery and Barrow dove in opposite directions. The ghost's

claws raked across the asphalt where Ellery had just been standing. But as she whirled to face it again, she stumbled, slipped, and fell painfully onto her back. Her vision spun.

"Barrow," she gasped.

On the creature's other side, Barrow had toppled to one knee, his training wand shuddering against the wind. Spell after spell erupted toward the monster, but the ghost recovered from each blow instantly, strengthened by the storm's power.

"I-I can't do this anymore." The frostbite had spidered up Barrow's neck, and his chest heaved as he braced a hand against the ground. His panic seemed a living thing all its own.

Ellery stared at the ice-encrusted chassis of a nearby car, shattered headlights staring out like vacant eyes. They weren't strong enough. They were going to die here. Them and everyone else in Mercester Square.

"I-I'm going to try something, all right?" Ellery rasped. "Be ready."

"Try whatever you want," Barrow choked.

The winterghast lumbered closer. Ellery squeezed her eyes shut, tears freezing before they could trail down her cheeks.

And just as she had back in Nordmere, she stopped fighting her magic.

Instead, she surrendered.

The power within her coalesced, brutally cold, as she desperately fed it into her training wand. And then Ellery *recognized* the winterghast's magic. It was as though its ice coated her own skin, as though its roar was her own voice.

Ellery gathered it all, her magic, her terror, and cast the strongest spell she could.

Instantly, the wind slowed. The cold ebbed, warmth flooding through her until Ellery's cheeks stung not with snow or sleet, but with melted tears.

She opened her eyes.

The winterghast towered over her, utterly still. A fierce

white light shone from her training wand, revealing the creature's fearsome snarl, its fangs perfectly positioned to rip out her throat. Its piercing blue eyes were dulled. Snow hung around her and Barrow, twinkling like constellations, as if they stood within the night sky.

The monster was Winter itself, a brutal horror, the villain of every Aldrish story.

And she'd frozen it.

She scrambled to her feet and cried, "Now!"

Immediately, Barrow pushed himself upright. Sunlight bloomed out of his wand like a flower unfurling, blazing brighter and brighter until it speared through the creature's throat.

The winterghast wailed, thrashing against Ellery's hold. But its sounds weakened as its body began to melt. Its blue eyes winked out like dying stars. Steam hissed into the air as its chest collapsed in on itself, its claws clattering apart until its body crumbled into a heap of slush at their feet.

The storm collapsed alongside it. The winds quelled immediately, frost misting away, snow pattering into a soft rain. It mixed with Ellery's tears and slid down the back of her dress. She scarcely cared, shuddering with relief as the city came back into focus.

The incandescence of Barrow's magic swept across Mercester Square, banishing every last trace of the storm. It illuminated mangled streetlamps and dented cars, smashed windows and scattered trash bins. It shone upon the broken marquee, sparkled in every puddle, every windshield, every shard of glass.

Yet *he* was the brightest shape in Ellery's vision. He rose to his feet, panting but steady. Water streamed down the curve of his brow, the hollows of his throat. He looked valiant. He looked radiant.

A final gust rustled out a death rattle, then stilled.

The winterscurge was gone. The winterghast was slain.

Mercester Square was safe. *Gallamere* was safe.

Barrow lowered his gaze to hers. For several heartbeats, neither of them looked away. Both of their training wands had broken—hers splintered, his snapped clean in half.

The longer Ellery stared at him, the less she recognized the boy whose reputation preceded him for all the wrong reasons, whose tragedy clung to him like a shadow.

Instead, she saw a powerful magician—shaken but still standing.

"Fuck," Barrow said at last.

Ellery swallowed. "Fuck, indeed."

She swayed, and Barrow caught her sleeve. Her entire body trembled, her clothes soaked and freezing. His warm grip melted the frost on her forearm. Steam sizzled through the air.

"Are you okay?" he asked. "Y-you're . . ."

Hollering drowned out the rest of his words. People flooded out of nearby buildings, their voices rising in a boisterous uproar. They pushed open storm shutters. They rushed from within the darkened movie theater and the department stores, from where they'd huddled in alleys.

The crowds were clapping and cheering—for them.

But Ellery couldn't muster any true triumph.

For years, she'd believed her childhood was nothing more than a twisted, unreliable nightmare. Until tonight, when she'd surrendered to the very *thing* she'd convinced herself had never existed at all.

"I'm sorry," she whispered, pulling back.

She turned away from Barrow, from the growing crowd, and fled.

V

DOMENIC

SUMMER

Thirty minutes after Domenic staggered home from Mercester Square, he soaked his blistered, frostbitten hands in the bathroom sink. He couldn't stop shivering.

I told you a cataclysm's coming, Hanna had said that night in the Vault. *And even with Valmordion to save us, we all need to be ready if we're gonna survive it.*

What Domenic's favorite movies about heroes never got right about surviving a disaster was that the whole of you didn't. Pieces of yourself would always remain there, buried amid the other bodies and the wreckage. Because when you desperately, agonizingly clawed your way out, you couldn't carry everything with you.

But he hadn't simply lost pieces—he'd lost almost everything. And he feared if he did survive whatever horror the cataclysm held, nothing of himself would be left at all.

He startled as the front door burst open. Heels clacked from the foyer.

"Dom?" a voice called frantically—Iseul. "Dom, are you home?"

"I'm here." He emerged into the parlor, where Iseul rushed to inspect the ghastly white of his fingertips, the terror still etched on his face.

"It *was* you. I knew it. As soon as we heard, I raced home, and . . . Oh, Dom." She threw her arms around him, and though Domenic still shivered, finally, he was warm. "Are you all right?"

"I'm fine," he answered automatically.

"But you're shaking. And your hands. Come. Sit." She steered him to the sofa, and they both sank into the velvet cushions. Iseul withdrew Calynia from her purse. It was a beautiful wand, its walnut wood laced with perforations as delicate as a butterfly net. Iseul claimed it was her lifeline. It maintained the details of her schedule, attentively handled the combined storm of three untidy magicians under a single roof. Already, its housekeeping enchantments got to work at her arrival. In the kitchen, pots and pans clattered as they set about preparing supper. The candle on the coffee table ignited, smelling soothingly of gardenia.

As Iseul examined his hands, Domenic asked, "What did you hear?"

"The NDC called us as soon as they reached the square. A winterghast in *Summer*! And in Gallamere! It's unprecedented. The only reason it broke through the city's defenses was because we weren't prepared, not off-season. The office—it's already in havoc. Tenney's rushing down from the border of the fallen territory, and Sharpe and the rest of the team are scrambling to draft a statement."

"Shouldn't you be helping them?" As the Director of Public Relations for the Council, Iseul Seong acted as the primary spokesperson of the Magicians Order. Amid the fog of foreboding since Valmordion's awakening, it'd been Iseul reassuring the public each night on the radio or each morning in the papers. And though Iseul never complained, the increased stress of her already stressful job was taking its toll. Purple pooled beneath her dark eyes that not even powder could conceal. Her short gray hair, normally neatly curled, hung limp and flat. And a pallor seeped across her already fair skin.

"I had to make sure you were all right," Iseul answered. "Hanna wanted to come, too, but Glynn needed her to consult Syarthis's Archives about any past unseasonal winterghasts. But maybe I should call her. You haven't developed frostmaul, but corporeal magic isn't Calynia's specialty. . . ."

"No, I don't want to bother her. And I'm not going to the hospital." He couldn't handle more people—not tonight.

Iseul heaved out a breath. "Fine, fine. I'll do my best. But you need to hold still."

But Domenic couldn't stop quivering, and Iseul's brow creased in concentration as she cast Calynia. Gradually, his blisters receded, and pink bloomed across his fingers.

"Thanks." He drew away and wrapped the blankets tighter around himself. "But I don't get it. How did you know I was there?" He'd fled Mercester Square shortly after Caldwell.

"Because of the eyewitness descriptions. Male, slender, fair, very freckled, about six and a half feet tall. How many academy students does that sound like to you?" Her soft laugh wilted into a sigh. "Ellery Caldwell was recognized at the scene, which is no surprise, given how famous she is. But it's only a matter of time before reporters identify you as well, if they haven't already."

Domenic stiffened. He remembered all too well how flocks of reporters used to accost him outside the Citadel, the months he entered and exited this house through the back door.

"But you c-can't . . ." Domenic stammered. "I mean, you can't stop them—?"

"I can't keep your name out of it. I'm sorry. But it won't be like last time. A pair of teenage magicians slaying a winterghast with training wands? Dom, that's incredible. That's—"

"I never would've been able to without Caldwell. She was the one who kept a level head, who told me what to do and helped me do it. She was . . ." He couldn't even think of a word for Caldwell in those moments: her voice clear over the whirling wind, her determination unfaltering even as the world caved in around them. "Yeah, I cast some strong magic. We saved all those people. But I never thought of them—not once. All I was thinking about was getting out of there alive. Because for a few minutes, I really believed I wouldn't. Just like . . ."

He clenched the blankets in his fists. His windpipe felt narrowed to the size of a drinking straw.

"Hey. *Hey.*" Iseul rested her hand atop his. "It's all right. You're safe now. You're home."

Domenic nodded, sucking in shallow breaths. He was safe. He was home.

Six years ago, gossip had flared across the Order after Councilor Seong had volunteered to take in two fledgling magicians. And not just any two, but a thirteen-year-old girl who'd bonded with a notorious wand under the most traumatic of circumstances, and the automotive tycoon's son who'd been the sole other survivor. While most had chalked up her decision to her recent divorce, Domenic and Hanna knew better—Iseul understood how it felt to survive a disaster. When she was a student herself, a classmate had tried to murder her after already killing two of her friends, all to decrease the competition for Calynia, one of Alderland's most powerful enchantment wands.

"I don't get how it could've been me again," Domenic rasped.

"What do you mean?" Iseul asked gently.

"Ever since Valmordion started thawing, all I've been able to think about is what's coming. It doesn't matter if I'm here, at the Gardens . . . I can't stop, like I can feel doom breathing down my neck. And just when I try to do something fun and take my mind off it, what happens? I'm face-to-face with the first fucking winterghast to breach Gallamere in centuries." He laughed darkly and smeared the tears out of his eyes. "All these years, I've been trying to get better—really, I have. I've told myself over and over that what happened was bad luck, and this cataclysm that's about to show up, it won't touch me. But then *this* happens, and it's getting a hell of a lot harder to ignore that voice in my head, you know? The one that keeps reminding me that bad luck finds me. It *always* finds me. And so if this cataclysm could really destroy Alderland, well, even if Alderland survives, there's no way I'm making it out."

"Oh, Dom . . ." Iseul wrapped her arm around his shoulder, and he crumpled against her, so tall he could only rest his chin atop the crown of her head. He felt ridiculous. He felt pathetic.

For nearly a whole minute, neither of them spoke. Domenic stared at the artwork and decorative porcelain on the wall.

"Can I confess something to you, Dom?"

"Sure."

"I'm scared, too. I'm terrified. All these meetings I take about how bad this Winter is expected to be . . . I just want this family to be safe. And Hanna—we both know how proud that girl is, how hard she pushes herself. But it's you I worry about most. What you did tonight was incredible, but without a Living Wand, you're vulnerable. You know that, don't you?"

Shame curdled in Domenic's gut. Iseul had enough burdens without him adding to them.

"You and Hanna win, all right? I'll do it. I'll bond with a Living Wand as soon as possible."

She lurched back from him and frowned. "This has never been about winning. And just because you need a wand doesn't mean we should be hasty about a decision that will define your entire life."

She said "entire life" like it was so substantial. Like Domenic ought to care about a future he could barely fathom beyond tomorrow.

"Sometime soon, I'd like us to talk about wands, just you and me," Iseul continued. "And—"

"We can talk now, if you like."

"You've suffered an ordeal tonight—"

"One of my advisors suggested Hestiel to me." He furiously wiped his face on his sleeve. "Its vigil is in a few weeks."

"That gloomy enchantment wand? No, your advisor doesn't know you."

"There's Octorion."

"Octorion isn't even in the Vault yet. What about Ravfiri?

Its vigil is next month, and Nellow's is the week after. Though if Ravfiri isn't a match, I hesitate to suggest you wait until Guinvallah—"

"Ravfiri is too powerful," Domenic couldn't help but blurt. "And so is Guinvallah."

Iseul's gaze could be surprisingly sharp for someone who so often fussed over the trivial details of his well-being. But it wasn't her tender instincts that had earned the daughter of immigrants and the once-wife of a current director a fellow seat on the Order's Council; it was her cunning.

"Listen to me, Dom. You are an exceptionally talented magician. Even before what you did tonight, I've always known that, no matter your performance in school. And Hanna and I, we love you, and we know what you've lived through. But it kills us to see you torturing yourself. So please, help me understand. Why do you still deny your potential?"

"I'm just afraid, all right?" he snapped. "I know it doesn't make sense. But even if I did want a powerful wand—"

"Do you?" she asked quietly.

"I . . . Of course I do." The confession hurt, like prying a thorn out of his heart. "I've always known I was special, even when I was a kid. And I used to be really proud of it. I used to think that, one day, I was going to be someone extraordinary."

Truthfully, Domenic hadn't just thought it; he'd *known* it, even before he'd developed magic. He'd known it with a deep-down certainty that had never truly disappeared after what had happened, only festered.

"You still could be extraordinary," Iseul murmured.

"No, I *can't*," he hissed, his voice scraped raw. "Because whenever I look at a powerful wand, all I see is . . . is . . ."

"Syarthis."

Domenic suppressed a shudder. He couldn't bring himself to answer. He owed Hanna so much; even a nod would've felt like a betrayal.

Instead, he shoved his hand into his pocket and withdrew the withered dandelions he'd picked that morning from the Gallamere Gardens, their spores fallen and smooshed—countless wishes wasted. He fiddled with their stems anyway, not looking at Iseul.

"What if I'm not ready for a Living Wand?" he whispered.

"I'm sorry. I wish I could give you more time. But the truth is, you might never feel ready. And Winter's cataclysm will come whether we're ready for it or not."

She was right. And Domenic had always known his fixation on Octorion was illogical—of course he had. But he hadn't been prepared for how abruptly his future would shift, how suddenly such weighty decisions would be thrust upon him.

Iseul patted his back. "It's late. You should try to rest." She stood and walked toward the foyer. Obediently, Calynia's enchantments readied for her departure: her heels drifted off the rack, her keys soared into her pocket, and one of the umbrellas prodded her side—there was a chance of rain.

"What? You're leaving already?"

"I only came to check on you, and unfortunately, I have to get back to the Citadel. Will you be all right if I go? Calynia and I will leave the enchantments running."

"Yeah. Yeah, of course."

Again, Iseul scrutinized him, her hand perched on the doorknob. "I know what happened tonight is the last thing you wanted, but I'm proud of you. I hope you're proud of yourself, too."

"I am," Domenic said, for her sake. And as Iseul smiled sadly and left, he tried hard to summon it, pride. But like every other piece of himself he couldn't carry that day, it was lost, and no amount of wishing would bring it back.

# VI

ELLERY

SUMMER

The night after Ellery fought the winterghast, she dreamed of a memory.

An alban tree.

Not the alban in the Citadel grove—the one in Nordmere. As a child, she'd climbed often in its bone-white branches, high enough for the wind to tousle her hair and sting her face. High enough that when she closed her eyes, she could pretend she'd escaped her hometown, that she belonged somewhere, anywhere else.

It was no wonder, then, that this alban tree was where she first did magic.

Ellery had just turned seven, and the world was buried beneath a quilt of snow, the air clear and quiet. When she grasped the lowest branch, silver crept from her fingertips across the trunk, then froze into a shimmering coat of ice. Then the canopy bloomed, flowers unfurling, until a perfect silver plum appeared.

Alban trees did not bear fruit.

Ellery ate it greedily, triumphantly. Juice dribbled down her chin, until only a diamond-shaped pit remained. Even in the dream she remembered the taste of its flesh, tart and crisp.

She'd done magic. She *was* magic. And magic was wonderful.

Then, as always, a different memory invaded.

The snow rumbled, cracking beneath her feet. The gentle flakes whipped into a terrifying barrage. And a winterghast advanced upon her. In the glassy sheen of its ice, she saw her own reflection. Her eyes gleamed a glacial blue.

Ellery woke in a cold sweat to the weak sunrise spilling into her dorm room. She fumbled through her nightstand drawer, pushing aside spare training wands and magazines until she found the alban pit. It was her only memento from childhood. A stubborn reminder of those simple, early days where she'd loved her magic.

Ellery clutched the pit tightly. She tried to draw comfort from the familiar clippings of fashion ads and movie posters adorning the walls, the photographs tacked to the corkboard above her desk. But panic pinned her to her mattress, her breaths sharp and fast.

Something tapped her shoulder. Ellery yelped and jolted up. But it was only an enchanted envelope, flitting impatiently through the air like a bird.

Ellery tucked the pit into her satin pajama pocket and snatched the envelope. It bore no name or address, but the thick, rich paper and wax seal of an alban tree signified that it came from an Order magician.

She tore it open.

Seven o'clock sharp. My office. We have much to discuss.

It wasn't signed. It didn't need to be.

Ellery grimaced and crumpled it into a ball.

* * *

Edgar Glynn's office had belonged to generation after generation of the Order's Directors of Education and Recruitment, each determined to make their mark. The resulting space had become a cornucopia of enchantment magic. A bespelled record player crooned the latest stylings of the Gallamere Philharmonic Orchestra. Paintings offered small windows into other parts of the country, sunlight dancing off the Portmere coast, clouds shifting above the dense forests outside Danmere. An Aldrish flag hung in the corner, rippling in an imaginary breeze. And a special calendar, a twin to the one in the student lounge, kept meticulous track of upcoming vigils.

"Ah, you're finally here." Glynn peered up from a pile of paperwork, sounding harried.

Ellery glanced at the clock—she was early. Frowning, she sank into the familiar leather seat across from his desk. He was surrounded by newspaper clippings and dusty books, along with three mugs of tea: two empty, and one long since gone cold. She could barely make out the photograph of Glynn, his husband, and their toddler amid the mess.

"Did you sleep?" she asked him.

He waved dismissively. "I'll get around to it. Did *you*?"

Ellery grimaced. "I tried."

"I gave you as much time as I could, but I'm afraid I can't hold off any longer. We need to talk about Mercester Square."

He reached for his wand Aetherium and waved it. Dust flecked off its simple oak tip, and the piles atop his desk shuffled until a crisp copy of the *Gallamere Gazette* emerged.

UNSEASONAL WINTERGHAST DEFEATED BY ORDER TRAINEES

Ellery had known this was coming, but that didn't make the words any easier to read. "The whole city must be terrified."

"The Council was up all night ensuring otherwise. Seong has an address planned for Parliament, as well as a public statement promising everyone that this was a terrible fluke. What matters most is that no one was hurt, and everyone's safe now. And, Ellery . . . it's all thanks to you."

It was unusual for an administrator to call a pupil by their first name. But Ellery's relationship with Glynn had always been unusual. When they met, her name was splashed across every headline: the tragic heroine orphaned in Winter's conquest of the fallen territory. Glynn had expected a prodigy who'd slain a winterghast. Instead he found a thirteen-year-old terrified of her own magic.

In more affluent parts of Alderland, all children were tested for magical aptitude. The most talented were fed into a network of prestigious public schools, where they trained for the Citadel's famously difficult entrance exam.

But Ellery had grown up in the rural North, where limited resources meant that few ascended beyond the ranks of hedge magicians. Many fell through the cracks. And Ellery hadn't just fallen—she'd plummeted. Her parents forbid her from being tested for magic. No one ever questioned them.

Yet Glynn, intrigued by her potential, designed her a custom curriculum, intending to train her for a year before she caught up to her peers.

She finished three months later.

Ellery cared for Glynn deeply—she owed everything to him. But he expected more from her than anyone.

"Thank you," she said anxiously, setting down the *Gazette*. "But I didn't fight that monster alone. Barrow and I did it together."

"Right, right, Seong said as much, and of course we're all happy he rose to the occasion. But given your history, I imagine you took the lead."

An unexpected defensiveness flared in her. "Barrow struck the killing blow. He's not who I thought he was."

Ellery had seen plenty of girls indulge in Barrow as a distraction, but he hadn't drowned the world out—instead, for a few hours, he'd made her feel less alone in it.

He'd also seen her bolt after they slayed the winterghast. Ellery tried not to dwell on it.

"Perhaps I've misjudged his capabilities. Regardless, you and Barrow prevented a terrible tragedy at the heart of the country. And yet . . ." Glynn leaned forward intently. The Gallamere Philharmonic Orchestra played on, its steady beat pounding into Ellery's skull. "I still haven't received your application for Valmordion's candidacy."

On some level, Ellery had expected this. Of course she had. The deadline was tomorrow. Everyone else at the academy was all too eager to vie for the grandest of destinies, even Julian, who'd scoffed at the would-be NDC members just days ago. She'd hoped her own lack of an application would be eclipsed by the glare of her peers' ambitions.

How silly that hope had been.

"No, you haven't," she said. "Because I'm not applying."

"What? Why?"

"It's not the right wand for me. I know it. And I'm not going to change my mind."

Glynn's glasses magnified the concern in his eyes. "I hope you don't mean that. Because in light of the unseasonal winterghast attack, the Council's made a decision. It'll be announced later this morning, but I wanted you to hear it from me first: Valmordion's vigil will be held on the final day of Summer, in one week. And it is now mandatory."

Ellery's heartbeat stuttered out of time with the music's rising, swelling strings. "But I-I can't, Glynn. I can't."

"Why not?" He rose from his seat, his gaze a spotlight that seemed to sear her skin. "The country needs you to step up. You could be our Chosen One. The hero we—"

"It happened again."

Glynn blanched, then flicked Aetherium. The music cut off with an abrupt scratch.

"What, exactly, are you saying?" he asked carefully.

Her parents' voices echoed through her mind, their words overlapping through a hundred anguished memories.

Monster, they snarled.

"The things I told you when you first started training me. From before I was at the Order. When I fought that winterghast, its magic felt . . ." *like mine.* She sniffled. "I-I can't go near Valmordion. I can't risk it. Maybe I shouldn't even be at the academy at all."

She stared fixedly at her lap. Silence stretched on, until she felt Glynn's hand on her shoulder. He'd rounded his desk and crouched beside her. He held out a tissue. She took it with a trembling hand.

"Oh, Ellery. I apologize. I should've foreseen this potential complication. It makes sense that being confronted with a winterghast would reopen your old wounds." He regarded her gently. "However, it would be a terrible waste if you let fear break you after you've come so far."

Yet despite what Glynn thought he knew of her fear, no one had ever seen the heart of it. Ellery might've no longer borne external marks of her childhood. But her feelings, her thoughts, even her dreams were threaded with scar tissue.

"May I show you something?" Glynn continued.

Ellery nodded numbly. Glynn rose and pointed Aetherium at the papers on his desk.

Glynn's relationship with Aetherium was proof that when it came to Living Wands, power wasn't everything. Aetherium was a relatively minor enchantment wand, but Glynn had climbed higher in the Order's ranks than anyone had anticipated. Since Aetherium was connected to the enchantments woven within the Citadel, he used it primarily as an administrative assistant, keeping track of student files, wand histories, and recruitment efforts.

A map fluttered to the giant window, then plastered across it. The Gallamere skyline disappeared, replaced by a bird's-eye view of Alderland. The island nation was largely isolated from the rest of the world, a world Ellery would likely never see. For an Order magician, there was simply no point. Living Wands didn't function past the Aldrish border; although other nations had magicians of their own, they relied on other methods for their spellwork.

A marker for each of the alban trees glimmered gold, scattered across the country like fallen stars.

"The Order's most important task is to keep Alderland safe," Glynn said. "Yet Winter worsens every year."

The map changed as he spoke. Color leached from the country's northernmost tip, leaving an entire region of alban trees grayed out.

Ellery's gaze fixed on one of the cities within the region, labeled NORDMERE. A shiver crept down her spine.

Six years ago, Winter had conquered the North, now known as the fallen territory. Within it, the long Summer most of Alderland enjoyed was gone. Instead the land was plagued with endless Winter unlike any endured in centuries—since the single cataclysm a Chosen One had failed to thwart, known as the Thirty Years' Chill. The only people who remained in the fallen territory were too stubborn to leave, clinging to a homeland that no longer existed.

"There are rumors that winterghasts are evolving," Glynn went on. "A select few seem to be capable of executing coordinated attacks."

Ellery stiffened, disturbed. "I thought winterghasts were mindless monsters."

"Not anymore. And we fear that ghast in Gallamere may be just the beginning of their larger strategy." He flicked Aetherium, and the map zoomed in on Gallamere. There was a gap at the city's edge that she'd never noticed before. It wasn't gold or grayed out. It was white. Blank.

"What is that?" she asked.

"There is a second alban tree within the Gallamere city limits."

"Why don't I know about it?"

"Because for generations, the Council has kept it a secret. The tree is dead."

"There's fallen territory *inside Gallamere*?"

"No, not fallen. Destroyed. The alban has been sapped of life, and the land around it is a grave. We call it the Barren because nothing grows there, and even our finest nature magicians can't heal it. Even Valmordion's past wielders failed to restore it."

"B-but there's nothing stronger than Valmordion."

"Not even Valmordion can bring back the dead, I'm afraid." Glynn flicked his wand, and the map rolled up again, revealing the Gallamere skyline once more. "But the trees in the fallen territories *aren't* dead. Not yet, anyway. And as long as they endure, we believe Valmordion's next wielder can find a way to bring them back to Summer. To make Alderland whole again."

All at once, Ellery understood.

"You really think it could be me, don't you?" Her voice quavered. "Th-the Chosen One."

"I do," he said solemnly. "I know you don't like to speak of destiny. But now that Valmordion has thawed, even you must admit that if anyone is meant to wield it, it would be the very student who's already lauded as one of the heroes of Nordmere."

"I . . ." Ellery didn't know how to finish. She didn't know what she believed.

"The way I see it, if you're not meant for Valmordion, it won't Choose you. But if you are, running from your destiny will only draw out this war. So tell me, Ellery. What will *you* choose?"

VII
Domenic
SUMMER

Five years ago, the tragedy of Hanna Mayes and Domenic Barrow unfolded like this.

Flushing, the pair of them scooped up their books and trudged to where they'd been banished to the back of the classroom. The other students snickered as they slumped into their seats.

"What are *you* pouting about?" Hanna hissed at Domenic. "This is your fault for talking too much."

"You were talking back!"

"Because otherwise you never shut up. Not all of us have a rich family as our plan B, you know."

He scoffed—Hanna was fighting dirty. "What do *you* need a plan B for? You're the top of our class."

"Yeah, well, we've only been at the academy for two months." Yet as she ignored him to resume her diligent notetaking, her frown warred with a smile.

For several minutes, Domenic too tried very hard to focus on the lesson—or at least on the rude doodle of their teacher he scribbled vindictively. But even as his fury faded, his eagerness still blazed white hot. Their promised guest would soon arrive.

While their teacher faced the blackboard, Hanna tossed a square of bubble gum across the aisle into Domenic's lap. A peace offering.

He gratefully popped it in his mouth and whispered, "I don't get it. You and I mastered bruise-healing ages ago, but they won't even let us practice it yet! This whole class is just *theory*. I thought the academy was supposed to be hard."

"Not for the 'Danmere Duo,' clearly."

They'd invented the nickname on the train to Gallamere, when they'd spat on each other's hands, shaken them, and solemnly vowed to join the Order together. After all, they were lifelong best friends, both powerful, both brilliant, and the only two students from Danmere to pass the academy's competitive entrance exams. And that was just the beginning, Domenic was sure, because theirs was a great story in the making.

"I bet we'll be the first in our class to get Living Wands," Domenic said. "I bet we'll be the youngest members of the Order ever. What kind of wand do you think you'll bond with? I think I'll bond with an enchantment wand. No, a *nature* wand. But a corporeal wand would be cool, too, I guess. That's what the guest speaker has, right? Do you think he could heal *any* wound? What about reattach a limb? No, a *head*? Maybe if I had a Living Wand, I could—"

"Mr. Barrow, Ms. Mayes, do I need to ask you both to stand outside?" their teacher asked coolly.

Will Haden snorted into his sleeve. Connie Massey twisted around to sneer at them.

Hanna muttered a word Domenic had never dared use before. Then, louder, she answered, "No, ma'am."

Domenic echoed her and slumped lower in his seat.

He sighed, shifting, fidgeting. His attention drifted to the window, to the dappled sunlight winking through the treetops of the grove.

He startled as the door opened, and even as tall and gangly as he was, from the rear of the room, Domenic had to stand to glimpse the newcomer: a stark-looking man, with a ruddy gaze and a wispy comb-over. But far more captivating than the magician was his *wand*.

Syarthis, Domenic thought it was called.

The ugly name suited it; it was an ugly thing, pale and emaciated. Even as the guest introduced himself, Domenic couldn't hear, couldn't quite look away from it. The dark rings in its shaft disturbed him. They looked like eyes, darting back and forth, up and down. As if searching for something.

Until they froze, locked directly on *him*.

Like the wand recognized him, somehow. Like they'd met before.

Hanna smirked. "What's the matter with him? He looks like he's gonna keel over."

Domenic wrenched his focus from the wand to its wielder. Indeed, the magician wore a strangely vacant expression. His face slackened. His mouth sagged ajar.

"Um, sir?" their teacher spoke.

The magician heaved out a strangled gasp. Then, as one, the eyes of both the man and wand rolled back in their sockets. The coiled tip of Syarthis unfurled like a tongue and lashed out in all directions.

"What's happening?" wailed Annie Page in the front row.

"Each of you, stay calm," their teacher snapped, drawing her own wand. "We're going to—"

She exploded in a torrent of red.

Domenic blinked several times, hard and with intention. He touched something undeniably warm and wet and real trickling down his cheek.

In a sudden roar, the windows shattered, and students screamed.

Domenic pressed his forehead against his desk and shielded himself with his arms. When he peeked up, he saw blood: the blood of his teacher splattered across the chalkboard, the ceiling; the blood gushing from the guest magician's eyes and gaping mouth, puddling onto the floor. Students shrieked and shrieked, but no one did anything. They couldn't. Even as the magician crumpled, a terrible pressure and heat emanated from Syarthis, writhing in his limp hand. Domenic cried out as it drilled into his eardrums, his eyelids, his chest. And just as he dropped to the ground, as he swore his skull would crack, he saw things. Terrible things.

Memories.

A reel of shame and embarrassment, things he'd blurted out when he hadn't stopped to think. Every fear he'd ever felt, from the brutal monsters of Winter to his dormitory in the dark. The way his parents looked at him that time he'd wandered home coated in wilderness and burned blistered from the sun, like he mystified him, like he wasn't theirs.

He thoughtlessly kicked out, and pain burst across his back as his chair tumbled onto him. He gasped and opened his eyes, smearing away crimson tears. Five feet away, Kannan Thevar, his roommate, stared at him, his empty stare leaking red.

Domenic shakily pushed himself to all fours. His memories still battered him, all the worse each time he blinked. So he forced himself not to close his eyes. Not as Annie Page collapsed in the center aisle, gory tracks raked down her cheeks from her own fingernails. Not when Connie Massey vomited into her friend's arms. Not even when Will Haden's sobbing abruptly cut out.

Domenic twisted his head to glimpse Hanna, who lay curled in a fetal position. He called to her, and to his relief, she craned up her neck.

But she didn't look at him. Instead, her gaze trailed to the front of the classroom. Domenic followed it, then cringed at the sight of Syarthis—sputtering, jerking, unbonding.

A desperate idea seized him. When the wielder of a Living Wand died, a new magician could succeed them, even on that very same day. And the wielder, so exsanguinated that his gums had shriveled back from his teeth, was certainly dead.

This would be the start of Domenic's great story. He would rise to become the hero. He would save them all.

Yet as he tried to crawl forward, he couldn't. He was paralyzed, aching, petrified. And when he turned to look again at his best friend, for three agonizing seconds, they held each other's stares, and they knew.

Nothing they'd promised was ever going to happen.

Then, as Domenic braced himself to die, Hanna's expression hardened.

Whimpering, she dragged herself forward.

Domenic tried to shout to her, but he couldn't speak. He tried to reach for his training wand in his backpack, but he couldn't move. He could only watch, worthless, as Hanna crawled over each broken body of their classmates, until at last, she grasped the Living Wand around the handle, and she let out a piercing scream.

* * *

The Gardens were Domenic's refuge in Gallamere. Unlike Valley Park, which was flocked with tourists and reeked of days-old garbage and cigarettes, in the Gardens, you could almost forget you were in a city at all. The trees shrouding the pebbled trails obscured the high-rises. The chorused birdsongs and buzzing of honeybees muffled the all-hours din of traffic. And though it didn't compare to the meadows where he'd grown up, when Domenic lay here, cradled in clover and wildflowers, he could almost grasp that feeling—when magic had been nothing but wonder.

"I thought I'd find you here."

Domenic peeked open one eye. Hanna stood over him.

"Guess you've heard," he said blandly.

"Yeah. Glynn told me. Said he scheduled the vigil for the first day of Winter. Thinks that'll make it seem fortuitous or some bullshit."

One of the many reasons Alderland believed Valmordion Chose its wielder from birth: they could bond with the wand at any time after its thawing, regardless of the previous wielder's death day.

Hanna nodded at the dandelions piled atop his stomach. He'd been mindlessly plucking whichever ones were within reach. "You look like a corpse, you know."

"I'm practicing."

Hanna didn't laugh. Instead, she sat on the ground beside him and gazed grimly around the Gardens. They were always crowded as Winter approached, but this year, every wrought-iron bench was occupied, every plot of grass claimed by a picnic blanket. People basked in the sunlight with collars unbuttoned and lips stained red from the last of Summer's fruit. They counted the passing clouds as if counting their blessings.

It would've been a pleasant sight if not for how starkly it contrasted with the rest of Gallamere. Already, salt littered the sidewalks. The supermarket shelves had been gutted clean. Half the windows were boarded, nonessential shops closing for the season. Toilet paper was selling for twice its usual price.

"Syarthis has a collection about Valmordion, you know." Hanna's words were half-garbled as she simultaneously bit at her cuticles. "A whole wing. Goes practically all the way back."

Domenic stifled a cringe, wondering if that was what had filled Hanna's overtime hours these past five days—visiting the bowels of Syarthis's Archives. Domenic had heard rumors it was a ghastly process to watch, but Hanna always spoke about it casually. Maybe that was for his benefit. On more than one occasion, Hanna had come home with blood crusted in her lashes or the veins of her eye sockets bulging like burrowed roots. She always avoided him those nights, her door closed but her light still on. And he, like a coward, never knocked.

"What Valmordion is capable of . . ." Hanna continued. "It's more dangerous than anyone realizes."

Domenic forced a chuckle. "And to think, it'll soon be in the hands of some lousy seventeen-year-old."

Hanna squinted at him as if searching for some detail she hadn't noticed before, some fine print she hadn't read.

"What?" he asked.

"You're not worried it might bond with you?"

He scoffed as he propped himself on his elbows. "I'm more worried about blowing up the moment I lay a finger on it. I'm the last magician that wand will Choose."

"Well, you should hear some of the stuff they're saying about you, since you and Caldwell took on that winterghast. That was . . . pretty incredible, Dom. No one knew you had it—"

"I'm not a hero, no matter what anyone thinks," he snapped. "And I'm pretty sure that's a prerequisite."

With fingers already stained yellow with pollen, Domenic ripped dandelions from the grass, one then three then six of them. Hanna sucked on her bleeding nail bed. And before Domenic even uttered another word, her face crumpled. Like she already knew what he was going to say.

The two of us—we promised to join the Order together.

Thoughtlessly, he blurted, "After Valmordion's vigil, I'm gonna try to bond with Ravfiri. And if it doesn't work out, I'll try for Guinvallah, too."

Hanna smiled, wide and goofy. "Yeah?"

"I . . . Yeah."

That same dread ached within him, the roots squeezing over his heart. But as Domenic anxiously twisted a dandelion between two fingers, he realized he'd meant what he said. The only thing he loved more than magic was her.

Still grinning, she lay beside him and fished out a packet of bubble gum from her pocket. She flung a piece onto his stomach. "You know my barista this morning gave me a whole earful about destiny?"

He snorted as he unwrapped his piece. He and Hanna were seemingly the only people in Alderland who thought destiny was bullshit. "Really?"

"Oh yeah. He saw my Order pin and went off. Asked me what I thought about Valmordion. If I had any guesses who the

Chosen One was. I think I offended him when I said I pitied whoever the poor kid would be."

Domenic had been so preoccupied with his own possible demise that he hadn't given much thought to his fellow classmates. Truthfully, he hated most of them—their obsession with status, with gossip. And maybe it was childish, but even if Domenic didn't believe Valmordion's wielder had been *Chosen,* he still thought they should be someone gallant, someone strong, someone noble. And he could only think of one candidate who matched that description.

But he refused to wish that fate upon Caldwell. No matter how direly Alderland needed a hero, he struggled to wish that upon anyone who didn't want it.

Pained, Domenic lay back down and shakily breathed in the last remnants of Summertime. And though it didn't catch his notice, as he sighed, every tree, every flower, every blade of grass rustled. As though attuned to him. As though in a bow.

VIII
Ellery
Summer

Ellery arrived at the waiting room outside Valmordion's vigil chamber exactly on time. Tapestries of illustrious wands throughout Order history hung upon the rough-hewn stone walls. Unlike their frayed brethren stranded elsewhere on campus, these were meticulously enchanted to move like images on-screen. Magicians coaxed crops from arid ground, healed the sick, constructed Gallamere.

Students bustled everywhere, looking for their seats among the rows of wooden chairs. A nervous excitement hovered in the room, buoyed by whispers that increased the moment Ellery stepped inside.

"I heard she didn't even have a scratch on her after the winterghast attack."

"I don't get why she's not going first."

"I don't buy that Barrow helped. Who wants to bet he doesn't even show up?"

Although Ellery outwardly ignored them, internally, she was coiled tight as a spring. She reached into her pocket and clutched the alban pit.

It was the last day of Summer.

By the time Winter fell at dusk, Alderland would have its hero. Candidates would take their turn at bonding with Valmordion based on age and grade level. Ellery was among the first fifty. If all of them failed, another fifty would be brought forth—until Valmordion finally Chose a wielder.

A ray of warmth brushed her cheek, like sun streaming through a window. Ellery turned as a lanky form ducked through the door. He scanned the room as if assessing a battleground.

Their eyes locked.

Since Mercester Square, Ellery assumed she'd exaggerated the intensity of Barrow's stare in her memories. Now she realized she'd diminished it.

Before she could overthink it, she strode toward him. The surrounding whispers crescendoed.

"Barrow." She was surprised by how calm she sounded.

"Caldwell," he said cautiously, leaning in close so as not to be overheard.

Over the last week, Ellery had been besieged by unwanted attention while he lay low. She'd considered trying to contact him, but given his absence from class, she'd suspected he didn't want to hear from her. And now, although *she'd* approached *him,* she didn't know what to say.

"How are you feeling?" It was a pointless question—of course they both felt terrible.

"Out of my fucking mind," he said flatly. "*This* is why I've been avoiding this place. Because they all just look at us like . . ."

"Like they expect something."

"Yeah, that you'll spare them all this nightmare, and that I'll—I don't know—collapse. Something dramatic." He shoved his hands into his pockets, slouching as if vainly trying to make himself small. "Let's hope we both disappoint them, then."

Ellery let out a surprised snort. Surprised he could joke during such a serious moment. Surprised by how good it felt to laugh. Surprised that not only had he remembered she didn't want this, he hadn't questioned her choice.

"I've never wanted to be a disappointment before," she drawled.

He grinned. "Ah, a first timer. Care if I offer you some advice?"

"Only if it's good advice."

"Well, contrary to popular opinion, disappointing doesn't hurt so much the first time. But the third time? The tenth? However long it takes that they come to expect it?" His smile widened even as it dimmed. "That's the one that stings."

As Ellery grasped for a response that didn't sound like a platitude, he blurted, "I should find my seat before, you know, the swooning sets in. I'll see you, then?"

"Uh, yeah. Good luck?"

Barrow hurried off, leaving Ellery to stare awkwardly after him.

Then she sighted Demelza and Julian among the magicians shamelessly gawking. She joined them by her assigned seat. Ellery was slotted eighth—directly behind Julian, in the midst of the Order favorites. She suspected she wasn't ahead of him because of her tearful conversation with Glynn, although the rumor mill had run wild with their own explanations. Barrow, by contrast, was the final magician in their class.

Ellery sank into her chair. Demelza, a grade year behind, was seated several rows back, but hovered beside her and Julian anyway. Since the announcement of the vigil, the three of them had agreed not to discuss Valmordion. But she knew they both wanted it, especially Julian.

"Well, now I get it," Demelza murmured to her.

"Get what?"

"Why so many people think you and Barrow were on a date before you fought the winterghast."

"We're at Valmordion's wand vigil," Ellery hissed, "and you want to talk about my love life?"

"Only if there's something to talk about."

"There isn't."

"Of course there isn't," Julian said pointedly. "Ellery's sworn off dating."

"But you *were* at the movies at the same time," Demelza said.

"Alone," Ellery countered. "It was a coincidence."

A loaded word—Alderland didn't believe in coincidences. Neither did Ellery's friends.

"Look, we all know you don't kiss and tell," Demelza said. "But if you *did* . . . I'm just curious: did he live up to his reputation?"

Ellery's mind unhelpfully conjured an image of Barrow's full lips, slightly parted. She flushed. Julian cracked his knuckles ferociously.

"Here's the entire sordid story," she said coolly. "We ran into each other after the film. We had a casual conversation. Then we fought the winterghast, which as you both know is *famously* an aphrodisiac."

Demelza coughed to hide a laugh. Even Julian chuckled, his shoulders relaxed. But Ellery still felt the color in her cheeks.

"Attention, everyone," called Glynn from the doorway. "Good afternoon. Please, take your seats."

Demelza gave Ellery and Julian quick hugs, mouthed *good luck,* and hurried off to her own seat.

"I'll be your proctor for today's vigil," Glynn continued. Proctor duty was typically a task for lesser magicians, not Councilors. But of course, this was no lesser wand vigil.

He scanned the room until he found Ellery. His gaze was even more expectant than her classmates'.

If there's something wrong with my magic, Valmordion won't Choose me.

If Ellery repeated it enough times, she could almost believe it.

"But before we begin, I'd like to remind you of our security rules." Glynn opened his jacket and pulled out a small bouquet of training wands. "Each of these were confiscated from a student before they entered this room, all of whom conveniently 'forgot' that training wands are expressly forbidden from vigils."

Training wands weren't allowed in vigils to prevent sabotage. Decades ago, before widespread reform, it wasn't unheard of for students to attack fellow classmates to reduce competition for prestigious Living Wands.

"Inside the vigil chamber," Glynn continued, "are some of the most important people in Alderland. Right now, you are all potential Chosen Ones and you will behave accordingly. You will remain quiet and undisruptive until it is your turn. If your attempt to bond with Valmordion ends unsuccessfully, you will peacefully depart the premises. There will be no second chances, no loitering, and no complaints. Understood?"

Some of the crowd responded with eager assent, while others stared at their laps or worried at their cuticles. Their anticipation was its own kind of magic, a promise that something momentous was about to happen. Something extraordinary. Something that would one day merit its own piece of Citadel artwork.

"Excellent," said Glynn. "Now, if the first candidate would follow me?"

The academy's oldest magician rose warily to his feet. As soon as the vigil chamber's ornate wooden door shut behind him and Glynn, the whispers resumed.

Again, Ellery clutched the alban pit in her pocket.

After what could've been seconds or minutes, the door opened again, and Glynn returned, face impassive.

"Tej Kumar?" he called.

The second magician disappeared into the vigil chamber. Five remained between Ellery and Valmordion.

Despite already being seated next to her, Julian leaned closer until their shoulders brushed. "Are you nervous, El?"

"Aren't you?" Ellery muttered. "Everyone else is."

"Actually, they're not. Because everyone in this room thinks it's you."

Ellery shifted away. "We agreed we wouldn't talk about this."

The room silenced while Glynn escorted candidate three off to the vigil. But as soon as they left, Julian rounded on her again.

"I know what we agreed," he said. "And I tried, but I can't

stop wondering . . . Why am I testing for Valmordion before you are?"

"It's not like you to question your accomplishments." Ellery attempted to sound teasing, but her words came out stilted.

"Oh, I know I'm qualified. But you're the name in the headlines. You have the grades. The history. You should be going for that wand before me. Hell, you should be going before everyone."

Ellery's chest clenched. "Julian—"

They paused again as Glynn fetched candidate number four.

"The only thing I can think of," Julian hissed, "is that you don't want it. And I can't figure out why."

"Why I wouldn't want to be single-handedly responsible for the fate of the country? Or a wand that burned its last wielder alive?"

"Those are good reasons, but they're not *your* reasons," he countered. "Not all of them, anyway."

Ellery winced. "Don't push me. Not right now."

"I try not to. I've tried for years. I know you're private. But we're supposed to be best friends. You know everything about me, good, bad, embarrassing. And lately, I . . ." His voice dropped even lower. "I feel like I don't know you anymore."

Ellery could admit that things had frayed between her and Julian since she'd broken up with him. But she still wasn't prepared for him to force the subject. Especially here. Especially now.

"But . . . but you know me better than anyone. And this is the worst possible time to ask me about—"

"Is it?" He caught her gaze, his expression imploring. "Whenever I try, you deflect. You deny. And I just wish we could go back to how it was. Before we ever—"

"That's what I'm trying to do!"

"Except you're not. You just keep pushing me away. And maybe you're fine pretending otherwise, but I want to fix whatever's going on with you."

But she was no hangover or headache, easily mended by a

training wand or a tender word. Ellery squeezed the alban pit so hard, it stabbed into her palm.

"It was never about us," she murmured, then rubbed at her eyes. "So please. Leave this alone."

Julian sighed in surrender and turned away from her. "If that's what you want."

Ellery watched miserably as candidate number five filed out. Only three people remained between her and Valmordion.

A scream rang out from beyond the wall, followed by muffled commotion. Several students lurched to their feet; others stiffened. Ellery thought anxiously of the fifth candidate—a nineteen-year-old who'd smuggled wine into last year's Winter solstice party.

Glynn returned, ash dusting his jacket. "Do not be alarmed," he said, sounding harried. "I'll return for the next candidate as soon as possible."

"What happened to her?" Ellery demanded. "Is she all right?"

Glynn didn't make eye contact. "She'll be fine."

He slipped away before anyone could get another question out. But the mood in the room had changed. Ellery's classmates fretted to their neighbors. Some fiddled with their clothes or hair.

Candidate six left the room, but when no sound came from beyond the walls, the room's tension began to subside.

At last, it was Julian's turn. Once he rose, he spun around and studied her. The last five years hung between them, and Ellery felt something crack, then crumble, as the moments ticked by, as the right words didn't come.

Ellery bowed her head, defeated, as he disappeared into the vigil chamber.

She tried to focus on what it would mean if Valmordion Chose Julian. He could be an excellent hero. And selfishly, if he bonded with Valmordion, it would mean she hadn't.

A gigantic burst of heat exploded from the vigil chamber.

Smoke billowed beneath the door. Then it flung open, crashing wildly into the wall.

Julian stood at the threshold, screaming and coated in flames.

Ellery cried out as he collapsed. She leapt up and reached for her training wand, but it wasn't there.

She couldn't help him.

People shrieked and scattered, overturning chairs as they stampeded for the exit. A dark haze suffocated the room, rendering students into silhouettes. Healers charged through the smoke.

"Everyone out!" one of them hollered. But Ellery froze. She couldn't leave him.

Two healers knelt beside Julian as he thrashed upon the ground, flames still flaring across his clothes. He wailed, the sound so raw he scarcely sounded human. Healing magic surrounded him, a golden, shimmering mist that hovered over his skin. But even as his burns closed, the flames smoldered as fiercely as ever.

"Why haven't you put the flames out?" a healer snapped at her nearby colleague.

"I can't," he hissed back.

Horror surged in Ellery as Julian clawed at his face with blistered fingers.

Glynn rushed up beside her, panting. "Ellery! Get out! *Go!*"

But it didn't matter that Valmordion's magic was greater than any Ellery had ever felt. That these magicians had Living Wands and she didn't.

Her fear dulled, replaced by something else, something stronger.

"The training wands," she gasped. "Give them to me."

Glynn hesitated, then pulled them from his jacket. She snatched them and lunged toward Julian.

Healers shouted protests, but she ignored them as she crouched beside her best friend. One of his eyes was swollen shut; the corner of his lip had ripped away, revealing bloodied teeth and jaw. The fabric of his academy uniform was melded gruesomely into his flesh. The heat was nearly unbearable, as was the smell, hot and thick as tar. His wand hand, the hand that had grasped Valmordion, was charred nearly to the bone. Ellery forced her nausea down.

"It's me," she choked, unsure if he could hear her. Tears trailed down her face; her eyes stung from the fumes. "I'll fix this. I-I'll try."

She summoned a torrent of water to douse the flames. But almost immediately, it hissed into steam. Her first training wand splintered, yet she grasped the second, undeterred.

Memories flashed in her: time after time when Julian had healed her. Paper cuts and bruises. A sprained ankle. His hand on her wrist as he traced his wand along her lifeline.

Ellery poured everything she'd been unable to say into her spell. He'd always wanted more from her than she could give. But she could give Julian her magic now, as much as she could manage.

Until at last, the flames dimmed, then sputtered out. Ellery dropped the fragments of her final training wand and stared at Julian, stunned. Someone seized her shoulder, and she turned, panting.

"How did you . . . ?" The Order healer gawked. "Never mind. We'll take it from here."

Ellery shrank away as the healers closed ranks again. Their golden mist shimmered, thicker than before. Julian's screams faded as he lapsed into unconsciousness.

The adrenaline that had carried Ellery this far ebbed, replaced by a numb exhaustion. Glynn reappeared and took her gently by the arm. He spoke, but she couldn't make out his words. She let him lead her to a chair.

Time passed. Ellery didn't know how much. The others hauled Julian out on a stretcher, still cocooned in light.

Ellery wanted to go with him, but Glynn softly dissuaded her. He helped other magicians repair the damage done to the room. Someone conjured an artificial scent to drown out the smoke. It didn't do much. Finally, one of the healers returned, then murmured something to Glynn.

"Norwood is stable," he told Ellery. "They cannot promise a full recovery. It's too soon for that."

"B-but he'll make it?"

"He'll make it."

Relief lanced through Ellery's shock. Tears trickled down her cheeks.

"We've told the other students to leave if they wish," Glynn continued. "We won't force anyone to forfeit their life for Valmordion. I know after everything I've put on you, you might feel as though you have no other choice. But you do. Of course you do."

You should be going for that wand before me, Julian had said. *Hell, you should be going before everyone.*

"I won't run," Ellery said vehemently.

"I thought you might say that." Glynn sounded proud, yet there was a tinge of mournfulness to his words.

Gradually, students returned, solemn as attendees at a funeral. Around a third didn't return at all.

Demelza was among those who did, alongside the other Order favorites. Barrow slipped in last and slouched low in his seat. Other students seemed surprised that he'd come back, but Ellery wasn't surprised at all.

Ellery walked to the front of the waiting room. Her hair was frizzed. She smelled of death and charred flesh. People gaped at her soot-stained clothes, but she scarcely cared. She pushed the door open.

It was her turn.

The vigil chamber was located deep within the belly of the Citadel, adjacent to the Vault. Its high, arched ceilings had been fortified, and its tiled floor and drains made for easy clean-up should a magician's attempt to claim a wand go brutally astray. Ellery had entered it eleven times before, and on each occasion, the rows of observation benches—all shielded behind enchanted glass—had been virtually empty save for the vigil's proctor.

Today, every important magician she could name was packed inside. So were members of Parliament and industry bigwigs. The Prime Minister herself sat front and center.

The chamber was swelteringly humid. Scorch marks marred the floor, and crimson pooled around the drain. The rank of ash permeated the air.

All because of the infamous, legendary Living Wand atop the pedestal in the room's center.

What struck Ellery first was its ugliness. The white alban wood had never been less appealing to her. Below the wand's handle, roots hung limply like clumps of burned hair, its thorns bloodied from the candidates before her.

She reached for it without hesitation.

Immediately, she was struck by a sense of *wrongness*. The thorns bit into her palm, and heat flared up her arm and through her chest, toward her heart. She staggered backward, trying frantically to uncurl her hand from the hilt. But she couldn't.

A terror coursed through her unlike anything she'd ever known, alongside the absolute certainty that Valmordion would not let her leave this room alive.

And then her magic steeled itself, frost hardening in her veins, in her blood. A furious slice of cold against Valmordion's unceasing heat. Her grip loosened—just enough to free her.

Ellery Caldwell screamed, and dropped the wand, and ran.

# IX
Domenic
SUMMER

Domenic felt as though he was burning.

Sweat dappled atop his brow and above his lips. He wrenched at his collar, gasping as quietly as he could without drawing more attention. But the remaining candidates hardly paid him any mind now. One girl hugged her knees to her chest. A boy to Domenic's right sat rigid, his face dipped low, his fingers intertwined behind his head. Someone else muttered to themself, and the noise of it all, the battering of his heart, the reek of burnt flesh, the heat scorching like a fever across his skin, made Domenic teeter on the edge of a breakdown.

Hanna, he reminded himself. *I'm doing this for—*

Caldwell's scream rang out like a death knell, startling Domenic so much he lurched to his feet.

No. Caldwell was an incredible magician. She couldn't be hurt. She couldn't be . . .

He collapsed back into his seat.

Finally, Glynn returned. His clipboard trembled in his grasp.

"El—Caldwell is fine," Glynn assured them, and the horror in the room eased.

Until Glynn summoned the next candidate.

As more and more students filed into the vigil chamber, gradually, Domenic became aware of the stares he was attracting. At first he avoided them out of habit. But then he realized it wasn't pity on their faces—it was curiosity. Caldwell had already failed. So what of him, the supposed second hero?

He retrieved a withered dandelion from his pocket and worried at its stem.

All too soon, Glynn called, "Barrow?"

Domenic didn't move. Those same roots of dread tightened around his heart.

"Domenic Barrow?" Glynn repeated, even as he shook his head and his wand struck through Domenic's name on the clipboard. He hadn't so much as glanced around the room, assuming Domenic had joined those who'd fled.

Domenic crushed the flower in his fist.

"Haruto—"

"I'm here," Domenic heaved. "I'm coming."

Ignoring the surprise on Glynn's face, Domenic brushed the ruined petals from his palms and followed Glynn through the door. His footfalls echoed on the ancient stone floor, and for several torturous seconds, his gaze ricocheted around the audience. Iseul paled but offered him a comforting nod. Hanna cringed. She mouthed something, but he couldn't make it out.

Then his eyes fell upon Valmordion.

From that moment on, he couldn't look away even if he'd wanted to. Power emanated from the legendary wand, so oppressive that his every step felt like walking into the embrace of a wildfire. The room around him faded as if swathed in smoke. He saw nothing else, heard no noise other than the calamitous sputter of his breaths.

And then he stood before it.

Now that Valmordion had thawed from its icy slumber, Domenic beheld its appearance in all its devastating glory. Scarlet thorns bristled like fangs along its shaft. The fingerprints that adorned the alban wood seemed to unspool the longer he stared at them, the threads of destiny swirling and knotting together.

A bead of sweat traced down Domenic's cheek.

It wasn't too late to run.

But the thought was fleeting, replaced by ones far more potent.

He thought of Hanna, who'd sacrificed so much to save him—too much. He thought of Iseul, who'd loved them both from the moment she'd met them, simply because she understood. And most of all, he thought of a boy he used to know, who dreamed about stretching his magic to its furthest limits—if he even had any.

As Domenic reached out, something stirred inside him, something he'd long thought lost.

His fingers closed over the handle.

Immediately, his magic swelled, petals unfurling, bramble exploding. All of the air burst out of his lungs, but he didn't dare gasp for more. A pressure bloomed inside his chest, so tremendous and agonizing that he swore his bones would buckle, that his skin would rupture as the power forced its way out. His vision flooded gold, as if he'd looked directly into the sun.

And now the sun would incinerate him.

Time slowed. His heart drummed at an erratic, breakneck speed, and he realized with a start that the light that had momentarily blinded him was not death, but the radiance shining from Valmordion's core.

Every detail in the room returned to him magnified a hundredfold. Colors so vibrant the names he'd always called them no longer satisfied. The clamoring onlookers. And faintly, an inexplicably humid breeze, smelling of flowers.

But stronger than all of that, stronger than anything, was Domenic's panic.

"Y-you've done it," Glynn choked. "Valmordion Chose *you*."

Domenic's knees quivered under the weight of the wand's power, and a myriad of images and sensations invaded his mind. Branches reaching skyward. Earth of incarnadine red. Rings like those of a tree, hundreds and thousands and millions of them, records of some unknowable, primordial time. And a heat—an immense, magmatic heat—scorching him from within.

Domenic let out a strangled sob and gripped the wand with two hands, squeezing even as the thorns stabbed into his palms.

Already, the power was overwhelming him, and soon it would rip him and everyone around him apart.

Slowly, applause trickled through the chamber. And though it was scattered, even wary, to Domenic, it sounded like a roar.

Hanna leapt from her chair and dashed toward him.

But Domenic didn't want her near him, didn't want *anyone* near him. So he surrendered to his instincts, and he ran.

# X
ELLERY
SUMMER

Ellery bolted through the Citadel, her palm weeping blood. Terror and humiliation warred in her as she stumbled up seemingly endless stairs, past magical marvels and stone corridors, past people who gaped but didn't try to follow. A stitch stabbed in her side. Her breaths grew labored and painful. And unbearable cold stormed within her, as though still purging Valmordion's fire.

It wasn't until she burst into the grove that she realized she'd stopped running *from* Valmordion and started running *toward* something else.

Ellery slowed, panting, and stared at the alban tree. Branches spiraled toward the sunset, and the trunk was alight with the molten glow of Summer's final moments, as though the season itself bled out across its bone-white bark. Winter was only minutes away.

Crimson splashed onto the dirt. Ellery could barely make out her palm amidst the bloodied blisters and rows of lacerations. The scent of scorched flesh still lingered in her nostrils.

She needed a healer. But as she made to leave the grove, her legs locked. Her shoulders stiffened. In a freezing flood, her magic sluiced through her, submerging her until her surroundings were muffled and distant. Ellery's mind gave no protest as her body turned back to the tree of its own accord.

The alban groaned and shifted. Its wooden trunk creaked open, revealing an indent in the ancient wood.

Dimly, Ellery recognized its diamond shape.

Her fingers closed over the alban pit from her pocket. Her feet carried her to the tree.

And just as an alban in Nordmere had given that pit to Ellery eleven years ago, Ellery pushed it into the trunk, and gave it back.

As she drew away, silver gleamed across the divot. The pit vanished, and frost spiraled across the bark.

A single branch lowered and brushed her forehead, gentle as a kiss.

Ellery's blood-soaked hand reached for it. As soon as she grasped it, her magic burst forth, swelling, *yearning*. It seeped into the alban wood—and collided with power of an unfathomable magnitude. She gasped for breaths that couldn't come as she was assailed with inexplicable images. Snow so bright it seared her retinas. Iridescent ice crusted across a river. Silver plums blooming, a banquet, a bounty. Winds that gusted across entire forests with the ease of a sigh, a laugh.

Frost crept up Ellery's arm, and a chill like none other stole through her. Like a veil draping over the world, her vision changed, colors muting but details sharpening, the grove now cast in a cool-toned glow.

The branch cracked off in her hand.

And transformed.

Vines sprouted from the gnarled wood, studded with thorns. They looped and coiled around the shaft, gleaming, while the hilt of the branch molded perfectly to Ellery's hand. Silver light pulsed inside its core, like a heartbeat. And finally, ice clustered atop the wickedly sharp tip, then froze into a crystalline crust.

Winter arrived in Alderland, and Ellery felt it roaring free, a hold loosened, a dam burst. The rest of the grove withered, Summer leaves mottled with decay as the wind tore them from their branches, tugging at Ellery's hair. Her breath fogged. Snow flurried through the air.

Ellery's reverie shattered as she took in what she held.

Something impossible. Something terrible.

A Living Wand that belonged not to Summer, but to Winter.

XI

Domenic

SUMMER

Domenic ran.

He felt delirious, feverish. In his right hand, he white-knuckled Valmordion, blood oozing down his wrist. Yet he barely felt the pain of its heat, its thorns. He barely felt anything except the panic snarling around his core.

It couldn't be him. It should've been anyone but him.

Magicians followed him. One or two called his name. But Domenic didn't dare stop. His magic detonated within him, every second growing larger and fiercer and more agonizing. As if his body contained the force of a star.

By the time he finally clambered outside, he'd lost his pursuers amidst the mazelike passages of the Citadel. The moment the cobblestones gave way to grass, he fell to his knees, his bloodied fingers digging into earth.

Then, like a creature dying, the earth went cold.

All at once, leaves fell, withering to gray before even brushing the ground. He squinted as his surroundings brightened, the barren branches exposing the auriferous blaze of sunset. Then abruptly, the daylight dimmed, as if a burial shroud draping over the world. And as the first wind of frost swept over Alderland, Domenic felt it like a breath down his neck. The very land seemed to shift beneath him. As if something seismic was breaking, something terrible was coming loose.

"Barrow?" a voice asked, and Domenic scrabbled backward, crushing decaying weeds beneath him. Valmordion burned hot in his hand.

Wildly, he locked eyes with Ellery Caldwell. She stood beneath the Citadel's alban tree. In the strange, saturated filter of Valmordion's magic, snowflakes shimmered in an iridescent crown upon her hair, and the blue of her irises had deepened into the azure of a descending storm. Yet she didn't look distorted—she looked more beautiful than ever, strikingly so.

He dragged his gaze away to the desolate grove around them, bewildered that they should find themselves here, alone, beneath the very tree that had born Valmordion.

Caldwell took a cautious step toward him. Immediately, Valmordion's golden core flared and hissed with smoke.

"Get back!" he barked, squeezing the wand tight. "I—I don't want to hurt you."

Only as Caldwell recoiled did Domenic notice the wand clutched in her own wounded hand. However, it was no training wand. Silver gleamed across its handle, and thin veins of bramble looped and twined up its shaft into a lethal point. It was the same white as the alban tree looming behind her, the same white as Valmordion.

Her eyes widened as she took in *his* wand.

"It's you," she breathed—not with shock or pity, but with awe. "Valmordion Chose *you*."

Domenic couldn't answer, straining so as not to cry out as Valmordion's power surged violently in his chest. As though the wand *wanted* to hurt her. He tried to let go, but his fingers felt calcified to its wood. Inside, his magic was exploding, exploding, exploding, and he didn't know when it would stop, if it would ever stop.

And so, with a gasping shudder, Domenic smothered Valmordion's power. Pain thrashed against him, as if contorting his insides into an unnatural shape. Valmordion's power, his own power—there was no difference, he realized. Already the two were intertwined, his own self unrecognizable. But he didn't relent. He'd sooner perish than risk its power overwhelming him and repeating what had happened with Syarthis.

Within moments, the pain diminished, and his breaths steadied. Though he could still sense magic within him, it was buried deep.

Domenic heaved himself to his knees, his body shivering, his fingers dripping crimson.

"What wand *is* that?" he asked.

Caldwell gripped her wand with both hands. Scarlet-tinged ice had crusted across her fingers, shackling them to the wand's hilt. When she spoke, the terror in her voice echoed his own.

"Its name is Iskarius."

XII

DOMENIC

WINTER

Two hours later, Domenic sipped a bland cup of tea. His stomach heaved. He set the cup back on the conference table, his bandaged hand trembling.

"Something else I can getcha, Dom?" Councilor Peak asked brightly. "Coffee? Water?"

Domenic shook his head.

The rest of the Council's voices drifted in from an office down the hallway. Though Domenic couldn't make out their words, their furor exploded off the stone walls, each echo sharp as shrapnel. The Council's wing was considered the most revered sanctum of the Citadel, and despite the few occasions Domenic had visited to deliver Iseul or Hanna a late-night dinner, he hadn't truly explored it. If not for the Gallamere skyline glittering out the windows, he would've felt transported back in time. Here, electricity didn't dare disgrace any shared workspace or cubicle, each sconce and chandelier instead alit by motionless flame. Every piece of furniture was antique. Even the vending machines were enchanted and framed in ornate panels of hardwood.

Suddenly, the argument quieted as a single word rang out, ugly and immaculately clear.

Peak hastily shut the conference room door.

Councilor Tennyson Peak headed the Nature Defense Corps, and Domenic had heard countless tales of Peak at the academy. That he held the record for more winterghasts slain than any member of the Order, living or dead. That he'd once taken on a horde of them single-handedly, with an unconscious rookie slung over his shoulder. That he'd staggered upright even after a ghast had torn the flesh right off his leg—then he'd decapitated it.

Domenic would've bet anything that the people who spread those rumors had never actually met Peak. Peak had impulse-purchased a swanky penthouse condo but still slept most nights in his truck in the Citadel parking garage. He knew the names of nearly every magician in the Order as well as their spouses, children, and pets, yet he misplaced his wallet so often that Domenic had once witnessed him try to bribe a hot dog vendor with his own autograph. He sneezed like a bomb. He had an unseasonable devotion to shorts. And he was the only person other than Hanna and Iseul who called Domenic by his nickname, despite them being barely acquaintances—Peak and Iseul had divorced the year before she'd taken in him and Hanna.

Then, despite the many empty chairs in the room, Peak chose the one beside him, groaning as he did so. He smiled, dimples creasing his pale skin at the corners of his beard, and he clapped Domenic's shoulder—hard. "Between you and I, I always knew you had it in you."

Domenic choked out a deranged laugh. "Did you?"

"What, you never had a hunch growing up that you were Chosen? Not even an inkling?"

After hours spent refusing to acknowledge it, finally, Domenic's gaze swiveled to Valmordion. It looked surreal, a millennium-old relic of incomprehensible power resting on a conference table beside a forgotten fountain pen and a sooty ashtray. His blood still stained its thorns, and his wounds still ached, wounds no wand had managed to heal. Yet his magic reached for it, like flowers craning toward the sun.

Again, Domenic's stomach lurched violently.

"If destiny really Chose me," he rasped, "it Chose wrong."

Peak's smile snuffed out, replaced by an expression he didn't recognize. Domenic didn't care. In all the time since he and

Caldwell had been removed from the grove and Domenic had been instructed to wait here; he'd been told nothing. *Nothing.* It was growing harder to convince himself that this was all a nightmare when the nightmare refused to end.

At last, the door opened, and Iseul and Hanna hovered at the threshold.

Both Domenic and Peak stood with a start.

"They all done?" Peak asked.

"Not quite," Iseul answered. "But Tenney, would you mind giving us three a moment alone?"

"Yeah, sure thing. You need anything, though? A drink? Those crackers you like?"

Iseul smiled weakly. "No, but thank you."

As soon as Peak closed the door behind him, Iseul threw her arms around Domenic. Domenic leaned into her, inhaling her gardenia perfume. A sob shuddered through him.

It was a relief, to finally break.

"I can't be the Chosen One. I-I can't," he blubbered. "And that's why they're all arguing, isn't it? Because I'm the last person anyone would want near that wand, let alone wielding it. And—"

"Dom." Iseul drew away, her features etched deep with concern. "I know you're upset right now, but we need you to calm down—"

"Calm down? I watched that wand torch one of my classmates tonight!"

"I know. But it's not so much you the Council has been arguing about. For Caldwell to create a Living Wand—it's unprecedented. We haven't told anyone yet, but Sharpe's been on the phone with the Prime Minister about you for the past hour, and I've been fielding calls from radio stations—"

"The *radio stations*? They— They already know about me?"

"They're already airing the story, and—oh no. Hold on. Here."

With a swish of Calynia, the waste bin launched across the

room into Domenic's arms—a second too late. He puked all over the historic hardwood.

After Iseul enchanted the puddle away, she steered him back into his chair. He hunched over the bin.

Cautiously, he glanced up at Hanna, who lurked utterly still in the corner holding a leather-bound book. Though Hanna spent nearly all her time in the Council wing—Syarthis's wielder was a permanent member of the Council, regardless of age—she looked childlike amidst the vaulted ceilings, the track-hung oil paintings, the candelabras several heads taller than her. Like a student lost on a field trip. Like a girl playing dress-up in a blazer and waistcoat.

Yet as he stared, his best friend didn't offer him any words of reassurance—not even a smile. Instead, she clutched Syarthis against her heart. Its heat pulsed, suffocating. When she squeezed her eyes shut, so, too, did the eyes of the wand.

Iseul knelt in front of Domenic. "As you already understand, to wield Valmordion is an enormous burden. For that burden to be yours . . . It's the last thing I ever wanted for you. But if it bonded with you, that's because you were always destined for it. Which means that, whatever the future will ask of you, I want you to remember that you're capable of it."

Domenic managed a nod.

"But even so, you're not in this alone. Hanna and I, we'll do everything we can to help you. The rest of the Council will help you as well, but they also have expectations of you. It doesn't matter that you didn't ask for this or what your past is. You are our Chosen One, and the future of the entire country is at stake. You understand that, don't you?"

He did. Even he knew of the Thirty Years' Chill from history class, when Winter had terrorized the country and claimed over a third of the population. All because a Chosen One had failed.

Domenic didn't know their name. It was considered bad luck to speak it.

"Even if I *could* stop the cataclysm," he murmured, "Alice Rhodes died saving Alderland, didn't she?" It occurred to him that being Valmordion's last wielder, Rhodes was his *predecessor*. Her face was on the ten-cent coin. "Is that what's gonna happen to me? I'll light up like a firework?"

"O-of course not," Iseul told him.

"How can you know that? Is she the only wielder who died?"

As Iseul hesitated, Hanna answered, "No."

"How many did, then?"

"Only two." As Domenic's mind stuttered like a scratched record as he attempted the math, Hanna added, "That's two out of thirteen. Those are good odds, Dom."

"But not zero."

"No, not zero."

"And did any of them . . ." His knuckles whitened around the waste bin. "Did any of them unbond with Valmordion?"

For years, Domenic had thought the worst thing he could glimpse on anyone's face was pity. But as Hanna exchanged a look with Iseul, he glimpsed that same something in both their eyes as he'd seen in Peak's, something else, something worse.

Fear.

Not fear for his sake, but for theirs—for everyone's.

Domenic had thought he could be honest with Iseul and Hanna about how he felt. But from now on, he was no longer simply their friend, their family—he was their supposed savior.

"N-never mind," he blurted. "Of course they didn't. Stupid question. I mean, there'd be no Alderland left, right? And . . ."

The door opened. The three other members of the Magicians Council strode inside to take in their Chosen One, stooped over a trash can, vomit still dribbling down his chin.

Sharpe pursed his already thread-thin lips. At eighty years old, Alexander Sharpe had been a permanent fixture in Aldrish politics for so long that half a dozen buildings, scholarships, and foundations were already named in his honor. He held two positions within the Order: the Director of Infrastructure and Administration, overseeing magician affairs as well as the maintenance of every roadway, sewer, and enchanted broadcast tower throughout Alderland; and, as the senior-most member of the Council, he was also its president.

At his entrance, Domenic's chair squirmed beneath him. At first, he thought it was only urging him to stand out of respect, but as he did so, it scooted back with a screech. Domenic realized he'd accidentally taken Sharpe's seat at the head of the table.

Domenic scrambled aside. He set the bin on the floor and wiped his face on his sleeve.

"Um, sorry. Sir."

Sharpe's pitch-dark gaze roamed up Domenic slowly, his frown ever-deepening. As if with every excessive inch of him, he found another thing lacking.

Then Sharpe withdrew Ballathim from his side, along with a cigarette. He lit it from a flame at Ballathim's tip and sucked in a long drag. Smoke leaked from his nostrils, like a dragon.

"To be Chosen by Valmordion is a great honor," Sharpe began coolly, "and the five of us would like to offer you our sincerest congratulations."

The first time Domenic had met Sharpe was in his hospital room after the Syarthis Disaster, when the Council had offered him their sincerest apologies.

As Sharpe claimed his seat, the others took those flanking him on either side—Iseul and Peak on his left, Glynn and Hanna on his right. Domenic shakily lowered into the one at the opposite end. The heat waves of Valmordion radiating on the table between them distorted their faces into dreamlike blurs, and in the room's corner, an enchanted typewriter clacked like gnashing teeth.

"However, this honor comes with great responsibility," Sharpe continued. "The cataclysms our nation has faced throughout its history have been tremendous. One hundred and fourteen years ago, Alice Rhodes single-handedly quelled a winterscurge that would've razed half the eastern coast. Before her, Sewall Heard defended against a ghost invasion that would've claimed thousand of Aldrish lives, and Odierne Artell had Collinsmere evacuated while she burned through the last of Winter's power—and burned the city along with it."

Domenic glanced fearfully at the frost that crept like skeletal fingers across the lancet windows.

"I . . . I understand," he managed.

"Do you?" Sharpe demanded. "Because, Chosen or not, it would be a betrayal of our duty not to impress upon you how serious of a task you have been assigned. Between your student records, your panicked run from the vigil—"

"I get it. You think I'm not taking this seriously? What do you think has had me bent over a . . ." At Iseul's warning look, he cleared his throat. "I mean, I do understand. I promise. The last thing I want is to fail *all of Alderland*."

Sharpe tapped his cigarette over the ashtray. "Then let's cut right to the heart of the matter. Mayes, if you would."

Domenic had nearly forgotten about Hanna's book. She opened it, and with a wave of Syarthis, a golden leaf peeled off from where it had been pressed into its yellowed pages, and it fluttered across the table to Domenic. He squinted at the strange writing webbed through the leaf's veins.

> *as Summer wilts and Winter lays its siege*
> *and prophecies of yore come to an end*
> *an ancient peace denied must be restored*
> *or see the land destroyed forevermore*

Domenic burned under the heat of every eye in the room, including Syarthis's. "This is it, isn't it? The prophecy?"

"Yes. The words of the prophecy appeared on the night Valmordion first began to thaw. We've been safeguarding it in the times since." Sharpe waved impatiently. "Well, what do you make of it?"

Domenic scanned it again, and again, and again. The Councilors leaned forward, so silent Domenic wasn't even sure they were breathing. He felt as if he'd been summoned to speak in the front of the class only to discover he was ass naked.

"Given Winter's conquest of the North," Hanna said, "we can presume that—"

"You are a junior member of the Council, Mayes. You will *not* speak unless addressed," Sharpe snapped, and Hanna recoiled, pressing into the back of her chair. "As you know, the Aldrish people believe that the destiny of Valmordion's Chosen begins even before their bonding. During her academy years, Alice Rhodes warned her classmates over and over that a new cataclysm was coming. And when they asked her why, she responded . . . Mayes, now is your chance to be a know-it-all."

A muscle in Hanna's jaw clenched. "She said, 'Because I was born.'"

Domenic stared at Hanna desperately, wondering if she, too, was wrestling down a deranged urge to laugh. Who knew his years of disruptive behavior had been inherited from such an illustrious legacy?

Hanna didn't look at him.

"Even before Valmordion thawed," Sharpe said, "the Council has been expecting a Chosen One for five years—ever since Winter began claiming territory. Such a conquest is unprecedented, even during past cataclysms. And given our lack of success reclaiming it, we assumed the task of reunifying our country would fall to a coming Chosen One. Apparently, to *you*."

Domenic nodded and wiped his sweaty hands on his trousers. He pored over the words of the prophecy until they blurred in and out of focus. He tried tracing his finger across the leaf only for it to crinkle, delicate as spider silk, and he wrenched back.

"So, um, given Winter's conquest of the fallen territory . . . that's the laying siege bit, right? Makes sense that Winter wants more. Winter's probably gunning for all of Alderland." He rubbed at the chills prickling up his arms. "And this line about the prophecies. What does it mean, that they'll end?"

For some reason, it was the wrong question to ask. Iseul and Peak exchanged a look Domenic couldn't name. Glynn fiddled with his Order insignia pin.

Sharpe gritted his teeth and gestured at Hanna to answer.

"Beneath the Citadel's alban tree, its roots form a cavern," Hanna explained. "Every prophecy we've ever received bloomed from them at Valmordion's making."

"You mean the Order has always had all the prophecies?" Domenic asked.

"We've had the leaves, but the words of the prophecy only appear as Valmordion thaws and another cataclysm looms. But what's important, Dom . . . this leaf, it's the last of all of them."

Domenic grappled with the magnitude of that statement. Despite Alderland's reverence for Chosen Ones, the Order glossed over the details of the past prophecies in school. Maybe he simply hadn't paid attention—the cataclysms had always felt like ancient history to him. But he didn't think it was his fault he was clueless. No, the truth was, for a millennium, the Council had *known* exactly how many cataclysms were coming. And every time Valmordion thawed, they'd counted them passing, telling no one, until only this final prophecy remained. Again, he read the last line.

or see the land destroyed forevermore

So that was why this prophecy was the grand finale. If he failed, the cataclysm wouldn't merely wound Alderland—it would destroy it.

Domenic stabbed his nails into his kneecaps.

Wake up, he begged himself. *Wake up.*

When he didn't, he stammered, "S-so I'm supposed to... I'm supposed to restore an ancient peace? How? By reclaiming the fallen territory, like you said?"

"Well, this isn't the entirety of the prophecy. These are only the first lines." Hanna spoke tentatively, as if prompting him. Right—this Domenic did know from school. The prophecies functioned as instructions. The original piece led the Chosen One to another, then another. Until either the Chosen One prevented the cataclysm before it began, or thwarted it just as it unfolded.

Domenic forced in air, trying vainly to calm himself. "How many pieces do I have to find in total?"

"Past Chosen Ones received between six and eight additional pieces, excluding the original prophecy," she answered. "The prophecy pieces each require a task to fulfill them. Sometimes how that task relates to thwarting the cataclysm is clear; other times, it's mysterious in the moment but makes sense in hindsight. Regardless, it's always the final piece that's the hardest, that requires the greatest power to fulfill. And we'll know for sure when you receive that final piece, as it'll have four lines like the original prophecy, whereas each piece in between has two."

"All right," Domenic said, struggling to absorb it all. "But how am I supposed to get more pieces if there aren't any leaves left?"

At once, he knew he'd spoken wrong again, because Hanna and Iseul cringed, Sharpe coughed out smoke, and that same expression flitted across every other Councilor's face.

Fear.

"What?" he asked. "What is it?"

"I knew it. All the questions you've been asking—you haven't heard it, have you?" Glynn gasped. "Destiny always speaks the next piece of the prophecy to its Chosen when they bond with Valmordion."

"Oh?" His whole body trembled. "And what if—what if I didn't get that memo?"

The silence echoed. Domenic wouldn't even mind bursting into flame right then. He would've welcomed it.

Peak chuckled, but it sounded forced. "There's some sort of explanation then, I'm sure."

"Yes, I'm sure there is," Sharpe said, pounding his cigarette into the ashtray. "We're all fucked."

Iseul blanched. "Sir, that isn't—"

"*No*. You and Mayes are too biased, and you swore before we came in here that you wouldn't meddle. The two of you, coddling him, fighting his battles for him. It's pathetic." His chair screeched as he stood. "Valmordion may have bonded with this . . . this *boy,* but just because his destiny is to save us doesn't mean he'll succeed! I mean, *him,* the champion of Summer? Where do you see Summer's fire? Its strength? Its fervor? The only reason he wasn't expelled years ago was because according to the Prime Minister, the Order—who provides every service to this country, whose magicians give their lives each year fighting Winter—*we* apparently can't afford to look heartless. As if the Syarthis Disaster was our own doing! *No.* We each have a destiny to lead this country, and I refuse to lead it into ruin!"

Domenic lurched to his feet and paced in front of the fireplace. Furious, mortified tears spilled down his cheeks.

"I-I get it. You think I *want* that wand? You think I *want* every life in Alderland on my shoulders? I don't even believe in destiny. Just because you hand me mysterious instructions on some leaf doesn't mean I buy that I've actually been Chosen from the day I was born. Because if my whole life has led up to Valmordion, what the hell does that make what happened to me? What happened to both of us? Our classmates?" He jerked his head at

Hanna. "I refuse to believe that every event I've lived through has been . . . been . . ." He couldn't find the words.

"By design," Hanna spat, and nodded in agreement.

"Right. Exactly. So I'm sorry I'm not your perfect Chosen One. Or, what was the better word you called me earlier—a disgrace?" He grinned at Sharpe maliciously. "Yeah, I heard you all arguing. But guess what? *I wouldn't have Chosen me either.*"

The other Councilors seemed to have forgotten how to close their mouths. Hanna fiddled with something in her lap.

Sharpe fumed, more furious than ever.

Domenic resumed pacing. "What about Ellery Caldwell?"

"What about her?" Glynn asked warily.

"Well, she's a part of this. She made a Living Wand. An *alban* wand. Seems to me you do have your perfect Chosen One, right there."

Sharpe cocked a brow, as if amused he finally agreed with him. Then he barked, "Mayes, it's decided. Go to her."

Domenic hastily smeared his cheeks on his sleeve and smoothed down his rumpled hair. "You're bringing her here?"

"No. Or at least, not until she provides answers about her wand that finally make a shred of sense."

Domenic startled. Caldwell's wand might've been unprecedented, its appearance strange, but Caldwell was the Order's darling. And they were describing her like a criminal.

Hanna rose grimly. Her fingers flexed over Syarthis, and its tip curled around the crook of her thumb.

"Sir, I feel adamantly that this step is unnecessary," Glynn said. "Caldwell has proven herself to be nothing but loyal. Is this really how we wish to reward—"

"Now is *not* the time to test me," Sharpe snapped.

"Wait. You're going to invade her memories?" Domenic balked. "But you can't. That's not fair. She didn't do anything wrong."

"So Syarthis will judge, I'm sure," Sharpe said flatly.

"What if I spoke to her? Maybe I—"

"Barrow, you've spoken quite enough."

"But—"

"Dom, don't," Hanna said, her voice oddly strained. "I'll be back soon."

She left.

Domenic clenched and unclenched his fists, hating himself. All he'd been thinking was that maybe, just maybe, Caldwell could save him. She had an alban wand, after all. No doubt she'd make a better Chosen One than he did.

Instead, he'd condemned her.

Fuckup, he told himself.

"What if destiny is just taking its time?" he asked frantically.

"A minute ago you were throwing a tantrum about how you don't believe in destiny," Sharpe muttered.

"Yeah, well, this Chosen One thing is new to me. If destiny needs to tell me another piece of the prophecy, maybe—I don't know. Maybe I just need to give it another chance to try."

Truthfully, he had no idea what he was saying. But once upon a time, Domenic had sensed greatness within himself. Maybe Valmordion had, too. Maybe it was still there, had always been there, and he really was capable of this.

As Domenic grasped the handle, every color in the room brightened, dizzyingly vibrant. The wand's heat seared through his gauze, as though he gripped an iron over an open flame. Yet he forced himself not to let go.

And he waited.

And waited.

And waited.

Finally, when he could no longer stand it, he dropped the greatest wand in history onto the table with a clatter. Fresh blood bloomed through his bandages.

Sharpe's lips curled. "If *you* are all that stands between Alderland and the end of its days, then we are all damned."

Domenic didn't—couldn't—defend himself. Instead, he lunged toward the trash can, falling onto his hands and knees. He vomited. He missed.

XIII

Ellery

WINTER

Curtains were drawn over the windows in Glynn's office. The scenes of a sunny Alderland were frozen in their frames, the record player silenced. Ellery waited in her ash-smothered clothes, still reeking of burned hair and flesh. Despite a healer's best efforts, her wounded palm remained raw beneath its bandages.

Order magicians had confiscated Iskarius as soon as they found her in the grove, then escorted her here. Glynn questioned Ellery while President Sharpe hovered behind him. Ellery scarcely remembered what she'd said, only that she'd created a wand of alban wood, a wand whose name had come to her in a rustle of dying leaves. A wand that wielded the magic of Winter. But all thoughts of what that might mean were submerged deep within herself. Reality rippled as though she were underwater; she was distant, lost.

Time passed. An untouched tray of refreshments cooled on Glynn's desk.

She sank. She drifted.

The door creaked open.

"Evening." Hanna Mayes fixed Ellery with a hollow stare. The door thudded shut behind her.

Since Mayes's brief time at the academy, she seldom crossed paths with her former classmates, and Ellery had only occasionally spotted her consulting with Glynn about duties to the Council. Mayes never acknowledged her. Then again, Mayes rarely acknowledged anyone. She stalked everywhere with her head bent low, always in a rush, always with an eerie, faraway glaze to her eyes. But never had she looked worse than tonight. Stringy ash-brown hairs slipped from her ponytail and clung to her neck, and several zits on her jawline bled, freshly picked.

Dread seeped through Ellery, slow and steady as a tide.

"Why are you here?" Ellery asked.

"The Council would like a few more answers."

"I already told them what I know." Her voice sounded small and distant to her own ears.

"You told them your wand possesses Winter magic, which doesn't make sense. Winter magic is wild. And the reason Living Wands are all that can defend against its storms and monsters is because they're instruments of Summer. These aren't just pretty notions. They're the facts that have guided a thousand years of Aldrish history. So either you're delusional, or you're lying. Regardless, Syarthis and I will uncover the truth."

Mayes dragged Glynn's chair around the desk beside Ellery and sank into it. She scrutinized Ellery, as if there was fine print hidden within her soot-clogged pores.

Ellery white-knuckled her armrests but knew better than to protest.

"The sensation will feel like a needle," Mayes explained, in the rote style of having given this speech before. "It won't be comfortable, but the more you tense up, the more uncomfortable it will be. You'll feel a pinch in your temples and at the soft spot at the base of your skull. You might also feel a pressure . . ." As Mayes kept speaking, her words fuzzed in and out. ". . . You might re-experience old emotions that can vary in intensity from faint echoes to quite visceral. These reactions are all normal and nothing to panic about."

"And . . . and after?" Ellery asked numbly, uncertain she'd caught any of it.

"After, Syarthis and I will leave and report our findings to the rest of the Council. Someone will speak to you as soon as we're finished with Dom. And—"

"Barrow?" The afterimage of him in the grove flared in her mind: vibrant when everything else had been so muted. For one precious instant, Ellery roused, gulping for air. "Have you seen him?"

Emotion cracked through Mayes's expression. She grimaced. "I have."

"How is he?" Ellery hoped he was all right. As all right as anyone could be after Valmordion had Chosen them.

"He . . ." The other girl shuddered, and her gaze drifted to some aimless point over Ellery's shoulder. Each of her blinks was unnervingly slow, as if it was the darkness of her eyelids that truly held her focus, not the room. Until Mayes tore at a cuticle on her thumb and said, "Again, I think we should proceed."

Ellery remembered what Barrow had told her back in Mercester Square. *I'm not in search of a grand destiny.*

One had found him anyway. And although she knew he didn't want it, she'd seen the wand in his hand, seen the truth.

He suited Valmordion.

And *she* suited . . .

Mayes reached into the inner pocket of her blazer and withdrew Syarthis. She stroked her thumb along its handle, and its tip curled and uncurled, like a cat stretching out its spine.

Ellery's gaze followed it, disturbed. The Syarthis Disaster had happened before her arrival at the Citadel, but she knew its details intimately from her classmates, many of whom had lost roommates, friends. And if the rumors about Syarthis were true, it could lay Ellery's whole life bare, every thought, every moment.

"There's no other way?" she croaked.

"I'm afraid not," Mayes answered.

After everything the Order had given Ellery, she trusted them. If this was what it took for them to trust her too, so be it.

"I understand. Just make it quick."

Mayes rested Syarthis against Ellery's temple. The wand licked her, like a warm, oily tongue.

"Focus on your memories of creating the wand," Mayes told her. "We'll do the rest."

Syarthis's magic jabbed at the base of her neck, and a gradual pressure built behind her eyes, then her throat. Ellery gagged but held still. She shut her eyes and pictured the pit. The alban tree. The branch descending, her hand reaching for it.

The pressure began to burn, so hot that sweat beaded on her forehead. Then Ellery's own magic swelled, a cool sensation that numbed the pain. Syarthis's heat fizzled out; its pressure receded. In a matter of seconds, both vanished entirely.

Ellery opened her eyes. Mayes stood, her shoulders heaving, then shrugged off her blazer. And while Syarthis's eyes darted wildly around the room, Mayes gawked, frazzled, at Ellery. A burst blood vessel wept across her left sclera.

"How did you do that?" she snapped.

"W-what do you mean?"

"You locked us out. That shouldn't be possible." Mayes leaned against the wall and hugged her wand against her chest. Each time she blinked, so did Syarthis. Then abruptly she kicked the stand of the record player, making the vinyls jolt on their shelves. Ellery jolted, too. "What the fuck is going on tonight? Why doesn't anything make *sense*?"

The girl's brusque professionalism had been intimidating, but this was far, far worse. Unbondings were rare, but they typically occurred when a wielder was distressed. And even if Mayes wasn't showing other signs, given the wand's history, Ellery couldn't help but glance at the door.

Which was precisely when it swung open, and President Sharpe and Councilor Seong entered.

Sharpe frowned, examining the gap between Ellery and Mayes. "Well, are you finished?"

Immediately, Mayes lowered Syarthis and squared her shoulders. "We can't see into her mind, sir."

"What?" Seong said. "You're sure?"

"Of course I'm sure," Mayes grumbled.

Sharpe shut the door behind him with a flick of Ballathim, then strode toward Ellery until he loomed over her. She felt pinned to her chair like an insect on a corkboard.

"How are you shielding yourself?" he demanded.

"I d-don't know."

"Of course you don't," Sharpe said coolly. "You're quite the enigma, Miss Caldwell. As soon as we confiscated that wand of yours, we sent it to our best magicians to examine it. And it would seem the story you told us, no matter how far-fetched, has at least some truth to it. Iskarius, as you've called it, is a proper Living Wand. The first new one in recorded history." Yet Sharpe's tone did not suggest congratulations. "And it was crafted from an alban tree."

The significance of that hung between them, but Ellery couldn't bring herself to speak. Words were trapped like air bubbles in her lungs, and she felt just as she had in the grove, apart from herself, apart from everything.

Sharpe reached into his wool jacket and pulled out a tall, thin box made of alban wood. He rose and placed it on Glynn's desk. Then he waved Ballathim, and the top of the box creaked open. Ice crystals puffed into the air, shimmering.

Inside, terrible and beautiful, was Iskarius. There was a single thumbprint on the hilt, smeared with blood. Hers.

The rest of the world stayed blurred as the wand came sharply into focus. It was the only thing that felt real.

"As if all those facts already weren't fucking enough to swallow," Sharpe went on, "you tell us this wand's made of *Winter magic*. Now, it certainly looks like it. We've all got eyes. But our magicians can't say for sure. Neither can Mayes, apparently."

Behind them, Councilor Seong squeezed Mayes's arm and whispered to her. Mayes scowled and smeared the blood on her face across her sleeve.

"Syarthis's corporeal magic is second only to one wand," Sharpe continued. "And given who's wielding that one wand, I'll admit that I'm inclined to hear you out. You *do* understand what I'm saying, don't you?"

Ellery nodded numbly. "You think my wand could be like . . . like Valmordion."

"We've been watching you for a long time. A national hero when you could scarcely wave a training wand. Glynn's little pet project. He always swore you'd be a good investment." Sharpe leaned closer. His breath reeked of cigarettes. "Now's the time to show us he was right. Can we trust you, Caldwell?"

The full implications of his words yanked her up to the surface, to reality. Ellery shivered, painfully alert.

"Of course," she choked out.

He gestured to Iskarius. "Then show us this so-called Winter wand of yours. And prove that we should place some hope in you rather than destroy this wand and whatever threat it could pose."

Ellery didn't know how to prove something to the Order that she didn't understand herself. But she needed answers just as much as they did.

She stood and picked up Iskarius.

It was freezing to the touch. Yet the longer she grasped it, the more her body grew used to the cold. Glynn's office sharpened into hyper clarity, every color muted and cool. Ellery felt an all-encompassing *rightness.*

Then a voice hissed in her ear.

It was the same voice that had given her Iskarius's name, old and dry as dust and yet commanding, impossible not to heed. With chilling certainty, she repeated each word it spoke.

> *the unveiled truth of everything you are*
> *is power that will rise from your own ruin*

Long, stunned seconds of silence ticked by before Mayes demanded, "Where did you hear that?" Syarthis quivered in her hand.

"Something told me." Ellery shivered again. "Something that wanted—n-no, it *needed* me to listen."

Seong gaped. "Was that a prophecy piece?"

Ellery staggered backward. It was all too much: Julian burning in front of her, Syarthis's tip at her temple, and the wand in her hand, an alban wand, a *Winter* wand. Suddenly each inhale felt as they had when she'd fought the winterghast, as though she were drowning, subsumed by a current too overwhelming to fight. Magic surged through countless tributaries within her, magic greater than anything she'd imagined.

Then it burst outward, into a spell.

Brutal cold exploded across the room in a shockwave. Ice shredded the curtains and speared into the paintings. It hardened across the floorboards and atop the record player, crushing the stylus. The other three magicians screamed as Ellery's spell shattered their hasty shields. Frostbite blistered across their hands.

As Ellery tried to wrench back control of Iskarius, the door banged open. Councilor Peak rushed inside, wielding his wand, Targath. Its tip flared an ominous orange, like molten metal. Even from across the room, she smelled burning. His gaze ricocheted from Ellery to Seong to Mayes, then back to Ellery.

"Drop your wand!" Peak commanded.

Ellery struggled to pry her fingers from the hilt.

"Now!"

She forced her grip free and threw Iskarius down. It clattered to the floor. Its silver core extinguished.

"I'm sorry," Ellery rasped. "I didn't mean to hurt anyone, I swear."

Without lowering Targath, Peak asked the others, "Are you all right?"

Ellery stared in horror at their injuries. Mayes and Seong both bore signs of frostbite, while Sharpe's had progressed to frostmaul. Ice fused gruesomely with his engorged, bloodied skin.

"Mayes," Sharpe snapped. "Get over here."

Mayes held Syarthis against her wounds. "Hold on a sec. I need to heal myself first."

Sharpe seethed and cradled his hand to his chest. Then he barked at Peak, "Why are you here? Why aren't you with Barrow?"

"Our western team just called," Peak answered. "We got a winterscurge forming outside Oldermere."

Yet as the others gasped, Peak advanced toward Ellery. Ice crackled beneath his boots as her heartbeat ratcheted faster.

"What *are* you?" he asked, with equal parts awe and terror.

But Ellery knew they'd already made up their minds.

Monster.

XIV
Domenic
WINTER

"—But does he really have it in him, is the question," spoke radio personality Floyd Wilder. *"And it's a question I think a lot of folks, myself included, have found themselves asking tonight."*

"Destiny wouldn't have Chosen him if he didn't," political correspondent Amos Cheng pointed out.

"Sure, but just being Chosen isn't a guarantee you'll succeed. And as his classmates told us, they never expected Barrow to bond with Valmordion. Aloof? Lazy? He turned tail and bolted from the vigil, even! I mean, come on! Do you think that sounds like the best man for the job?"

Domenic stared with bloodshot eyes at the ceiling of his train car.

No, he thought. *I don't.*

The door slid open, and a frigid wind whirled through the compartment. Beyond the windows, the Aldrish countryside blurred past. Winter had stripped lush forests into desolation: every tree gone skeletal, every hillside barbed and barren.

"How'd your call with your family go?" Peak asked, shutting the door.

Amid every frantic minute of tonight, this night that would seemingly never end, Domenic had only just informed the Barrow family that their youngest, forgotten son was suddenly the most important person in the nation. Domenic had braced himself for shock, maybe a few tears, but no. As soon as his mother had finished blustering about the embarrassment of first hearing this news from her best friend-slash-nemesis at the country club, Domenic had learned his family was *proud*. His father had even boasted how this would rocket up the company stock price. This had relieved Domenic, who, of course, cared about nothing more than shareholder value.

Never did they state whether they were surprised that their third born was a Chosen One. Domenic had considered asking whether they'd failed to mention some tale of falling stars or serenading songbirds that had heralded his birth. But he doubted his parents would remember even if there had been.

"I think I've made their year," Domenic answered Peak dryly.

On the table beside him, the radio continued to blare.

"*—slayed that winterghast in Mercester Square two weeks ago, didn't he? Well, Floyd, maybe he lived through the Syarthis Disaster for a reason, too,*" Cheng declared. "*That's the way destiny works. It always has a grander purpose—*"

Peak switched the radio off.

"That's enough of that," he rasped, clapping Domenic hard on the shoulder. "Sorry, Dom, but that can't be good for you. It just can't." Domenic was about to argue that actually, listening to people publicly debate his trauma was great for him, when Peak slid into the booth across from him. "How are you feeling?"

"Well, five hours ago, I bonded with the most powerful wand in Alderland. Then I spent the whole evening being told how worthless I am by a man who's been around since prehistory. And now I'm being thrown into a category-three winterscurge. How *should* I be feeling?"

At Domenic's description of Sharpe, Peak stifled a laugh. "Look, um, Dom. The Council knows what the past day has put you through. You're only being sent out so that our forces and the public see you on the ground, already helping them. But we don't expect you to do anything."

"Yeah, because you all think I'll fuck it up."

"I definitely don't. Hell, after blasting a winterghast with a training wand, this storm might be a cakewalk, yeah?" Peak flashed him a smile, goofy-wide, his dimples visible even beneath his gray scruff. Domenic wondered what he'd ever done to make this man so fond of him, if it wasn't too late to reverse it.

"I didn't do that alone." And then, as if a horrible pendulum, Domenic's mind veered from impending mortal peril to the other subject that had haunted him all evening:

Ellery Caldwell, radiant and ethereal at the base of the alban tree.

Ellery Caldwell, wielding a Winter wand.

Ellery Caldwell, who'd heard what sounded an awful lot like a prophecy piece.

And he hadn't.

"I know Caldwell hurt Hanna and Iseul," he said. "I just—she never would've done it on purpose."

"Whether she did it on purpose or not doesn't matter," said Peak. "The thing is, that wand of hers having Winter magic? Take it from someone who's been fighting Winter his whole career. I've lost a lot of friends over the years. Made some . . . some pretty big sacrifices, too. Put Caldwell outta your mind. That wand will be destroyed. All that matters now are whatever plans destiny has for you."

Maybe Peak was right. Yet each time Domenic thought of Caldwell, a feeling wormed deeper inside him, a weed he couldn't uproot.

Domenic laughed nervously. "You really trust destiny, don't you?"

"Yes and no. I do believe destiny is a guiding force for all Living Wands, but ultimately, I believe the only person or force who can give you purpose is you. And purpose can make you capable of extraordinary things." He tapped Targath's sheath jutting out from his breast pocket.

Domenic's gaze swiveled between the wand and wielder, considering.

"Tell me what it's like, fighting ghosts, being in a scurge. I know I've done it before, technically. But it all happened so fast that I don't remember much."

Peak's smile sharpened on one end, curved up like a sickle. "There are two ways to end a scurge. The first is to slay all the ghasts within it. The more ghasts there are, the more powerful the scurge grows. So you gotta move fast. And the big storms . . ." His tongue swiped over his teeth. "You can get some real nasty monsters in those. The sort right outta nightmares."

Domenic shuddered. "And what's the second?"

"The second way is to breach the eye of the scurge, the central point of all its magic. There you can stop the storm from within and wipe out all the ghasts in one blow."

"I've never heard of that before."

"That's because it's only been accomplished a few times in history. By that wand you got lying right there." Peak jerked his head toward Valmordion, resting sheathed beside the radio.

"Oh," Domenic said, because he wasn't sure how Peak wanted him to respond.

But Peak betrayed no disappointment. He stood with a groan and lightly slapped his left knee. "Well, it's been a long night. You should try to get some sleep before we arrive."

"Yeah. All right."

After another hard clap, Peak returned to the rest of the team in the adjacent train car.

Domenic slumped across the bench. His eyes drifted toward Valmordion, like a fly drawn fatally to a flame.

He'd already believed destiny was bullshit. Maybe prophecies were just bullshit, too.

Still, he jolted up and switched the radio back on, even if it meant hearing prime-time star Floyd Wilder warn the whole country to kiss their hope goodbye.

It was better than hearing nothing.

* * *

Domenic cringed as he forced open his car door against a barrage of icy wind. Orange Nature Defense Corps vehicles clustered on the highway bank, their headlights shining across the craggy field toward the winterscurge raging a hundred yards beyond. It rose from earth to sky and stretched out endlessly in either direction. Although glints of silver frost whirled across the storm's surface, no light penetrated within it, the blackness so absolute that Domenic swore he was staring at the very edge of the world.

Immediately, a young magician scampered to greet their team, then gawked at Domenic. In his bulky Winter gear, it took Domenic a moment to place him as Elijah Kleid, a boy from the class above him who'd bonded with a mid-tier nature wand two years ago.

"What is this?" Peak demanded. "I was told thirty minutes ago the storm was at the 306 mile marker. Just how fast is this thing moving?"

"That's the thing, sir. Th-the winds just broke a hundred and twenty knots. At this rate, it'll hit Oldermere before sunrise. And there's been two more winterghast sightings, as well—small ones, we think. We dispatched another scouting squad thirty minutes ago, but they haven't returned yet."

Peak's expression darkened. "Osakwe, radio Oldermere, then Gallamere. Tell them I'm reclassifying the scurge as category four. Matthews, get me a full roster of every magician here. And Barrow, suit up. You and I need to lead a unit into the storm."

Domenic swallowed down a noise of alarm—he'd barely braced himself for a category three. But Peak and his retinue had already dashed off to join the other officers, leaving Domenic alone with Kleid, who stared at him with something uncomfortably close to awe.

"This way, um, sir." Kleid led Domenic to a large utility vehicle, which Domenic immediately noticed from the logo was manufactured by his father's company. A pair of magicians huddled behind it to escape the onslaught of wind. Judging from the gray insignia on their uniforms, they were hedge magicians—magicians without Living Wands whom the Order hired to fill the gaps in their ranks.

Recognizing yet another former classmate, one he'd rather not acknowledge, Domenic hastily turned his back to them. Kleid dug through the crates in the trunk and began thrusting gear into Domenic's arms.

"—aren't real," Former Classmate grumbled. "The Dire Three are just conspiracies made up by rookies who saw a ghast for the first time and shit themselves."

"I'm telling you, my friend swore he saw Decibel," her companion hissed, shivering as he smoked a cigarette. "Spotted it while patrolling the border of the fallen territory. Said it must've been ten feet tall, with the spikes and everything."

"Well, if ghasts like them *are* real, then there's no way your friend would've survived . . . *Barrow?*"

Domenic cringed as he zipped his coat and spun around. "Hi, Sanford."

Vivian Sanford's companion balked. "Barrow? You're here? And you . . . ?" His eyes locked onto the white sheath poking out of Domenic's pocket—alban wood.

When Domenic had last spoken to Sanford, she'd asked him not to tell anyone about that time in the empty lecture hall, or in the alley off Elm Street, or in her dorm while her roommate was gone for break. Everyone knew his reputation, she'd explained, and she intended to be a serious magician.

Her bonding window had closed three weeks later.

"Are even more dashing in person?" Domenic finished dryly. "I get that a lot. So . . . what's the Dire Three?"

"I-it's nothing," Sanford's companion stammered. "Just rookie superstition."

A proper Chosen One would take the high ground.

Domenic, however, flashed a smile. "No, Sanford's too serious of a magician for that. So tell me. I want to know."

Sanford's already wind-bitten cheeks flushed fiercer. "They're three really powerful winterghasts, supposedly. They've never been seen together, and it's not like there's ever been a confirmed report or anything—"

"But there's been enough rumors that people have started giving them nicknames," her companion cut in. "All the rumors claim that they don't look like normal ghasts. They look almost *human*. Like, I've heard Decibel stands upright, but it's got spikes all over it. But it's also hard to be sure—apparently it's not easy to get a look at it. Cadaver has never technically been sighted, but its victims always look the same, just totally mangled. And Thundersnow is the biggest. I mean *huge,* as big as a building."

Domenic barked out a laugh. "As big as a building. Sure. Because why not, right?"

None of the others laughed with him.

Instead, there it was again. On Sanford's face. On her companion's. On Kleid's.

Fear.

Domenic's smile fell; his pettiness extinguished.

He muttered a quick goodbye and stalked away. Kleid scurried after him with the rest of Domenic's supplies piled in his arms.

Once he'd finished donning the dozen layers of warmth and armor, Domenic joined Peak where he addressed a squad of five magicians. Beneath all their gear, Domenic couldn't differentiate any of them, and he only picked out Peak by the sight of Targath in his hand. It was even more impressive unsheathed, its calcified oak handle ridged with igneous veins.

"Our primary goal is to locate the scouting team," Peak said. "If they need assistance, Matthews, Young, you split off to help them. The rest of us, we'll be hunting whatever ghasts are left.

We can't afford to stall. Blink, and a category four can turn category five real fast. And the longer we're in there, the more time we give frostmaul to set in. So we stick to formation. We keep our wands out and warm. And we keep moving. Got it?"

"Got it," the other magicians echoed.

"Then let's go."

As the group hurried across the field, Peak jerked his head at Domenic to walk beside him. Domenic was all too happy to do so. Peak seemed a better leader than Domenic had given him credit for. And Domenic intended to stick closer to him than a hemorrhoid.

"We're getting a bit more than we bargained for, huh?" Peak said, not sounding the least bit distressed about it. "But the plan's the same. You stay by my side. You keep a heat spell going. And that's all you gotta do, Dom. Got it?"

"Yeah," Domenic answered weakly.

Peak beamed and clapped his shoulder. "Attaboy."

The team halted at the edge of the winterscurge and assembled into a two-three-two formation, with Domenic at the center and Peak on his right. Each magician slid their wands into the narrow slits of their gloves, their collective radiance swathing the group in a warm, golden net.

Domenic mirrored them, and several heads whipped toward him as he unsheathed Valmordion. He stifled a wince as its thorns scraped his wounds. Then, carefully, nervously, he released the smallest fraction of his magic into a spell. To his amazement, the net brightened tenfold, its every crevice sealing into a shield. With a training wand, such power would've taxed him. With Valmordion, it'd cost him nothing at all.

Though Domenic couldn't see their expressions, the other magicians continued to stare at him, and Peak shot him a thumbs-up. A measly sprig of pride sprouted in Domenic's chest.

"All right!" Peak shouted. "We enter in three . . . two . . . one!"

It felt like plunging into ice water. The winds struck Domenic as if a punch to the gut, and he staggered so as not to be blown over. Though the cold didn't pierce through the shield, the frozen sheet across the ground cracked like glass beneath their boots, and the storm's roar thundered in his eardrums, rattling him down to his bones.

He'd hoped that the ghast he and Caldwell had faced in Mercester Square would've prepared him for this moment. But the scurge that single monster had summoned bore no comparison to this.

They moved at a slow jog. As bright as it was, their shield only illuminated several feet ahead of them, and Domenic took in every boulder, every tree, bracing for a beast to emerge from the dark.

They didn't sight the lost team until they collided with them.

It was immediate chaos: magicians shouting and barreling into each other, enchantments flickering, wands haphazardly blasting into the sky. And while the rest of the rescue party dashed back into formation, Domenic froze. It was no wonder the scouts had yet to return; they had encountered not one winterghast, but an entire pack. The closest resembled a crude approximation of a wolverine, its limbs bent at unnatural angles, its fang-bristled mouth encompassing nearly the entirety of its skull. Behind it, ghasts like a spider, a serpent, and a fox swarmed the few scouts still standing. In the saturation of Valmordion's filter, the eyes of every monster glowed an otherworldly, piercing blue.

Immediately, Peak shouted, "Get back!" A golden spell blasted out of Targath toward the wolverine. It burned clean through its abdomen, and its balance buckled as its wound seeped with water.

"You're here," one of the scouts gasped with relief. He knelt beside a wounded magician. The gash that raked across his gear had exposed him to the storm's magic. Already, bloodied frost-maul crystallized across the side of his jaw, down his neck, and across his shoulder. His breaths heaved out in spurts.

Domenic reeled back. Each time he blinked, he saw red. He saw Syarthis.

"We need to evac Varley, sir," the scout continued. "But the ghasts..."

All around, the ghasts advanced. One of the spider's many mangled legs jabbed toward a pair of scouts, who toppled back as their shield shattered above them. To the left, the hole in the wolverine's abdomen resealed, and it charged toward the rescue team. Domenic ducked as their frantic missiles of fire or beams of sunlight flared at it through the blackness.

"Change of plans!" Peak shouted. "Kim, Matthews, Young—escort the scouts back to camp! The rest of you, move on to hunt down whichever ghasts are left."

"The rest of us?" Domenic choked. "What about you?"

Peak turned to him, and to Domenic's shock, Peak tore off his balaclava. But Peak's skin wasn't flushed from the cold—he was sweating. He shrugged off his coat, left only in the armor.

"I'm gonna stay behind to take out these ghasts," Peak told him. "I know this isn't what we planned, but this storm's a bit dicier than we thought. And we can't afford to waste time—"

"You're taking on all four of these ghasts *alone*?"

Peak's sickle-edged smile looked all the sharper in his wand's orange glow. "Oh, don't go worrying about me and Targath. But Dom, I need to hear that you can do this. *Can you do this?*"

Domenic's throat clamped shut. But he couldn't admit his cowardice to the very man risking his life for the sake of the mission. "Y-yes. I think so."

Peak winked. "Good, 'cause I know you can."

Domenic and the remaining pair of magicians ran off. Their formation shifted into a triangle, and Domenic happily claimed one of the spots at the rear. Shards of frost whirled past, scraping like claws across their shield.

"In a category four, there will be six ghasts. Maybe seven," one of the others said—Osakwe, Domenic thought. "That means we have two or three left to hunt down. So keep your eyes peeled for any—"

Abruptly, Osakwe stopped, and Domenic barreled into his back.

Without warning, the winds quickened. The snowflakes thickened into a barrage, and a glowing silver shape coalesced above them. It had wings. Talons like scythes, a beak like a raptor.

"Look out!" Osakwe called.

The three of them threw themselves aside as the ghast swooped. It grasped the other magician by the leg, wrenching him up as if to carry off its prey. Then flames spewed from Osakwe's wand, and the ghast released him with a screech.

As Domenic scrambled upright, the winds hurled him back onto his side, and he rolled until he cast a rooting spell to tether him to the ground. While Osawke yanked the other magician to his feet, Domenic pointed Valmordion at the ghast. Light exploded from his wand, so gigantic it utterly consumed the ghast—and in an instant, obliterated it.

Domenic shuddered with relief as he lowered his wand. Yet there was no chance to celebrate. Even with the ghast gone, the winds continued to accelerate, and the darkness crushed down on them, a force unto itself.

Osakwe cursed. "This is a category five."

Category five storms were caused by ghasts gathered in the greatest numbers. They could level an undefended city, could freeze civilians solid in their own beds.

"Wh-what do we do, sir?" stuttered the second magician.

Domenic waited for Osakwe to respond, only to realize he'd been asking *him*. "What?" he croaked.

"Peak sent us to slay a few ghasts—not an army of them. And even if we could hunt them down, we're getting tired, and if our shields give out . . ." The magician shivered as he clutched his wand against his chest.

Domenic agreed. This wasn't the mission Peak had given

him. Which meant, no matter how much the storm worsened, it wasn't Domenic's responsibility.

And yet, it was. Because even if Domenic would give anything to thrust this burden on someone else, someone better, he didn't *want* to do nothing while a category five scurge decimated Oldermere. He didn't *want* the Council to think he was worthless. He didn't *want* Floyd-fucking-Wilder broadcasting across the nation that they were all doomed.

"I'm gonna stop the scurge," Domenic said. "How far is it to the eye?"

"The *eye?*" Osakwe repeated. "Sir, the last magician who fell into an eye was literally shredded. And that was a category three—"

"I'll be fine. Go find Peak, both of you."

"But—"

"That's an order."

Domenic tried to match Peak's authoritative tenor. He was pretty sure he sounded like a cartoon.

But to his surprise, Osawke said, "The eye is at the storm's center, where the dark is deepest. G-good luck. Sir."

And just like that, Domenic was alone.

Heart hammering, Domenic raised Valmordion higher. He spun, and in Valmordion's filter, even the blackness of the scurge had color, layers and layers of it. But there, to his right. It was as though the darkness had substance.

He ran into it.

Monstrous sounds pierced through the wind: wails and howls, shrieks and growls. Domenic ignored them, pressing onward into such obscurity that Valmordion's light only penetrated a few feet ahead of him.

Just as Domenic feared that it would be—not a ghast—but the cramp in his side that murdered him, he saw it: a column of whirling magic, spearing up through the storm into the sky.

Colors shattered across it, blues and violets and silvers of such vibrancy that Domenic's mouth fell ajar.

It was horrible.

It was beautiful.

Domenic didn't pause to doubt. He threw himself into the eye of the storm.

He broke through with a gasp and fell to his knees. The winds lashed at him, sharp with frost. But when he looked up, he glimpsed stars. They speckled the small pinprick of clear sky above, everything else swallowed by the great vortex of the storm's gullet.

Peak hadn't explained how to dispel a scurge from its eye. And so, desperately, Domenic pointed Valmordion skyward. A golden beam detonated from it, so bright it blinded him, so powerful he had to grasp the wand with both hands to hold it steady. And as the rays pierced through the solid blackness of the storm, Domenic felt every wind that slowed, every shard of frost that melted. He felt the very storm shudder.

But he also felt fire.

His skin warmed, feverish, and Domenic ripped down his hood, tore off his goggles and balaclava. Immediately, he pictured Alice Rhodes, incinerated in a pyre of Valmordion's own making.

"Don't burn me," he pleaded, then he coughed, smoke pluming from his mouth. *"Please."*

But maybe that'd be for the best. Maybe the most heroic deed Domenic Barrow could ever do for his country was to die.

Yet for all he'd grown to hate himself, he knew that wasn't true.

Domenic thought of his magic, as he'd always felt it to be. He thought of vermilion sunsets and viridian leaves. He thought of meadows blooming, of forests rising. He thought of hope that sprouted like weeds, impossible to prune.

He thought of Summer.

He squeezed his eyes shut as he felt the power burn hotter, hotter, hotter. And just as he braced himself for death, a ray of warmth burst from above, casting down on him as if a spotlight of radiance. Then the enchantment flooded across the scurge. In Valmordion's filter, it shimmered in fractals, vibrantly incandescent.

Monsters howled throughout the storm, but the sounds dimmed as, one by one, Domenic's magic consumed them. Gradually, the cold lessened. Raindrops fell as frost melted midair. And, like a sigh, the winterscurge dissipated.

"Fuck," Domenic breathed. "I did it."

He collapsed onto his back, his fingers lacing through thawing grass. He marveled at the stars. He let himself cry.

Dimly, he made out hollers of victory.

For several seconds, he did nothing but listen. His shoulders heaved as he caught his breath, and after wiping the sweat off his brow, he gaped at his hands. His wounds from Valmordion's thorns—they were gone.

Suddenly, a voice like the crackles of flames hissed in his ear.

what long laid buried lies only in wait
silent land in need of resurrection

Domenic stiffened. It couldn't be.

But even if it was, even if some parts of destiny *were* real, why would he only get the first prophecy piece now?

The realization poured over him like a sunrise. Prophecy pieces were instructions, each stanza granted once the previous one had been fulfilled.

He *hadn't* heard the first prophecy piece.

He'd heard the second.

# XV
ELLERY
WINTER

Julian's chest barely moved below the blankets on his hospital bed, and the fine golden mist of a healing spell hovered around him. But Valmordion's wounds were not easily healed. Bandages swathed half of his face, his shoulder, and his wand hand. Ellery hated seeing him like this, so still, as though his sharp focus had been dulled.

Gaudy flower arrangements and stuffed animals crowded the room, enchanted to change color or spout a jingle when pressed. Condolence cards from classmates and his parents' colleagues cluttered the nightstand. Ellery frowned at one in particular.

Better luck next time, it read, which seemed a grotesque misinterpretation of the situation.

"I told the nurses to toss all the roses," she whispered to Julian, her bandaged hand clutching his own. "What's that ridiculous thing you used to say? 'Why would you ever hold a flower that could hurt you?'"

Their argument at the vigil was a fresh bruise. Ellery had kept secrets and dodged questions for so long, hoping her suspicions of her Winter magic were mere paranoia. But instead they'd been confirmed in the worst way possible. And now that Ellery desperately wished to tell Julian the truth, the Council had forbidden it.

Although they'd deemed her to be no true threat without Iskarius, they'd released her last night with severe restrictions: she was not to leave the Citadel, she was not to use magic, she was not to breathe a word of the previous night. She couldn't even visit her injured friend without a magician standing guard in the hall.

Ellery was a prisoner in the only place that had ever felt like home.

After wounding three Council members, she deserved to be.

Glynn must've thought so too, otherwise he would've come to see her, would've been there when the rest of the Council—

A radio crackled on the nightstand.

"*—no reported casualties, minimal damage to property. It seems Barrow pulled off a win after all.*"

"*I'll admit I had my doubts,*" said Floyd Wilder. "*But hey, Valmordion doesn't Choose wrong. I said that, didn't I?*"

The door creaked open. Demelza set down her own flower bouquet and rushed to wrap Ellery in a hug. Ellery hugged her back uncomfortably, aware that Demelza was trembling.

"Where have you been?" the other girl asked, drawing away. To the untrained eye, Demelza looked polished and peppy. But Ellery knew the defensive power of a full face of makeup.

"I've been in my room," Ellery answered carefully. "After last night, I didn't want to see anyone."

Demelza grimaced. "It was horrible, wasn't it? Apparently, Julian's parents will be here in a few hours."

Ellery knew Julian's doting parents from their regular visits. His mother was sure to find flaws with his doctors' care regimen. His father was sure to find loopholes in the academy's safety policies.

"They're taking him home as soon as he's cleared for such a long journey," Demelza continued. Normally the flight to Julian's hometown would take no more than an hour, but all airports had been shut down for Winter due to the threat of scurges. His parents would have to take a train instead. "I heard they're even suing the Order."

"What? They're pulling him out of the academy?"

"Yeah, I think so."

Ellery stared at the half of Julian's face that wasn't bandaged, aghast. She couldn't picture life at the academy without him, the surprising loudness of his laugh or his insistence that he knew every shortcut on campus or the way he paid attention to the credits of every movie, stubbornly shushing his friends when they dared to talk through them.

"He'll come back," she insisted. "He wants this too badly."

"If you say so." Demelza studied Julian's prone form dubiously. "Between a cataclysm coming and now the vigil, everyone's totally shaken up. A few students have left. I mean, there was a category five scurge on the very first night of Winter! My parents called me last night after the news broke. They begged me to drop out, come home. They don't want me fighting ghosts on the front lines."

"Are you going to listen to them?"

"No, I'm not." Her expression hardened. "When I decided to study magic, my parents assumed it was more out of curiosity than anything else. And I've heard the rumors—that I'm some shallow starlet, here on a lark. But magic isn't a game to me. It's the realest thing I've ever known. I won't pretend that Winter doesn't freak me out, but I know magic is the only way to stop it. So I'm going to use my magic to change things. To help people. And considering *Domenic Barrow* is our fated Chosen One, Alderland needs all the help it can get."

Ellery bristled. "He stopped that category five winterscurge, didn't he?"

"Sure. But you have to admit, he was an unconventional Choice."

Judging solely by Barrow's reputation, that was true. But nothing about the boy who'd fought beside her in Mercester Square resembled the apathetic person she'd thought he was.

And Ellery knew more than most how much a reputation could hide.

"He was Valmordion's Choice," Ellery countered. "Isn't that all that matters?"

"Huh." Demelza studied her. "There really *is* something going on with you two, isn't there?"

Ellery tensed. Her eyes flickered toward Julian, still unconscious. "Seriously? This again?"

"So you're telling me you weren't with him last night?"

"Of course I wasn't—"

"Oh, come *on,* Ellery. Barrow might be the talk of the country right now, but the entire academy's talking about you, too. People saw you both escorted out of the grove right after he bonded with Valmordion."

Ellery's heart thrummed and she tried to keep her expression still, all too aware of the magician lurking outside.

"I'm not saying you're together," Demelza continued exasperatedly. "I'm saying you're involved in the prophecy, somehow. Or are you telling me the magician in the hall isn't guarding the door, like the Prime Minister's inside?"

"I'm not . . . whatever you think I am," Ellery said helplessly.

Demelza arched a perfectly manicured brow. "Sure you're not. You saved Julian's life, you know."

"I'm pretty sure the healers did that."

"I saw it. You put out Valmordion's flames with a training wand. That's unbelievable!"

Ellery winced.

"Clearly you can't get into it, or maybe you just won't," Demelza went on. She smiled cautiously at Ellery, with a sort of sweet, tentative trust. "But knowing you're part of this, even if I don't know how yet—it makes me feel a little better about what's coming."

Ellery couldn't return her smile. If Demelza knew the truth, she would fear her. And if she'd actually had the chance to tell Julian, he'd probably fear her, too.

* * *

Back in her dorm room, Ellery shucked off her uniform blazer and rolled up her sleeves. Despite the Wintery chill, she was too warm.

Branches rapped against her window like knucklebones. She jolted at the sound, then dismissed it.

It happened again, louder.

Ellery approached the glass slowly. In the courtyard below stood a lanky figure, leaning against a leafless tree.

Ellery gasped and yanked up her window. *"Barrow?"*

The presumed savior of Alderland slackened with relief. "I was starting to worry they had you locked in a dungeon somewhere."

Surely Barrow had more important things to do than knock on Ellery's window, as though she were some storybook princess in a tower.

Then he added, "If you're worried about your guard overhearing us, don't. I've cast a privacy enchantment over the two of us. Chosen One perks." Barrow patted the sheath that jutted from his coat pocket—alban wood white. Ellery glanced at a pair of students passing by the trails, oblivious to the most famous person in the country making a scene only yards away. "So are you gonna let me in?"

"Um . . . sure," she said weakly. "Come in. Or up, I guess."

He hoisted himself up the tree. At each foothold he left behind, buds sprouted from the bare Winter branches—small but vibrantly green. With surprising ease, he reached the top and ducked beneath her window frame.

"That was fast," Ellery muttered as he straightened, dusting bits of bark off his hands.

"Yeah, well, believe it or not," he said sheepishly, "I've done this before."

Ellery flushed self-consciously as he examined her bedroom decor—paying particular attention to the posters of Kent Sinclair, her favorite movie star. "And here I was thinking all those rumors about you were exaggerated."

She only spoke lightly because she didn't know what to say. Dark bags sank beneath Barrow's bloodshot eyes, and he locked his shoulders tight, like he might jolt into action at the single tick of a clock or creak of a door. Yet beyond his exhaustion, there was something different about him she struggled to identify. He seemed to stand taller, but he was already so tall it was hard to say. There was the way the light caught him, winking along his silhouette.

Ellery's gaze fell upon Valmordion's sheath, decorated with a rim of solid gold. A memory flashed through her mind of Julian burning, screaming, that oppressive, terrible heat. She shuddered and looked away.

"I appreciate you paying a visit to my tower and all," she said awkwardly. "But shouldn't you still be in Oldermere?"

"My train got in an hour ago. The Council decided I'd earned myself a chance to sleep."

"So the Council doesn't know you're here."

"No, they don't." He fiddled with something in his pocket. "After the scurge, I was up all night, thinking. The Council told me what happened yesterday in Glynn's office, with your wand. But they're wrong about you. I know for a fact that your prophecy piece is real."

Ellery gaped. "*What?* How could you possibly know that?"

"Because I . . ." Barrow's throat bobbed, and without warning, he sprang into a frantic flurry of action. He yanked a throw blanket off her bed and draped it atop her desk chair, then spun it around. Next, to her utter bewilderment, he dragged over her waste bin. "Here. Why don't you sit? You want some water? I can conjure some—"

"Stop," Ellery said fiercely. She stayed standing. "Just tell me. Why are you so convinced my prophecy piece is real?"

He exhaled shakily. "Because I fulfilled it. And now I have another."

That couldn't be right. Ellery reached for an alban pit that was no longer there. She clenched her empty hand into a fist, quaking.

From that point onward, Barrow didn't look at her. He paced, recounting his last eighteen hours in grim, occasionally humiliating detail—right down to the need for a wastebin.

"I-I'm sorry, Caldwell. I know this is a lot. And I know you didn't want this. I sure as hell didn't want this either. A day ago, I thought I was the last person who should ever be wielding Valmordion. And now I . . . I don't know. Maybe that isn't true. But I still feel like I'm losing my fucking mind." He raked a hand through his already disheveled hair. "The point is, your prophecy piece—'power that will rise from your own ruin.' During the scurge, there was a moment when I-I really thought I was going to burn. Just like Rhodes. But I didn't. I pushed through. I defeated it. And I heard a prophecy piece for the first time. And it didn't take that long to hear one because I'm a mistake, it took that long because I was supposed to fulfill *yours*. So don't you see? *This* is what the original prophecy means, that 'an ancient peace must be restored.' It's Summer and Winter. It's you and me. We're both Chosen Ones, and we're in this together."

For however compelling his argument, however fervent his tone, Ellery struggled to absorb the full weight of his words.

"You're wrong," she murmured. "The cataclysm is always Winter. I wield Winter magic. I lost control and I *hurt* people. How could I possibly be a Chosen One?"

"When I ran from the vigil, I thought I was about to lose control, too." Barrow regarded her gently. "Think about it. How many people have you already saved from Winter? In Mercester Square? In Nordmere? It seems to me like if anyone would be Chosen to save Alderland and reclaim the fallen territory, it'd be you."

Ellery cringed at the mention of Nordmere. "It's not that simple."

"Then explain it to me. Because I don't see it. I don't see how someone as heroic as you could ever—"

"Because I knew I had Winter magic!" Ellery shouted, making Barrow stiffen. "I knew the whole time, okay? I convinced myself it was all in my head, and I made myself believe it, because I wanted so desperately to believe it. Because Winter is Alderland's greatest enemy. *Your* greatest enemy. I've worried about this my whole childhood, my whole *life* . . ."

Ellery stepped away from Barrow, trembling. She stared at her bandaged hand, remembering how it had felt to hold Iskarius. So inevitable. So right.

"I think some part of me has always understood I was destined for Winter. Destined for Iskarius. I just can't hide from it anymore. I know I didn't mean to hurt anyone, but the Council is still right to be afraid of me. So I'm sorry, but . . ." She blinked back tears. "I can't be whoever you want me to be."

Barrow blanched. "Do you mean that?"

"Of course I do. I'm not—"

"No, about destiny. You always knew you were a Chosen One?"

Ellery paused. "You didn't?"

Barrow's hand hovered above Valmordion. He swallowed. "I'm still not sure I'm the destiny sort."

It was unusual for anyone in Alderland not to believe in destiny, let alone a Chosen One.

"If you're not sure about fate, how can you be so sure about me?" When he didn't answer, she pressed, "Seriously. You lie to the whole Council. You sneak in here. You spill confidential information. *Why?*"

"Because . . ." Barrow dragged a hand down his face. "I guess I thought, maybe, just maybe, I wouldn't have to do this alone."

Ellery hesitated, feeling a strange mixture of agitation and guilt.

He choked out a laugh. "Let me guess. You think I'm a coward."

"No, I don't. If anything, what you've done is brave. Maybe

a little deranged, but brave. I just need a moment to think. Like you said, this is a lot."

Barrow nodded vigorously. He was slightly pink.

Ellery chewed her lip as she considered his theories. Her own doubts aside, it was hard to focus with him watching her. Despite everything she'd told him, she could find no trace of fear or revulsion in his expression.

This close, his freckles accentuated the honey brown of his irises.

"You said you got a new prophecy piece in Oldermere," she spoke at last. "What was it?"

"'What long laid buried lies only in wait,'" he recited. "'Silent land in need of resurrection.'"

It perfectly matched the prophecy piece Ellery herself had received, in rhythm, in tone. She parsed through the riddle of the words. Resurrection implied death. And there was only one piece of land she could think of that was gone, that was silent.

"It's the Barren," she breathed, remembering what Glynn had shown her: that blank space on the map of Gallamere, the site of the dead alban tree.

"The what?"

"It must be. And I know exactly where we need to go. It's right at the edge of the city."

Barrow sucked in a breath and withdrew from his pocket, oddly, a dandelion. No matter how much he worried the stem, it never wilted, and its petals never drooped.

"What are you suggesting?" he asked carefully.

"That the Council won't believe any of this. Not without proof. So maybe we should try to find some. If we're supposed to fulfill each other's prophecy pieces, then I would get one next, yeah? And that would mean that I, that we . . ." Ellery couldn't bring herself to say it, to dare to hope. She continued hastily, "If there's any chance at all you're right, we owe it to Alderland to give this everything we've got."

Barrow's chest swelled, and Ellery swore that the rays of sunlight streaming through her window brightened. "I agree with you."

"Okay then." Ellery exhaled. "If you snuck in, you can definitely sneak me out. But we've got a problem. The Council told me they were going to d-destroy Iskarius."

Her voice quavered on the last words. No matter how terrible the wand was, it was still *hers*.

He snorted. "Oh, I know. They've been trying, but I found out when I got back that they haven't even managed to scratch it. And I know where they're keeping it."

Relief flooded through her. "Then how long do we've got before anyone notices you're gone?"

"Hmm . . . I'm supposed to meet with the Council this afternoon." The corner of his mouth quirked. "So what do you say, Caldwell? Up to play a little hooky?"

Ellery let out a surprised laugh. "Gee, Barrow. I thought you'd never ask."

 XVI

Ellery

Winter

The car's headlights beamed onto the frosty gate at the entrance to the Barren. An ominous sign was fastened to the chain links:

TRESPASSERS WILL BE PROSECUTED

Barrow cranked down the passenger window and pointed Valmordion at the gate. Obediently, it swung open. Beyond stretched a thin dirt path, crowded by forest and crusted with ice.

"Quite the rap sheet we're growing here," Barrow muttered. "Trespassing, breaking and entering, carjacking . . ."

"Technically it's not carjacking if we borrowed it."

"Don't worry. Hanna's car has definitely seen worse."

Ellery didn't doubt it. Gum wrappers littered the floor. Spare shoes were piled in the back alongside stacks of overdue library books. And Iskarius sat in a sticky cup holder, shoved in a plain brown sheath, ancient and unknowable and perilously close to a sloshing thermos of mystery liquid.

She still couldn't believe what the two of them had done. Barrow had cast an illusion of Ellery sound asleep in her dorm. Then they'd taken Iskarius from the Vault, supposedly the most secure place in the Citadel, a place Barrow claimed he'd somehow broken into *before*. They'd stolen a Councilor's car. And to top it all off, if they were wrong, she'd be tried for treason.

Ellery Caldwell, perfect hero, was well and truly gone. In her place was Ellery Caldwell, rogue Winter magician.

Ellery drove on until the paved road abruptly stopped, replaced by inhospitable underbrush. She pulled over, and they stepped out into a cluster of trees, birches with bare branches, pine still adorned with green bristles.

"The forest looks normal," she said as she tucked Iskarius inside her uniform blazer.

"But it's not," Barrow said. "You feel it too, right? It's like . . ."

"Like there's something wrong about this place. Even if I can't see it, I *know* it. And I feel this awful dread."

"Exactly." He approached the tree line. "You said there's a dead alban here?"

"According to Glynn, yeah. And I don't think he was lying."

"Well, knowing the Order, they're hiding it with more than a trespassing sign. Do you see anything? Any flickers? Seams?"

Ellery studied the nearby branches. Illusions often bore a telltale golden shimmer of magic or an unrealistic feature, like impossible symmetry. "Not yet."

Then, mere moments later, Barrow gasped, "There! You see it? By that oak?"

Ellery joined him beside the oak in question. There was the slightest hint of a magic seam on its trunk, like a loose stitch in a piece of clothing. "Yes, I do."

Barrow drew Valmordion. Ellery reached for Iskarius, then hesitated, images of Sharpe's frostmaul vivid in her mind. She couldn't lose control again.

Barrow swiped Valmordion down, as if slicing a crease through the air. Instantaneously, the illusion dissipated.

"Well, damn," Barrow breathed.

The Barren was much larger than Ellery had expected, a forest of death that blotted out the horizon with its clawed branches. The hollowed husks of trees were packed together tight as headstones. Striations of scarred earth snaked through the dirt like veins.

"It's like a horror movie set," Ellery said. "All that's missing is some cheesy fake fog."

"I should warn you. I'm terrible at horror movies."

"Even the ones with bad special effects? Come on, those are only scary if you're a kid."

"Hey now. My past two days have been one continuous horror movie. So be prepared—if there's a jumpscare, I might leap straight into your arms."

Barrow offered her the same charming smile he'd worn back in Mercester Square. And although Ellery was tempted to return it, the weeks since that night already felt like a lifetime, the enchantment they'd made together inevitably long since faded.

Besides, flirting probably meant something very different to him than it did to her.

She strode into the forest.

The crooked canopy shrouded the sun, making her feel as though they wandered through an endless twilight. The wood felt utterly removed from Gallamere. They could have been thousands of miles away. They could have been in another world.

Ellery understood why the Order had concealed this place. It disturbed her to know an alban languished in such a dismal grave.

The two of them kept up a seemingly lighthearted conversation, ranging from more horror films to magazines, most of which Barrow had never heard of. Yet Ellery's dread grew more and more difficult to ignore, a pervasive, unmistakable sense that each step she took was closer to her doom.

Until she tripped on a root—an alban root. But instead of the familiar white, this one was gray.

"Found it," she whispered.

They followed the shriveled roots to a nearby clearing, where an alban tree awaited them, split nearly in two. Each half was twisted, mangled, with deep, ugly grooves carved within the bark. The branches were emaciated, devoid of life, devoid of Summer. And the scarred, ruined land twined around it, like the center of a knot. Somehow, it still stood.

Dread seemed to ripple outward from the tree itself. Ellery

was gripped by the sudden sense that something terrible had happened here.

"What could possibly be powerful enough to kill an alban tree?" she murmured.

"Beats me." Barrow treaded toward it wearing a haunted sort of wonder. His grip tightened around Valmordion. "But you were right about this being the place from the prophecy piece. I'm sure of it."

"I think so, too. The question is what we do next. The prophecy piece said, 'silent land in need of resurrection.'"

"Wild guess: this alban tree's dead. We revive it."

"I'd agree with you, but Glynn said past Chosen Ones couldn't heal this. So if we're meant to save this tree, I'm not sure how."

Barrow's charming smile returned. "Well, none of the past Chosen Ones were part of a Chosen Two."

Ellery knew this was what they'd come here to prove. But she struggled to meet his eyes. And when she drew Iskarius, she stiffened. Its power—*her* power—poured through her, plunging to unfathomable depths.

Barrow rolled his neck, shook out his limbs. As if readying for a sports match. His smile was gone. "All right. We've got this. On three?"

He pointed Valmordion at the trunk. Ellery mirrored him with Iskarius.

"One," she counted, "two . . ."

Yet as she spoke "three," it was only Barrow who cast a spell, not her. A soft golden glow emanated from the tree, then spread up its branches and down its roots. For several seconds it shone, until it gradually faded.

The tree remained unchanged.

Barrow glanced cautiously toward her.

"I know," Ellery said. "It's just that last time I used Iskarius, I . . . Forget it. I'll try."

Ellery grasped Iskarius more tightly, then leveled it once more. Barrow paused, looking like he wanted to say something.

But before he could, wind whipped through the clearing. With it came a soft susurration that crescendoed to a frantic howl.

In front of the tree trunk, flickering furiously, a monster materialized.

An outline of liquid silver coagulated into a humanoid form, but far taller than any person, stretching at least ten feet high. A ridge of spikes rippled down its back, and blue eyes blazed within a gaunt, sunken face. Yet its form was ephemeral; pieces of it shifting, always shifting, as if it were made from the static of a broken projector screen.

Ellery gaped. "Is that a *winterghast*?"

"Um," Barrow croaked, "according to an acquaintance of mine, it's called Decibel."

"What—"

Before Ellery could finish, their surroundings shifted. Trees warped and bent at impossible angles, and Ellery staggered, stricken. A winterghast who conjured illusions, not storm.

"It's using enchantment magic," she rasped.

"That's not possible."

"Well, does that look like nature magic to *you*?"

"No, but it's a monster. It can't—"

"Glynn told me the winterghasts might be evolving, somehow. Getting smarter."

Barrow uttered a choked noise. "Is there anything else Glynn filled you in on that you wanna—"

The monster lunged for them. Barrow hurled a torrent of flames, blindingly luminescent. But before the spell could connect, the ghast vanished.

"Where did it go?" Ellery asked anxiously, as seconds passed.

"I don't know," Barrow answered. "I didn't know ghasts could cloak—"

Decibel reappeared at the opposite end of the clearing. Barrow instantly shot a golden beam at the creature, and it shrieked as light struck its chest. The sound was unlike anything Ellery had ever heard, neither human nor monstrous. Like the thunderous crackle of white noise, serrated enough to slice through an eardrum.

As she willed herself to fight beside him, a rhythm pulsed behind her sternum. Just like the battle in Mercester Square, her magic felt like the ghost's magic. But now that she wielded Iskarius, that connection was deeper, more intimate—as though she could sense Decibel's heartbeat beneath her own skin.

And for the first time in her life, when faced with danger, Ellery didn't move.

Without warning, the earth around them tilted. Like a dial turned, the sky dropped clockwise as the ground reared up into a great wall. Ellery's balance tipped, and Barrow crashed into her, sending them both sliding into a tree. While she toppled onto her side, he scrambled up and fired another blast of nature magic at the ghost.

Decibel dodged as it advanced upon them. The spikes on its back seemed to grow sharper. The blue of its eyes flashed as a row of spikes sloughed off, then spun around its body, hovering in the air like throwing knives.

All at once, they launched toward them.

Barrow hastily conjured a shield, and as the spikes collided with its translucent dome, they disintegrated into speckles of silver. Keeping the shield intact, he whipped around to face her.

"Caldwell. Caldwell." When she still didn't respond, Barrow knelt beside her. "*Ellery.* I know you're scared, but we're in this together, aren't we? I need you to . . ."

Whatever else he said, Ellery scarcely heard him. Magic writhed in her, but she choked it down, nearly gagging from the effort.

Barrow's expression hardened, grim and resolute. He stood and turned back to Decibel. And as he raced toward it, the clearing brightened with Valmordion's radiance.

Ice crackled around Ellery's hand, welding it to her wand. Each breath was a tiny rasp, barely able to break through the frost crusted across her lips.

Valmordion had burned Alice Rhodes alive. But Iskarius was about to freeze her solid.

And part of Ellery, a terrible, selfish part, reached for the death it could give her. It would be so easy to fade into oblivion. There would be no more pain. No more terror.

But as her limbs went numb, as her lungs stiffened in her chest, she knew, she *knew*: she had to live. Maybe she didn't have proof of the prophecy yet, but she could no longer deny the unshakable feeling that she'd first had in the Citadel grove. That they truly were in this together.

Ellery's gaze snapped to Iskarius, its glowing silver core, its hilt majestic and thorn-studded, engraved with her fingerprint and hers alone. She stopped fighting her power. Instead, she reached for it.

Instantly the gashes on her hand began to close, until the throbbing pain in her palm ceased. Awe rose in her, and with it came a rustling wind, a discordant whisper:

> *join an old legacy to a new fate*
> *uncover the tangled roots of the past*

Ellery clambered to her feet. Tears spilled down her cheeks and dribbled onto her chin, but she paid them no mind.

"Domenic!" she called.

He whirled around, and at the sight of her, his expression slackened with relief. "You're up."

"I'm with you. And I'm not going anywhere."

Another row of spikes rocketed toward them at an impossible velocity. Cool silver light erupted from Iskarius's tip. Beside her, Valmordion blazed with a matching gold.

Their combined spells met the spikes in a great explosion. Ellery gasped from the force of it, then reeled away, instinctively bracing her back against Domenic's. She could feel each shudder of his breath, his form strong and reassuring against her shoulder blades.

Before Decibel could conjure another attack, Ellery raised Iskarius, magic already crackling across its thorns.

Again, the ghost vanished.

"That thing is *playing* with us," Domenic groaned. "How the hell are we supposed to hurt it if it keeps disappearing?"

"We need to outwit it," Ellery said. "Does nature magic actually hurt it?"

"Well, it definitely didn't like my fire. It's more of a matter of getting through its illusions to land a hit."

Ellery's heartbeat hammered with the rhythm she'd never wanted to hear, the pull she'd never wanted to heed.

"If I concentrate, I can hear Decibel's heartbeat. I think it's a Winter magic thing, and it might make me able to track it. If I can, I'll break its cloaking spell."

Ellery readied herself for Domenic's unease about her magic bearing any connection to the monster. But he only nodded.

"Then you find it. And I'll take it down."

"Perfect." She grasped Iskarius with both hands.

Sounds sharpened; colors muted. Ellery caught the smallest of details: glimmers of frost in her exhales; blades of frozen grass crunching beneath her feet. Power spilled from her as the world melted into a harsh chiaroscuro.

She heard it then, faint but unmistakable. A *thud* inside her chest, beside her own. Another heartbeat. Another source of Winter magic.

A silver outline shimmered to their right, studded with spikes.

"Found it," she said triumphantly, then tore apart the monster's cloaking enchantment as easily as paper.

The ghost let out a whine of panicked static as it reappeared. Its spikes glinted; its eyes rolled wildly, blue beams darting like searchlights through the clearing.

Immediately, a ray like a solar flare detonated from Valmordion and lanced through the monster's chest. Decibel collapsed, writhing and howling as it melted from within. Throughout the clearing, snow dissolved from Valmordion's heat. Yet even as Domenic's arms trembled from exertion, the spell never diminished, only strengthened.

Until at last, Decibel was gone.

Domenic lowered Valmordion and braced his hands on his knees, cursing with every heaving breath.

"We're not dead," Ellery croaked, sheathing Iskarius.

"Speak for . . . yourself," Domenic panted. "I might . . . keel over here." Yet the moment he straightened, he laughed. "Fuck, we really pulled it off."

Ellery laughed too, spinning dizzily as she basked in the sunlight that seemed to drench them both, dreamlike. There was no more dread. No more fear.

"The Council will have to take us seriously when they hear about this," Domenic babbled. "I mean, poking around the Barren might've not gone down exactly the way we thought, but if the superstitions about the Dire Three are real, then maybe they're what will lead us to the next prophecy piece—"

"I already have the next prophecy piece."

Domenic balked. "You . . . really?"

"Yes." Ellery craned her neck up at him, grinning. "I heard it during the fight. I-I guess that means, um . . ."

Her throat clogged, and she sniffled. She couldn't remember the last time she'd cried because she was happy.

"You—*we*—were right," she told Domenic. "I'm a Chosen One. We both are."

With a delirious, victorious holler, Domenic pulled her into a hug.

Ellery gasped at the suddenness of it, of him. His arms folded tightly around her back. Her face pressed against his chest. His touch felt familiar, as though they'd known each other for years instead of days. An incredulous giddiness bubbled in her as she wrapped her arms around him, too, and as they leaned in to each other, his fingers brushed against the back of her neck. Immediately, Ellery's magic roared in response. As if it had been utterly diverted to this one point in the universe, to the pads of his fingertips against her skin. They broke away from each other, gasping. Heat radiated down her back. Her stunned expression mirrored his own.

"I . . ." Domenic's mouth hung open, but he seemed to have forgotten how to speak.

Ellery flushed and wiped away a final stray tear, searching desperately for something to say. Her gaze settled on an odd rock behind him. It shimmered blue amid the debris of the fight, like a gemstone.

"What's that?" she asked, hastily changing the subject.

Looking similarly relieved, Domenic turned. "Is that from the winterghast?"

"I don't know." Ellery walked over and knelt beside it. It was about the size of her fist, unnaturally smooth and spherical, glowing with a faint cerulean sheen that reminded her of Decibel's eyes. She drew Iskarius and pointed it at it, just in case. "There's nothing left of ghosts after they're destroyed. But you knew this one was different. How have you heard of Decibel before?"

"From some NDC superstitions. So, get this . . ." Domenic explained what he'd learned about the so-called Dire Three, finishing with, "But the rookies never mentioned them leaving pieces behind. I don't think any of them have ever been defeated."

Ellery tentatively touched the stone. It was cold, but seemingly harmless. She rose, clutching it.

"We should probably take it with us," Domenic said. "The Council will want to see it."

Ellery's excitement ebbed, reality flooding back in. "Oh. The Council."

"Hey, we've got our proof now," Domenic said firmly. "They have to believe us."

Ellery swallowed. "I really hope you're right."

XVII
Domenic
Winter

Domenic sauntered out of Iseul's study and halted at the kitchen's edge, marveling at the image of Ellery Caldwell rooting through the cabinets. Twin mugs of coffee steamed atop the counter.

"What are you looking for?" he asked.

"Um, sugar."

Domenic unsheathed the greatest wand in history and gave it a flick. The pantry door opened, and the jar floated out and set itself neatly beside the mugs.

"Thanks," Ellery said. Then, as a teaspoon sailed from the silverware drawer to join it, she smirked and added, "Wow. What manners."

"Yes, I'm a man of many facets." Ignoring the sugar, Domenic snatched one of the mugs and downed it. He was the kind of exhausted where just to stand was to strain against gravity, yet his thoughts whirled, delirious and drunken and jumbling together like crashing traffic. His hands shook as he lowered the mug.

"How'd the call go?" she asked.

"I think I gave Sharpe's secretary a heart attack. I said my name and she made this sort of shocked squeaky sound, like a rabbit. Do rabbits make sounds? Actually, never mind. That's not important. I told her I wanted the Council here as soon as possible. She mentioned Sharpe had another call with the Prime Minister in an hour, and you know what I said? I said, 'Cancel it.' Just like that."

Ellery Caldwell quirked a brow. Ellery Caldwell standing

in his kitchen. Ellery Caldwell barely a foot away from him, spooning far too much sugar into her mug.

Then her amusement dissipated, like the steam wafting off her coffee. "So the Council's really coming here, then."

"Yeah, they are. I didn't tell them that you're here or what we have planned, but I'm done letting them bully us. We're the Chosen Ones, for shit's sake! And we've fulfilled two prophecy pieces in twenty-four hours. From now on, *they* come to *us*."

Ellery chewed on her lip, an expression Domenic already knew to mean she was worried. "I think we did the right thing. But the most powerful people in the country won't appreciate being strong-armed."

"Actually, breaking news, *we're* now the most powerful people in the country. I mean, one day, this place will probably be a museum." He gestured around grandly. "Welcome to the residence of Domenic Barrow, Chosen One. Also Councilors Iseul Seong and Hanna Mayes. It's within this humble abode that our great story began."

Ellery studied him as she sipped her coffee, and he feared she disapproved of joking about such dire circumstances—but Domenic couldn't fathom treating them any other way.

Then a smile crept across her face.

"Because a full set of electric appliances and expensive antique furniture really screams humble," she drawled, then pointed at the breakfast nook. "Don't tell me—is this really it? *The* table where the Chosen One ate his morning toast?"

"What an eye you have! Indeed, that is the very one! And here, come on." He bounced through the dining room and into the parlor. "It's on this settee where he had many a breakdown. And this! The powder room he once slept in during that week last Winter when all three of the house's occupants had the flu and he, ever the gentleman, claimed the only toilet downstairs."

"How chivalrous of you."

"How *heroic,* you could even say."

Ellery snorted lightly and examined the small portrait of Domenic along the stairwell, the one Iseul had insisted on commissioning for his and Hanna's fourteenth birthdays, less than a month apart. Then her gaze strayed to the second-floor landing. "What's upstairs?"

"Our bedrooms." When she moved to pass him, he leapt up and braced one hand against the wall and another on the railing, blocking her path. The room tipped rather excessively sideways as he did so. He tallied how much coffee he'd consumed in the last forty-eight hours, but either math was beyond him at the moment or he wasn't remembering right, as that number couldn't be correct. Unless he was *invincible* now. Perhaps he was.

"Oh, you expect an invitation?" he asked.

"I thought I was getting a grand tour," she said dryly. "Besides, you barged into *my* bedroom this morning. It seems only fair."

"I, uh . . ." He hoped he was invincible. Otherwise, should Ellery Caldwell enter his bedroom, he might actually die.

Rather than test it—or even answer—Domenic spun and bolted up the stairs.

"Are you cleaning it ahead of time?" she called, charging after him. "That is *cheating*!"

"I'd never!" He slammed his door behind him and frantically drew Valmordion, cursing himself for ignoring Iseul's frequent prods to tidy his space. With an intended swish that was more like a jerk, enchantments exploded across the room. The window curtains yanked aside so violently that Domenic ducked for cover as a rod shot toward his head like a javelin. The dresser drawers hurled open, and dirty clothes crammed into them with such force that the whole structure toppled over, scattering the mountain atop it—loose coins and crinkled gum wrappers, emptied training wands and used subway tickets—across the carpet in an avalanche of trash. The singular picture frame crashed down. The hoard of empty glasses and mugs on his nightstand teetered into each other with calamitous clatters, spilling stale dregs of water and orange juice. Only the bed (thank everything) obeyed him: the quilt tucked itself beneath the mattress, the pillows arranged themselves upright—though they did belch out a loose feather or two.

Ellery threw open the door and yelped as she tripped on the crumpled curtain. Her arms flailed out for balance until she fell and caught herself on the floor—only a foot from where Domenic was still crouched, like a soldier in trench warfare.

They locked eyes, then burst into simultaneous, hysterical laughter.

"It looks like you tried to clean with a bomb."

"Believe it or not, this is . . ." He gasped for breath, tipping dramatically onto his side. "This is actually an improvement."

"Is it? There's barely any decorations in here. It looks like a guest room."

"It *was* a guest room. I just never bothered to gussy it up." Surveying it, he spotted his discarded Enchantment Theory III textbook lying beneath where the dresser had once stood. "Well, what do you know? I've been looking for this! You think I'll still need it?"

This only made Ellery laugh harder, a real laugh, like the one he'd heard at Mercester Square. She, too, tipped over and rolled onto her back—eight, maybe ten inches away from him. "This is . . . This is real, isn't it? It's really us."

"It's really us."

"Alderland's saviors."

"The Chosen Ones."

"It's up to us to stop the cataclysm. Us!"

They continued cracking up on the floor for what might've been a minute or might've been an hour. Time had gone sludgy, like the leftover grounds at the bottom of that seventh mug of coffee. Valmordion's heat simmered deep in Domenic's center, and he kept picturing himself like a planet. Like if you peeled back his layers, the crust of his skin then the mantle and flesh or however the order went, you'd find the exploding magma of his core. Power of the most incredible, unfathomable sort.

"Do you think we actually can stop it?" Ellery murmured. "Whatever grand feat of magic it asks of us, you really think we can pull it off?"

She looked so strange in Valmordion's filter. Not strange in a bad way—definitely not in a bad way—but like whatever vibrancy Valmordion lacquered over the world didn't apply to her. She was all contrasts. Light glinted off the planes of her face, and iridescence limned the frizzed waves of her hair. Shadows laced down the slopes of her neck, her cheeks, her mouth. Shadows that he swore moved as he stared at them, hypnotic as the eye of a storm.

She looked like a fixed point. Like it was impossible not to notice her.

"Yeah. I think we can," he answered truthfully.

Ellery smiled, and so did he. Her eyes were glassy, and so were his. Their worlds were reorienting in indescribable, terrifying ways, two stars colliding, yet he was no longer the least bit sorry about it.

He felt compelled to touch her.

He inched his hand forward until his knuckles skimmed hers. Much like when they'd hugged in the Barren, an electrifying rush swept over him as if he'd been doused in ice water. Reflexively, he wrenched away, and the two of them sat up and scrabbled back, panting and gaping at each other. His every hair stood on end. His magic shivered down to that exploding magma core. And despite the past two-or-singular day, despite everything, he was suddenly wide awake.

"I, um . . ." Domenic said, because he felt the need to say something. Ellery's cheeks blazed pink.

Downstairs, the back door slammed open. Footsteps clobbered through the kitchen.

"Dom!" Hanna yelled. "Dom, are you here?"

Domenic's mood crash-landed like a meteor.

"Oh, shit." He scrambled up and rushed downstairs, where Hanna had already reached the foyer. "Hey."

"*Hey?* Dom, from the bottom of my heart, what the *fuck*? Why didn't you show at the Council meeting? I've been everywhere—at the Gardens, every movie theater uptown, driving around in an NDC vehicle because I've been so panicked I—I lost my car. And Iseul, she's beside herself. She even went to Peak, asking how you were behaving on the train home, if—"

"Woah," he said. "Take a breath. I'm fine."

Yet Hanna uttered a noise between a growl and a scream. "I should've known leaving you here was a bad idea. This isn't class, Dom. You can't just flake on a Council meeting—"

"I didn't *flake*."

"Well, you look like shit, so you sure as hell weren't sleeping. So what were you—" Hanna cut off, sighting Ellery, who stood by the banister. She'd tucked Iskarius's sheath beneath her sweater.

Hanna threw up her hands and stalked across the ground floor. "There it goes!"

Domenic careened after her, tripping repeatedly. "There what goes?"

"The last shred of my sanity! I cannot *believe* you. You're so . . . so . . ."

Domenic seized her shoulder and twisted her around. "So what?"

Hanna glared up at him. "Caldwell is supposed to be on house arrest, not *in your bedroom*—"

"It's not like that! Listen. I—I know how it looks. And I'm sorry I sprang this on you. I'm sorry you had to go searching for me, that we stole your car. But—"

"You *what*—"

"But ever since I saw Ellery in the grove, I'd had this gut feeling that she's part of the prophecy. That she's Chosen, too. And now we can prove—"

"Oh, *that's* why you've done this? A gut feeling? And you're sure it's got nothing to do with the fact that this is the same girl you've been in love with since before your balls dropped?"

Domenic recoiled as if she'd struck him. Then he cast a panicked glance behind him, but Ellery hadn't followed.

When he whipped back to Hanna, he hissed, "Are you serious? What the hell do you take me for? Over the past twenty-four hours, I've thrown myself into the eye of a winterscurge. I watched a kid burn *right in front of me.* I've listened to Sharpe and every reporter in the country debate how big of a piece of shit I am. And you think that's what's on my mind right now? Getting *laid*?"

Hanna jutted up her chin. Domenic hated that look, like she was so sure she saw straight through him. Like he was so predictable.

"Hanna, I'm just asking you to trust me. Do you trust me?"

Hanna hesitated. Her mouth twitched like she was chewing on her answer, as if it was wadded between her molars like a piece of bubble gum.

Then a knock rapped on the back door.

Domenic brushed past her to open it, revealing Peak shifting side to side on the patio. Despite the sub-freezing temperatures, he wore his usual shorts. "Dom, there you are. You all right? What's this about?"

"Yeah, I'm fine," he answered, trying not to sound annoyed. What had they assumed, that he'd tried to flee the country the moment he was left unsupervised? "I just wanted to talk."

"Right. Of course, of course." Peak clapped his shoulder as he entered, but Domenic got the sense Peak had barely caught his words. Peak scanned the kitchen as he stepped out of his shoes.

"Iseul redecorated a bit, it looks like. Don't remember those porcelain plates on the wall. And the breakfast nook . . . That new?"

Domenic had entirely forgotten that Peak had lived in this house before he did.

"Oh, uh, I guess?" He glanced at Hanna, who'd jumped atop the counter, her boots swinging idly, her own mug of coffee already fully vertical as she downed it.

Muffled voices sounded from outside—the rest of the Council had arrived.

But rather than greet them, Domenic told Peak: "Gather everyone in the parlor." Then he dashed back upstairs to find Ellery hovering, pale, in the hallway.

"Are they all here?" Ellery asked Domenic.

"They sure are." Domenic shoved his hand in his pocket and fiddled with the worn dandelion stems, the same ones that had sat there since the vigil. His emotions all simmered dangerously close to the surface. He regretted the coffee. "How are you feeling?"

"I'm braced for a complete shitshow," she deadpanned.

"Even if this meeting isn't pretty, all that matters is that they believe us. About the shared prophecy. About the Chosen Two."

Ellery nodded, then she laughed lightly. "Is it bad I'd rather face Decibel again than Sharpe?"

She was six, maybe eight inches from him, so close that his skin prickled from the cold of her magic, that his mind was already replaying the sensation of his fingers just barely brushing her own, already considering how it might feel to touch her again, to trace lazy circles around her palm, to press his lips against the inside of her wrist.

But Hanna's accusation still stung, a thorn he couldn't pry loose. If they were going to convince the Council to take them seriously, he needed to act like a real Chosen One. Noble. And the way he was thinking about Ellery Caldwell was anything but.

Domenic forced a chuckle in return. "Y-yeah. You and me both."

Side by side, they descended the stairs and braved the parlor.

Clearly, Hanna hadn't informed the others about Ellery's presence, because as soon as they sighted her, chaos broke out across the room. Peak and Iseul's conversation abruptly died as Peak leapt in front of her and yanked Targath from one of the pockets of his cargo shorts. Glynn fumbled with the wine bottle he held, splashing pinot across the coffee table. And Sharpe, like a crack of thunder, bellowed, *"ARE YOU OUT OF YOUR MIND? WHAT IS SHE—?"*

"Thank you for coming," Domenic said smoothly. "We hoped a change of scenery might—"

"BOTH THAT GIRL AND THAT WAND ARE SUPPOSED TO BE UNDER OBSERVATION. SO HOW IS IT THAT—"

"I understand why my being here with Iskarius is a lot to take in," said Ellery, gesturing at the sheath at her side. "But I promise that if you listen to us, it will all make sense."

Domenic gazed at her admiringly, the strong stance of her posture, the determined set of her jaw. For all the fear he knew drifted beneath her surface, he couldn't glimpse a single shard of it now.

Indeed, Sharpe's shouts diminished to seething, and the other Councilors gazed at each other uncertainly. Hanna lurked in the corner, biting her cuticles.

"And why should we listen to you?" Sharpe demanded. "I'm lucky to still have all my fingers after your display last night. You and that wand are clearly dangerous. And yet, here you are, flaunting the crimes you've committed."

"I'm truly sorry that I hurt you, and Councilors Seong and Mayes." Ellery nodded at Iseul and Hanna. "But I swear Iskarius is now fully under my control."

"I can vouch for her," Domenic jumped in fiercely.

Sharpe scoffed. "Yes, because *your* opinion is so infallible."

"I pulled off a win in Oldermere, didn't I? Just give us a

chance. Hear us out. And afterward, we'll answer every question you've got."

Sharpe grinded his teeth. Then he lowered onto one of the sofas and gave a show of making himself comfortable: enchanting away the spilled wine, seizing a glass, and leaning far back into the striped upholstery, an ankle crossed over his knee. As if to say, *By all means, make fools of yourselves.*

Domenic and Ellery claimed the opposite sofa. Noticing Hanna's scrutiny, Domenic left an exaggerated amount of space between them.

Domenic cleared his throat. He'd always dreaded class presentations. "When I heard the prophecy piece in Oldermere, I realized something . . ."

He recounted the full story, from how he'd connected their parts of the prophecy to their battle in the Barren. As he described killing Decibel, Ellery withdrew the strange glowing stone from her skirt pocket and set it upon Iseul's never-opened architecture coffee table book.

"You all see how great this is, right?" Domenic asked. "If prophecies have six to eight pieces in total, then we've already found *three*. We could already be halfway done beating this thing. And if not, then close to it!"

Except once he finished, rather than congratulate the two of them, Sharpe asked Peak, "Well? You ever heard of this Dire Three bullshit?"

"Yeah, I have." Peak's forehead creased. "They're rookie superstitions. Claims of winterghasts of true intelligence. They're apparently large—ridiculously large, mind you. I've heard one described as tall as a skyscraper. And they've all got some combo of ghast and human features. Standing upright, but with some other horror—like the spikes you mentioned. But there's never been an official report. They're just rumors, that's all."

"So you don't believe us," Domenic said flatly.

Peak blinked. "What? 'Course I believe you. The way you

took down that scurge? Valmordion knew what it was doing, Choosing you. I never doubted it."

Domenic fidgeted, somehow both flattered and embarrassed. Peak's unerring optimism could give a man sunburn.

Then Peak strode toward the stone. "And this thing... It shines winterghast blue, all right. Is it safe to touch?" When Domenic nodded, Peak scooped it up. The cerulean light glinted off his stubble, illuminating a pale scar across his cheek. "I've slain my fair share of ghasts, but I've never seen anything like this before. Have you, Hanna?"

Hanna didn't answer. Her attention was fixed enigmatically upward, as if tracing the flourishes of the crown molding. At her side, she squeezed Syarthis.

"Mayes?" Sharpe barked.

Hanna jolted. "Oh, um, no. Syarthis doesn't recognize it."

Peak passed the stone to Iseul. "And what do you make of it?"

Iseul slid on her tortoiseshell reading glasses and inspected it. Then she pointed Calynia. Gold flooded through the wand's perforations, casting shapes across the ceiling and carpet.

"It's not an enchanted object," she said. "But it certainly contains magic. It feels... Well, for lack of a better descriptor, *cold*."

Peak stuffed his hands in his pockets, pondering. "I'll admit, Caldwell, I'm no fan of that wand of yours. But this prophecy is about balance—and it's the last of them, at that. And hearing you say you've fulfilled each other's pieces, I kept thinking about that ghast you fought in Mercester Square. The city watch still can't come up with an explanation for it. And the fact that it was you two... I'm no believer in coincidence. I—"

"Yes, yes, all right. Spare us one of your sermons," Sharpe snapped, rising to his feet. "We've already wasted an entire day debating why Iskarius exists while these two deemed us, the *most important magicians in the country,* unworthy of knowing matters of national security."

"Only because you treated us like. . . ." Domenic struggled to avoid a curse.

"Do not whine to me," Sharpe snarled. "Do you realize the stakes we're all playing with? There are five million people in Alderland. Five million lives. You may have pulled off a victory in Oldermere, Barrow, but even you must have a clue about the effect your naming has had on the nation. The Order is a public institution. Your academic record, your *disciplinary* record—they're all out there. The stock market had already been falling since Valmordion began thawing. Yesterday, it plummeted. Every supermarket is sold out of essentials: milk, eggs, toilet paper—"

"I get it," Domenic choked.

"No, you don't. Because what would you have had us do? Hand what could be the most dangerous wand in existence to a teenage girl without hesitation? If you believe just because you're Chosen that we'll trust your judgment with no questions asked, then *grow up!* Destiny isn't some storybook narrator that gives you permission to run off playing heroes! Destiny is duty! Sacrifice!"

"But—"

"Did you think that by forcing us to meet you here, somehow you'd be in control? In this house that isn't even yours? That you live in as a *dependent*?" Sharpe laughed cruelly. "You have both confessed to lying, breaking and entering, theft, trespassing, and treason—yes, Barrow, treason! And you think we owe you an apology for the way we've treated you? You think being permitted to return to your dormitory after creating a *Winter wand* is anything less than generous? You have no idea what lengths I will go to for the sake of this country. If I decide you're a threat, then destiny be damned—*I* will be the one to have the last word."

Domenic slid his hands beneath his legs to hide their trembling—whether out of distress or fury, he couldn't be sure. Beside him, Ellery had gone statue-still.

Sharpe strode toward the fireplace and glared into the flames. "I think I speak for all of us when I concede you both seem correct about the prophecy pieces. But even if you *are* both Chosen, the public won't have it, I can tell you that."

"They won't like the idea of a Winter magician, at least," Iseul said grimly.

"But the country already knows Ellery," Glynn protested. "I understand all of you consider me biased as far as Ellery is concerned, but you have to admit, if there was ever a candidate to bolster the public's faith that we'll reclaim the fallen territory, it'd be her."

"It's not just the public I'd worry about," Peak muttered. "My guys have lost life and limb fighting ghasts. And the way she looks when she uses magic isn't a whole lot different."

"Then we hide her," Sharpe declared. "As far as anyone is already aware, Barrow is the only Chosen One."

Domenic's and Ellery's gazes snapped toward each other. This wasn't fair. This wasn't how this was supposed to go.

But after Sharpe's tirade, it felt perilous to argue. Yet as Domenic laid a finger against Valmordion in the sheath at his side, its warmth wasn't steadying—it was propellent.

"That won't succeed," Glynn urged. "Rumors about Ellery are already spreading through the student body. It's only a matter of time before—"

"Then we deny them," Sharpe countered. "Tell them Caldwell left the academy because her window closed, that—"

"No," Domenic said vehemently.

Sharpe paused to glare at him. "Excuse me?"

"Ellery and I, we're *both* Chosen Ones. She deserves to be recognized as one."

"Dom," Iseul said warningly.

"No, I'm not backing down. I-I'm sorry about the panic. I really am. But you want to talk about destiny? Do you know what it's like to wield so much power that you can feel a winterscurge shudder in your grasp? That you could summon a volcanic eruption if you fancied a lighter? Because I do. And so does Ellery. So you want us to throw ourselves into more storms? To face down monsters more powerful than you can even imagine? Fine. We'll fulfill the prophecy, whatever it takes. But if you want us to trust *your* judgment, you don't get to ask us to put our lives on the line and then treat us like shit. Either Ellery and I are honest with the public—we tell them about restoring balance, about Iskarius, Summer and Winter, all of it. Which the public deserves, by the way. Or we save this country without you."

After he finished, Ellery regarded him incredulously, smearing away tears. The Councilors gawked. But none of them gawked more than Hanna. Her stare darted from Valmordion in his hand to his socks. Glancing down, Domenic realized that—despite casting no magic—he had no shadow.

Sharpe's eyes bulged. "How *dare*—"

"Their next prophecy piece, the 'uncover the tangled roots of the past,'" Hanna cut in hastily. "Syarthis knows what it is. Underneath Alderland, the roots of every alban tree intertwine, forming a network. Several of the past Chosen Ones connected to it in order to fortify the land amidst each cataclysmic Winter."

"So we need to do the same, is what you're saying," Ellery said. "But how?"

"I don't know. But the first step will be accessing the network through an alban tree."

Domenic's chest swelled. "We could go to the Citadel's grove, right now. We could—"

"Dom, you need to sleep. You've earned it. *Both* of you," Iseul said pointedly, peering at Domenic and Hanna. "The country will survive until morning."

"That seems a sensible path forward for this next piece, yes," Glynn said. "But what of future pieces? Mayes, do you feel they really could already be halfway finished with the prophecy?"

"It's not possible to be sure," Hanna answered. "But if past precedent holds true whatsoever, then yeah, there should only be three to five pieces left."

"So we can hope," Sharpe muttered. "That being said, when you access this so-called network, it *won't* be from the alban in Gallamere. I won't risk you taking out the whole city if something goes wrong. We'll use an alternative tree, somewhere remote. But before all of that, there's another matter to consider. The *public*." He swiped his tongue over his teeth with distaste. "Tomorrow, the pair of you will be presented to the country, as Summer and Winter. However, the people will have expectations of their Chosen Ones, and given *your* record and *your* magic, neither of you are enough to keep them sleeping easy at night. So you will play your parts as we assign them. That is the compromise. Is that clear?"

Domenic and Ellery exchanged a smile. They'd done it. Shitshow or not, they'd actually proven themselves.

"Perfectly," he said.

"Absolutely," Ellery chimed in.

Domenic locked eyes with Hanna next. *Thank you,* he mouthed.

Except Hanna didn't join in their triumph. Her expression remained blank, unforgiving and unreadable.

But in her fist, her knuckles whitened around Syarthis.

# XVIII
Ellery
WINTER

Ellery reapplied her lipstick, a light rose shade called First Blush. Then she studied herself in the vanity mirror of the Citadel dressing room, finally satisfied.

Ellery had only just begun to believe she was a hero. But in minutes, she needed to make the country believe it, too.

A ray of warmth grazed the back of her neck, and someone cleared their throat. Ellery spun to spot Domenic hovering in the doorway, beside two clothing racks and a discarded pair of heels. If not for his distinctive lanky frame, Ellery might not have recognized him. His normally unruly hair had been slicked into a gleaming side part, the divots of the comb still raking through the pomade. Bronzer framed every peak of his face to make his angles sharper, his features older; foundation masked his freckles; concealer softened his usually heavy stare. Complete with a tailored russet suit, waxy loafers, and Valmordion's golden sheath at his side, Domenic looked like the leading man on an Aldrish movie poster.

He stretched out his arms in mock surrender. "Go ahead. Tell me how ridiculous I look."

Ellery cocked a brow. "I don't know what you're talking about, Mr. Alderland."

Domenic scowled as he bent to examine himself in her mirror. He tugged at his bow tie. "Right? I look like I'm about to break into the national anthem."

Then he straightened and looked her up and down. Ellery was suddenly overly aware of every detail of her own appearance.

Ellery's hair was flawlessly finger-waved, her makeup applied by professionals who'd wielded brushes and pencils as artfully as wands. Councilor Seong had outfitted her in a cream two-piece velvet jacket and blazer, with matching suede heels. Ellery had seen a similar outfit in a magazine ad billed as the stylish choice for the modern young career woman. Her favorite part was her necklace, a dainty chain studded with crystal teardrops that dripped elegantly down her throat.

"Well?" Ellery asked dryly. "What do you think of Miss Perfect?"

"*You* look great. The necklace, whatever wavy thing they did with your hair—it all suits you. Are you happy with it?"

"With the outfit? Sure." Ellery heaved out a breath. "It's the performance I'm worried about."

"You're telling me. I mean, who's gonna buy *this*?" He shook his wrist, where a hideous, clunky designer watch jangled. "Have you seen the stuff they've printed about me in the papers? Half our classmates jumped at their five seconds of fame all to tell the country I'm a jackass. And now I'm going up there pretending I'm . . . I'm . . ." Even through his makeup, his skin went green.

"Hey. *Hey*. Why don't you sit down?"

Domenic nodded and collapsed into the vanity chair. Ellery pulled Iskarius from its fancy new silver sheath and fetched him a glass of water.

"Drink this. And yes, the irony of the situation isn't lost on me."

"Ha. Ha," he grumbled even as he accepted it. "I just—I know today isn't as important as fulfilling the prophecy. But I don't want the whole country panicking because I'm . . . because of who I was."

"I get why you're nervous," Ellery said. "But if it makes you feel better, if the country's going to panic about anything, it'll be me. It doesn't matter how good I look." She grimaced and sheathed her wand. "I mean, I could go out there naked, and the only thing anyone would stare at is Iskarius."

Domenic choked on his sip of water. Ellery flushed as she realized exactly what she'd said, and to whom.

"Oh, come on," he said hoarsely. "I'm sure the reactions would be mixed."

Ellery's flush only deepened. "You flatter me."

Domenic set down his glass and stood. This close, the heat of his magic radiated against her. "How about this? Whatever parts we have to play to make Alderland happy, we do it. But when it's just us, no bullshit. Deal?"

"Deal."

He extended his hand for her to shake. Ellery hesitated.

"Look, in the interest of no bullshit . . ." She curled and uncurled her fingers. "Don't take this the wrong way, but when we touch, I—no, *we*—feel something, don't we?"

Something intimate flickered in his gaze, like the glint of candlelight. "I feel your magic. It's kinda like being thrown in a full-body ice bath."

"An ice bath? Really?"

"Well, what's it like for you, then?"

When Domenic had touched her, she'd felt his magic kindle like a flame, and her own magic had drawn toward him, so sharp, so alert.

"Uh . . ."

The door creaked open. Ellery and Domenic lurched away from each other just before Councilor Seong strode in, a stack of notecards in one hand and Calynia in the other. She frowned and flicked her wand, and an additional notecard soared in from the hallway to join the others.

"Caldwell, your remarks are all finalized, and if you're ready we can . . . Oh, Dom. I didn't realize they'd finished with you. You look . . ." Seong pressed her palm over her heart.

Domenic chuckled. "That bad, huh?"

"No, you don't look bad," she managed. Then, collecting herself, she smoothed down his sleeves that didn't need smoothing. The gesture was so familiar, so parental, as though she'd done it dozens of times before. "You look the part."

"I can play the part," he told her firmly.

Seong squeezed his shoulder. "I know you can. I've always known how talented you are. It's just . . . Never mind. I'm so proud of you."

Ellery knew that Domenic lived with Seong and Mayes, but over the last day she'd come to realize that the Councilors weren't just his mentor and his friend. They were his family.

It was impossible not to see parallels to her own situation, except for all that Glynn had tried to defend her to the Council, he'd always kept her at arm's length.

Maybe he'd suspected she had Winter magic all along. Maybe that was why.

Seong distributed notecards to both of them. "Now I ought to warn you: I'll do my best to corral the reporters, but they're impatient and riled up. However, so long as you stick to your scripts and maintain calm, that should minimize any problems. Understood?"

"Yes," Ellery said.

Domenic gulped as he tucked the notecards into his blazer. "Yeah, I can do that."

"Then come on. It's best not to keep them waiting any longer."

Ellery and Domenic followed Seong, Domenic's posture rigid, Ellery's sensible heels clicking against the floor.

They emerged onto the Citadel's front steps, through the arched stone gate separating its campus from Gallamere's iconic Main Street, the star of a million postcards. Neat rows of trees ended in two gigantic flagpoles, each proudly flying the Aldrish green and white.

Immediately, cameras flashed, smoke coughing from their

shutters and swathing everything in a disorienting, dreamlike haze. Behind the reporters were a series of barricades, blocking off traffic and holding back the crowds of spectators. There were hundreds—no, thousands of people, blanketed by a heating spell, their breath fogging as they chattered excitedly.

The roped-off first row was crammed with faces from the newspaper's front pages, including the Prime Minister. Nerves stirred in Ellery as she walked to the podium with the same polished poise that she'd honed at the academy, then positioned herself behind Seong, Domenic at her side.

"Thank you all for gathering here today," Seong said into the microphone. "Since Valmordion's vigil, the Magicians Order has worked tirelessly on behalf of this nation's future. And as the Director of Public Relations, on behalf of the Council, I am proud to now address the Aldrish people regarding the developments of the past several days."

The rest of the Council sat amongst the Gallamere elites. Yet Mayes was notably absent, a chair for her missing entirely.

"Over the last millennium, our country has been given a series of prophecies to ensure our survival against Winter. Along with each prophecy comes a hero. Again and again, they have shielded us from cataclysm, and as a new one approaches, for the first time in history, we have been granted a Chosen Two: one who wields Valmordion, the great wand of Summer . . . and one who wields Iskarius, a new wand of Winter."

The crowd began to rumble, but Seong continued, seemingly unfazed. Ellery kept her countenance unfazed, too.

"It is with great confidence that I introduce Alderland to Domenic Barrow and Ellery Caldwell."

The crowd applauded sparsely. Many murmured. The reporters craned closer, scribbling in their pads and raising their cameras higher.

"They have some remarks they'd like to share," Seong said. "So please hold any questions until afterward. Thank you."

She descended the steps to sit with the rest of the Council. Ellery's heartbeat quickened as she and Domenic approached the podium.

"Hello, my name is Domenic Barrow," Domenic read off his notecards, his voice oddly stilted as he chronicled his own life story: his birth in the industrial city of Danmere, and his excellent scores that earned him admission to the Order's academy. "Being considered as a candidate for a Living Wand was already a great honor. But it was two days ago, when Valmordion Chose me as its fated wielder, that I was given—no, um, granted—the absolute greatest honor, and the greatest responsibility: to save Alderland from the cataclysm ahead. But of course, this came as no surprise to me. As I"—he paused, frowning—"have always known that I bear a great destiny."

After he finished, they transitioned awkwardly, bumping elbows as Ellery took his place. The microphone crackled as she lowered it.

"I'm Ellery Caldwell," she said calmly. "You may remember me from five years ago, when my hometown, Nordmere, fell to a category five winterscurge. But although I was only a child, I was a light against the darkness. While I tragically lost my parents in the attack . . ." Ellery had told this particular story enough times that her tone didn't change, even as an acrid taste rose in her mouth. "I slayed a ghast and saved dozens of lives. Then I came to Gallamere to study at the national academy." After a highlight reel of Ellery's time at the Order, during which she dutifully recited canned versions of her student accolades, she said, "When destiny calls, we must answer. And destiny led me to create Iskarius, the first new wand in a thousand years. It is a counterpart to Valmordion. And yes, as you have heard, it is a wand that wields Winter magic."

At the words "Winter magic," the crowd shifted, their voices an indistinct, ominous chorus. Ellery kept talking as though she hadn't noticed, even as a warning shifted within herself.

"But you can rest assured that such power is safe in my hands.

With the backing of the Order's wisdom, the prophecy, and the strongest Living Wands the world has ever known, I have no doubt Alderland will emerge from this challenging chapter of our history stronger than ever—and the fallen territory will be united with us once more."

At the notecard's urging, she reached toward Iskarius, and together, she and Domenic drew their wands.

Valmordion might've been terrible to behold, its ugly roots, its jutting thorns, but Ellery still thought it looked resplendent in his hand, the glow of its core gilding his features.

But when she raised Iskarius, people blanched. Its icy hilt shimmered in a flurry of camera flashes as the crowd recoiled. Their murmurs turned to shouts.

Their fear struck directly to the fault line in Ellery's heart. She'd had this nightmare dozens of times: herself on display, unmasked as a Winter magician, unable to run or hide. Still, she plastered on a confident smile as reporters rose in their seats, crying out questions.

"Barrow! Do you have any comment on how the Syarthis Disaster has played into your life as a Chosen One?"

Domenic's grip tightened over Valmordion. He hunched toward the microphone. "Um, no. No comment."

"How about the rumors that it's rendered you unfit for this responsibility?"

Seong rushed to reclaim the podium. "To ensure we answer as many questions as possible, I ask that we proceed with order. Please wait for us to call on you before speaking. Now, Wallace, I appreciate you having your hand raised. What is your question?"

A reporter wearing the badge of a business newspaper asked, "Caldwell, does the fact that your wand bears Winter magic make you nervous about its potential danger?"

"Not at all. It's no more dangerous than Valmordion." Defensiveness crept into her voice, and she squeezed Iskarius with an increasingly clammy hand.

Seong called on a reporter from the *Gazette*.

"My question is also for Caldwell. Given that no magician has ever wielded Winter magic, what makes you so different? How do we know we can trust you?"

Before Ellery could respond, the spectators' panic escalated. A barricade crashed to the ground and Ellery jolted, stumbling back from the podium as the audience's faces smeared like paint. Their voices dampened to a dull roar as her pulse thundered in her ears.

She and Domenic were losing them. This wasn't going to work.

But Ellery had remade herself for a role before. She would remake herself again, right here, right now, until she was undeniable, until she was everything Alderland could ever want. She stepped up to the podium, tucked a lock of hair behind her ear, and gave the crowd a slightly sheepish smile.

"Well, gosh," Ellery said, with a soft chuckle. "The truth is, I'm not different at all. Like any other kid with big dreams, I was determined to take my humble roots and grow them into a wonderful future. You can trust me because I'm just as Aldrish as any of you. Because I love a sunrise over the Gold Cliff Mountains or the rolling hills of the countryside. Because I love a scoop of caramel ice cream and a picnic at the beach. Because I want to protect everything we value, everything we are. Just like any other magician would do. Just like any of *you* would do."

The crowd hushed into a cautious calm, broken only by several appreciative cheers.

The next reporter aimed her question at Domenic. "And trusting you, Barrow? How are people supposed to rest easy at night knowing that their Chosen One was at the bottom of his class?"

Domenic drummed his fingers against his thigh. He looked first to Seong, who bit her lip. Then he locked eyes with Ellery.

Bullshit, she mouthed.

He sucked in a breath and nodded slightly. This time, he approached the microphone with a smile. It didn't resemble his true ones—a little too wide, but shining brightly all the same.

"I won't pretend that I was a proud student. But I've *always* been a proud magician. Take a look at Oldermere, at Mercester Square, and ask yourself—when it comes to protecting the country, who would *you* choose: someone who's only proven themself in a classroom, or someone who's proven themself on a battlefield?" As the murmurs dissipated, his chest swelled, and he continued, "Like Caldwell, I grew up with big dreams. In fact, upon arriving in Gallamere, the first thing I did was hike up Poplar Street to compare the skyline to a postcard I'd always had tacked onto my bedroom wall. And having watched my father succeed as a businessman—now owning the largest vehicle manufacturer in Alderland, every part Aldrish-made—I've seen the power of dedication. And I promise you, I'm absolutely dedicated to serving this country."

"Service and dedication are part of every decision we make," Ellery said, trading off on the microphone. "Because service is at the core of who we are as magicians. We are your Chosen Ones. Your champions. And soon enough, your heroes."

First a few staggered claps came from the audience. Then more, and more, until the entire crowd cheered. Flashbulbs popped from all directions. Bursts of illusion magic rose from training wands, sparkling like fireworks.

The applause shattered through Ellery's lingering sense of a nightmare until it felt like an impossible dream. Domenic grinned at her, and Ellery grinned back, just as wide, just as false.

Together, they would give Alderland the performance of a lifetime.

XIX

DOMENIC

WINTER

No matter how many times Domenic scrutinized the front page of the *Gallamere Gazette,* he couldn't be sure he'd read it right. THE CHOSEN TWO, its headline declared, above a photograph of him and Ellery side by side, brandishing their wands and beaming like they were in a toothpaste advertisement. He didn't know whether to be proud of giving such a grand performance or embarrassed for the public so gleefully swallowing bullshit.

"You do realize you've been staring at that for basically two hours, right?" Hanna groused beside him.

Domenic slapped the paper onto the table of their booth. To their left, the morning daylight cut out as their train hurtled through another mountain tunnel. Automatically, the enchanted sconces throughout their private carriage brightened.

"And why shouldn't I?" he said. "Look at me! I mean, I'd still rather lose the bow tie, but Iseul must've told them to get my good side."

Across from them, Ellery deadpanned, "Huh. I don't have a bad side."

A dirty joke singed the tip of Domenic's tongue, but he didn't dare utter it with Hanna present.

"Next time, I think they ought to give us capes," he replied instead.

Hanna rolled her eyes.

"You should be focusing," Glynn reminded them, hunched over his work at one of the other booths. Aetherium was balanced precariously at the table's edge; with every rock of the train car, it rolled closer to falling. Glynn didn't seem to notice. "We'll arrive in Undermere in less than an hour."

According to Hanna's theory, the next prophecy piece required them to access the magical network of alban roots that spread across the whole country and fortify it against the worsening Winter. The Council had selected the outskirts of Undermere as their test site because its alban tree was the most remote of any in Alderland, far from settlements that risked damage should their experiments go awry. And there was a real chance they could, considering no one—not them, not Hanna, not Glynn—had any idea how to connect to the network in the first place.

"Have you found anything?" Hanna asked.

"No, not yet," Glynn answered, sighing and flipping through what looked like a torturous magical theory book.

Hanna rose into the aisle. "I'm going to keep looking for a memory of Rhodes connecting to the network. See if it—"

"Keep looking?" Domenic cut in, alarmed. "I thought you found one yesterday?"

Hanna tensed. "O-oh. I mean, I want to study it again."

"But is that *wise*?" Glynn asked. "You shouldn't spend so long in Syarthis's Archives. It's not good for you."

Hanna scowled at all of them and muttered, "And here I thought it's the greater good we're supposed to be worrying about." Then, without waiting for anyone to argue further, she yanked open the sliding door and stalked into the adjacent carriage.

No one spoke for some time. They were, seemingly, focused dutifully on their upcoming task. Glynn returned to his research. Ellery stared at a book of her own, gnawing on her lip. Domenic's attention, however, drifted back to the front page, to the photograph of him and Ellery looking so much like a set.

Those times we flirted, he thought, *it's not like we were in our right minds.*

Maybe he still wasn't. Because even if he knew saving Alderland was the only thing that mattered, a traitorous part of him still wanted her. Even more than he always had.

His leg jittered. He glanced at his hideous designer watch.

"Does accessing the Archives normally take Hanna this long?" Domenic asked, making Ellery and Glynn look up.

Glynn peeked at his own watch and frowned. "Hm. Perhaps I ought to check on her." He picked up Aetherium. At first, Domenic assumed he meant to perform an enchantment. It was only once he pointed it grimly toward the exit did Domenic realize it was for his own protection.

Domenic jumped to his feet. "No, I'll do it. I'll check on her."

Before Domenic could change his mind, he barged past Glynn into the neighboring carriage. It was a sleeping car. Private compartments lined the aisle, each door bearing a window of murky reeded glass. Domenic peered into the first compartment, only to find it vacant. As was the next, and the next.

"What the hell, Hanna?" he hissed, flitting down the aisle. "Why would you go so far . . ."

Finally, in the last compartment, he spotted a small shadow.

He knocked tentatively. "Hanna?"

She didn't answer.

Domenic wrenched open the door. Hanna slumped across the cot, Syarthis still clutched in her lap—like she'd been sitting and had toppled over. Both her eyes and the wand's were clenched shut, and though she didn't appear to be conscious, her expression twinged with pain.

"Hanna." Domenic lunged for her, then froze, unsure if it was safe to touch her, if he should call for Glynn. Syarthis's heat filled the compartment, so humid that sweat broke out on Domenic's brow.

Then Syarthis's eyes shot open—pupils focused, as they seemingly always were, on *him*.

Hanna gasped. Her own eyes opened, and she made a revolted face.

"Wh-what is it?" he sputtered. "Are you all right?"

Hanna's head whipped toward him in surprise. The cot creaked as she wearily pushed herself upright. "I'm fine. I just bit my tongue. It happens sometimes when I . . . *Don't* look at me like that."

"Like what?"

"Like you're worried. It's never looked pretty, Dom."

Domenic flinched and retreated a single step, knocking into the narrow desk. "I've always worried about you."

Somehow, his words only deepened her scowl. She ignored him as she withdrew a tube of eyedrops from her trouser pocket, then leaned her head back as she applied them, as if she'd done so a thousand times before. Domenic didn't even know she owned eyedrops.

"Are you mad at me about something?" he blurted. "Whatever it is, just tell me, and I'll fix it. Because I don't know if you've noticed, but I've spent the past few days trying not to lose my mind, and I could really use my best friend actually having my back."

"Really? You'd accuse *me* of not having *your* back?" Hanna glared at him through watery eyes. One of her sclera had burst when she'd been unconscious, making a splotch of red join with her brown iris. "I've seen every past cataclysm, you know. *All* of them, even if Syarthis's memories are cloudier the older they are, even if it's awful, digging so deep. But that's what I've done, ever since Valmordion woke. Because that's the duty of Syarthis's wielder. I'm the historian. I'm the one who has to remember. But now that *you've* bonded with Valmordion, shit, do you know how many times I've watched the Thirty Years' Chill descend? Over and over and over again. And I know you, Dom. I know the way you get your hopes up. But just because you apparently pulled it together so far doesn't mean this will all be easy. You can't slack off. You can't get distracted."

Domenic's frustration warred with his shame. But as he opened his mouth to refute her, his focus snagged instead on the purple caverns below her eyes. Her choice of the farthest compartment. Her own admission: *Over and over and over again.*

Warily, he studied Syarthis. Its tongue curled back, stroking Hanna's thumb. Yet she didn't shift away, either because she didn't notice or she didn't mind.

"When's the last time you slept, Hanna?"

She seethed and smoothed down her hair. "Just . . . get out. Please."

Domenic squeezed the doorknob. Words roiled deep within his chest, ugly and awful and coated in mire. He couldn't bring himself to speak a single one.

Then, as he opened the door, Hanna murmured, "It's not as bad as it looks." She sounded almost apologetic, and Domenic hovered on the threshold, waiting for her to take back what she'd said, to at least acknowledge he wasn't the same person she'd dragged into the Vault. But she added nothing else.

He wondered what it would take for her to see that he'd changed.

He wondered if it was his own fault if she never did.

* * *

After they arrived at the station, it took another three hours by off-road vehicle to reach the most isolated alban tree in Alderland. It grew within the country's largest national forest, cradled between two mountain ranges and dappled with frozen lakes and marsh. Though Winter had stripped away its leaves and smothered the underbrush beneath a hard layer of snow, this wood bore no resemblance to the Barren's graveyard. Ice glazed every branch, as if the entire world had been dipped in glass. The conifers preened in lush green glory. A squirrel darted up the slope of a trunk.

While Glynn and Hanna debated over a map, Domenic and Ellery wandered off the gravel and into the tree line. Now that they'd arrived, his nerves sizzled like static.

"If this root network really does span the entire country," he said, "whatever we're about to try is big. Bigger than any ghast or scurge."

"Are you scared we'll mess up?"

"Mess up. Blow ourselves up. Blow the whole damn country up."

Ellery's laugh cracked, brittle. "Oh, is that all?"

Domenic pitched his voice at Sharpe's throaty baritone. "Five million people in Alderland. And you two exploded them. You were too busy frolicking or being happy or whatever it is kids do these days, and you just obliterated them in a single instant."

Ellery snorted. Then she propped her hands on her hips and, in a bizarre accent, she proclaimed, "'Breaking news: Everyone dies, horribly.'"

Domenic howled with laughter, wheezing so hard he had to brace himself against a nearby oak.

"What?" she demanded. "What's so funny?"

"That voice! What were you trying to be, a wind-up toy?"

"I was Floyd Wilder!"

"Wow. Lucky you're a Chosen One because I'm not sure you'd make it on prime-time radio."

She shoved him playfully. "You're the worst."

"Hey, consider the bright side: if we annihilate the whole country today, you'll only be stuck with me a few more minutes."

They laughed more, and more, until not even the darkest jokes could cast their task as light by comparison. Then, once Glynn and Hanna settled on a route, the group trundled off through the wooded trails. Domenic swathed them in a warming spell, but it required little concentration, and in the solemn silence, again, his attention roamed. He marveled at how vivid Valmordion's filter could render nature, how he could now perceive a thousand shades of green and brown and silver he'd never noticed before.

Then his gaze stopped at his feet. Despite the blazing sun, he still had no shadow.

Maybe it's 'cause you're Summer's Chosen, Domenic told himself. However, even if he'd conceded to believing in prophecy, like the bow tie and the designer watch, the title felt too grandiose to suit.

Then the hairs on his arms prickled. He halted.

"There it is," Ellery said, speaking the very words about to tumble from his lips.

The alban tree stood tall and apart from the others around it, as if the forest genuflected out of respect. Its leaves burgeoned in all of Summer's splendor, so golden and paper-thin that even the tree's shade could be mistaken for daylight.

Hanna crouched to examine the gnarled, white roots threaded across the ground. "In every memory I found, the past Chosen Ones accessed the network by touching a tree. I realize that's not much to go on, but it's a start."

"Fortifying the network could take a great deal of magical energy, and according to Hallemund's Third Law of Magic, magical energy cannot be created or destroyed." Glynn adjusted the bridge of his glasses, sounding uncannily like Mr. Abney, whose excruciating Continued Studies in Enchantment lecture Domenic had skipped only five days ago. "Thus we must assume that it's *your* magical energy the network will draw from. Even for magicians of your caliber, you run a risk of draining yourselves . . ."

While Glynn droned on, Domenic treaded toward the tree. The thought of touching it stirred one of his most distant, most fragile memories, withered from years of doubt. His hand against ghost-white bark, his skin sunburnt and crusted with dirt, his focus sharpening as if finally rousing from a dream.

"Yes, we understand Hallemund's Third Law," Ellery said, with a sort of weariness that made Domenic wonder how deep Glynn's admiration for Hallemund really went. "But Glynn, even you have to admit theory can only take us so far right now. Domenic and I are as ready as we'll ever be. So let's just give this a try."

Something clouded across Glynn's face, but he nodded. "Very well, then."

"How far away should we stand?" Hanna asked, not looking at Domenic. She'd spent the entire hike seemingly incapable of looking at Domenic.

"Far," Domenic grunted. *So if we blow up, maybe you won't, too,* he almost added. But Hanna didn't need another reason to doubt him.

As soon as Hanna and Glynn had retreated to a distance, Domenic said to Ellery, "Well, any last words? Just in case?"

Ellery tugged on the crystalline pendant at her throat and mumbled, "We better not die. I refuse to have spent my last day alive getting lectured by Glynn in the middle of nowhere."

He channeled his own inner Floyd Wilder. "'Such chipper words from your Chosen One, folks.'"

"Oh, come on. You can't tell me this is how *you'd* have wanted to go out."

Domenic mourned several dirty jokes he knew better than to say. How onerous nobility was.

He wagged a finger. "I really think we ought to focus here."

"Mhm, how mature and responsible of you." Then, biting back a smile, she strode to the base of the tree. "All right. Are you ready?"

She placed her hand on the tree.

He set his next to hers. Only an inch between them.

"Ready," he echoed.

Cautiously, Domenic reached into the tree with his magic. The moment he connected, like a match dropped in kerosene, a flash detonated behind his eyelids. His power exploded, spearing automatically out from him like lightning pulled to the earth. It splintered across countless paths of roots, miles and miles of them. Until he could *feel* the entire land awaken from a silent slumber, sizzling with energy.

No, not the entire land. In the far reaches of the North, his connection cut out—the border of the fallen territory.

But Domenic didn't have the chance to dwell on that disturbing notion, as suddenly, he sensed Ellery's magic. Not simply within the roots, but beside him where he stood, startlingly, exhilaratingly cold. And even as he touched the bark, he swore her palm lay against his own. As if reality had severed any distance between them. As if in connecting to the network, so, too, had their magics connected to each other.

They wrenched back from the tree, each leaving behind a handprint: one silver, one gold.

Domenic's awareness of the roots faded away. But even as both he and Ellery bent over, panting from exertion, he felt each shudder of her breath like a breeze against his neck.

"You feel it, too," Ellery whispered, somewhere between a statement and a question.

"I sure do."

They straightened and stared at each other: Ellery seemingly with bewilderment, Domenic with alarm. He staggered back, but two steps, four—it made no difference. He wondered with mortification if she could somehow sense the yearning that scorched within his stomach, if her every sense was as attuned to him as his felt to her.

As if he hadn't already felt that way about Ellery Caldwell. As if he didn't automatically angle his body toward her or keep constant measure of the distance between them or think of her beside him when she wasn't.

This is it, he thought direly. *Not a scurge. Not a ghost. This will be what kills me.*

All around them, the trees swayed, a melody of rustles and scratches and creaks. And in it, Domenic heard words.

when the darkness descends to its deepest,
a hero's flame illumes the cast of night

"We did it," Domenic gasped.

"I know Mayes—Hanna—called it fortifying," Ellery gushed, "but it felt more like . . . awakening. Like beneath the country, there's an ancient living *thing*. And our magic revived it. It's so much stronger. It's . . . What? Why are you laughing to yourself?"

"I heard the next prophecy piece."

She hitched her breath, and even with four feet between them, the graze of it made goose bumps prickle down his spine.

Another laugh escaped him, a little unnerved, a little thrilled.

Ellery pressed her hand against her check. She'd felt his breath, too.

Simultaneously, they smiled.

# XX
Ellery
WINTER

Ellery sat on her hotel bed, restless. After a long afternoon debating what the newest prophecy piece might mean, they'd come to a consensus: "darkness descends to its deepest" and "flames" had to refer to the Aldrish solstice ceremony, when the country lit candles to brighten the longest night of the year.

The solstice was two-and-a-half weeks away—a long wait after their breakneck last few days. But with potentially only two to four pieces remaining, Ellery had assured herself it was a wait they could afford.

However, the prophecy wasn't the only reason she felt restless.

She drew Iskarius and cradled it in her lap. Despite the hours since she and Domenic had fortified the alban network, so long as she held the wand, the connection between them remained as steady as ever. Heat gusted behind her shoulder in what she now knew was the rhythm of his breaths.

The hotel phone rang shrilly.

"Hello?" she answered.

"Hey. Hi. You're up," Domenic spluttered. "The draft that's blowing around my room right now? That's you, right?"

"Uh . . ." She focused on Domenic, three doors down in his hotel room. "Did it just get stronger?"

"Yeah. *How* are you doing that?"

"I don't know! Since this afternoon, I've still . . . felt you?" Ellery cringed. "I can try to stop it—"

"No," he said hastily. "I mean, just tell me how you did it. I want to try."

"Are you holding your wand?"

After some shuffling and muttering noises, Domenic returned. "Okay. Got it."

A few moments later, Ellery *sensed* Domenic, as though he'd sank onto the bed beside her. If she closed her eyes, she could half-convince herself he was there. The unmistakable scent of honeysuckle drifted through the room. And a sudden warmth chased away any hint of cold.

His presence was an overwhelming sensation, but not an unwelcome one.

"Ha!" Domenic exclaimed into the phone. "That worked, didn't it? It's like you're right next to me."

Ellery suddenly, desperately wanted to know how her presence felt to him. "Guess you don't have to knock on my window the next time you want to get my attention."

"Hey now." Domenic's exhale brushed against her ear. "I'll be honest, even if you hadn't done . . . whatever you just did, I don't know if I could've fallen asleep."

"What, because of the prophecy piece?"

"No, it's not that. I thought magic on the scale of what we did today would be terrifying. But it wasn't. It was easy. And I can't stop wondering what else we can do, what else we might be capable of."

Ellery's grip tightened nervously around her wand. "Oh?"

"So I guess what I'm asking is . . ." He paused dramatically. "Wanna go find out?"

* * *

"Why do I always have to drive?" Ellery teased as she turned onto one of the bumpy back roads away from the quiet village of Undermere. This time, they hadn't stolen the car; they had keys to the same Order vehicle they'd taken into the forest that morning.

Beside her, Domenic waved Valmordion, and frost melted from the windshield. "I thought you liked driving."

"I mean, I'd think you do, too. Doesn't your dad own Darby Motors?"

"He sure does. It's the family business. My two older brothers work for him." Domenic's voice sounded falsely cheerful, no different than when he'd mentioned his family during the press conference. "But believe it or not, they never taught me how to drive. Up until recent events, they barely remembered I exist."

Typically, Aldrish citizens were honored to have a magician in the family. But when it came to family, Ellery refused to pry.

"Do you think things with them will be different now?" she asked.

"Shit, I hope not." Domenic lowered his seat, then pushed it as far back as it would go, claiming the maximum amount of legroom. "What about you? Do you think your parents would be proud, if they knew you were Chosen?"

Ellery white-knuckled the wheel. The road outside seemed to narrow as snow whipped past the windows. "I seriously doubt it."

Craving a distraction, she cranked the radio dial. A familiar melody crackled through the airwaves.

"Oh, I love this song," she said.

"Huh. I've never heard it before."

"How is that even possible? It's the biggest hit of the year! You can't go anywhere without hearing it." As she spoke, she felt a painful twinge of nostalgia. This was Julian's favorite song.

Ellery hadn't heard from him since his parents had brought him home from the Order. She'd called, only to be told he was awake and recovering, but unavailable. She'd been trying not to think about whether he was dodging her or not. Maybe he was still angry about their fight. Or maybe he was upset that she'd confessed to the entire country she was a Winter magician, but in the five years they'd been friends, she'd never told *him*.

"I don't pay attention to that stuff," Domenic said. "You know, celebrities and all."

Ellery swallowed and pushed her memories away. "I hate to break it to you, Dom, but we're both celebrities now."

"So, what, will the next prophecy piece quiz us on pop culture?"

"If so, you really ought to get out more. Go to a concert or something."

Domenic folded his hands behind his head and grinned at her. "Well, when we wrap up this whole Chosen One business, I grant you permission to take me to one."

Their conversation carried on in the same witty, easy way that Ellery had come to expect as she steered the car down the snowy roads, deeper into the night.

Ellery parked on a deserted trail on the forest's outskirts. She left her coat in the car. She was tired of pretending to need it, and with Domenic, at least, she didn't have to play pretend.

"So," Domenic declared as they traipsed through the woods, "up until today, obviously I've been a bit preoccupied with the notion of saving the country. But Val and Izzy are—"

"Val and Izzy?"

"What, too irreverent? They're our wands, aren't they?"

She let out a soft, surprised laugh.

He beamed. He was all giddy momentum, walking so quickly Ellery jogged to keep pace. "As I was saying, Val and Izzy, being Summer's Chosen, I thought it all had to be a joke at first. Sure, my whole life, I've had to hold back because otherwise I blew through my training wands. And before I got to the academy, Hanna and I—we received some of the highest grades on the national entrance exam. But now that I'm starting to buy this whole Chosen One thing, that means I really have been one of the most powerful magicians in the country, haven't I?

Ha! What I wouldn't give to have seen Mr. Abney's face when he found out it was *me*. Two weeks ago he called me the most shameless student he's ever had the misfortune to teach!"

Domenic waved Valmordion, and illusions spun throughout the forest, so vivid and precise Ellery could spot no seams. An image of rolling green hills reared into a backdrop, cast in the rosy, fuzzy filter of a film screen. A castle perched upon the farthest one, flags waving merrily in an imaginary breeze. Fireflies danced to the drifting music, a tune old and stirring, but strange, as if played through a warped phonograph.

It felt real and fantastical all at once, as though Ellery stood at the edge of one of his daydreams. Perhaps she did.

"It's gorgeous," she said.

"I thought we'd both like it. Like a movie set, right?" Domenic lifted Valmordion, admiring it. The golden light of its core bathed his features, emphasizing the honey undertones of his eyes, the freckles dusting his face like pollen. Then he tossed Ellery an expectant look. "The set is pretty and all, but it still feels like it's missing something. I can't put my finger on it."

Ellery drew Iskarius and conjured a phantom waterfall. It trickled down one of the hills then grew into a river, rushing across the clearing in glittering tributaries. Tiny projections of fish rippled through it, blue and indigo and silver, their scales bright as coins.

"Yeah, I think we're getting somewhere." With a flourish, Domenic added a trail behind the waterfall, wandering into wilderness. Thistle and clover sprouted across the hills in a polka-dotted blanket. The Winter air suddenly smelled of petrichor, as if coaxed from a fresh rain.

Emboldened, Ellery added daydreams of her own to the illusion. A city thronged around the castle. Buildings speckled the hills, some clustering into neighborhoods, others sharpening into the modern points of skyscrapers. The rhythm of life emanated from within the winding streets, people chattering and laughing; the melodic chime of the Gold Line; wind rushing between the alleyways; the drumbeat of pedestrian footsteps—the same sounds that had soothed her so when she'd first arrived in Gallamere. *Welcome home,* they'd seemed to say.

She smiled at Domenic. "Your turn."

He shook out his limbs, jumped a few times, then expanded their set threefold. Whereas before they had gazed upon their illusions ahead, as if an audience viewing a stage, now the stage circled them. Cobblestones tufted with weeds quilted the earth beneath their shoes. The buildings took on detail: gleaming glass storefronts and milling customers and chimneys sighing smoke. Carriages wove among motorcars. Pigeons perched upon a wishing well.

Domenic gestured grandly at an ornate bench, and they sat upon it. The slats of wood pressed against her back. The iron handle was cool against her palm. Their shoulders touched.

"It feels real," Ellery said hoarsely.

"It sure does." Domenic craned his head back and marveled at it. His leg bounced. "Maybe this is why I could never focus. All this time, *this* is the power I've had inside me. And somehow, I've been expected to sit still."

Ellery hesitated as the illusion's performance carried on around them. It was the most masterful one she'd ever experienced, overwhelmingly complex, unfathomably vast. And although her magic felt no strain, suddenly, she couldn't stop worrying that it would explode somehow. That it would be all her fault.

Domenic studied her. "What's wrong?"

Ellery stood abruptly. It wasn't instinctive for her, thinking out loud. But it was easier if she wasn't looking at him. "My power's always been tremendous, too. It keeps me focused, but not in a good way. It's more that I'm always so alert, so on edge, because I know how awful the consequences could be if I lose control." She walked toward the nearest shop, then halted before a department store window. Her reflection regarded her, and although she could recognize the loveliness of it, she also saw the winterghast blue of her eyes, the fractal ice crusted at Iskarius's tip. Her shadow feathered behind her, layers and layers like the train of a gown. Its edges undulated even while she stilled.

"But the truth is," Ellery continued, "I've only ever lost control out of fear. And even though I've proven I *can* control my power, it's still hard to let the fear go. Especially when I see how everyone looks at my wand. At *me*."

"Not everyone," Domenic murmured.

Tears welled in her eyes as he joined her at the window. She studied how they looked side by side, their wands in their hands, the miasma of their magic around them.

For all that they were different, in every way that mattered, they were the same.

She sniffled. "The way you've risen beyond everyone's expectations, I know the rest of the country is saying that was inevitable. But for all the ways you were already special, I see the effort you've put into embracing who you are. And it makes me think that maybe I can, too."

He clasped a hand over his mouth, then laughed breathlessly. "You have no idea how much I needed to hear that."

Ellery gently knocked her shoulder against his arm. "I think it's my turn."

Over the next half hour, she and Domenic transformed the world around them again and again. Ellery luxuriated in her magic, reveling in each spell she cast. Until at last, the only piece of the scenery they'd yet to change was the sky. Ellery parted the clouds, revealing the constellations between them. Then, one by one, they fell, an illusory star shower that graced the whole firmament. Yet as the twinkling rained upon them, Ellery realized they were snowflakes, each the size of her palm. She reached for one, and it burst into a cloud of shimmering frost, winking into the night.

It was Winter magic. And it was beautiful.

Domenic gaped at her, his mouth ajar. The frost melted where it touched him, silver sparkles hissing into steam. And as the last of her magic faded, he raised Valmordion.

A hint of color peeked across the eastern horizon. Then, as Domenic traced Valmordion in a steady, careful arc, the light followed him, lilac and cornflower and calendula, as if he painted the entire sky in dawn. A false morning flooded over them, sunlight so convincing Ellery felt the kiss of its warmth on her cheeks.

As Domenic lowered his wand, it almost hurt to stare at his vibrancy: his lips pink, his irises umber, some of his loose strands of hair nearly red in the halo of daylight. Like looking directly into the sun.

Yet Ellery couldn't bring herself to turn away. He was absolutely extraordinary.

And so was she.

"What?" he asked softly.

Ellery clutched her wand with both hands, lest she reach for him. She wanted to indulge in an entirely different sort of fantasy than the one they'd conjured all night.

"Nothing," she said, turning away.

For all Ellery could embrace herself, this was the one thing she couldn't have, the one line she couldn't cross. They still had a duty to Alderland, and they couldn't risk distraction. Not with so many fates at stake.

XXI

Domenic

WINTER

"So I think we've got time for one last round of questions before taking a few calls. Mr. Barrow, several weeks ago, your classmates painted a pretty colorful picture of your reputation. But here you sit, clearly a changed man. So which version of Domenic Barrow is the truth?"

"Well, Floyd, I wish I could deny those reports—I'm not proud of them. But even Chosen Ones have our rebellious teenage years." Domenic laughed good-naturedly. "What matters is that when Valmordion woke up, so did I."

Domenic peered at Iseul observing from behind the window of *Wake Up, Gallamere!*'s recording studio. She nodded, which was good. Domenic could never tell when he was laying it on too thick.

Floyd Wilder laughed with him, so he mustn't have thought so, either. In person, he looked exactly how Domenic imagined, which was to say, like an absolute jackass. He leaned back in his seat, ankle bobbing atop his knee, cigarette perched lazily between two pale fingers. Maybe this was how he'd lounged when he'd declared on national airwaves that Domenic was doomed to fail.

Wilder turned to Ellery next. "Do you agree with his statement, Miss Caldwell?"

Ellery smiled primly, which Domenic knew to mean she, too, was envisioning strangling this man on live broadcast. "I think there's always been much more to Barrow than meets the eye."

Beneath the table, Domenic bumped his knee against hers.

Since they'd fortified the alban network, Alderland hadn't suffered a single winterscurge. Thus, in their weeks waiting to fulfill the next prophecy piece at the Winter solstice, the pair had little to keep them busy except to woo the public. And so far, in Domenic's humble opinion, they'd been doing a fantastic job. He'd transformed his golden boy routine into an art. He'd shaken hundreds of hands. Scrawled his barely legible signature on thousands of postcards. He'd even been asked to hold a baby once—a random person had just thrust their offspring into his arms. Domenic had never held a baby before. It'd smelled weird, like sour milk.

Yet Ellery's performance still put his to shame: accomplished ingénue, Alderland's sweetheart, and fashion trendsetter. And though Domenic knew shit about clothes, even if this was only a radio appearance, Ellery looked incredible. She shined, the glint of her necklace, the crisp white of her dress, the rolling waves of her hair. Of course the public was in love with her.

"Now as for you, Miss Caldwell," Wilder said. "Our listeners wanna know: how does a girl from the sticks wind up creating the first Living Wand in a millennium?"

"Well, one of the most wonderful things about being a magician is that magic can find you no matter who you are or where you come from. I'm so grateful to the Order for seeing my potential—I was a real diamond in the rough, you know? But it's thanks to their support that I wield Iskarius. They took a chance on me long before I knew I was Chosen."

"And what's your take on her response, Mr. Barrow?"

"Oh, Caldwell is too modest. To tell the truth, I was a bit intimidated when I found out she was my partner. I thought, wow, even Chosen myself, it'll be pretty hard to hold a candle to her."

Under the table, Ellery bumped his knee back.

Wilder smirked. His teeth were bleached white. "Bet it helped that she's so easy on the eyes, huh?"

Ellery laughed with him, aggressively prim as ever. Domenic didn't.

Wilder's smile faded as he stubbed his cigarette into his ashtray. "Let's not leave our callers hanging." He pressed a button on his switchboard. "Hello there. You're our lucky first caller. What's ya name?"

"My name is Marion Wheelock, from Fellmere."

"Ah, from way up in the mountains! Thanks so much for calling in, Marion. Must be real pretty, living in the clouds. What question do you have for our Chosen Two?"

"So, Ellery: I was lucky enough to snag a necklace like yours, but the jacket you wore last week is sold out everywhere. *So* annoying. Anyway, are you planning on releasing your own collection now that you're a fashion icon?"

Ellery touched the necklace in question before leaning toward her microphone. "Wow, I'm flattered! But for now, my focus is on my Chosen One duties."

"No one ever calls *me* a fashion icon," Domenic lamented.

Ellery snorted. Then she cleared her throat and kicked his ankle.

Marion Wheelock giggled as well, and with swift goodbyes, Wilder cruised onto the next caller.

"Hey there, caller number two. Who are we speaking to?"

"M-my name's Basil," he stammered.

"And where are ya callin' from, Basil?"

"From Enmere. My question is for both of them. Now, I know you two aren't much like the rest of us, being Chosen and all. So maybe this is a silly question . . ."

"No such thing, Basil," Domenic told him. "That's what we're here for. And, ultimately, we're all facing this cataclysm together, aren't we?"

"A-all right. What does it feel like to have been born with destiny watching over you? Did you always know that you were different from everyone else?"

Domenic shifted, but there was no getting comfortable in these seats, hunching low to his microphone. Thankfully, Ellery jumped in. "Well, goodness. I think you can understand why I might've been surprised to find out I'm Winter's Chosen."

Domenic marveled at how seamlessly she could lie, that he was the only one who could see it.

"And you, Barrow?" Wilder asked.

Domenic managed a chuckle. "Believe it or not, I do put my pants on one leg at a time."

Wilder grinned crookedly, like he did see Domenic's seams. "That's Barrow, folks. Always a charmer. But you don't have to play humble here. We're trying to get to know the real you."

The harsh red of the on-air light seemed to glare down on Domenic.

"The, uh, the funny thing about childhood memories is that it's hard to trust them," he answered. "But as far back as I can remember, even before I developed magic, I knew there was something waiting in my future. Something extraordinary."

"Of course there was," Wilder said cheerily, and Domenic released a subtle sigh. "Now, up next we've got a caller from . . . Where are ya calling in from?"

Static crackled through the airwaves.

"Hello?" Wilder spoke.

A coarse voice garbled over the poor connection. "This question's for Ellery. What plans do you have for your retirement?"

Ellery's brow knitted. "Excuse me?"

"After you and Barrow are done with the prophecy, will your wand even work anymore? Seems to me like the only reason you could make it is because Winter is the strongest it's ever been. So what happens when Summer conquers all of Alderland again?"

Ellery and Domenic met each other's gaze with alarm.

Carefully, Ellery answered, "There's no reason to believe Iskarius would—"

"Do you really think Winter's Chosen is meant to destroy it?"

Ellery recoiled and fell silent. In all their interviews, Domenic had never seen her at a loss for words. He touched her sleeve. But as he prepared to jump in, it was Wilder who rescued her.

"How 'bout that, folks! Looks like it's already time to say goodbye. On behalf of myself, everyone here at Capital Broadcasting Studios, and—if I may—the whole country, we thank you both for giving us a chance to get to know the real Chosen Two. Next, a word from our sponsors: Humphrey & Lee's menthol cigarettes—they'll soothe your throat and keep your breath minty fresh. There's no better way to finish off a meal! And our second sponsor, *Foretold*. Now that's a blockbuster you won't want to miss. It follows the story of Alice Rhodes . . ."

Domenic and Ellery shut the door of the recording studio as they fled.

"What was that about?" he asked Ellery. "Are you all right?"

Ellery smoothed down where her dress cinched into her belt. "There's never been a magician like me before. We can't expect the whole country to understand how it works."

"You took the words right out of my mouth," Iseul said kindly. "Still, it might be prudent to start limiting public questions at future events."

Ellery nodded gratefully. "Thank you."

"And Domenic, I wanted to say I was very impressed by how gracefully you handled that second caller asking about destiny. I know you still have complicated feelings about it, but your answer really did sound believable."

Domenic held tight to his grin, knowing Iseul had truly meant her words. She just had no idea that he'd meant his, too.

* * *

"No, you're right. It's been years. I figured it was a long shot. I . . . Yeah. Well, guess we'll talk again soon. Tell Dad, Robby, and Oliver hi from—Oh. Sorry. Yeah, I know it's late. Right. Goodbye."

Domenic hung up the phone on his nightstand and slumped onto the edge of his bed. He should've known that'd be bullshit.

All day, Domenic had simmered over the call-in question from the interview that morning, asking if he'd always known he was different from everyone else. And if he couldn't get answers from his family . . .

He snatched Valmordion from atop his quilt and slid it from its sheath. Immediately, a cool draft kissed the back of his neck.

The phone rang.

He answered it.

"I was starting to think you'd fallen asleep on me."

He grinned. "Says the one who's usually dozing off. Isn't it past your bedtime?"

"Yeah, I . . . I can't sleep."

Domenic fell back on his mattress, Valmordion clutched in his hand, the phone propped between his shoulder and ear. Twenty-seven blocks separated Iseul's home from Ellery's new Order-provided apartment, but when they both held their wands, distance was meaningless. She was here. And he was there.

"So which of this week's PR events takes the cake?" he asked. "The one where someone asked for locks of our hair, or the voice like a winterghast asking you about your fifty-year plan?"

"Oh, definitely the hair thing." Then her voice went soft and unsure, so different from how confident she'd sounded on the radio. A voice Domenic only ever heard her use when it was just her and him. "Do you think that caller had a point? *Would* Winter's Chosen be meant to destroy it?"

"That caller had no idea what they were talking about."

"How can you be so sure?"

"Look at the prophecy. Look at our track record. This time last Winter, there'd been *five* scurges. But we haven't had a single one since Oldermere. If that isn't peace, I don't know what is."

"You're right. Of course you're right." She let out a sigh, and it was one thing to hear it. It was quite another to feel it shudder across his room.

"To be honest, I've been dwelling on the interview, too," Domenic admitted. "Specifically, the question Basil from Enmere asked about destiny."

"I thought we had a standing agreement not to bring up the *d* word."

He laughed. But he was only stalling. Not because he didn't trust Ellery, but because *this* was what got him through day after day of asinine, cartoonish bravado. Knowing that when the curtain closed, they'd shirk off their costumes, one of them would call the other, and for hours, they'd joke about work, about everything, about nothing. But so far, this conversation didn't feel like joking at all.

"It's just you and me right now," she said gently.

A knot loosened in Domenic's chest. "Say, theoretically, there's this Chosen One. He's talented, handsome, valiant—the whole package."

"Mhm, theoretically," Ellery drawled.

"Sure, he's heard the supposed words of destiny with all these prophecy pieces. But everyone claims destiny is more than that. That it's been watching him or prodding him along his whole life. And when he looks back, he can almost see it. He can almost . . ." He groaned and pressed his left palm into his eye socket. "Would you believe I called my mom?"

Her muffled laugh made chills prickle up his arm. "Oh, so it really is dire, then."

"Yeah. Some of my memories—I was so young. I thought maybe she could help. But even though most magicians brag about being the pride of their families, you'd think my mom usually forgets she has a third son. And she's always been like that—they all have. There was this one time. I-I was seven." Domenic didn't mean for his voice to catch, but in truth, the memory was no footnote. "I wandered into the woods. It's a bit hazy what happened, but for a long time I was convinced I'd found an alban tree. I claimed that it bloomed when I touched it, and I was so excited to tell my parents. I was sure this meant that I had magic."

Ellery let out a startled sound. "That's how I figured it out, too. *Exactly* how. There was an alban tree, and I hadn't been tested for magic yet, but . . . it was like it recognized me."

The memory had been no dream, then. And despite how many times Domenic had proven himself, for a moment, there was relief. He squeezed his wand tight.

And yet, ever higher, the evidence mounted—like the walls of a prison, or perhaps a castle.

"Then, when I returned from the woods, do you know how long I was gone? *Three days.* I'd had no idea. But my family didn't seem to either. It's like there's a . . ." He struggled to find a suitable word. "A fog. Like they've barely ever been able to see me. Like I never belonged to them, and on some level, they always knew it. And yeah, I guess it'd be relieving, if destiny was always the reason and not that I—I don't know—was never worth anything to them. But then I think about what happened to me, to me and Hanna and our whole class, and I can't buy it. It'd be nice to stop hating myself for it being Hanna who had to bond with Syarthis. But to think that destiny would've just sat back and done nothing—or worse, to have played a hand in it . . . I can't believe in something like that. Even if I get to be special."

"I understand why you don't believe in it," Ellery said.

"But you do, right? You told me you do."

She fell silent for a long time, long enough that Domenic feared he'd dampened their night enough to ruin it, to ruin all of their future ones, forever.

"S-sorry," he stammered. "I didn't mean to go so dark. I'm just tired. I—"

"I understand about your family and Syarthis," she blurted.

"Whether it's all destiny's fault or not, I can't be sure. But I promise I-I understand."

Domenic swallowed. Ellery never brought up her childhood.

But rather than elaborate, she asked, "What about Hanna and Councilor Seong? They're your family, too."

"Yeah. Definitely. If anything, they're my actual family. But..."

He glanced at the door that adjoined his room to Hanna's. Light still spilled from beneath it, and so he cast a hasty soundproofing enchantment.

Yet he whispered his betrayal all the same.

"I don't think Hanna and Iseul see me either. Not—not like how my family can't. But they don't see *all* of me. Like I'm just *me* to them, not a Chosen One. When really, I think I've always been both."

He twisted Valmordion, examining its many illustrious fingerprints until he found his own, set just above the handle. Its whorl blurred as he blinked away tears.

"I'm sorry," Ellery said. "For me, it's always been the opposite. There's always been this wall between me and the people I care about—Glynn, Julian... Maybe that's why I believe in destiny. Because they could always see that I was meant for something, but they couldn't see *me*."

Even when they were different, always, *always* they were the same.

As per usual, Domenic's emotions stoked his magic, and he worried she could sense it flaring. Embarrassed, he leapt up, desperate to move. He rummaged through his dresser.

"Now, going back to more important matters—what *of* our retirements?" Domenic asked. "The cataclysm won't last forever, not with the short work we're making of it. We ought to start planning soon. What did other Chosen Ones do in the after?"

"You mean aside from Rhodes?"

"Yes, obviously. I won't be bursting into flames if I've got you next to me." He yanked out the bundle of striped red flannel bunched in the corner.

"Huh. I don't think the academy taught us that, actually," Ellery said. "The lessons usually stopped right after the Chosen One saved the . . . What's that noise?"

"I'm changing. You're not the only one up past their bedtime. Though you should know, your magic feels quite a bit colder when I'm half-clothed."

Domenic hated every word as soon as they left his mouth. He and Ellery had admittedly toed the edge of propriety before, but only because the collars of Mr. Alderland and Miss Perfect were tight enough to choke. No matter how many lines they'd crossed tonight, Ellery knew better than to cross this one. And so did he. Theoretically.

"Ah, what an image," Ellery joked. "You, naked and shivering."

"Hey, if you printed postcards of it, I could sign those, too." He staggered, yanking up a pant leg. "Anyway, unlike the past Chosen Ones, I don't plan on peaking as a teenager. I better do something notable after the cataclysm. A few impressive feats. Maybe a scandal or two."

"A scandal? You? *Never*."

"Oh, fuck, you're right. I keep forgetting I'm a changed man."

Ellery laughed. "You know, once we're through with this, I'm sure you could get a date with anyone you want."

Domenic fumbled with his shirt buttons. "Could I, now?"

"What, have your eyes on Phillipa Chastian?"

"Should I know who that is?"

"She was in that movie we saw in Mercester Square! The femme fatale?"

"Oh. Right."

Ellery snorted. "You're ridiculous."

Domenic flopped back onto his bed, suddenly not the least bit tired. "What about you? I seem to remember a lot of posters of some dreamy, excessively muscular heartthrob on your walls."

Ellery paused, and Domenic wondered if she could sense he was holding his breath, if she was knowingly torturing him. Because he'd let Ellery Caldwell torture him all she wanted, so long as he survived to know what awaited at the end of it.

"*First* of all," Ellery said finally, "he's Kent Sinclair. He played the teen runaway in that spy flick. Secondly, he's thirty-five. And married."

"What a shame," Domenic said.

"Besides, I don't know if I'd retire from the Order entirely. I used to think I wanted Glynn's job, but now I'm not sure I could deal with Sharpe as my boss."

Domenic's hope withered. No doubt Ellery had changed the subject because, unlike him, she was too sensible to risk distraction.

"Fair. Sharpe will outlive us all," he joked. Then he sobered. "You know, I might hate all the costume stuff. And the destiny stuff . . . I guess I'm still making up my mind. But saving the country, it's terrifying, yeah—but we're really doing it. And if I got to go back and tell that to my kid self, that he was gonna be a hero? He'd be thrilled. He'd probably love the costume, even."

"I know what you mean," Ellery said. "Yeah, the costume is still bullshit, but the good we're doing feels real. And the fashion stuff . . . I suppose it's silly, but is it bad that I'm flattered?"

"You say 'silly' like it's a bad thing."

She laughed softly, then murmured, "Wielding Izzy and Val, it really is an honor, isn't it?"

"Yeah. It is."

Domenic twisted onto his side, facing the wall. And though the way he felt Ellery through their magic was not touch, he could feel her, next to him.

Then the cold of Ellery's magic dissipated. He didn't know why, but now she was the one holding her breath.

But oh, he could think of *reasons*.

He should get up. He should splash some water on his face. At this point, he was only torturing himself.

"So tomorrow, that meet and greet," he said. "I've been trying to decide what to say to the Prime Minister. And I figured, hey, you can never go wrong with a pun."

"No, no—that's what I was planning to do!"

"Shit. How do you think she'd react if we both—"

The line clicked as a third voice came over the phone. "Dom?" Hanna sounded deeply tired. "You do realize you're not the only one who needs to make calls, right?"

Domenic was so startled and mortified that he chucked the phone across his bed, making its coiled cord tumble to the floor. By the time he'd scrambled to grab it, Ellery had hung up.

But he could still feel her. She hadn't released Iskarius.

I'll let go when she does, he thought as he slid himself beneath his sheets and tried vainly to settle himself, even as his stomach fizzed like a shaken bottle of soda pop.

She never did.

He didn't either.

Until hopefully, shamefully, blissfully, Domenic fell asleep across the City of Magic beside her.

XXII

ELLERY

WINTER

When the darkness descends to its deepest, Ellery recited to herself, *a hero's flame illumes the cast of night.*

In the nearly three weeks of waiting to fulfill their previous prophecy piece, Winter had remained docile. No scurge or ghast attacks had been reported since Ellery and Domenic had fought Decibel. Now, at last, the Winter solstice had arrived, and Ellery was more confident than ever that the Chosen Two would receive their next piece at sundown during the solstice ceremony, when they'd be the first in the country to light their candles on the longest night of the year.

Domenic peeked behind the stage curtain and scoffed. "This is just as ridiculous as I remember."

"Wait, you've gone to the Solstice Gala before?" Ellery asked.

"When I was ten, Darby Motors was that year's primary sponsor. My dad dragged the whole family." He gestured with false grandness at the logo on his electric candle, then he tugged at his gaudy Summer-gold bow tie.

"Oh, how you've suffered," she quipped. "You know, *I* used to dream of attending the gala. It's got the best red carpet looks."

Domenic's gaze strayed over her. His brow quirked. "I'll admit, I'm not suffering so much this year."

Ellery flushed beneath her makeup, pleased. For her own red carpet look, she'd chosen a dress that she hoped befitted her status as a fashion icon, cut from deep indigo silk that draped and flared and flattered. Her hair was an airy halo around her cheeks, her now-trademark necklace prominently displayed at her throat and paired with matching earrings. The back of her gown dipped daringly low, leaving her aware of the rustle of air against her shoulder blades. And even as Domenic looked hastily away, she couldn't stop wondering how his hands would feel, skimming her spine. Despite still being careful not to touch skin to skin, their flirting was growing more difficult to deny.

Ellery was spared from having to respond when the CEO of the Aldrish National Bank, this year's gala sponsor, announced, "Give a warm welcome to our special guests: the Chosen Two!"

Applause thundered as Ellery and Domenic emerged onto the stage overlooking the dim ballroom. The Solstice Gala was always hosted in the political district's Crystalline Pavilion, as the venue's glass exterior offered the perfect sunset view. The guests ranged from businessmen and politicians to actors and other celebrities. Golden-hour light cascaded upon their fine clothes and coiffed hair, their electric candles raised aloft like champagne glasses in expectation of a toast. It was all a far cry from the Winter before, when Ellery's festivities had consisted of a messy student party at the Citadel.

"And now," the CEO said, as the sun sank below the horizon, "let the Chosen Two be the first line of defense against our bleakest night."

The entire room descended into an expectant hush. Beyond the windows, lights doused across the skyline until the City of Magic was swathed in shadow. Even though Ellery knew it was all for show, the sight still made her breath hitch.

Together, Domenic and Ellery switched on their electric taper candles. Soon more candles joined their own, until the room was illuminated by a hundred tiny spotlights.

Ellery waited, listening. This was the moment. It had to be. And since Domenic had received the last prophecy piece, presumably it was her turn. But as seconds dragged on, she heard nothing.

Domenic leaned down and whispered. "Anything?"

"No. I'm guessing you didn't hear anything either?"

"Nope."

"Put your hands together for Alderland's heroes!" crowed the CEO. The crowd clapped again. A band broke into a jaunty tune. And the Solstice Gala began in earnest.

The two of them hurried offstage, where Glynn and Hanna waited expectantly in the greenroom. Yet when Ellery and Domenic explained they'd come up empty, their questions turned from eager to anxious.

"Should we find the rest of the Council?" Ellery asked nervously.

"No, we don't have time for a meeting," said Glynn. "If the piece really does refer to tonight, we have a mere fifteen hours until dawn."

Domenic blanched. "What happens if we don't get the next one in time?"

"Then I suppose we'd better hope we were wrong about the solstice. Otherwise, we'll have to wait another year."

Ellery and Domenic exchanged panicked glances. Each time in history Valmordion had thawed, it had never been clear precisely when the cataclysm would descend. Although it always occurred during Winter, sometimes it arrived the year Valmordion thawed, while sometimes it waited several winters more. But even if they *could* try again at the next solstice, the risk was astronomical. They couldn't fail. They couldn't.

"No, we're not waiting," Ellery said. "We'll figure this out. There must be something we missed."

"Well, given the solstice's significance, its history, where else could the prophecy be leading?" Glynn asked. "Mayes? Any thoughts?"

Hanna's gaze hovered on an aimless point on the floral wallpaper, her finger resting atop Syarthis's sheath within her jacket. She wore a full burgundy tuxedo, and a black satin cummerbund accentuated her wide hips.

"Hanna?" Domenic pressed.

Hanna cursed, and her eyes rolled as they righted. "I'm trying to focus. This gala is the largest solstice celebration in the country, and I did *not* just spend an hour small-talking to some pompous prick about his second yacht for this all to have been bullshit."

Domenic gestured at the logo on his candle snidely. "Oh, I'm pretty sure this has been bullshit either way."

Something in Ellery snagged on that word. The sponsorships, the electric candles . . .

"I've got an idea," she gasped. "Glynn, you know about the student solstice party, don't you?"

"Oh, goodness, the fire hazard?" His brow furrowed. "You think the prophecy could be referring to *that*?"

"I do. It might be silly, but it derives from ancient tradition, right?"

Glynn absently adjusted his tie in a way Ellery knew meant he was thinking. "Mayes, how long would it take you to verify the tradition's history in Syarthis's Archives?"

"Um, considering I have no idea what party you're even talking about," Hanna said flatly. "A while."

Glynn turned to Ellery. "And how long would it take you to check?"

"I'm not sure. An hour or two?"

"Then in the meantime, we'll speak to the rest of the Council and prepare some alternatives, just in case." Glynn paused, and Ellery sensed there was something else he wanted to say. Then he grimaced and urged, "What are you waiting for? *Go*."

* * *

The siren above their car wailed as Ellery sank into the backseat beside Domenic and slammed the door.

"How long until we reach the Citadel?" Ellery asked their driver.

"Normally with the siren on I'd say fifteen minutes," he answered. "But with the holiday traffic and road closures, we're talking twenty minutes at best. Maybe more."

"Thanks." Ellery wrenched up the partition and cast a soundproofing enchantment. Then she hissed out a long, vicious string of profanities.

"Took the words right out of my mouth," Domenic muttered, drumming his fingers against his kneecap. "Tell me about this student solstice party. I've never heard of it."

"It's an informal tradition. There's this creepy cave on the north side of campus. Everyone builds a fire pit inside it and lights candles, and there's always a bit of a pissing contest over who can enchant the strongest graffiti on the walls."

Ellery and Julian had gone every Winter. The previous year, he'd mended a few burns from overeager NDC groupies who'd brought fireworks instead of candles. She'd accidentally won the graffiti contest after Demelza cajoled her into participating. They'd all talked about how excited they were to be done with school, how their first wand vigils were fast approaching.

Three weeks had passed since she and Julian had last spoken. He still wasn't taking her calls.

"So we're about to, what," Domenic said, "burst in and shut down the party early?"

"It'll probably be done by the time we show up. The real fun starts at the after-party in someone's dorm room."

Domenic uttered a quiet laugh and stared out the window. "Huh. I really missed a lot, didn't I?"

Ellery thought of the Domenic Barrow she'd known only as the occasional ghost in the back of a classroom. Whenever his name was mentioned, it was either to whisper about his tragic backstory or the rumors of which students were bold enough to "go there." And so Ellery could understand why he preferred to live off-campus and avoid it all. But she couldn't deny that he'd lost something he couldn't get back.

"And if it's not this party, if the Council doesn't think of an alternative, what then?" Domenic asked tightly. "Just because there hasn't been another scurge doesn't mean there won't ever be."

Ellery swallowed and tugged at her necklace. "Every other time we've trusted our instincts, we've been right."

"I know. Sorry. I-I trust you. It's just, fifteen minutes ago, we were so sure. We were good. And now, one night . . . it's not a lotta time." He reached into his pocket, seeming to fish for dandelions that weren't there. Then he withdrew his hand and flexed his fingers.

"It's not," Ellery admitted. "But—"

"We waited weeks for tonight. I can't wait another year." He pressed his back into the seat cushions and forced out a shaky breath.

Ellery had never seen him like this. Usually he was the comforting one, the steadying one, while she was always worrying, always doubting.

"Dom," she said gently, and when he didn't respond, she reached for his hand and laced her fingers through his. Her magic responded instantly, cold surging against heat, as exhilarating as it was disorienting. Ellery felt it in her head. Her chest.

Domenic jolted, and his eyes snapped to hers. But he didn't let go.

"I can't promise that we'll always get it right," she said. "But I believe in us. And I *can* promise you that whatever's coming, you're not in it alone. Not now. Not ever."

His throat bobbed. Gradually, his breathing eased.

"I, um," he said. "I can't say I love the idea that destiny steered my whole life, even with certain chapters excluded. But I think I believe now. And of all the people destiny could've paired me with, I'm really glad it was you."

"I'm glad it was you, too."

Left, then right, then right again, their car veered through city streets. Other vehicles jumbled out of the way, but it was still slow going to squeeze through traffic, and their car jostled as pavement shifted into the cobblestones of Gallamere's oldest neighborhoods.

But so long as she kept hold of his hand, Ellery felt calm.

She studied Domenic as he stared out the window again, his breathing steadier, his head leaning back against the cushion. His freckles peeked out from beneath his gala makeup.

Ellery had thought it impossible for her to feel so connected to another person. But she trusted Domenic wholly, truly, in a way that she had never trusted anyone.

"Can I tell you something?"

He turned to meet her eyes. "Of course."

"My parents." Ellery spoke matter-of-factly. "Everyone knows they died in the fall of Nordmere. What they don't know is how."

As Ellery searched for the right words, Domenic didn't push her. He waited patiently until she was ready to continue.

"Things were difficult at home even before I developed magic. And once I did, it was obvious that my magic was strange. I accidentally iced over my bedroom, and I covered our garden in snow in the middle of Summer. So my parents took my training wands away and refused to let me study magic. But after that, they were always afraid of me. They told me I was a monster. And I believed them."

Memories flipped through her mind like a film reel, as though she watched them on-screen, a spectator to her own life. During her first days at the Citadel, healers had mended three improperly healed fractures in her arms and legs. They'd never asked her where they'd come from.

"El," he said gently, but she didn't need to pause again. Her voice hadn't quavered. Her heartbeat was stable. And she *wanted* to tell him, wanted him to know her, all of her.

"Then, when the winterghasts invaded Nordmere, my parents thought I was partially to blame. I wasn't, of course, but they didn't believe me. So they took it upon themselves to play the hero. To slay . . . me."

Domenic sucked in a tight, furious breath and squeezed her hand tighter.

"I'd hidden a training wand from them. And I only wanted to protect myself, but I was so scared. I lost c-control." Ellery swallowed and fixed her gaze on the partition. "I tortured myself over what happened for years. Finally I convinced myself that I was too traumatized to remember it correctly, that no magician could possibly have Winter magic. But when I realized I was Chosen, it finally made things clear. Because if I'm destined to save Alderland, why would destiny want me to be horrified by my own power? Maybe I was always meant for Winter, but that doesn't mean I was always meant to suffer. My parents *chose* to treat me the way they did. It could've been different. But sometimes, I still hear their voices in my head. And I wonder if maybe they were right. Because only a monster could . . . could . . ."

Her heartbeat ratcheted violently, and despite her resolve, a hideous panic rose within her. Maybe she'd been wrong to trust him. Maybe it was better to hold herself apart, alone. Maybe—

"Listen to me, El," Domenic said fiercely. "There's nothing monstrous about fighting back."

Ellery felt his words as much as she heard them. Her pulse slowed, and she trembled, not with fear but with relief. She leaned against him, and he released her hand to slide his arm around her.

"I want to believe you," she said, sniffling. "I almost can. I just know that no matter what happens, I need to prove them wrong."

He kissed the top of her hair. "You already have."

As they neared the outskirts of the Citadel, the direness of the task ahead returned to Ellery. But even as she tried to train her thoughts on their shared duty, her focus slid back to the press of Domenic's arm, to the way she'd nestled against him. Their thighs pressed together. The scent of his cologne. Longing fluttered inside her like a flurry of snow.

* * *

Their car hadn't even reached a full stop before Ellery and Domenic threw open their doors, cloaked themselves, and raced through the maze of academy buildings. They found the cave already vacated.

It looked just as Ellery remembered, a space the size of a classroom carved into the mountain. Two trees flanked the entranceway, their roots and branches threaded into the stone. Enchanted graffiti shimmered across the walls. Embers flickered inside a pit in the dirt floor, sending weak puffs of smoke through a hole in the ceiling. Discarded cups, bottles, and candles lay scattered everywhere, crunching beneath their feet as they took in the mess.

"Okay, walk me through how this . . ." Domenic tapped an empty chip bag with his shoe, "*ceremony* works."

Ellery's certainty wavered. "The oldest students start the fire pit, and then everyone else lights candles and adds their own flames to it. I think we should start by lighting it, too."

"Makes sense to me." He was a silhouette amidst the cave's dim and the faint glow of Valmordion. The only sounds were the two of them catching their breaths. Side by side, they raised their wands, but neither cast a spell.

"You know," Ellery whispered, "if we're caught, we'll get a week's detention."

He wheezed out a startled laugh. "Shit. Another strike on my record, and I'm out."

"Then we'd better be quick." She nudged him with her elbow. He nudged her back.

"All right," she said. "On three?"

"On three."

As Ellery counted down, her nerves dissipated. For so long, the past had rooted her in a place of fear and shame. But whether they were right or wrong about tonight, they would find a way forward. She trusted him. She trusted *herself*.

Together, gold and silver flames ignited within the fire pit. But rather than blending into one, the colors intertwined into a spiral. They danced and blazed and churned until, suddenly, they exploded.

Magic swept across the cave. Flowers blossomed from the dirt, encrusted in ice that melted into dew. The branches in the ceiling sprouted fresh leaves, first a tentative, softer yellow before bursting into brilliant Summer green and then an alien, vivid crimson. They detached from the tree and tumbled through the air, their veined patterns as delicate as snowflakes.

"What is this?" Domenic gasped. They both sheathed their wands, then stared, stunned, as their accidental enchantment sputtered out. Ellery had heard of such phenomena in other lands, but never here.

Before she could respond, wind whistled through the now-shriveled leaves.

> *in treacherous land an enemy lies*
> *but what was lost invasion can reclaim*

She turned to Domenic and recited the piece aloud.

"I was right," she said breathlessly, victoriously—until it dawned on her exactly what the piece said.

"An invasion," Domenic croaked, echoing her own thoughts. "So it's finally happening. We're finally going to reclaim the fallen territory."

"This was our fifth piece. That means there's a chance the next one could be . . . the final one."

They stared at each other in mirrored shock. Then, as one, they broke into celebration. Ellery laughed into her palm. Domenic spun, glass shattering beneath him, before hollering so loud the sound of it reverberated across the cave.

"Careful," Ellery teased. "If someone hears us, we really might get detention."

He halted, his smile mischievous. "Oh no, can you imagine the scandal?"

Even as their laughter ebbed, the word lingered between them, growing all the more substantial in the silence.

Again, her gaze caught his.

"I can think of a better one," Ellery said.

Then she kissed him.

Domenic kissed her back, so immediately and so fervently that there was no question this want had ever just been hers. He clutched her hips, pulling her closer, while she snaked her arms around his neck. And although Ellery had kissed boys before, she knew in an instant that this, *he,* was different. Domenic was pure Summer even now, on the darkest night of the year. His lips were soft and honeyed, and he smelled of moss and wildflowers. His magic sang against hers, sizzling heat against shocking cold. Power pooled in her stomach, her throat, sluicing through her in an intoxicating rush of adrenaline.

Yet as their initial frantic touches faded, in their place something deeper unfurled, a tenderness that Ellery had never known, had never thought to dream of. His every touch felt laden with intention, as if trying not just to savor her but to memorize her. Each kiss was reverent and raptured; his lips trailed down her jaw while his fingers traced her spine, taking full advantage of her dress's daring silhouette. She buried a hand in his hair, mussing it from its sleek part into the disheveled style that better suited him. They sank blissfully into the rhythm of their mouths, their hands, their bodies. Until Ellery forgot why she'd ever denied this of herself, of either of them.

When something was right, it wasn't a distraction. It couldn't be. And nothing and no one had ever felt more right to her than Domenic Barrow. For all she'd wanted, for all she'd wished, she'd never wanted anything the way she wanted this.

XXIII
DOMENIC
WINTER

Their Order vehicle jostled over the pocked, neglected pavement of Alderland's northbound highways. Each time, Domenic relished it—his knee knocking into Ellery's, her shoulder bumping his arm. Every touch they let linger a moment too long. Every look bore the exhilarating weight of a secret.

"How much farther?" Ellery asked the driver anxiously.

"As soon as we clear the trees, you'll see it."

That left only a few precious minutes more of distraction. Since obtaining the next prophecy piece last night, they'd stolen such minutes whenever they could: in the elevator after their strategy meeting with the Council, in a phone booth near the Citadel's gate, in an empty compartment on the train here. Every instance had been so surreptitiously hurried, so deliriously giddy that Domenic couldn't be sure he hadn't fantasized them.

Subtly, he hooked his pointer around hers. The electric chill of her magic shuddered through him. He locked his shoulders to withhold a shiver.

Ellery hitched her breath, then bit down a grin.

Fuck, he was happy.

As their car emerged from the forest, a darkness loomed in the distance, vast as a city skyline. Domenic smeared away the fog on his window and tensed.

Ahead, a great wall swallowed the evening horizon from east to west, from land to sky. It resembled a storm in slow motion, snow eddying in lazy, ominous currents. And though Domenic could vaguely distinguish shapes beyond it—the jagged silhouettes of barren trees, the ghostly outlines of abandoned buildings—none of it had any color, not even when he grasped Valmordion. The wall divided two seemingly opposite worlds of Winter: one of life, even if that life meant a fight for survival, and one submerged entirely in silence, in shadow.

Domenic had seen pictures of the border before, in newspaper photographs and mission dockets. Yet those images had failed to capture how truly menacing the fallen territory was.

"It's worse than I remembered," Ellery murmured. He couldn't imagine how it felt to have once called that land home.

He squeezed his finger around hers. She squeezed back, almost painfully tight.

Ten minutes later, they pulled into a large Nature Defense Corps compound, all steel warehouses fortified with glimmering warming spells and guarded by barbed wire. Peak awaited them in its central courtyard, flanked by a retinue of officers. A lush golden alban tree swayed behind them in the frigid wind. It all would've made a more impressive sight if Peak hadn't been wearing shorts and a plain white T-shirt.

"Well, look who's hiked up North to pay us a visit!" Peak clapped Domenic's shoulder as he slid out from the backseat. "Looking good, Dom."

"Feeling good," he answered, resisting the urge to wink at Ellery.

"Good to see you, too, El," Peak told her.

Her mouth slanted into a bemused smile. Apparently she and Peak had also achieved nickname status. "Thanks."

While several officers unloaded their bags, Peak led them into the compound's largest facility.

"I'm sorry it's not much to look at," Peak said. "These bases are only active during Winter, so we don't go out of our way to make them cozy. But take it from someone who's been stationed here every Winter for forty-four years—you get used to it."

"I'm sure we'll find it more than satisfactory," Ellery quipped. Domenic cocked a brow.

They entered a command center of the sort Domenic had only seen in movies: maps splayed across corkboards and thirty different telephones and a table of stern-faced magicians with medals spangling their jackets, one for each Winter they'd served. Beyond the reinforced glass, the border's roiling haze gleamed crimson from the setting sun.

Peak gestured at the empty seats. "Please, make yourselves comfortable. Can we getcha anything? We know you had a long trip up here, but we've got a lotta ground to cover over the next few days."

"I'll take a coffee," said Domenic. "Just black, please."

"Same, but with sugar," Ellery said.

"You got it," Peak told them.

A corporal scurried away to fetch their orders, and Domenic and Ellery sank into their adjacent chairs while Peak claimed the head of the table.

"So, it's finally starting. The prophecy has asked us to invade Winter's territory. After all these years, we're going to get the rest of our homeland back," Peak said keenly, to nods of agreement all around. "Now, we've known this was coming, so we've been preparing for it for a long time—before Valmordion thawed, even. So brace yourselves. We've got a whole lotta ideas and plans to throw at you over the next few days. This meeting is just the beginning."

Domenic nodded, even as his boot found Ellery's beneath the table.

"Our scouts we've sent into the fallen territory have confirmed several things: that about five percent of the population stuck around, roughly forty to fifty thousand, so we estimate—and that they haven't been dealing with any ghasts or scurges. But it's like the Thirty Years' Chill up there: year-round Winter, regardless of what season it is below the border. Not my idea of a good time." Even the sternest magicians chuckled. "Obviously, you two will be at the head of the invasion. But you won't be alone. This morning, the Council authorized moving over half the NDC troops to this compound. We've also rush-ordered more training wands for our hedge magician units. Our goal is to back you up in every way that you need while minimizing casualties."

Domenic drew his foot away with unease. "Should we already be sending in an army without knowing how many prophecy pieces we have left?"

"Well, given that past Chosen Ones all got six to eight pieces, and you've now got five, that means going forward, we make our moves like every next piece *could* be the final one. Boys—and El—we're officially in the homestretch."

It was one thing to know they were nearing the prophecy's end; it was another thing to sit here surrounded by men at least three times Domenic's age, speaking of troops and casualties, while the border writhed at the edge of his vision.

"And how long until we finish all the preparations?" Ellery asked stiffly.

"Ideally, four days."

Four days. That was so thrillingly, alarmingly soon.

With so few pieces remaining, how soon, then, until they finished all of it? Until they were free?

This time, it was Ellery's foot that found his. It was such a simple touch, but Domenic felt everything in it.

"We'll review our more detailed plans of the invasion once the rest of our generals arrive," Peak said. "Today we'll focus on the Dire Three. Asker, you wanna show them the files?"

One of the generals withdrew their wand: Rhiannyd, Domenic thought it was called. Or perhaps Orth. Only so many wands were crafted from willow wood, its handle coated in the characteristic copper and gray bark.

With a wave of Rhiannyd-Orth, a binder slid from the bookshelves and fell open on the table. Photographs rose off the paper as if by projector: a town reduced to skeletal frames and rubble; a ravine gouged open as if by giant claws; a paved road flayed off the ground, pulverized cars littered around it.

"The Dire Three did this?" Ellery gasped.

"We believe so, yeah," Peak said. "Ever since you took out that first one in the Barren, we've been doing some research. Our magicians studying the enchanted stone Decibel left behind can't make heads or tails of it. But our interviews across the NDC have been real promising. It took a while to sift out fact from bullshit, mind you, but at this point, we've got a pretty good idea of what we're dealing with."

The projection shifted to a new image, and it wasn't until the enchantment zoomed in that Domenic even noticed the blur in the corner—Decibel. Its ephemeral form looked all the more haunting on camera, the glow of its eyes harsh as lens flares, its body a distorted jumble of static.

"Of the three, Decibel was the least likely to engage with our troops. But it also had the widest range of sightings, across nearly the whole country. We get the sense it's been acting as a scout and was probably the least dangerous of the three."

Panic sparked in Domenic's chest, and he forced in a deep breath before it could catch.

Again, the image changed: lightning crackling across a darkened sky, coalescing at a central point—a face, its mouth impossibly huge.

"Then there's Thundersnow," Peak said. "Like normal winterghasts, this one clearly wields nature magic. But it's no normal ghast. This photograph had to be taken at a distance, obviously, but according to our reports, this thing is massive. Take a look at those shapes at the bottom of the photograph, for scale."

Domenic leaned in, squinting at what seemed like pinpricks.

"Are those . . . trees?" he croaked.

"They sure are," answered Peak grimly.

The corporal returned with their coffees. Neither Domenic nor Ellery touched them.

The projection vanished.

"Last, there's Cadaver," Peak continued. "This one, we've got no idea what it looks like. There's never been a confirmed sighting, let alone a chance to catch it on camera. All the info we've pulled together is based solely on the victims. Corporeal magic. You can take a look at this binder to see their photographs if you'd like, but take my word for it—they're not pretty. If not for their wands, I'm not even sure we would've been able to identify who these magicians were."

Ellery reached for the binder and silently flipped through the pages, the cover blocking Domenic's view. But as he leaned over to peek as well, subtly, she shook her head. Domenic swallowed and righted himself gratefully. He'd seen enough victims of corporeal magic.

"Now, we don't know what tasks the future prophecy pieces will ask of you," Peak went on. "But it's our job to anticipate. All these rumors of the Dire Three, they only go back so many years—ten or eleven, so we think. And given how powerful they are, how soon after that we lost the fallen territory, these ghasts are significant. And we've got a hunch that we'll need to slay all three of them to make sure this cataclysm doesn't come to pass."

Domenic rested his finger upon Valmordion's handle at his side, focusing on his limitless expanse of power. However daunting this invasion seemed, they'd never lost. They never would.

They never would.

"Whatever it takes," he murmured, "we'll end this."

Peak grimaced, so quick and imperceptible that Domenic wouldn't have caught it if the expression didn't look so alien on him.

And just like that, Peak was smiling again. "So whaddya say, Dom, El? You up for hunting a couple monsters?"

* * *

As Domenic and Ellery exited the command center, Domenic squinted into the fluorescent lights of the facility hallways, the harsh cast of reality. He clasped his sweaty hands together so as not to reach for her. For however much he'd reassured himself, he needed fantasy. He needed distraction.

"Hey, Dom!" Peak called, jogging up behind them. Domenic halted, and Peak clapped him hard on the shoulder. "What would you say to the two of us having a little talk, man-to-man?"

Immediately, Domenic and Ellery exchanged a stricken look. Peak knew. He knew they'd crossed the line.

"Oh. Uh, yeah," Domenic answered weakly. "Why not?"

Peak beamed. "Come on. I'll give you the tour."

Domenic followed him into an officer lounge, which proved little more than several couches, a pool table, and a bleak kitchenette with a poster of some presumably famous, scantily-clad woman duct taped to the fridge. Several magicians saluted as they entered.

"At ease, all of you," Peak told them jovially. Then he procured two beers and steered Domenic toward a couch in the corner, beside a radio whose jazz music crackled over the long-distance airwaves. Peak stretched out wide, his arm draped over the back cushions. Domenic leaned his elbows on his knees.

Then a sudden warmth radiated against Domenic as Peak drew Targath. He flicked it, and his bottle cap popped off and plunked against the linoleum floor, slightly singed.

Why not? Domenic repeated to himself, training his own historical magical artifact on his beer. The cap crumpled and fell onto his lap.

"Well, cheers," Peak said, and they clinked bottles. Peak took a hefty swig. Domenic tilted his bottle back but didn't let any liquid pass his lips. He could control Valmordion, but he still wasn't about to drunkenly wave around a weapon that could raze mountains.

He did still have a few lines.

"I know Toddy Lite isn't anything fancy," Peak said, "but I'm fond of it. Me and a buddy used to sneak them into our dorm room. Got ourselves into some real trouble back in the day, if you can believe it."

"Trouble?" Domenic echoed hoarsely, still bracing himself. "Yeah, I think I can see it."

"I miss those days. Your whole time at the academy, all you're told to think about is getting your Living Wand. They don't tell you how your life changes"—he snapped his fingers—"just like that. The second I bonded with Targath, all of a sudden, I had a uniform. A rank higher than anyone in my class, even those who joined the NDC before me. People saluting when I walked into a room. I don't think I ever got used to it, to be honest. I'm sure you know the feeling."

Domenic laughed darkly. "Yeah. I do." Then, tentatively, he relaxed. Though if Peak didn't intend to scold him, Domenic had zero idea where this man-to-man talk was going. "But if you weren't ready, why did you sign up for Targath's vigil in the first place?"

"Oh, the same reason every student had their eyes on it from the moment my predecessor dropped dead. It guaranteed a future, glory. But after Hoover and Smith were killed before Calynia's vigil—and Iseul just about—my roommate and I used up almost all our training wands enchanting our locks at night."

Domenic shuddered to imagine what the academy must've been like before sabotaging competition was punishable by expulsion.

"Besides," Peak went on, "I never doubted I could handle Targath's power. But the responsibility? I had no idea what I was getting into."

"What changed?"

"Well, a few months later, that buddy of mine followed me to the NDC. He bonded with Fellis, which—don't get me wrong—it's a respectable wand. But that first time we went into a scurge together, technically, I was his commanding officer. It's the duty of Targath's wielder to lead, their destiny to protect their men. And I didn't grasp that." Peak blew out a breath. "Fellis has passed through a few hands at this point. It's with one of our cadets, now. I've never met her, but I've seen her from a distance. She's real dependable, I'm told."

Domenic winced. For however ridiculous Peak's lopsided smiles were, carrying around a burden like that, it was impressive he could smile at all.

"Can I ask you something?" Domenic ventured.

Peak tipped his beer toward him. "Ask away."

"Why were you so sure about me before you even knew me? Was it just destiny?"

Across the lounge, billiard balls smacked together. One of the officers whooped. Others laughed.

"I'll admit," Peak answered, "when Iseul first told me she was taking you and Hanna in, I was pretty surprised. Worried, even. Neither of us had ever wanted kids, and the pair of you, after what you'd been through . . . it seemed a daunting task. But Iseul's a smart judge of character, and she saw something in you two. And watching Hanna grow up all these years, that something was obvious. That girl's a force. Too stubborn and clever for her own good, mind you, but you gotta be, to make it to the Order from factory towns like Danmere—let alone to wield Syarthis. Now *that's* a responsibility I never would've asked for."

Domenic examined Targath's calcified sheath jutting out from one of Peak's pockets. He'd never considered the similarities between Targath and Syarthis before: both the most powerful of their class of magic, both accompanied by inherent expectations.

But there was more than that. Syarthis, Targath, Ravfiri . . . Domenic felt the heat of every Living Wand, but none compared to theirs. And when Peak drew Targath, when Hanna drew Syarthis, Domenic could always tell, instinctively. They each bore a presence of significance.

Domenic's stomach sank. "So you were only sure about me because of Iseul and Hanna?"

"No, that was only part of it. The bigger reason was when I first met you, when the Council visited you in the hospital. You were real quiet, real shaken up—understandably, of course. Anyone else would've dropped out. But you chose to stay. And I know the whole country's had a lot to say about your grades, your attendance. Even Iseul worried you were squandering your potential. But me, I always thought what you did achieve was pretty remarkable. Special, even."

Domenic fixed his gaze on the cinder-block wall. "Oh, um . . ." He cleared his throat. "That's nice of you to say."

"I mean it! And look at you now! Three weeks ago, you were so sick you were green on that train to Oldermere. You ought to be real proud of how much you've grown. I know I am."

"I mean . . ." Domenic shifted awkwardly. "It's not like I had a choice. It was that or fail . . . everyone."

This time when Peak grimaced, it lingered. And even though Domenic knew it was his imagination, he swore the radio's static sharpened, that the lounge's laughter dimmed as if moving farther and farther away.

Peak gulped his beer.

"Listen to me, Dom. Because there's something I've . . . I've really been wanting to say. Whatever choices you've got ahead, they're not gonna be easy." He rubbed the empty fourth finger of his left hand. "And yeah, wands like Targath and Valmordion, wands with the power to save a whole lotta lives, sometimes it feels like you don't have a choice but to put other people's well-being before your own. But there's real honor in sacrifice. And that sacrifice is always worth it."

* * *

Domenic unlocked his sleeping quarters to find Ellery sitting in his desk chair, one leg crossed atop the other.

He hastily slipped inside and shut the door. "How did you get in here?"

"Believe it or not, I've done this before," she said slyly, repeating his same words from when he'd climbed through her dormitory window. Domenic raised a brow, dangerously curious despite having no right to be.

Then Ellery's voice went worried. "So what happened with Peak? Were we too obvious?"

"No, if anything, Peak thinks too highly of me." Domenic paced as he struggled to find the words for their conversation. His chest felt oddly tight. "Peak said some things that sort of freaked me out, though."

"Like what?"

"All this stuff about duty, sacrifice. I don't think he meant to sound so dark. But . . ." He trailed off as Ellery's anxious expression began to mirror his own. "Actually, never mind. It was probably all in my head." He didn't trust himself when he was like this.

"I've been nervous since our briefing, too," she said softly.

For once, Domenic didn't know if it was better or worse that they felt the same.

He managed a smile. "I don't know about you, but I've had my fill of duty for today."

He grabbed her wrists and tugged her to standing. Swiftly, she slid her arms around his shoulders, pressed against him until their every slope and angle seemed to slot together.

"So have I," she whispered.

Finally, *finally*, he kissed her again, and as soon as their lips met, he felt as if he was resurfacing from beneath an undertow, as if he hadn't breathed since the air he'd last drawn from her. And even as he braced for it, he still gasped as the chill of her magic jetted through his core. It felt like a blast of wind from a thousand feet of free fall. It felt like a meteoric plunge into ice water. His own magic flared, but he didn't dare break away. Because now that he knew how it felt to kiss Ellery Caldwell, his survival instincts had been rewritten.

Ellery's hips moved against his, and Domenic was grateful to have her to lean against, otherwise his legs might've given out beneath him. Her mouth traced his jaw until she found the pulse point below his ear, pounding with adrenaline. Her nails skimmed the grooves of his spine, the strip of exposed skin above his waistband, the hook of his belt loop—

Without reason, his panic kindled again, and Domenic cursed himself. For weeks, he'd been better, and he refused to ruin this. Not just because of how long he'd fantasized about Ellery Caldwell, but because none of the girls he'd kissed had ever looked at him like she did. Like she saw him, all of him. And yet she wanted him anyway.

She guided him to the bed, and Domenic lay atop her, one hand propped against the mattress while the other wove into her hair. It took restraint not to rush, but he wanted to savor this. All the more, he didn't want to give her the wrong idea. She knew his reputation, and even if that version of himself had died the moment he'd grasped Valmordion, he didn't want her to think he expected anything, that he hurried because it all meant so little to him.

Ellery, however, had no such qualms. Her mouth barely broke for air. Her touches barely lingered on one place of him before reaching for the next.

She was afraid, too.

But he didn't acknowledge it. Not until her hands pressed against his bare stomach, and he could no longer stop himself. He paused, shivering, his forehead against hers.

"Swear to me you believe in us," he gasped.

Ellery panted as she clutched him tight. "I already have."

"Then swear it again. And I'll swear it to you."

Domenic tried not to count the seconds of her silence.

"I swear it," she rasped finally. "We'll survive this together. Just like we've survived everything else."

"We'll thwart it." He snaked his arm around her waist and crushed her against him. "We'll save each other. We'll save everyone. And I swear, we'll make our own destiny when this one is through."

He'd meant their words to steady them both, and indeed, the weight of their future lifted slightly. But the promise was so exorbitant as to have a weight of its own, and soon, there was no restraint from either of them. Ellery hitched her breath as he squeezed her thigh. Her hands roamed under his shirt, and wherever she touched, his magic scorched beneath his skin, so hot he almost swore he could taste smoke.

Then, outside, a siren blared.

XXIV
Ellery
WINTER

Instantly, Ellery and Domenic broke apart and scrambled to the door. As soon as Ellery threw it open, they both cringed as the alarm pierced their eardrums. Shouts cried out down the halls. Magicians barreled past, combat boots pounding, wands raised. Ellery wrenched Iskarius from its sheath.

"Are we under attack?" Domenic asked. Even beside him, Ellery could barely hear him over the siren's blare.

"I don't know," she yelled. "Let's go—"

BOOM!

Somewhere beyond the barracks, sound exploded. The ground shook, and Ellery and Domenic caught themselves against the wall. Then both the siren and the lights cut out, plunging them into blackness.

They hastily lit their wands and bolted after the flood of magicians, careening through the hallways until they burst through an emergency exit. They were greeted by a winter-scurge of horrendous proportions. Cold lanced through Ellery's skin, and although it didn't harm her, she could still feel its bite. Winds howled, and an oppressive darkness descended upon the compound. The more distant buildings were invisible to her, swallowed by the storm.

This was already a category four. At least.

To their right, fire poured through a warehouse's windows, engulfing the roof in an inferno that glowed a terrible beacon against the scurge.

She turned to the nearest magician and demanded, "What happened? What building is that?"

"It's the generator," squeaked the magician. She rapidly yanked on layers of gear, her pale fingers already violet from the cold. "It's supposed to be scurgeproof, but as soon as the storm descended, it blew up." Then she balked as she took in Domenic and Ellery. "Uh, ma'am, sir."

She stiffened as she stared at Ellery, who was suddenly hyperaware of her and Domenic's swollen lips, their mussed clothes. A pink mark bloomed on his neck, scattered amongst his freckles.

"The generator?" Domenic choked. "But they . . . They couldn't have . . ."

Rather than finish, he caught Ellery's gaze, and she knew they were thinking the same thing: it was no coincidence to attack the one building that would make the entire compound vulnerable. It was strategy.

"What are we supposed to do?" the magician blubbered. "I-I'm just a volunteer. I only just got here, and I . . ." Her words became gasps. She clutched her training wand to her chest—she was a hedge magician.

Ellery and Domenic didn't have time to linger, but Ellery said anyway: "We're here to protect you. You'll be okay. We'll make sure of it."

The woman nodded, but she didn't meet Ellery's eyes.

"Listen to me," Domenic told her. "If you go find the nearest NDC soldiers, they'll know the protocols, even if you don't."

At his voice, strained but steady, her expression changed—fear shifting into hope.

"A-all right." Her gaze flickered once more to Ellery, then Iskarius. But Ellery shook it off as the woman rushed away. There was no time to dwell.

"I don't understand. There hasn't been a scurge in weeks," Ellery hissed to Domenic. "And the same day we get to the border, there's an attack?"

"Even if a bunch of ghasts—I don't know—*planned* this somehow, we fortified the alban network. How did they break through?"

"Maybe there are just too many of them."

Domenic sucked in a shallow breath.

Even in the brief time they'd spent comforting the hedge magician, the wind had intensified. Strands of Ellery's hair whipped across her forehead, then froze there. All around them, people ran—some fleeing indoors, others distributing supplies and readying for battle. NDC soldiers strapped on goggles and secured their hoods. Yet with each passing second, darkness encroached further, until even those closest to Ellery and Domenic appeared as little more than silhouettes.

"We could get to the edge of the compound," she hollered to Domenic above the wind. "Try to defend it."

"No, the NDC probably had sentries guarding the compound already." Determination steeled across his features. "You remember how I told you that in Oldermere, I found the scurge's eye?"

Ellery did. "You think we should try to stop the storm from its center?"

"Yeah, together."

They took off through the compound, following the storm's magic to where the cold was most intense, the pressure crushing. But they'd barely made it across a single courtyard before whirling fractals coalesced into a shape several yards ahead.

The winterghast was hideous, and although it was not nearly as gigantic or eerily humanoid as the Dire Three, it was far more fearsome than the one in Mercester Square. Dirt and blood crusted its ice-sculpted body; a writhing mass of tentacles unfurled as it heaved closer to them. Its lone eye gleamed a haunting blue.

Instantly, Ellery and Domenic attacked.

With a burst of frost, she pinned it in place. Its body contorted grotesquely, and a screech emanated from deep within it. But she held it effortlessly while Valmordion's flames burned it in a blaze of gold.

It screeched again, then exploded into a spatter of ice.

But as its screech faded, another rose nearby. Then another, and another. Cries echoed across the storm in a terrible chorus.

Ellery thrust Iskarius into the air. Its silver light speared through the darkness.

Winterghasts swarmed everywhere, at least two dozen, maybe more. They were an army, a blight upon the compound. And each of their azure eyes were trained directly on her and Domenic.

Ellery had seen such an army once before, during the fall of Nordmere. She remembered peering through her dirty apartment windows, petrified. The ghasts rampaging through the streets.

Her memories devolved after that. Scrambling for her training wand. Her parents; a smear, a blur. Fleeing from what she'd done, running into the maelstrom outside. And the ghast, looming over a panicked crowd of people rushing to evacuate. She scarcely recalled what the monster looked like. Just its awful roar and the distant sound of her scream and the blood matted in her hair and her reflection in its body, her own eyes too bright, too blue.

Now, Ellery tightened her grip on Iskarius.

"If we want to get to the eye . . ." she started.

Domenic white-knuckled Valmordion. "We've gotta get through the swarm."

As the first of the winterghasts charged toward them—a creature with tusks that scissored and flayed out into countless points—Ellery pressed her back to Domenic's.

Together, they raised their wands and struck.

The NDC joined them, combating the initial wave of ghasts in squadrons of three or four, hurling coordinated barrages of nature magic.

Ellery fought as if a scurge unto herself, summoning a gale of frost that swept toward the winterghasts. Some fell prone. Others shattered. Behind her, Domenic's fire spiraled out in a vortex, impervious even to the winds.

The winterghasts shrieked as the flames consumed them, their forms sagging into even more gruesome shapes as they melted. Still, none compared to Decibel's power. But the monsters made up for it in sheer numbers, streaming endlessly through the compound as though conjured by the night itself.

Around them, magicians began to fall. Squadrons splintered and fled, until only Domenic and Ellery endured.

In some ways, it was a relief to be separate. Unburdened by the fear of collateral damage, they unleashed a tempest of magic. Domenic's very shape glowed with a halo so bright it hurt even to squint at him. Ellery's shadow elongated and spilled outward in a sea of darkness.

Their fight could've lasted minutes. It could've lasted hours. Until the final winterghast was slain. Steam hissed as its body melted into broken hunks of ice.

"You okay?" Domenic braced his free hand on his knee.

Ellery panted, "Alive. You?"

"Pretty much."

As she gathered herself, dimly, she realized a crowd of magicians had thronged around them. Many of them cheered, applauding, embracing. But not all. At least a third backed away, pointing with trembling hands.

Not at the carnage before them.

At *her*.

Ellery knew why: frost drifted from her every exhale; her blue eyes beamed like spotlights; her shadow coiled at her feet, eddying and shifting.

Yet as she moved to sheathe Iskarius, she felt a heartbeat, echoing beside her own.

Just like she'd felt Decibel's.

Whatever the other magicians saw, whatever they thought, she kept hold of Iskarius. She had no choice.

"Dom," she said hoarsely. "One of the Dire Three. It's here."

Domenic's eyes widened, then he spun to face the crowd. He yelled something at them, but not even Ellery could hear it as strange cobalt lightning detonated overhead. But rather than reach toward the earth, it stretched horizontally, as if a lattice of shattered glass covering the storm from edge to edge.

People scattered, screaming, as the lightning receded, each bolt drawing back toward a center. Then, in a cyclone of whirling snow and cloud, a giant shape loomed over them. Its icy body was as large as any building in the compound.

"It's Thundersnow!" Domenic shouted to her, horrified.

Before Ellery could even nod, above them, the lightning gathered to specific points: a twin set of eyes in a humanoid face; a crackling network of antlers. Its body was studded with debris, entire trees frozen within its torso.

Its heartbeat boomed. It rattled her rib cage. It chattered her teeth. And a name rose in her, erupting like thunder.

"No, Kythion," she corrected frantically. "Its name is Kythion."

Domenic gawked. Yet he didn't question how she possibly knew that. "But that sounds like . . ."

"Like a wand," she finished.

"Shit." He raked his fingers through his hair. "*Shit*. Well, if it has a name, what about the other two?"

"I didn't hear anything when we fought Decibel. But they must, right? The Dire Three aren't like other ghasts. And when one of them's close, like this . . ." Ellery stared up at the monster again. The storm swirled around its body, traveling with each of its tremendous, creaking steps. "I understand how this sounds. But I *know* them somehow. They feel . . . significant."

Domenic froze, and Ellery swallowed, aware of just how unnerving her statement was. Aware of their remaining onlookers.

"Targath. Syarthis. Ravfiri," he said gravely.

Ellery blinked. "What?"

"Everything you just said about those ghasts, that they're different, significant, that's how I feel about those wands. And there's three of them, the most powerful of each class of magic. El, that can't be a coincidence."

"So you think they're, what, *counterparts* to these things? You think wands are . . . are *monsters*?" Ellery's voice grew higher, shriller. "That's not . . . That can't be . . ." She trailed off as a figure detached from the darkness and jogged toward them. Ellery squinted at their unseasonal shorts, their utter lack of gear. Peak.

Domenic followed her gaze, then cursed. "You and me, we'll figure this out later."

"Y-yeah."

Finally, Ellery dared to examine the wand she had created, its silver core and icy tip, its thorn-studded vines. Ellery had used Iskarius to fling open her bedroom curtains and find spare pairs of shoes. She'd used it to fortify an ancient network of trees. She'd used it to slay the monsters she believed she'd been born to fight. And not once had she asked herself where such tremendous power had truly come from.

"But Dom, if what you're saying is true, then what the *fuck* are Val and Izzy?"

Hauntedly, Domenic glanced at Valmordion. Its golden heart seemed to blaze within his eyes.

"Later," he repeated, a promise, a plea.

 XXV

Domenic
WINTER

Through the storm's churning blackness, Peak only came into focus as he skidded to a halt beside them. He raised Targath. Its calcified wood gleamed like a hot coal, and its heat scorched across Domenic's skin as its warming spell expanded, making every magician in a one-hundred-foot radius slump in relief, even cheer. The darkness of the courtyard thinned, like smoke-tinged amber.

"You both all right?" Peak asked.

Domenic's panic blazed, a fuse dangerously close to explosion. Bearing the weight of the world had been burden enough before the world had shifted beneath them. He didn't know what to make of these ghasts who fought with strategy. What to make of Ellery, calling Kythion by name. What to make of the countless Living Wands around them, each burning with a presence that felt suddenly unnerving, monstrous. Least of all, he no longer understood the wand in his own hand, which seemingly possessed no presence entirely.

The boom of a collapsing building rumbled somewhere beyond.

"'Course we are," Domenic croaked, and Ellery managed a bleak nod.

"Have you two gotten a good look around?" Peak squinted through the whizzing shrapnel of snow. "I don't know how it's possible, but these ghasts are here with a mission, a goal. So the three of us, we figure it out, we stop it, and we save as many people as possible. 'Cause my guys—they're good, but they're not trained for this. And if I have any shot of bringing that thing down"—he gestured at Kythion overhead—"I can't be worrying about collateral damage, you hear?"

"*You* bring it down?" Ellery repeated. "It took me and Dom together to slay Decibel—"

"Well, Thundersnow isn't like Decibel, is it? It's got nature magic. No tricks or illusions to worry about." Peak tilted his head back, and he didn't flinch as Kythion's lightning detonated across the scurge. "Maybe Targath and I have finally met our match."

At first, Domenic swore Peak had reached their same conclusion. But as Peak smiled crookedly at the monster, the cracks between his teeth shining molten, Domenic realized that this, *this* was the truth of Peak. The man who ran into danger without a single thought for himself. Who strolled through Winter's cold without need for warmth, whose very presence had made the snow melt in a circle beneath him, had made the once frozen grass blacken with char. Who held Targath high—not to help him see in the darkness, but as a beacon to anyone else in need of hope.

"G-good luck, then," Domenic stammered.

With a final thumbs-up at the pair of them, who both awkwardly returned it, Peak charged off toward his epic war story in the making. A strange nerve tightened in Domenic's chest as he watched Targath's glow diminish through the scurge. Surely Peak was the last person he ought to worry about.

"Do you think he's valiant or deranged?" Domenic asked Ellery.

"Both," she answered grimly. "Now, with this many ghasts, I still think you're right—finding the eye is the only way we'll ever stop this scurge."

"But what about all the people here?"

The surrounding magicians shivered and shuffled around as one of that afternoon's stern-faced generals corralled them into units. With his magic like magma in his veins, Domenic had forgotten about the cold, and he hastily cast a warming spell of his own. The blackened grass greened, and the storm receded into a roiling dome overhead, their small pocket of refuge free from the smothering darkness and torrential winds.

As onlookers cheered again, Ellery answered, "Stopping the storm is the best way to save them."

"But that will take time. And you heard Peak—they're not trained for this. We need to get them out of here."

Ellery winced at another crash of thunder. "Then we split up."

"*What?* No. No way."

"It's the only thing that makes sense. One of us should find the eye, while the other should evacuate the NDC." Her lip quivered even as she bit it down. "A-and you see how they look at me. If they're going to trust anyone to lead them to safety, it'll be you."

Spite simmered in Domenic's core. While the pair of them stood there, still, Ellery's shadow lashed across the ground, alive and wild with magic. Several nearby magicians pointed at it. Some even lunged from its path as if it might strike them.

They didn't notice how even beneath the glare of Valmordion, Domenic had no shadow at all.

"Fuck what they think," he growled. "They won't give a shit so long as we're saving them from—"

"Dom, this is a better plan," Ellery snapped. "You know it is."

Domenic had never loathed his costume more than in that moment. That he couldn't reach for her. That he was bound to be noble. That he ought to care what anyone else thought of them when no one could ever see the entirety of who they were anyway.

"*Please*," he said desperately. "Be careful."

"You, too," she told him.

Ellery ran off, and Domenic raced toward the closest

building—a garage. One of its doors whipped in the storm. He ducked through it.

"Hello?" he called. Even inside, the wind wailed, and icicles speared down from the ceiling rafters. Shards of those already fallen littered the concrete.

"Over here! Help! Please!"

Mimicking Peak, Domenic raised Valmordion higher and sped toward the voice. He found a trio of magicians behind a utility vehicle. One slumped against the corrugated steel wall, wheezing—magical frostmaul crusted scarlet and crystalline over half her face. Another knelt beside her, his training wand quivering in his hand. The third was dead.

Dimly, Domenic's vision tinted red as he took in the body, and that scared him even more than the corpse did. That after all the agony of remaking himself into someone stronger, someone better, there was no version of Domenic Barrow that wasn't a little bit broken.

"It's you," the magician gasped. "Thank everything. I thought I'd lose her, too."

"We won't," Domenic assured him, then withheld a cringe. He sounded comical.

But the man only slackened with relief and scrambled out of the way so Domenic could crouch beside the wounded magician.

She reached for him, and Domenic clasped her blood-slicked fingers. His stomach turned in aversion, though he thought he hid it well.

Immediately, she stopped shuddering. "You're so warm."

"In a minute, you will be, too," he promised, training Valmordion on the creeping frostmaul. His hand trembled. Frostmaul this advanced would consume her in minutes. And healing required an uncompromising attention to detail that had always been Hanna's forte, never his. Yet gradually, the frostmaul melted, its sanguine water oozing down her neck and soaking into her scarf.

"Thank you. *Thank you*," the man sputtered, leaning so close over Domenic's shoulder that Domenic could smell the staleness of his breath. "The two of us came in here to hide"—he nodded at the corpse—"but when I went back to carry Manning inside, he was already . . ." He bit down on his fist, shaking.

"She's going to be fine, thanks to you," Domenic told him. Instantly, the fear on the man's face snuffed out, replaced by hope. And even if Domenic swore he was only wearing a costume, that hope felt almost real.

After Domenic finished healing the frostmauled magician, he led them to the edge of the compound, where an NDC team ushered others out of the gate. At his approach, the commanding officer rushed toward him. The man's jacket was spangled with medals earned in more winters than Domenic had seen in his entire life, yet he saluted him without hesitation.

"How many are left to evac?" Domenic shouted over the wind.

"The east side of the compound has been cleared. But the west . . ." The officer nodded dismally toward the lightning and explosions flashing through the obscurity, warning of some horror that awaited in the unknown. "We know Thundersnow took out at least half a dozen buildings. But that's the last we heard. Our recon unit still hasn't returned."

"Then I'll bring them back," Domenic vowed immediately.

The officer smiled—he didn't catch his falseness either.

As Domenic sprinted across the compound, he swore he was in a dream, a nightmare. It wasn't the light of *his* magic that lanced through the darkness. It wasn't *his* hands that tore and bled as they sifted through rubble. It wasn't *his* voice that urged other magicians away so he could battle winterghasts alone.

It couldn't be.

Their shoulders shook as they hugged him; their hair got in

his mouth, their blood smeared on his shirt. Many of them wept, in grief, in relief, in horror, in so many emotions that Domenic felt smoldering in them, like every tear was kerosene and he was ablaze. His hands burned from the grasp of desperate fingers. He bled where nails had stabbed into his skin. Once he swore he saved a man who'd already gone, had forced the air to return to his lungs and heard him choke back in his final breath. And it terrified him, how deeply their hope burrowed beside his own. He couldn't bear to be made a fool.

But it felt fucking real. The costume, the act—all of it did.

After scouring the final barracks and determining it empty, Domenic allowed himself a single moment to lean against a warehouse wall. Until a sudden, familiar warmth pressed against him, and Domenic threw up a noise muffling enchantment a second before thunder detonated directly overhead.

Then Kythion's antlered head reared over the warehouse, impossibly, grotesquely huge. Domenic clambered back, and his sight locked on a smaller shape atop the roof—Peak.

Peak aimed, and a torrent of flames spewed out of Targath toward the whirling ice of Kythion's form. On impact, fire and lightning erupted across the sky, so powerful that every window of the warehouse shattered.

Valiant, Domenic decided. Then he shook off his exhaustion and sprinted for the eye of the storm.

The darkness embraced him, abrasive like a shroud of burlap, so dense he couldn't breathe through his mouth without gagging. Blades of frost sliced his skin, and even as Domenic healed each scrape, leftover blood coated his hand and marbled Valmordion in crimson. He stopped twice: once to catch his breath and once to slay a ghast that lurked amidst a decimated vehicle, a corpse still dangling through the windshield where a pincer had skewered him through the glass.

When at last Domenic found the storm's whirling center, he didn't pause to despair at the immensity of it—far vaster even than the category five in Oldermere. He hurled himself within and broke through staggering and gasping. And for the second time, he found Ellery Caldwell at the base of an alban tree.

The scurge raged around them, ribbons of incandescence twisting through the blackness.

"Dom," she choked. "Help me."

Domenic had expected to find her trying to quell the storm from within. Instead, she pointed Iskarius at the tree, clutching the wand with two hands. The color of the leaves bled out, gold fading into brown then gray, as if in death. But no, not death—Winter. Just as the leaves tore from their branches, a frost replaced them, glittering and ominous, seeping over the canopy and down to the roots.

"No," he rasped, as the pieces locked together. The hundreds of ghasts, Kythion showing itself . . . *This* was the monsters' true goal. Domenic and Ellery had come to the border to reclaim the fallen territory, but as it turned out, the invasion the prophecy spoke of had been *Winter's*—and it was succeeding.

Domenic reached frantically into the very core of his power, the unfathomable depths of it. His magic radiated through the tree, and immediately, buds sprouted from its barren branches. Petals unfurled. Leaves revived to their lush, golden glory.

But the frost still came.

As the last leaf tore away and disappeared into the storm, a part of Domenic tore away with it. He doubled over, retching, as the warmth of Summer's magic ebbed from the alban roots beneath him. As Winter conquered this land as its own.

He managed to lift his head to spot Ellery a short distance from him, staring stricken as the scurge's vortex closed in.

Domenic threw himself against her and pulled them both against the trunk, and she clung to him as the world caved in around them, the feeble glows of their wands the only light against the all-consuming dark.

Even if this loss wasn't their fault, it might as well have been.

They'd gotten ahead of themselves. They'd gotten distracted. Whatever they felt, whatever they wanted, these stakes were too great to risk another failure.

There won't be another failure, Domenic promised. *Not ever again.*

As Domenic held Ellery against his chest, a cry of defeat wailed in the wind.

no battles can amount to victory
until Summer's traitor is condemned

XXVI
ELLERY
WINTER

Ellery watched worriedly as Domenic ducked back into their private train compartment. "All right. Peak went to the sleeper car." He slid the door closed and locked it.

"In that case, let's—"

"Wait." Domenic's soundproofing enchantment seeped down the paneled wooden walls, ruffling the curtains. Then he collapsed onto the bench across from her with a haunted, red-tinged stare. "Okay. Now we talk."

Their train hurtled south to Gallamere. Although the weak light of morning crept through the windows, neither of them had slept. Kythion and the rest of the ghasts had vanished after Winter turned the alban tree, and the worst of the storm had vanished with them. Yet even after Domenic and Ellery had reunited with Peak and the NDC, driving down the same highways that had taken them to the compound, several hours passed before they'd emerged from the fallen territory's new border.

Now, Ellery's fatigues were tattered and bloodstained, her feet blistered inside her combat boots. She was exhausted but unable to rest; starving but unable to choke down more than a few bites of food.

"I . . ." She swallowed. "I don't even know where to start."

"Neither do I. I mean, twelve hours ago, we were talking about retaking the fallen territory. And now Winter doesn't just have the North. It has, what—almost a third of the country?" Domenic slammed his fist on his own thigh. "What the hell just happened, El?"

"We lost. That's what happened."

The train car rumbled beneath them.

Ellery had fled Nordmere on a train much like this one, but instead of a quiet ride in a private compartment, she'd been packed in with other evacuees. Mile after mile of anxious chatter and babies wailing and pained groans from the wounded. The stench of sweat and grime and dried blood. Ellery whiled away the hours trapped in a corner seat, peeling back strips of wood from her armrest.

But her fear then was nothing compared to what she felt now. She'd been so confident, so convinced of their inevitable victory.

So wrong.

"At least we got another prophecy piece," she muttered finally.

Domenic choked out a laugh as he fixed his gaze out the window. "I still wish we could've told Peak."

"Me too. But you know we can't."

"Do I? The man took on Kythion single-handedly. Do you really think *he's* Summer's traitor?"

"Of course not."

"Then why aren't we telling the Council?" he demanded. "Because we think it could be Iseul? Hanna? Glynn?"

"I'm not trying to make accusations. But if Summer's traitor is a magician, which they probably are, then they're most likely an Order magician. And they could be *anyone*. Even a Councilor." Although Ellery kept her voice level, nausea rose in her at the thought.

"Yeah, but if it's not any of the Councilors and we *don't* tell them, we're only fucking ourselves over."

"I'm not saying we don't tell them! I'm saying we need a strategy before we do. Some way we want this to play out."

His leg jittered. "And what way is that?"

"I was hoping we could figure that out together." Ellery hesitated. "I know we lost. But we're not doomed. I mean, we learned that the Dire Three have names like *wands*. That they've got Living Wand counterparts. We should tell the Council that, at least."

"Yeah," he said solemnly. "They should know what they might be wielding."

"And have you thought more about . . . about *our* wands?"

Domenic drew Valmordion and studied it carefully: the whorled fingerprints, the gnarled wood, the thorns. "Val doesn't feel like some kind of Summer monster. It doesn't feel like anything."

Ellery drew her wand, too.

"Neither does Iskarius," she said softly. "As far as I can tell, there's no ghost inside. Its magic is gigantic, but it's *my* magic. There's no difference between me and it."

That notion was as disturbing as it was relieving. But even if Iskarius was somehow different, the implications of their discovery might be tremendous; for their understanding of Winter magic, for Alderland as a whole.

They both sheathed their wands. Then Ellery reached forward and squeezed Domenic's hand. His throat bobbed, and he squeezed back tightly, so tightly, and the terrible ache in her chest eased slightly, so slightly.

Then he slid his hand back.

"No, we're not doomed," he said firmly. "But we can't lose again, not ever. We can't fuck up. We can't get distracted."

From the way he said "distracted," Ellery knew exactly what he was talking about.

"We were careless, yes," she agreed. "But do you really think that's why we lost? There were hundreds of people at the compound, including Peak. The winterghasts surprised us all."

"I'm not saying it's our fault, but I don't want to risk it ever being our fault because you and I . . ." His gaze skittered away from hers.

"Right." Ellery's voice sharpened. "Sure. I get it."

"No, you don't," he said hastily. "I'm not . . . I don't want to do this. This is the last thing I want. But what we want—it doesn't matter, does it? Until we beat this thing, we need to be who everyone needs us to be. We need to be heroes."

"You think I don't know that? I've spent the past five years trying to be what everyone—" Ellery cut herself off, her cheeks burning. He knew. He knew everything. "Forget it."

"It's just, I-I haven't always been the hero." Domenic's words stumbled over one another, high-pitched and strained. "And I thought I forgave myself for not moving that day. I thought I was different now. But being tangled in bed while everything went to shit? That doesn't feel different. And I have to be."

But Ellery felt different. No—Ellery *was* different.

How naïve to think he might feel the same, to believe she might have changed him just because he'd changed her.

"You know what?" she said hoarsely. "You're right. We don't have time for some fling."

He flinched. "No, El, th-that isn't what I—"

"Please, just . . . just stop." Ellery forced back tears. She'd cried in front of him before, but the thought of it happening now was unbearable. "I don't need you to spare my feelings. In fact, let's just take the feelings out of it." She slid Miss Perfect on, expression steeled, posture straight, voice steady. "It's like you said. We've been distracted long enough."

"I . . ." Domenic's hand clasped over his mouth. He tugged it away, then stood abruptly, sniffling. "I'm gonna grab some coffee. Do you want any? No milk. Six sugars. Yeah, got it."

He bolted from the compartment. The door slammed behind him.

Ellery curled in the corner of her booth. She worried her fingernail beneath the armrest's mahogany varnish, then violently yanked back a strip of wood.

There was no place in her destiny for a broken heart.

XXVII
Domenic
WINTER

That night, as the nation mourned the loss of land and lives, as refugees crowded into Gallamere's train stations and camped in its parks, as overwhelmed magicians raced throughout the Citadel, the Council gathered solemnly in a conference room and locked the door.

"Well," Iseul said gravely, "I'm not even sure where to begin."

"So, not only have you posed that Living Wands and winter-ghasts are somehow equivalents," Sharpe spoke through gritted teeth, "but that there is a traitor within the Order working as an agent of *Winter*?"

"Yes, I believe you get the picture," Domenic answered flatly.

The frost over the lancet windows utterly obscured the gleam of Gallamere's nighttime skyline. The sconces burned dim. An enchanted typewriter clacked from a darkened corner.

Flames crackled in the ancient stone fireplace, casting every profile in stark shadows.

Domenic braced himself for Sharpe's outrage. Yet the President of the Magicians Order only chuckled. He leisurely withdrew Ballathim to light a cigarette, then held it perched between two wizened fingers.

From the opposite end of the table, Domenic crinkled his nose at the tobacco's reek and scrutinized Sharpe with disdain. It would take a heartless magician to betray the Order, and undoubtedly Sharpe fit the criterion.

Behind Sharpe, gilded paintings of famous Order figures and wands decorated the wall in an imposing backdrop. And for however much Domenic loathed the man, he couldn't deny that one day Sharpe's portrait would haunt the Council's wing, glowering at pathetic new generations of magicians for all posterity.

Domenic and Ellery exchanged a glance. It ached to look at her, but he couldn't dwell on the disaster of their conversation, not here, not now. They'd come to this meeting with a strategy.

As imperceptibly as he could, he shook his head.

Ellery's jaw clenched. She hadn't found Sharpe's reaction suspicious, either.

"Glynn," Sharpe said, his voice sinisterly relaxed in that way only he could manage. "What do you make of this notion that we're all strolling around with monsters in our pockets?"

Glynn paused mid-pour, his grip throttling the neck of the whiskey decanter he'd snatched from atop the sideboard. "Wandlorists have always postulated about what makes a Living Wand truly living."

"Oh, I see you're taking this all in stride," Sharpe quipped.

Though Domenic resented agreeing with Sharpe, he did. In less than twenty-four hours, the Council had shifted from strategizing an invasion to rethinking everything they knew about this war. And Glynn seemed far more curious than rattled.

Despite the weeks working beside Glynn and hearing countless stories of him through Ellery, Domenic didn't *know* the Director of Education and Recruitment. Not really. Domenic avoided small talk with him, lest he be held captive in a conversation about some mainland opera star or recent development in the riveting world of antique restoration.

Now Domenic squinted at him, trying to read his fine print. Glynn had to be ambitious to volunteer for a position no one else wanted.

Glynn capped the decanter and waved Aetherium. A glass floated over to Sharpe, amber liquid glinting in amber light.

"Under the circumstances, sir," Glynn said stiffly, "I don't see the merit in wasting time."

Sharpe smiled as he took a drag of his cigarette. "So for discussion's sake, let's say we agree with Barrow's and Caldwell's suggestions about the Dire Three's counterparts. Obviously, the corporeal ghost does suit this charmer over here." He jerked his head at Hanna, who scowled.

"But are you quite positive Decibel's counterpart is Ravfiri?" Glynn asked. "It could be Calynia."

"I certainly hope not," Iseul muttered as she rose to claim the two other glasses Glynn had poured. In one she dropped precisely two ice cubes. The second she left neat.

"It's Ravfiri," Domenic cut in. "I'm sure of it."

"Then it would seem destiny's on our side," Peak said confidently. "Its vigil is four days away, isn't it?"

"Assuming Ravfiri finds a wielder," Glynn responded. "It hasn't bonded with a magician in nearly five decades."

Sharpe tapped his cigarette atop the ashtray. "So what do you think of this, Peak? You fought Kythion, Thundersnow—whatever the hell that thing is named. Would you call it and Targath brothers?"

For the first time Domenic could recall, Peak donned a formal uniform, a black mourning sash draped across his torso and his chest adorned in medals. His broad silhouette was burnished gold as he stared into the fireplace.

"Truth be told, I believe them," Peak answered. "When Targath and I took that beast on, the scale of its magic, even its temperament . . ." He winced and shook out his left knee.

"You'd call your own wand a monster?" Sharpe's grip tightened on Ballathim's blackthorn hilt.

"I . . . Thanks." Peak accepted the iced whiskey that Iseul handed to him. "Don't get me wrong—Targath is a great wand. But that first time I took it into battle . . . you'd have thought it'd gotten impatient, waiting for its next wielder. Because when we went up against my first ghost, we didn't slay it—we obliterated it."

Peak grinned crookedly at the memory, dimples creasing above his beard. And despite dubbing Peak valiant the night before, a bleak question crept into Domenic's mind: Was it suspect that Peak had emerged from his battle with Kythion unscathed?

Immediately, he dismissed it. Peak had championed Domenic from the beginning. He was the entire NDC's symbol of hope. It couldn't be him. It *couldn't*.

"If Targath and Kythion are such behemoths . . ." Glynn swirled his glass thoughtfully. "What caliber of beings must dwell within Valmordion and Iskarius?"

Domenic and Ellery hadn't confessed their suspicions that their magic and their wands' magic were one and the same. But to pose their counterpart theory then immediately label themselves as exceptions—it sounded so arrogant, so preposterous as to undermine their theory altogether.

No doubt Sharpe would laugh himself into hysterics at the notion.

"I'm not sure any of us can really imagine," Domenic answered blandly.

"As disturbing as all these ideas are," Iseul spoke, "I'm far more disturbed by the idea of a traitor within the Order."

"Yeah, I mean, I'm not one to question destiny," Peak said. "But what motive would anyone have to side with Winter?"

"It wouldn't be the first time in the Order's history someone tried to take advantage of turmoil," Hanna said flatly.

"Turmoil?" Peak repeated. "This isn't some rigged election or bank crisis—this is war. What kind of magician would be corrupt enough to risk the whole damn country?"

Iseul brushed off her hands, dusted in the crumbs of vending machine crackers and jittery from too much caffeine. Her appearance might've been pristine—her crisp navy blazer, her polished pearls—but Domenic wondered if she'd ever faced such a catastrophic day in her whole career. Already, only half the whiskey remained in her glass.

"Motive aside," she said levelly, "a traitor implies a degree of sabotage. How can we investigate the existence of a criminal without even knowing what crimes have been committed? Tenney, did you notice evidence of sabotage at the border?"

"No. Nothing like that," Peak answered.

"Then could it have occurred here, at the Citadel?"

"There was the scurge in Mercester Square," Sharpe said. "The first ever recorded in Summer."

"Scurges are caused by ghosts, not magicians," Peak pointed out.

"Then, what, we have absolutely nothing to proceed with? Nothing but the words of the prophecy?" As Iseul regarded them all somberly, Domenic forced himself to consider it, that Iseul had honed in so emphatically on finding the traitor to conceal her own wrongdoing. After considering Glynn, it seemed only fair.

Yet the thought didn't simply nauseate him—it didn't make *sense*. Iseul might've possessed the cunning, the knowledge of performance, the wand of nearly unrivaled power, but she was the last person he'd accuse of lacking a heart.

"No, we do have something to go on," Sharpe responded. "Mayes, how quickly could you investigate the Order's ranks?"

Every gaze swiveled to Hanna. She was the only Councilor who'd maintained the same careful professionalism since the meeting's beginning. Yet on her lap, she white-knuckled Syarthis. Its tip curled around the crook of her thumb.

"You'd have us, what?" Hanna rasped. "Interrogate every magician in the Order?"

"That's quite the task for her, sir," Iseul said nervously.

"I didn't say I couldn't do it," Hanna said at once.

"Even if you can, to subject every one of our magicians to . . ." Glynn nodded grimly, though it wasn't clear if he was nodding at Syarthis, or Hanna, or them both. "There's the matter of their fortitude."

"Mayes will be on her best behavior," Sharpe said pointedly. "Seong, maybe you can do something about her hair. And those boots. You're a member of the Council. Would it kill you to dress like a lady?"

"Oh sweet fuck," Hanna muttered, then she ignored Iseul's disapproving look and tore open a packet of bubble gum. Automatically, she handed a piece to Domenic beside her, and for the thinnest sliver of a second, Domenic hesitated. As Sharpe had just mentioned, Hanna *was* an equal member of the Council. She could be the traitor, too.

Immediately, he scolded himself.

Don't be despicable.

"Surely interrogating every last one of our magicians is extreme," Peak said. "Dom, you must agree with me, right?"

Before Domenic could answer, Sharpe laughed. "Oh, don't be obtuse, Peak. As far as our Chosen Two are concerned, the interrogations have already begun."

Domenic felt his stomach plummet to his feet. "That's not—"

"The two of you, sitting there so silently, glancing at each other whenever we talk to decide if any of *us* betrayed the country. By all means, try to deny it."

Domenic's and Ellery's chairs creaked as they shifted uncomfortably.

Iseul's eyes widened. "You really believe one of us could be the traitor?"

Domenic cringed. "Of course not. But . . ."

"We can't make assumptions," Ellery finished. Then, hastily, she added, "Before we move forward, isn't there something else we should consider? If Living Wands and winterghasts are truly counterparts, what if we could turn winterghasts into wands?"

Domenic startled.

"To what end?" Sharpe asked gravely.

"Every winterghast that becomes a wand would be one less monster terrorizing the country. And one more wand in the hands of a magician who could serve it. Surely if I can wield Winter, other magicians can, too."

Ellery hadn't mentioned this idea to Domenic earlier, and even if he thought it was a fair one—a *good* one—the Council wouldn't. It was too late after a harrowing day, too soon after a devastating loss.

Yet even as Domenic willed Ellery to look at him, she didn't.

She was the only one not gilded by the firelight, blocked by the shade of a pillar. Yet she gleamed all the same. The almost silver luster of her hair. The bright blue of her eyes. She would shine to Domenic even in pitch darkness.

"How would you propose we make more wands?" Iseul asked cautiously. "You said you don't know how you created Iskarius."

"No, but I could help," Ellery insisted. "Maybe if I—"

"Your duty is to thwart the cataclysm," Sharpe snapped.

"O-of course it is. But do you really think this wouldn't aid in that mission?"

"To invite the very monsters we've fought for a millennium into the inner sanctum of the Order? Is it not enough that we must already contend with one traitor? Must we recruit them now, too?"

Ellery bit her lip. "I suppose you're right."

Her voice might've remained calm, but Domenic could see her mask slipping.

He fiddled with the flowers in his pocket. It was that or reach for her.

Sharpe stamped out his cigarette, then rose, his expression hidden in the blackness. "For now, I'd like to further our research into the Dire Three. Glynn, take a full account of everything Caldwell described about her connection to Kythion. You can take Peak's description of Kythion next. The rest of us, let's leave them to their work while we discuss Mayes's task."

As everyone but Ellery and Glynn made toward the door, Domenic hovered, confused at all the abruptness. Again, he willed Ellery to look at him. Words burned in his throat. He didn't know if they were good words, but surely they had to be better than what he'd blurted that morning. That he couldn't bear the thought that he'd hurt her. That *he* was aching too, that this was the last thing he wanted. That she meant more to him than he'd ever succeed in describing.

When she still didn't acknowledge him, he swallowed every word of it down and stalked after the others into the hall.

The five of them turned into Sharpe's office. Sharpe closed the door.

"When you first reached the alban tree at the border compound, you said Caldwell was already there, right?"

Domenic didn't answer. He was distracted, taking in the office. It turned out that portrait of Sharpe already existed—and was definitely already haunted.

"Well?" Sharpe barked.

Domenic realized Sharpe had stridden toward the waste bin beside the bookshelves, and he clutched a wad of papers—the minutes from the meeting.

"Yeah," Domenic answered. "Ellery was defending the alban in the eye when I got there."

"And you know for sure she was defending it?"

He frowned. "What are you suggesting?"

"It seems to me if there's anyone with the motive and means to play traitor, it's Winter's Chosen."

Domenic balked. "Y-you can't be serious. You all, you think this too?"

Iseul, Hanna, and Peak stared sheepishly at the carpet.

"Dom," Peak said gingerly. "If we're about to ask Hanna to go diving into the heads of every member of the Order, then I think it's fair to consider the one person whose head we can't get into. And you heard Caldwell in there. *Winter* wands? Can we really be sure where her loyalty lies?"

Only for Hanna's sake did Domenic bear considering that

Ellery might be the traitor. It felt wrong, not just to his logic, to his heart, but to every fiber of his being. The only reason he still found the strength to fight another day was because he knew—doubtlessly—that Ellery fought beside him.

But if the Dire Three each had counterparts, if this cataclysm was truly a war, what did that make him and Ellery?

Champions, the nation called them.

Domenic had always thought that title noble. Never before had it sounded so sinister.

He wrenched Valmordion from its sheath and cast a silencing enchantment over the office.

"You want to talk about loyalty?" he growled. "Ellery has sacrificed *everything* for the sake of duty. And the second there's suspicion, you'd point to *her*? The prophecy called for peace! That's what she and I have been fighting for every day, together. And—"

"It'd be the oldest trick in the book," Sharpe sneered, "to fool someone with a pretty face."

Smoke leaked from Domenic's breath. "Careful. I realize you've never thought much of me. But for you to rush to accuse who you feel is the most obvious suspect, despite all evidence otherwise? Are you deflecting, or are *you* just that much of a fool?"

Both Sharpes glowered at Domenic simultaneously, while the others only gaped.

Iseul squeezed Domenic's shoulder. "You're right, Dom. It doesn't do any good to jump to conclusions."

"And we do trust your judgment," Peak said. "If you say Caldwell's on our side, then we believe you."

However apologetic they sounded, Domenic didn't buy it. And Hanna didn't even bother to reassure him. Her eyes narrowed as they flickered between Sharpe and Domenic, as if unsure she trusted either of them. Clutched against her chest, Syarthis's muggy heat intensified the tobacco stench that permanently clung to the room.

Then Sharpe lifted Ballathim to the meeting minutes. A flame licked from the wand's tip, and the papers erupted in an instant. He dropped them into the waste bin to burn.

"All of you, out," he said firmly. "Except you, Mayes. You will stay, and you'll start with me."

XXVIII
Domenic
WINTER

"Domenic? *Dom?*"

Domenic resurfaced, his finger poised beside the last line he'd skimmed. "What?"

Ellery frowned from across the towers of yellowed wand registers between them. "I asked if you think we should've heard something about the vigil by now. It's been almost an hour."

Domenic swore it'd only been minutes since they'd sequestered themselves for their fourth day in a row in the Citadel library. But Ellery was right—as Domenic skimmed back through the endless cascades of fine print to where he'd started, he realized he'd already blown through several chapters.

"Didn't Glynn say every eligible student registered?" he asked. "That's a lot of candidates. It might just take time."

"Or Ravfiri hasn't found a wielder," Ellery murmured. "Again."

Domenic trained his focus back on the register. It did no good to worry. Someone *would* bond with Ravfiri, and as soon as they did, Domenic and Ellery would be summoned to meet them along with the Council.

Domenic almost pitied whoever they were. They had no idea what they'd really signed up for.

He'd barely continued reading when Ellery said, "I don't understand why the Council didn't want us to attend. It's an important vigil—would it be that strange to reporters if we were there?"

Domenic grunted noncommittally.

"And all this work they have us doing. Do you really think"—she squinted at a line in her own register—"someone who wields *Frithan* is the traitor? I've never even *heard* of Frithan."

"It specializes in herb gardening, apparently."

"Yes. That has high treason written all over it."

Domenic didn't glance up as he flipped a page. Not just because it ached to look at her. But because he feared one meeting of their eyes would give it all away. That the real reason they'd been omitted from the vigil's attendees was because the Council no longer trusted her. That he was terrified she loathed him. That simply to glance at her mouth would be to experience the phantom taste of it.

"You've really thrown yourself into this," Ellery said. "What are you even expecting to find at this point?"

"I don't know. A sign or something."

"A sign," she repeated flatly.

"What do you want from me, El? I'm just trying to . . ." *Exonerate you.* "It's going to take Hanna weeks to interrogate the whole Order. We can't just kick up our feet and do nothing in the meantime."

When she didn't respond, finally, Domenic braved her gaze—it was wary.

"You'd tell me if there was something I was missing, right?" she asked.

He stabbed his nails into his knee. "Of course I would. You know that—What? What's wrong?" Ellery's face had shuddered into an expression of horror.

Then abruptly she stood, her chair screeching. "Cadaver is here, in the Citadel," she gasped. "I feel its heartbeat."

"What?" He rose and grasped the back of his chair to steady himself. "Where?"

"It's . . ." She drew Iskarius to better concentrate, then she blanched. "Below."

Ellery took off, and Domenic scrambled after her. His mind fuzzed like radio static. Below meant the subterranean levels, and the subterranean levels meant the Vault, the vigil, and Cadaver was the . . . was the . . .

Suddenly, the elevator was opening, and he was in the same stone corridor that he'd last visited in another life. Some thirty yards down, the grand door of the waiting room lay in a shredded heap, and Domenic had paced outside that door only weeks ago, had just watched as a colony of Order magicians carried away Julian Norwood's charred, unconscious body. Now a throng of magicians bottlenecked that same entrance. Many had crumbled to the ground. They were gasping, moaning, and when Domenic looked down, he was shaking, shaking—

"Do you feel that?" Ellery hissed as they slowed to push past the fallen magicians.

"Yeah," he heard himself answer. But he didn't feel whatever she meant at all; not until they stood directly atop the threshold. A terrible pressure emanated from the room in a crush of gravity.

Hanna, a voice warned him, a voice he hated.

Yet as Domenic scanned the room, forcing himself to examine every unmoving body, every broken bone, every splotch of blood, he realized the students that lay around him weren't dead, only unconscious—and grotesquely, almost exaggeratedly injured, like a scene staged. There was their hands: bruised and mangled to every last finger. The several limbs bent at revolting angles. The obligatory puddles of blood.

Only one still stood. Her eyes were rolled back into their whites. Her mouth hung crooked, and blue light leaked out from her throat, her ears, even her nostrils, glinting against the slick trail of her nosebleed.

"Demelza," Ellery choked, lunging toward the girl. Dimly Domenic recognized her. That actress girl. Maybe a year or two below him.

He trained Valmordion on her.

"*Don't,*" Domenic said, making Ellery halt midstep. His breath fogged in the frigid air.

"Wh-what are you doing? She's—"

"The pressure in the room. It's coming from *her.*"

"Shit. *Shit.*" Ellery's hand trembled as she raised Iskarius. "But if Cadaver's possessing her, how do we get it out without hurting her?"

"C-can you expel it?" Domenic's voice wavered even as he fought to keep it firm. He glanced at the second door, flung haphazardly open, and realized with a clench of his stomach that a similar scene likely waited in the vigil chamber, that *Iseul* was in the vigil chamber.

Ellery's expression softened as she studied him. "I'll try."

As Ellery cast a corporeal spell, her eyes, too, rolled back into her head. Domenic stifled a blaze of panic.

Someone lightly kicked his calf. He turned to the lone conscious student on the floor behind him—Tej Kumar, from two years ahead. His black waves hung loose and disheveled across his shattered glasses, and he had dark brown skin and a single ruby earring.

"Barrow," Kumar croaked. "That ghast—"

"Not now," Domenic muttered, unwilling to look away from Ellery.

"That ghast is no normal one. It blasted through the vigil chamber door looking like a . . . Well, you don't want to know what it looked like. But I think—I think it's trying to stop anyone from bonding with Ravfiri. It's been possessing one student after the other, like it's searching for the wielder. And after what it did to all our hands . . ." Kumar winced, and Domenic realized that his hands were so mottled that white bone peeked out beneath a scarlet crust of frostmaul. "Even if the wielder wakes, I don't think they could move their fingers well enough to hold it."

"Here. Let me help you." Yet as Domenic crouched to heal

him, his gaze wandered across the students—there had to be at least fifty. And whoever Ravfiri's wielder was, he needed to heal them and get them to the wand as soon as possible.

Frost melted down Kumar's palms, and the boy cursed in visceral relief. Then he heaved himself onto his elbows, half-wheezing, half-laughing, entirely out of sorts.

"Kumar, listen to me," Domenic urged. "Do you know who that ghast has possessed already?"

"It went for Cutler first, then Ianetti, then . . ." Kumar paused to retch slightly. "Then Ramezani. Glover, his pinky just broke right off. Look at him—he's still holding it. Sort of ironic, when you think about it. It's not like gloves will ever . . ."

Kumar puked onto Domenic's loafers.

"Wow. Shit. I am *so* sorry," Kumar said, while Domenic quickly vanished it. "I cannot believe I just hurled on a Chosen One."

Something thudded, and Domenic whipped around to see Demelza collapsed on the floor, her eyes closed, the light gone. Frost coalesced through the air, so fast Domenic could barely track it, until another student's mouth began to glow. Domenic didn't even recognize him. He looked about fifteen, and he lay on his back, his white eyes staring blankly at the ceiling.

While Domenic straightened and trained Valmordion on him, Ellery stumbled, clutching her head.

"Are you all right?" he asked her sharply.

"I couldn't expel it without hurting her. But I heard Cadaver's true name. It's called Maltherius. And it showed me . . ."

"It showed you what?"

"An alban tree. I saw Nordmere's alban tree."

The hairs on Domenic's neck rose on end. But he didn't have time to dwell on why Cadaver—why *Maltherius*—would do such a thing. Already, the new student's body convulsed, and frostmaul crept across his lips, his cheeks.

Ellery hitched her breath. "He's not strong enough to withstand it."

"Th-then I'll expel it this time." He hated the way his voice cracked.

Like a needle, Domenic breached the student's mind—Zachary, Domenic learned his name was. Immediately, Domenic realized Ellery was right. Maltherius's power was freezing Zachary from within as it scoured his psyche, and even Domenic's spell was making violet blisters bloom across his pale skin.

Domenic honed in on the source of Maltherius's hold, like a shard of ice impaled at the base of the boy's skull.

With a wave of Valmordion, Domenic wrenched it out.

Again, the ghost's frost darted through the air, and despite Domenic trying harder to track it, soon, another student uttered a choking noise.

Kumar.

To Kumar's credit, he fought against Maltherius, nails scratching across the stone floor, knees and arms locked tight against the ground even as his back arched.

"Kill it," he sputtered. Bloodied spit dribbled down his chin. *"Kill it."*

Domenic hesitated. Even if Kumar could control himself to this level, attacking Maltherius from within him was a huge risk.

"He's trying to help us," Ellery said. "Let him."

"I could incinerate him, El," Domenic snapped.

Then Kumar spoke again, too garbled to make out. But as Kumar clawed his half-ruined hands insistently toward Domenic's ankles, Domenic surrendered and cast his spell.

He found Kumar's lungs bristled with frostmaul, so solid he could barely expand and compress his ribs. Yet his body still fought, still *lived,* and instantly, Domenic could tell why. Kumar's magic shined so bright it was blinding, so bright Domenic needed to squint his own eyes against its radiance.

Like Ravfiri's.

No sooner had Domenic had the thought than the cold exploded, and Kumar screamed as frostmaul sheathed his neck, sealed the crevices between his knuckles. His fingers swelled. Black splotches bloomed wherever his skin met ice.

"What happened?" Ellery called out. She now knelt beside Demelza, casting a healing spell. Her friend's head lolled back, then she coughed, her eyes blinking open. Trails of makeup ran down her cheeks. She touched a hand to her ice-encrusted neck, then stared at Ellery in horror.

"I-I think it's my fault," Domenic stammered. "Maltherius felt my excitement. Because it's him, El. Kumar is Ravfiri's wielder."

Ellery sucked in a breath. "I'll go get the wand. I'll bring it to him." To Demelza, she asked, "Will you be all right if I go?"

Demelza nodded, curling her knees to her chest.

While Ellery bolted into the vigil chamber, Domenic's grip on Valmordion trembled. Already, he felt Kumar's magic dimming, his pulse slowing. And so Domenic swallowed his own urge to vomit, and he unleashed more magic.

The effect was instantaneous. Kumar's heart jolted into acceleration. His blood ignited as his veins flooded with fire. Smoke leaked out from his nostrils.

"Please don't die," Domenic begged him, unsure Kumar could even hear. And yet he repeated it as his skin blistered. As the room reeked of scorched hair.

Until at last, Domenic burned every trace of Maltherius out.

Kumar spasmed, and frost escaped from his mouth like a dying breath. It whirled upward, and before it could disperse, Domenic's enchantment seized hold of it. Each crystal of ice fused into an awful skeletal shape—so tall it scraped the ceiling. But most nauseating was the monster's head. Every inch of it was covered in eyes. They rolled and blinked and roamed, none of them in sync.

A clangorous noise pierced through the room, high-pitched and deafening, and Domenic *felt* the awful static of it shoot down the entire length of him. Deliriously, he realized it was Maltherius's screech, though so far as he could tell, it bore no mouth.

Gold lanced from Valmordion's tip and speared straight through the ghast. Its scream silenced. The pressure vanished. And it shattered.

Domenic panted. His gaze flitted to Kumar, then he clutched his stomach.

Ellery skidded to a halt beside him. In her left hand, she held Ravfiri in its sheath.

"Is he still alive?" she whispered.

"He has to be." Domenic dropped to his knees beside Kumar and fixed Valmordion toward his chest. Subtly, his heart beat. "Give me Ravfiri. *Now*."

Ellery thrust the sheath toward him, then rushed to cast a healing spell while the magicians outside stampeded into the room. Voices shouted. Footsteps thundered. Around the room, students roused as Maltherius's magic faded.

Yet Domenic barely registered the havoc. With a levitation enchantment, he pulled Ravfiri from its sheath and rested it atop Kumar's mangled, limp hand. Ravfiri's heat sizzled across Domenic's exposed skin.

"It's not working," Domenic rasped. "He has to be awake."

"I'm trying," Ellery said dismally. "But h-his wounds are . . ."

Domenic twisted to one of the magicians behind him. "You, go get Hanna Mayes."

The magician paled. "But our healers here—"

"No, it has to be the best. Go. *Go*."

Once the magician sprinted away, Domenic and Ellery both fought to keep Kumar alive. But it was as if remnants of Domenic's magic still smoldered inside him. Each time Ellery healed one of his burns, new blisters bulged across his skin. And while Domenic worked on his internal injuries, Kumar's pulse sputtered, faint like a candle flame about to snuff out.

If he dies, Domenic thought, *it'll be me who killed him. Not Maltherius. It'll be me who—*

In a rush, Domenic cast an illusion over himself. Then he puked directly where Kumar had earlier.

When he returned to healing, Ellery's free hand drifted toward his shoulder. She squeezed.

Someone cursed behind them, and Ellery jerked her hand away. When Domenic peeked up, Syarthis stared back. No matter how much Syarthis revolted him, this close, Domenic couldn't quite look away. Valmordion's core brightened into the purest, most dazzling of golds, and Domenic *felt* the heat of Syarthis's magic flare in response, feverishly hot.

"What the fuck happened here?" Hanna hissed. "Why is this kid torched?"

"Can you save him?" Domenic asked desperately. "He's Ravfiri's wielder, Hanna."

Hanna took in Kumar and hesitated. Her grip tightened on Syarthis.

"Yeah," she answered finally. "I can." She knelt between them and aimed Syarthis at Kumar's sternum. A soft gold light shined beneath his eyelids, and the worst of his blisters at last stilled their smoldering.

Ellery cursed in relief. "How soon will he wake?"

"I've got no clue. Magic boosts the body's healing process, but the body has limits. Even for Syarthis."

What matters most is that he's alive, Domenic told himself. *But if Kumar doesn't wake by midnight . . . If he can't bond with Ravfiri . . .*

"What about Iseul?" Hanna asked. "The rest of the Council was in the audience, weren't they?"

"They were unconscious when I went into the vigil chamber, but they didn't look injured. I wanted to check on them, but there wasn't time . . ." Ellery paused. Then she rose and scooped something off the floor several feet away—a frozen blue stone.

"It's another one," Domenic breathed. "Just like Decibel."

"The Council should know about this, about all this. Hanna, if I leave to wake them, will you be able to get him to the infirmary?"

"We'll be fine," Hanna muttered. "Go."

After Ellery left, Hanna glanced at Domenic from the corner of her eyes. "How are you holding up? The magician who fetched me told me what ghast you fought."

"Oh, I'm peachy."

"So it's not your puke I'm kneeling in right now?"

"That depends. Would it be less disgusting if it were mine?"

"Nope, it still is," she grumbled.

Around them, the Order magicians tended to the wounded. Yet even with the threat gone, they gawked anxiously at Syarthis, all but shoving the students in their haste toward the exits.

"You get out of here, too," Hanna told Domenic. "I mean it. Take a breath."

"I can still help you."

"You're not. And the reminder's worse when we're with each other. Look at all these grown Order magicians, fleeing like they're the ones who just faced one of the Dire Three. By the time you get back, it'll just be me and Flambé here."

"It's Kumar."

"Don't tell me that. Not until after I save him."

And Hanna did save him. An hour later, Kumar stabilized enough to be transported to the infirmary. But he still didn't wake. And so, just as one of the greatest wands of Summer had finally found a wielder, midnight arrived. And Ravfiri's window closed.

XXIX
ELLERY
WINTER

The Gallamere skyline glittered through the frost-coated window in Glynn's office. Opera music crooned faintly from the record player, punctuated by the slam of the door as Sharpe stalked out. Seong had departed an hour ago to take Hanna home to rest. Ellery, Domenic, and Glynn slumped in their seats, exhausted and shell-shocked. It was one in the morning.

"I still don't like the idea of going to Nordmere just because that monster showed it to you," Domenic muttered. "It has to be a trap."

"Oh, it's definitely a trap," Ellery said. Although Maltherius, much like Syarthis, had failed to breach her mind, it *had* managed to force the painfully familiar image of Nordmere's alban on her. She'd sworn she'd never go back.

Ellery fiddled with the blue stone Maltherius had dropped after it died. Unlike the sharp, staticky chill of Decibel's, this one felt clammy, like a cold sweat.

"At least if we get ambushed up North," she continued, "we'll have a chance to kill Kythion."

Domenic forlornly studied the enchanted calendar on the wall. The previous day's date with its notation of Ravfiri's vigil had dimmed. "Even if destiny will eventually ask us to take out the Dire Three, that's not the piece we've got now. We're supposed to be finding Summer's traitor."

"And once you do, your next piece might well be your last," Glynn reminded them. He sounded more somber than celebratory, although after Maltherius had knocked him unconscious in the vigil chamber while it attacked his students, Ellery didn't blame him. "Barrow's right. Your job is still to focus on the prophecy first."

"I never said I disagreed," Ellery mumbled tiredly. "But for once, I think Sharpe had a point when he said Maltherius and the traitor could be connected. That's why Hanna's going to Nordmere with us, why . . ."

Suddenly, the stone in her hand pulsed. Once, then twice, until the sensation reverberated up her arm in a steady rhythm. Fissures spread across its frozen surface. Ellery gaped as light beamed through them, brighter and brighter until it flooded the office in an eerie blue. Domenic shouted in alarm and drew Valmordion, while Glynn hastily pointed Aetherium. But rather than explode into shrapnel or somehow resurrect Maltherius, the stone transformed.

Its icy shell crumbled away until Ellery clutched a large silver aspen pod.

"What just happened?" Domenic choked. "What did you do?"

"I don't know," she said hastily, examining it. "I wasn't doing any magic, I swear, just talking. And then it turned into . . ."

A seed.

All three of them fell silent as the gravity of the situation took hold. Hope unfurled in Ellery, surprised, wondrous, precious hope.

"This is proof," she exclaimed. "I mean, Maltherius is Syarthis's counterpart, and Syarthis is made of aspen wood, isn't it? So if this seed found the right wielder, then I bet they really could turn it into a wand. A Winter wand. Just like I did with Iskarius."

"What?" Domenic shook his head. "No. No, we can't."

Ellery startled. "What do you mean, we can't?"

"Ellery, please, think," Glynn urged. "You still don't know how you made Iskarius, nor do you know how you turned

Maltherius's . . . well, whatever it is, into a seed. The stakes are too high to play around with things we don't understand."

"But we're *so* close to understanding it," Ellery said. "I can feel it. I just need to think. Glynn, do you still have Decibel's stone stored here?"

Glynn hesitated. "Yes," he said finally, and flicked Aetherium. A filing cabinet opened, and a box lifted out and landed on his desk. Ellery set the aspen pod down and lifted Decibel's stone.

"I was talking when Maltherius's seed started to change," she said, thinking aloud. "But I've spoken while holding these things before, and it didn't have any effect. So what was different? What did I . . . *Oh*." Her breath hitched. "I said its name."

"All right," Domenic said slowly. "But even if that's what triggered it, we don't know this one's name. Not its real name, anyway."

Ellery huffed in frustration and replayed the moments before Maltherius's seed had transformed. How it had thumped in her hand.

Like a heartbeat.

Ellery drew Iskarius and focused, just as she had in the Barren four weeks ago. She shut her eyes. Decibel's staticky cold prickled against her palm, and she exhaled, trying to listen.

Faintly, she found a rhythm. Ellery fed her own magic into the stone—no, the heart—until it thudded steadily in her hand, until a name crackled in her mind.

"Eledrium," she said, like a command.

When she opened her eyes, a silver pinecone rested in her palm.

"Okay," Ellery said excitedly. "It's Ravfiri's counterpart. And they're both made of pine." She set Eledrium's seed down, then summoned one of Glynn's spare notebooks. Ellery dictated through Iskarius, each word appearing on the chart as soon as she'd thought it.

Magical Specialty	NDC Nickname	True Name	Summer Counterpart
Enchantment	Decibel	Eledrium	Ravfiri
Nature	Thundersnow	Kythion	Targath
Corporeal	Cadaver	Maltherius	Syarthis

"This is what we'll show the rest of the Council," she declared. "It's clear, it's straightforward, and when we pair it with the seeds, they'll have no choice but to take us seriously."

"The Council still won't go for it." Domenic had pocketed Valmordion and slouched against the wall, his arms crossed. "They think Winter wands are too dangerous."

"They'd be no more dangerous than the wands half of them are wielding," she argued.

"You know it's not the same."

"With the right magicians, it could be." Ellery turned away from Glynn and strode toward Domenic. "I don't get it, Dom. What's so wrong with this idea?"

Domenic straightened and raked his hands through his hair. "Nothing is wrong with it! I agree with you—I always agree with you. But we just lost Ravfiri. Maltherius invaded the Citadel. This isn't the time to take risks."

"Isn't it? If we don't do anything, we'll never figure this out. We can't just leave it alone. It's too major. Too important—"

"They won't go for this," he repeated.

"We don't have to do everything the Council says," Ellery snapped. "You didn't care what they thought when you climbed into my dorm room and convinced me I was a Chosen One. Or when you summoned everyone to your house, or when we went off-script during the press conference, or, I don't know, when we were *making out* right before Kythion showed up!"

Domenic's eyes bulged, and he shot a horrified look toward Glynn. Ellery whipped around to face her mentor, flushing. She'd almost forgotten he was there.

Glynn slid off his glasses and pinched his brow. Ellery decided she'd already gone too far to care and glared back at Domenic.

"I-I know all that. But El, we might be the strongest magicians in the country, but there are other strong magicians too." Domenic's tone was fervent, desperate. The horrors of the day lingered in his stare. "It's thanks to Hanna that Kumar's alive. And you saw Peak take on Kythion. We *need* the Council. And after losing more territory, after *today*, would you really rather we figure out the prophecy without their help? Would you rather face the cataclysm alone?"

Ellery swallowed. "Of course not."

"Then why are you pushing so hard? Why can't you let this go?"

"Because it could change everything!" Ellery's voice cracked, and a longing poured from her that she'd scarcely admitted to herself. "Because if Maltherius and Eledrium can become wands, then that might just be the beginning. What if we could double Alderland's power? Its magicians? What if every ghast was gone, and there was nothing left to fight?"

"Our only choice is to fight. We're in the middle of a war."

"But the prophecy said we'd restore balance to the land. What if *this* is what that means? What if this is how the war ends?"

Domenic tilted his head back and heaved out a groan. "I promise, I hear you. But that's a lot of ifs."

Ellery backed away from him. "You asked me if you'd rather we face the cataclysm alone? Well, I'm already alone. And if there were other Winter magicians, if I was the first of a kind instead of the fucked-up exception everyone else thinks I am, then that could all change."

Maybe it was a selfish thought. But it was too tantalizing to push away.

Domenic's expression collapsed into something anguished. He reached for her shoulder. "I'm sorry, El, but—"

Ellery pushed him away. "I don't need you to apologize. I need you to be on my side."

"I'm . . . I'm just trying to protect you."

"Don't," Ellery said coldly.

Domenic's hand quivered as it fell. "I'll see you tomorrow," he muttered. Then he flung open the door and left.

Glynn didn't even wait for it to click shut. "Ellery?" he asked tightly. "A word?"

Ellery turned, already braced. "Do you really think now is a good time to lecture me?"

"Apparently, a lecture is warranted. How long have you been romantically involved with Domenic Barrow?"

"It doesn't matter. It's over now, anyway."

"If that's what over looks like, I shudder to think of what it looked like when it wasn't. Oh wait, I don't have to. You already painted me such a vivid picture. I mean, goodness, were you truly carrying on at the NDC compound? I expected better of you."

His disappointment was a palpable, awful weight. After the countless times Ellery had stood in this office and smiled and strived to be perfect, she felt an overwhelming urge to apologize.

"I know you did," she said. "But we were careful, I swear."

"What I saw tonight wasn't careful. Do you have any idea the tremendous risk you've taken? Any . . . *dalliance* between the two of you is a national security risk. What if the public found out about this? You're both meant to have one thing on your mind and one thing alone. Given how young you both are and Barrow's history, even your most ardent supporters would see this as irresponsible. And if you undermine the public's trust in you, there could be a panic. Not to mention the complication of you two breaking up. Are you still able to work together?"

"We are."

"And if need be, can you put the well-being of the country before your own?"

"Of course."

"Before *his*?"

Ellery's throat burned. "Are you planning on calling Dom back in here, too? Lecturing *him*? We're both Chosen Ones, we both had feelings, we both acted on them. So when you tell the rest of the Council about this, at least have the decency to punish us both. Equally."

"Ah, but it's not the Council's punishment you should be worried about." Glynn flicked Aetherium. Newspaper clippings cascaded from a desk drawer, then splayed themselves across the surface.

Winterghast Infiltrates Citadel In Brutal Attack

Then a subheading: Does Winter's Chosen Pose Additional Risks?

"This is tomorrow's front page of the *Gallamere Gazette*. Seong shared it with me."

Ellery studied the picture of herself below the headlines, an unflattering shot from a publicity event. "This makes it seem like I could be dangerous. But they've never questioned me like this before. Wh-why now? What did I do?"

"You didn't do anything. But Maltherius's attack has stoked the public's anxiety," Glynn said gravely. "Some of your classmates gave fear-mongering interviews. They've included several anonymous NDC sources who spoke about your use of Winter magic during the fall of the border. Altogether, it poses a worrisome line of thought about the nature of who you are."

"But I used my Winter magic to protect those people," she protested. "I saved them."

"I know that, of course. But people are frightened. And in their paranoia, they're searching for something or someone to blame. Valmordion's destiny to protect Alderland has been proven time and time again throughout history. I'm sorry, Ellery, but Iskarius's destiny—*yours*—doesn't have such guarantees. You say you want to be punished equally? Well, you and Barrow aren't equal, not as far as Alderland's concerned. You never have been."

A fissure split through Ellery's heart, and she staggered away from the desk. Ugly, painful sobs clumped in her throat as tears streamed down her cheeks. She clapped a hand across her mouth. It only seemed to make her sobs sound worse.

"Ellery," Glynn said. "Oh, goodness. Ellery—I did tell you to sit down, didn't I? Well, if you'll just—"

He rounded the desk and gestured tentatively to the armchair.

"Stop!" Ellery choked out. "S-stop trying to comfort me."

"Please, if you'd just sit—"

"You don't get to be disappointed with me!" she said, still crying. "You don't get to lecture me about how you expect better and then say that Alderland was never going to accept me anyway. And you know what? Of course it was foolish of me to think I might win the country over when I can't even win *you* over. When somehow I'm still not good enough for you."

"Why would you ever think that?" Glynn asked, aghast.

"*Why?* Glynn, I know every wandlorist you admire. I can recite the plot of each important opera in the Aldrish canon and the details of your and your husband's hunt for the perfect antique dining table, but you've never so much as invited me over for dinner. A-and I thought it was fine, I really did, but seeing Dom with Seong, even Peak . . ."

"You think I don't love you," he said, and the look on his face was so wretched that Ellery instantly knew he did.

Maybe it wasn't so difficult to believe. When Ellery had first arrived in Gallamere, Glynn had tutored her through the academy curriculum, waiting patiently as she worked up the bravery to use her magic again. After she became a student, he'd made a point of seeing her once a week, answering her questions about magic and Citadel life. And although he'd never gone with her to explore Gallamere, he was the one who'd encouraged her to find a home within the city that had always been his home, too. Of course she'd wanted to become his successor. She was living proof of how much his work mattered.

And even after Glynn learned she wielded the magic of Winter itself, he'd stood by her.

But the knowledge that all this time he *had* loved her, that anyone had ever loved her, didn't heal the fissure in her heart. Instead, it cracked her open.

"Why the hell would I think you cared about me that much?" she rasped. "You've never said so."

"No, I haven't," Glynn said seriously. "I thought it would be easier that way."

"Easier," she echoed. "Why?"

"I . . ." Glynn muttered a curse. "Did I ever tell you why I took the job as Director of Education and Recruitment?"

Ellery blinked in disbelief. Surely he wasn't about to lecture her *again*. "You have. You took the job because nobody else wanted it."

"No, they didn't." Glynn used Aetherium to arrange two armchairs beneath the window. He sat in one, then gestured to the other. Ellery sat, although she refused to meet his eyes. Instead she stared fixedly at their reflections in the warped, frosty window, his face solemn and drawn, hers blotched and swollen.

"After the Syarthis Disaster, I don't blame people for being wary of the position," Glynn continued. "But from the moment I bonded with Aetherium, I understood my greatest strength wouldn't be my magical aptitude, but the work I could do within our institution. Magicians *are* Alderland. We set it apart. We move it forward. And each member of the Order begins as a student at the national academy, a student who deserves to be protected. But we failed in that duty when Syarthis unbonded from its wielder. I know people believe me to be ambitious, and pedantic, and, well . . . the point is, the primary reason I took this position is because I care about our new recruits. Quite a bit. I audited every wand in the Vault. I made the qualification exams necessary to ensure no student laid a hand on a wand they weren't ready for. And of course, I attempted to give Hanna Mayes the best support I could."

Ellery dabbed at her eyes with a handkerchief. "I get it. You take your job seriously. But what does any of that have to do with me?"

"Well, it was only a few months into my tenure that I found you. We'd just lost the North, and after such an assault by Winter, the Council knew it wouldn't be long before Valmordion thawed. We kept a close eye on the students who seemed like potential candidates for the wand. There is no way to be utterly certain someone is Chosen before they bond with Valmordion, but there are signs. Past Chosen Ones have claimed to know they were magicians before manifesting any magic. They have an immense innate talent for all categories of magic; they barely need to be taught. And they seem ill-suited to other Living Wands despite being strong enough to wield any of them, often failing to bond with many before Valmordion thaws. There are also personality and social signs. Most were loners who struggled to connect with others, even their own families. They had a strong sense of duty and occasional grandiosity. Alice Rhodes, for example, was considered both off-putting and extraordinary by her classmates before she was revealed as Chosen."

"I wasn't a loner at the academy," Ellery protested, although even as she spoke she recalled herself at party after party, always invited yet plagued by the feeling that she didn't—*couldn't*—belong.

"Alone, these anecdotal parallels may not have struck me as significant. But you arrived here as a hero from the fall of Nordmere, the very event that heralded a Chosen One's arrival. So from the moment we met, I was certain you were fated to wield Valmordion. And I was determined to ensure you'd be ready when the time came."

"So all those lessons. All those lectures." Ellery shuddered as the last five years of her life shifted into a new, brutal focus. "You really did expect me to be flawless. You say you love me, but did you ever actually care about *me* at all? Or was it only ever about my potential? My destiny?"

"Of course I care about you," Glynn said fervently. "I cared about you from the very start. And when I visited you in that hospital, I didn't just see a Chosen One. I saw a girl who'd endured horrors well beyond the fall of Nordmere. Yet you seemed utterly unaware of the strength you possessed—not just your magic, but *you*. And over your time at the Order, I've been astounded by your ability to adapt to any circumstance. But although I wished that I could protect you in a way no one else ever had, I knew I couldn't. Because one day, you would have to protect us all . . . no matter the cost.

"I'm so sorry, Ellery. I know it wasn't fair to keep you at a distance. I knew it even then. But seeing how deeply it has hurt you now . . ."

He buried his head in his hands. His shoulders shook. Not once had Glynn cried in front of her before.

Ellery stood and stared at herself in the newspaper atop the desk. She watched that girl's life flash through her mind as though it were someone else's, each trial and tragedy all leading to one duty, one goal, one impossible purpose: Winter's Chosen.

To always hold herself apart. To always hold herself together. To be a hero.

She was responsible for Alderland's safety, whether she cared about it or not. And as much as she wanted to rip the paper to shreds, to decry everyone who'd ever doubted her, she *did* care. As someone who'd spent so much of her life controlled by fear, she hated that people might fear her, fear that wasn't even justified.

Ellery could still show them that peaceful future she saw. And she knew exactly where to start.

"Don't tell me you're sorry," Ellery snapped at Glynn. "It's too late. And don't you dare tell me you love me. I'm the Chosen One you wanted so badly, so treat me like one." Then she snatched up Maltherius's and Eledrium's hearts and tucked them in her pocket. She regarded Glynn coolly, silently inviting him to protest.

Instead, he nodded in acquiescence. "If anyone discovers the seeds are missing, Mayes and Syarthis may question me again. They'll know you took them. But by then, I hope you have whatever answers you need."

"So do I," Ellery said quietly.

More Winter wands *would* change the tide of this war, and they'd change the way Alderland understood Winter magic, too. So she'd find a way to make them, even though it meant lying to the Council.

Even though it meant lying to Domenic, too.

XXX
Domenic
Winter

Side by side, Domenic and Ellery braved the battalions of journalists at *Foretold*'s red carpet premiere.

"How does it feel to be back in Mercester Square?"

"Do you have any comment on Danmere's mayor closing the city to more fallen territory refugees?"

"What brought you here tonight? Shouldn't you be at the border?"

Domenic plastered on his most golden of smiles. "Caldwell and I both felt tonight was an important occasion to honor Rhodes's legacy and our nation's history. But we have two more weeks of Winter; we wouldn't have spared the time if we weren't confident time was on our side."

For added effect, Domenic drew Valmordion. Speckles of golden light jetted into the air and scattered throughout the crowd. Gasps of wonder swept around them. Many cupped the lights, as if catching fireflies. More cameras flashed. Several guests behind them even applauded.

Ellery kept her wand sheathed.

"You don't think you're overselling it?" she muttered to him through her own prim smile.

"The people deserve a little hope."

So Iseul had told Domenic when she'd helped him knot his tuxedo bow tie earlier that evening. And Domenic agreed. Even if the border invasion still haunted him, he remembered how it felt watching hope kindle in people's eyes. He clung to it.

Certainly delaying their departure to Nordmere by two nights would be worth it if it dulled the public panic.

Ellery must've felt the same, because she waved while looping her other arm around his. Even with no contact between their skin, Domenic had to resist the whole of his concentration pooling to their touch.

It didn't help that she looked incredible: her silver dress paired with matching gloves, her hair pulled back to accentuate the long curve of her neck and slopes of her collarbones. Since exiting their limo, Domenic had only allowed himself to look at Ellery sparingly, lest his gawking be caught on camera.

In his effort to distract himself, Domenic scanned the crowd. But that ached too, in a different way. Every one of these people, all someone he needed to save.

Then he made tragic eye contact with a reporter. She pounced in an instant.

"Mr. Barrow, care to comment on the rumors that you were seen leaving the Gallamere Grand Hotel with Phillipa Chastian?"

Domenic blinked. "With who?"

"Come now, our readers aren't fools. She's here tonight, isn't she? Are we really supposed to believe you've changed your ways so quickly?"

Ellery's smile, if anything, widened.

Domenic forced a chuckle that sounded objectively constipated. "At the risk of disappointing your readers, I assure you, my focus is entirely on the cataclysm. And I think the country will sleep sounder at night knowing I'm sleeping alone."

He and Ellery only made it a few more steps before another reporter accosted them.

"Miss Caldwell, what was the inspiration for your look tonight?"

"It's from Arden's upcoming Summer collection," Ellery answered.

"You've been awfully focused on fashion all Winter. What sort of example do you think you're setting for the young girls who look up to you?"

Fury ignited in Domenic's stomach. Yet Ellery's mask remained perfect as ever.

"As Barrow mentioned," she said lightly, "our focus is entirely on the cataclysm."

Another reporter emerged, like beetles from a shit mound. "As Winter's Chosen, you must feel a special responsibility to those victimized by its magic. Do you feel you've faltered in your duties given a winterghast's attack on the Citadel?"

Domenic stepped in front of Ellery and growled, "*Both* of us feel a deep responsibility for Ravfiri's vigil. But the prophecy is still unfolding. And when it's through, we promise, we *will* reunite Alderland. Together."

They didn't linger in that spot.

"I can fight my own battles," Ellery hissed.

"But you shouldn't have to."

Domenic allowed himself this one chance to meet her eyes, if only so she could see the seriousness in his.

Her shoulders relaxed ever so slightly. It felt like a victory. "So . . . Phillipa Chastian, huh? Wherever did you find the time?"

For a peace offering, it carved the deepest of wounds.

"Yeah, you caught me," he played along. "In those five hours a day I don't spend at the Citadel, I've been with the actress who played . . . um . . ."

"Wow. You still can't remember. Dare I ask who's starring in the movie we're actually here to see?"

"Hey now."

In the theater lobby, attendants handed out snacks and promotional gifts. Domenic awkwardly accepted a toy replica of Valmordion.

Ellery raised a brow as he poked its rubber bristles. "Why didn't you just get the popcorn like I did?"

"The attendant didn't give me much of a choice. Did you see his face when he realized who I was? What was I supposed to say? 'Sorry, already got one'?"

She smirked. "Did you consider joking about how yours is bigger?"

Domenic barked out a laugh. He worried perhaps the wound was fatal.

Ellery's gaze strayed from him, and Domenic followed it across the lobby to a gaggle of other gussied-up, undoubtedly famous people.

"Hey!" she called to them. "Demelza!"

Some starlet turned around, blond hair tumbling down her shoulders. If Ellery hadn't spoken her name, Domenic wouldn't have recognized this Demelza Turner from how she'd looked two days before: the blue light of Maltherius beaming from her rolled-back eyes.

Demelza excused herself from the others as Ellery approached, Domenic trailing behind.

"I didn't know you'd be here." Ellery offered her a realer smile than she'd given all night.

Demelza didn't return it.

"Yeah, you know," the other girl mumbled. "Family obligations. Mom played Rhodes's mentor."

"I saw her on some of the posters. The reviews say she's great."

"Uh-huh."

"Well," Ellery ventured, "I'm glad to see you're doing better. I tried to visit you, but they said you were resting."

Demelza flinched. "I'm fine now. Totally fine. I just . . . I didn't expect to see you here, either. After Ravfiri's vigil, don't you think it's kind of irresponsible?"

Domenic seethed. But Ellery wanted to fight her own battles, so he bit his tongue—hard.

Ellery's voice flattened. "We're heading back North tomorrow."

"You still should've stayed home. Or at least left that *thing* behind." She glared at the sheath at Ellery's hip. "If you ask me, Winter magic isn't safe. No one should be wielding it."

Then she stalked off.

Domenic clenched and unclenched his fists. Beside him, Ellery stilled, her expression neutral, but he knew her enough to glimpse the storm churning beneath.

"Are you all right?" he murmured.

She heaved out a breath. "I'm fine."

"Really, El? Can we cut the bullshit, just for a second?" He didn't mean to snap, but he couldn't play their games anymore. They were bullshit, too. "We promised we wouldn't perform. Not for each other."

"Oh, really? Isn't that all we've done since . . . since . . ." All too quickly, whatever indignation he'd coaxed from her faded, buried, vanished. Her voice leveled. "I can't risk another headline, Dom. So can we please just go inside and get this over with?"

He sighed. "Yeah. All right."

But even as Domenic tried to dowse himself, he still burned. He glared at the employee who handed him his cherry cola while watching Ellery nervously from the corner of her eyes. He ignored the celebrity who offered his hand to Domenic but not to her. He all but cursed at the usher who muttered something under his breath as he guided the Chosen Two to their reserved seats at the front of the theater.

But more than he hated all of them, he hated himself. That he couldn't reach for her.

After this is all over, we'll have a real future, he assured himself.

Assuming Ellery forgave him. She sat rigid and silent. She didn't touch her popcorn. He didn't touch his cola.

Once the rows filled, the cast assembled beneath the screen.

"Welcome to the premiere of *Foretold*," said the director, a man with an atrociously thin strip of a mustache. "From its onset, this picture was an exciting project for the entire team at Croswell Production Studios. But given recent events, this film has never felt so timely. Alice Rhodes's victory and sacrifice altered the course of our nation, and to have her successors in this very audience—it's a tremendous honor . . ."

Domenic didn't catch another word of the director's speech, all too aware of the hundreds of gazes searing into the back of his skull. He resisted the urge to slump lower in his seat—he sat nearly a head taller than their whole row.

At last, the lights darkened, and it was all so familiar—the Mercester Square theater, his favorite soda, the anticipation stirring in his stomach—that for a delirious moment, he wasn't Domenic Barrow, Chosen One. He was Domenic Barrow, skipping class to catch a matinee, counting the minutes until Hanna and Iseul got home.

Then the movie began.

Drip.

Drip.

A dim picture came into focus on-screen: Valmordion encased in a hazy sheath of ice, melting atop its pedestal.

Drip.

Drip.

Domenic white-knuckled his armrests.

"What's wrong?" Ellery whispered.

"Oh. Uh. Nothing."

She squinted at him, like she knew better. Then she swallowed and fixed her focus back on the screen.

Gradually, the ominous opening image faded, replaced by text: *Leetmere*. The screen brightened with daylight, and birdsong filled the theater. A young girl scampered barefoot across a forest floor. She moved quickly, with purpose.

Goose bumps prickled up Domenic's neck.

He peeked over his shoulder at the party in his family's garden, celebrating the first day of Summer. No one had noticed him slip away. He crawled beneath the hedges, soiling the knees of his trousers. Something squeezed tight in his chest, eager and exciting, urging him to follow. Instinctively, he knew where it led. He'd always known, had struggled his entire life to sit still, to pay attention. He wasn't good at being patient.

On-screen, sinewy white roots threaded through the detritus, and the girl halted. The camera panned up, following the trunk of a massive alban tree.

The grass parted, and he ran down its path until at last, the forest eased into meadow. Pollen whirled in a soft, dreamy vortex, and at its center, there stood an alban tree.

Rhodes halted beneath it.

Domenic craned his neck back, sunlight kissing his cheeks.

Rhodes reached up. A branch bent toward her, and briar entwined her fingers.

He climbed, and once he emerged at its top, he gazed triumphantly at the surrounding field. The meadow bloomed for him. And for the first time, finally, his magic bloomed with it.

In the present, Domenic squeezed Valmordion. Beside him, Ellery, too, looked haunted.

As the film continued, Domenic was unsure he blinked, even breathed. Though Rhodes's story didn't perfectly match his own, he had the uncomfortable impression it was his life on-screen, his most intimate moments laid bare to an audience who watched, not with understanding, but with morbid fascination.

After what felt like hours but couldn't have been more than ninety minutes, Alice Rhodes stood on a mountain summit. Sweat poured down her forehead, mixing with a bloodied cut on her brow. Icy storm clouds ruptured above her as if she'd cleaved a crater across the sky. As the winds stilled, the score cut out. The only sound was the pounding of Rhodes's heartbeat.

She lowered Valmordion toward her lips.

"Thank you," she whispered.

Domenic braced himself. Ellery hitched her breath. But neither dared to break character. Even in the dark, stares pressed against them from all sides. Stares that looked but didn't see.

The theater brightened as Rhodes ignited.

The special effects were dramatic and crude. Flames caught across her skin as easily as tissue paper, yet even as they consumed her, as her profile thinned from round cheeks to the sharp angles of bone, she didn't so much as whimper. Flecks of gray peeled off her face and flurried into the air. The locket dangling from her neck glowed molten. Too quickly, all that remained of her was a charred, mangled shape, somehow still standing, still dignified, already a monument beneath a glorious, Summer-blue sky.

One hundred and fourteen years later, her successor, every bit as dignified, hurled up a cloaking enchantment and bolted outside.

How welcome the night's cold was. Domenic darted through Mercester Square and ducked into the half-privacy of the bus stop, gasping as he wrenched the bow tie from his throat. The image of Rhodes and the alban tree seeped over his own memory, staining what few precious parts of it he hadn't already lost to its excruciating aftermath: the realization that he'd been gone not hours, but days. His family's realization that he'd been gone at all. And worst, the way they'd looked at him from then on—like he was alien to them, unknowable to them.

Dead to them.

Domenic's fingerprint had always been among a dozen on Valmordion's shaft. But it still disturbed him how closely his story mirrored one that ended in tragedy.

Our prophecy is different.

Ten minutes later, after Domenic recovered each broken piece of himself, he caught sight of the transport map. To his shock, magic shimmered across it: a butterfly fluttering across the Gold Line, starlight twinkling atop the Gardens, diamond-bright radiance illuminating the Citadel from within.

Ellery's and his enchantments were still here, all these weeks later. Even when cast by training wands.

Suddenly, reassurances were not enough. He needed to know the line between significance and coincidence. He needed to know if there even was a future worth waiting for.

Domenic walked his usual route home. No one noticed him through his cloaking enchantment, but several people paused their shivering as he passed, as if crossing a nighttime patch of sun. (He tried spitefully several times to shut this off, but it seemed he couldn't.)

In the foyer, he set his shoes on the rack, shrugged off his spell like a heavy coat. His heart thumped as he climbed the stairs and approached the door that adjoined Hanna's bedroom to his own. He rarely ever used it.

He knocked.

"Yeah?"

He pushed it open and treaded inside, wary in more ways than one.

Sure enough, Hanna held Syarthis. Light poured from its tip over the open pages of her science-fiction novel. Its eyes peered at Domenic over the cover.

She smirked. "You look like a waiter."

He smirked back. "You look like a grandmother."

"I like nightgowns. I feel like I could bake banana bread. Or, I don't know, roam the hallways at three a.m. and make weird moaning noises, like a ghost."

"Shit. This whole time, I assumed that was Iseul."

They both laughed, but their jokes had the same cautious pattern as they had for weeks. They teased. They deflected. They pretended things were as they'd ever been.

It was better than fighting.

He navigated around the mounds of clothes to the foot of her bed. He sat.

"Why did Alice Rhodes burn, Hanna?"

Hanna's smile caved in. "What?"

"The only other Chosen One who died was the one who failed. So why was she the unlucky one? What did all the others do right that she didn't?"

She didn't answer.

"What did the other Chosen Ones do, after they thwarted their cataclysms?"

She picked at her cuticle.

"Why did Peak haul me aside at the border for some man-to-man talk about sacrifice?"

Nothing.

"Damn it, Hanna. I don't want to fight with you. And I don't care if you hate me right now. You have to tell me the truth."

"I . . ." Hanna dragged her gaze, not to him, but to Valmordion. Something dark lurked in her stare, something haunted. "I could never hate you, Dom."

He was crying now. He was always the worst at arguments. "*Please*. How many of the past Chosen Ones survived? How many?"

Hanna tilted her head back, scowling as she blinked away tears. She crawled toward him, then she wrapped her arms around his shoulders and propped her chin atop his head.

After several seconds passed, Domenic finally spared her the burden of telling him. He answered for them both.

"None of them did."

XXXI
ELLERY
WINTER

The car lurched down yet another winding, snowy road, barreling heedlessly through the Northern hills. Ellery sat in the backseat, trying not to vomit.

"Woah, slow down," Domenic croaked, white-knuckling the handle above the passenger door. "There's a—"

"I see it," Hanna grunted, swerving at the last possible second to avoid a fallen tree. She was so short, she sat propped on an extra seat, her foot barely touching the brakes.

They were headed to Nordmere to uncover why Maltherius had shown Ellery a vision of her hometown's alban tree. Ellery, Domenic, and the Council still believed Maltherius had set them up for a trap. But the danger would be worth it if they finally gained a lead on Summer's traitor.

Because Syarthis was best suited to verify the traitor, Hanna had paused her interrogations of the Order to accompany them. But the Council had contained the mission to the three of them, unsure of who else to trust and unwilling to risk rumors of internal discord leaking to the public.

"We won't even survive until Nordmere at this rate," Ellery grumbled. "I can just see the headlines. ALDERLAND'S DISAPPOINTING CHOSEN TWO DIE IN TRAGIC CAR CRASH."

Domenic choked out a loud, awkward laugh. Hanna shot him an unreadable look. The two of them had behaved strangely the entire journey, keeping Ellery's nerves fraying faster than her seat belt. Before a third of the country had fallen to Winter, the drive from Gallamere to Nordmere would've taken twelve hours. But the ravaged road conditions beyond the border had slowed what could've been a single-day trip into two.

Anxiously, surreptitiously, Ellery slid her hands into her pockets, reassuring herself the winterghast hearts were still there.

Ellery had her own plans for this trip. Back in Gallamere, she'd tried touching each heart to its corresponding tree—Maltherius to an aspen, Eledrium to a pine—in an attempt to create a Winter wand. It hadn't worked. But she refused to give up. It stood to reason that she had the best chance to make a Winter wand within Winter territory. So once they got to Nordmere, she'd slip away and try again. If her gamble worked, she'd tell Domenic everything. And if it didn't . . . he'd never have to know she'd lied to him at all.

Abruptly, their car skidded across a patch of ice.

Domenic cursed and braced himself in his seat. "Hanna. *Hanna*—"

"You're not helping!" Hanna wrestled the steering wheel.

Ellery hastily grasped Iskarius. Ice dissolved across the highway, and the snowbanks lurched backward. She'd only meant to clear the road immediately in front of them, but her magic poured effortlessly through her, until pristine pavement stretched hundreds of feet ahead.

"Thanks," Hanna muttered.

Ellery inspected Iskarius, bewildered. "You're welcome."

At long last, Nordmere came into view. The city was nestled into a valley, bordered by a frozen river on one side and thick forest on the other. Like most cities in the North, it had begun as a mining town, then grown large enough for other industries to take root.

"Huh," Hanna said. "I thought it'd look worse."

"Hanna," Domenic gritted.

"No, it's fine," Ellery murmured. "I did, too."

Although Peak had told them that some Northerners stubbornly remained in the fallen territory, Ellery had assumed year-round Winter would be as bleak as the textbook descriptions of the Thirty Years' Chill. Yet flourishing farms circled the city, crops rising through the snow in what could only be regular magical cultivation. New neighborhoods had sprung up amidst the rubble. In the city center, they passed entire blocks under active construction. Although Nordmere was far from the bustling metropolis Ellery remembered, there were still people on the streets, open storefronts, even a park.

It unnerved her more than ruins would have. Ellery had girded herself for the fallen territory to be a wasteland of memories. Not this. Not *life*.

As twilight fell, the three of them elected to begin their mission after a night's rest. So they stopped at what seemed to be the only hotel left in town. Marks gouged the lobby floor from what had likely been a winterghast's claws. Hanna and Domenic lingered near the door with their luggage as Ellery marched to the front desk. The receptionist read a pulpy romance novel propped against an ashtray.

"Welcome to the Nordmere Grand Hotel," she said, with the throaty rasp of a heavy smoker. "What brings you to town?"

"Oh, we're just passing through. We'll need three rooms."

"Sorry, sweetie. We're nearly full up. Just one room left."

Ellery gulped. "We'll take it."

The woman rummaged for the key, then leaned forward. "You look awfully familiar. And your accent . . . Have you got family in town?"

"Sorry, no," Ellery mumbled.

She returned to find Domenic and Hanna in an intense debate.

"—think I don't know why you're here?" Domenic hissed.

"*I* didn't want to be here," Hanna snapped. "I didn't want any of us here! I was overridden!"

"And yet you volunteered."

"Oh, would you rather it'd been Sharpe with his nose up your—"

As Domenic spotted Ellery, he jabbed Hanna with his elbow. "Any luck?" he asked Ellery.

Ellery studied them both. Hanna chewed a wad of bubble gum, seemingly unfazed. Domenic flushed.

"Kind of." Ellery held up the single room key. "Everything okay?"

"Y-yeah," Domenic said. He was a terrible liar. "Are *you* okay? You know, um, being back here?"

"I'll live," she said flatly. Somehow, this made him flush fiercer.

The trio hauled their luggage up several dilapidated flights to their room. The fixtures were outdated. The bathroom had seen better days. But it wasn't the yellowed wallpaper and moth-eaten carpet that set Ellery's heartbeat ratcheting. It was the bed, singular.

She and Domenic glanced at each other, then looked hastily away.

"So, I don't care who's cozying up next to me, but I'm sleeping on that bed," Hanna announced. Then she flopped unceremoniously onto the drab comforter.

Ellery perched primly on the other side of the mattress. "Don't hog the covers."

Domenic heaved out a dramatic huff before setting down his suitcase. "Great. Fine. Well, I'm calling first dibs on the shower."

As he stalked into the bathroom and closed the door, Hanna rolled over, then propped her head on her hand. She still wore her slushy boots.

"So," Hanna drawled. "Any bets on what kind of trap's waiting for us up here?"

Ellery removed her boots in the hopes that Hanna would follow suit (she didn't), then crawled onto the covers and leaned against the headboard. The mattress creaked in protest. "Kythion ambushing us, probably." As terrifying as that notion was, at least they'd get a chance to slay the last remaining monster of the Dire Three. "Sorry. I'm sure you're thrilled at the prospect of fighting a building-sized winterghast."

"Psh, compared to spending every day learning way more about random Order magicians than I ever wanted to know, this is practically my vacation."

Ellery knew Hanna had yet to uncover evidence of Summer's traitor, but she'd never spared much thought for what *else* she might have uncovered. The enormity of sifting through so many minds, so many memories, was a tremendous burden. Perhaps not as great as saving the country, but a burden all the same.

"I guess I'd prefer Kythion to that, too," she said quietly.

"Don't worry. At this point, nothing surprises me anymore. I've seen it all—every lurid secret, every horrible thought, every humiliation." Hanna popped in a new piece of gum, then stuck her old one beneath the nightstand. "I mean, have you *seen* the way Peak looks at Iseul? It's tragic."

"Oof." Ellery tugged a piece of hair around her finger, curious despite herself. "What about the rest of the Council?"

"Glynn devotes way too much mental energy to his pretentious hobbies. And for all Iseul tries to keep things tidy, her mind is so cluttered. She's always thinking about twelve things at once in two different languages and not one of them is remembering to pay the electric bill."

"And Sharpe?"

"His mom preferred his older sister and he never got over it."

Ellery snorted. "So . . . exactly what I've always suspected, then."

Hanna burst into a cackling laughter, like a hyena. Then, abruptly, she sobered. "This how you always pictured your great homecoming?"

Ellery blinked, surprised at the topic change. "If I had my way, I'd have never come back."

Hanna cocked a brow. "Oh?"

"Gallamere's where I belong."

"Makes sense. I mean, you basically went right from being the Order's darling to Alderland's sweetheart." Hanna imitated a rising airplane with her hand.

Ellery's nerves drew taut as she thought of Demelza and the reporters at the *Foretold* premiere. Hanna knew Ellery most certainly wasn't Alderland's sweetheart anymore. "Sure."

"Until, well, recently. Probably not feeling so glamorous anymore." She crashed the airplane into her lap. "I'd actually be feeling pretty damn bitter, if it were me."

Hanna watched Ellery so carefully. Too carefully. Like even though Syarthis couldn't breach Ellery's mind, Hanna still wanted to glimpse what she was thinking.

Ellery replayed the conversation she'd overheard between Domenic and Hanna in the lobby, the strangeness of the car ride, Domenic's insistence in Glynn's office that he was only trying to protect her. And it all clicked, so obvious and yet so terrible that of course she hadn't seen it until now. The Council's priority was finding Summer's traitor and fulfilling the most recent piece of the prophecy. Hanna never would've deviated from that just to chase down a half-baked chance at a lead.

Which meant they thought *Ellery* was the traitor. And Domenic hadn't told her.

Truthfully, Ellery did have an ulterior motive up North. But she'd only smuggled the winterghast hearts to Nordmere because the Council had refused to listen to her in the first place. And she was doing this for the good of the country, no matter what they might think.

For weeks, Ellery had tried so hard to play her part. But she was suddenly, thoroughly done with bullshit.

"You really think that's a solid motive for Summer's traitor?" she asked Hanna coolly. "Being *liked*?"

Hanna, too, dropped her pretenses in an instant. "That whole hero routine of yours while the country casts you as a villain—I don't buy it. No one could keep it up that long."

Ellery wanted to laugh, or maybe scream. "No one? Or just you?"

"I don't see what any of this has to do with me."

"Oh, please. Is that why you stopped bothering to win people over? Or have you always been this charming?"

Hanna blew bubble after bubble, each bursting with a jarring *pop*. A voice drifted in from the bathroom: Domenic, still in the shower, singing the pop song Ellery had forced him to learn.

Finally, Hanna murmured, "You know, for all that everyone loves to call me charming now, I wonder what they'll call me when I stop trying."

* * *

As evening turned to night, Ellery cloaked herself, then retrieved her coat with the hearts still discreetly tucked in the pockets. She intended to return before either Domenic or Hanna noticed she was gone, but just in case, she left a note on the bedside table.

Outside, a person hovered beneath the hotel awning. Ellery nearly collided with them, then lurched back, holding Iskarius.

She recognized him instantly. Julian Norwood, his lean frame wrapped in a heavy coat, his dark coils peeking beneath his hat, his intent gaze trained on the hotel doors. Scar tissue sliced through one eyebrow and the corner of his lip, white and umber striated against his light brown skin. Incredulous tears welled in Ellery's eyes, that he was *here* of all places. It couldn't be a coincidence.

She sheathed Iskarius and dropped her cloaking enchantment. "Julian," she whispered.

He uttered a shocked noise, then cleared his throat as he noticed her stares. "El. Right, well, we might as well get the gawking over with. I know the scars are—"

Ellery rushed forward and wrapped him in a hug. After a moment of surprise, he squeezed back.

These past few weeks were the longest they'd gone without speaking since they'd first become friends. Now here they were again, not atop the mountain of Gallamere but in the middle of nowhere, surrounded by gently falling snow. Just like Nordmere, he felt familiar and unfamiliar, a relic of a life that was no longer hers and still part of her nonetheless.

"I missed you," he said as she pulled away.

"I missed you, too. But what are you doing this far north? And how did you know I was here?"

"You assumed I was here to see you, huh?"

"Do you really expect me to believe you wandered over to my hotel by accident?"

He chuckled. "Well, it's not every day the Chosen Two visit Nordmere. Word traveled fast. Although I was trying to figure out how to get you down here by yourself. I never assumed you'd show up on your own. I mean . . . isn't it a little past your bedtime?"

"Asshole," she said, sniffling.

"Guilty," he said, grinning. One corner of his lips stayed downturned, as though pulled into a permanent scowl.

"But if you wanted to talk to me . . . I've been trying to contact you since you left the academy."

"I know. Honestly, for the first week or so, I wasn't up for talking to anyone. My parents paid every doctor and healer they knew a truly exorbitant amount of money to patch me up, and by the time I'd started to feel better, you were all over the news. A Chosen One. And I . . . I'd almost died. I didn't want your pity."

"I never pitied you," Ellery protested. "I just wanted to know you were okay."

"Well, I am. I swear. The scars are the only part they couldn't fully heal."

"I'm glad," she said quietly. "And I'm sorry."

"What are *you* sorry for? You saved my life."

Ellery expected her next words to be a struggle, like they'd been so many times before. Instead, they were simple. "For that fight we had. For shutting you out for years. And for being a pretty terrible girlfriend."

"Girlfriend, huh?" Julian arched a brow. "As I recall, you refused to label it."

"Hence the *pretty terrible* part. You were my best friend. I should've treated you better after we crossed that line."

"I get it. I was kind of a dick, too," he said. Ellery laughed in surprise, and Julian's own grin widened. "What, you think I can't be self-aware? Back at the academy, I was so convinced I was destined for a powerful wand. And I kept telling myself I'd return to the Citadel as soon as possible. Keep trying before my window closes."

"So why didn't you?"

"Because I heard rumors about a magician up North. They claimed to be a Winter magician. Like you."

A Winter magician. Ellery had dared to hope she might not be the only one, but it was completely different to hear Julian confirm it with so much conviction. She felt the same way as when she'd watched the winterghasts' hearts turn into seeds, when she'd marveled at an impossibly grand illusion amidst a forest and realized her magic could be beautiful, when she'd first heard destiny speak. Like she stood at the precipice of something tremendous, something extraordinary.

"Can you take me to them?" she breathed.

Julian smiled again, wider. "What do you think I came here to do? They've wanted to meet you for a long time."

He gestured for her to follow, but she hesitated.

"What about Dom? He should come, too."

His smile wavered.

"No," he said carefully. "Not Barrow. Just you. Do you trust me?"

Ellery's hope shattered. If there really was another Winter magician out there, they'd kept themself a secret all this time. They'd only contacted her once she arrived in Nordmere, lured here by a vision from the Dire Three. And they wanted to see her, but not Domenic.

Maybe Ellery *would* find Summer's traitor on this mission after all.

"Of course I trust you," Ellery lied, and followed her best friend into the night.

XXXII
Ellery
WINTER

Ellery and Julian walked down dark, half-remembered streets from her childhood until they found one where the trees pressed close like nosy neighbors. People milled in and out of pubs, their laughter mingling with faint music, the streetlamps haloed in flurried snow.

Julian led her into one such pub, called Altitude Sickness, shabby yet surprisingly cozy. Gas lanterns flickered on the tables and on the bar, and a record spun merrily in the corner, playing a song Ellery hadn't heard in years. Ellery pushed through the crowd under the shroud of her cloaking spell, dodging elbows and shoulders.

But her spell was far from the only one. Everywhere, from people lounging in the booths to leaning against the walls, were magicians. Magicians dyeing their drinks different colors. Magicians conjuring tiny gusts of wind to cheat at darts. Magicians drawing designs into the frost on the windowpanes. And none of them wielded a Living Wand.

"Reminds you of the academy, huh?" Julian murmured, as Ellery gaped incredulously.

"How many hedge magicians are in Nordmere?"

"More than there were a few months ago. Just like me, they came here looking for *them*."

He gestured to an alcove not unlike the one at the Order's student lounge, where a large corner booth was filled with excited, chattering teenagers. Ellery didn't need to ask who the supposed Winter magician was. They sat in the center, holding court.

They looked around Ellery's age, if not younger. Yet they carried the presence of someone who'd long since grown up. They were striking, with a mane of wild brown curls, hazel eyes, and fair skin. A patched-up coat and trousers hung on their rail-thin frame, cinched by a brown belt. They held a training wand, but plenty more jutted out from their pockets, their waistband, even their sleeves.

Julian strode toward the alcove. The crowd parted for him, greeting him, as he slid into the booth beside the Winter magician, just as effortlessly as he'd done back at the academy.

He held out his palm triumphantly. "Pay up, Kester."

The person—Kester—lifted a brow and flicked their gaze behind him, and although Ellery knew they couldn't see her, she swore they looked her straight in the eyes.

"Get out of here, everyone," they said lightly. "Suddenly, Julian and I have evening plans."

The magicians around them rose without protest and scattered throughout the bar. Kester stood, then pulled a crumpled bill out of one of their many pockets and thrust it at Julian.

Ellery flicked Iskarius. Her cloaking spell extended over the three of them. Kester seemed remarkably unfazed by Ellery's sudden appearance, as though a Chosen One dropping in was just another night.

"You bet I wouldn't come," Ellery said warily.

"Yes, well, I like to win," they said, without a hint of an apology. Then they stuck out a ring-studded hand. "I'm Kester Wright. You're you."

Their grip was strong. Their hand was callused.

"It's a pleasure," Ellery said automatically.

Kester's mouth twitched in amusement. "And that's Iskarius you're holding, I presume?"

Ellery braced herself for a recoil, for a grimace. But Kester only peered at it curiously, then whistled. "Now *that's* a wand."

"We should talk." Ellery gestured to the booth.

"I'll leave you both to it," Julian said, standing.

"Wait," Ellery protested. "You're not staying?" If Kester proved to be Summer's traitor, she didn't want to be left alone with them.

"I think you should get to know each other. You've got a lot in common," Julian assured her. "And Kester . . . play nice."

Kester frowned. "Don't I always?"

Ellery was surprised he was so eager to go. But Julian would never lead her into a trap, which meant he must've considered Kester trustworthy. And maybe it would be easier to prod Kester for answers without Julian present, anyway.

"Okay," she said cautiously. Julian departed as Ellery sat on the opposite side of the booth. The table was sticky from spilled drinks and littered with spare crumbs. Kester sipped a dark beer, unbothered by the mess.

"So you think you're a Winter magician," Ellery began, resting Iskarius in her lap beneath the table. "Why?"

The cloaking spell muffled the rest of the bar; sound and light felt distant as Kester leaned in, studying Ellery shamelessly. Usually Ellery knew what part someone wanted her to play. But with Kester, she had no idea.

"Well, I didn't at first," they answered. "But you know how kids manifest magic. Mine was a little odd." They waved their wand, and a tiny storm cloud spun above the table. Nature magic. With another flick, it dissipated. "My training wands kept doing *that* no matter what sort of spell I tried to cast. But they were just some wind and snow, and they didn't hurt anybody, unless you count the occasional mailbox as an innocent bystander."

Ellery had been prepared for obvious lies, born of a grab for attention. But Julian was right; although Kester's story wasn't identical to her own, it was close enough to make her breath hitch.

"But you conjured storms?" she asked. "Didn't anyone else care?"

"Once I got to one of those Order primary schools, some teachers definitely thought I was strange. So I just learned to conjure rain instead of snow."

Ellery couldn't decide if their nonchalance about their magic was an act or not. If it was, it was a convincing one.

"And what about after primary school?" she asked.

"I didn't pass the Order academy's entrance exam. And then Nordmere fell." Kester grimaced. "But when my family stayed behind, I stayed with them."

"Why? When I left, Nordmere was in ruins. It was . . ." She trailed off, trying to shake the memories.

Kester took a long draught of their beer. "I won't pretend my family's had an easy time sticking it out. But Nordmere's my home. I'm glad we didn't abandon it."

Ellery, who'd never felt such a devotion, only nodded.

"Eventually, we started to rebuild. And as time passed, my magic felt stronger. At first I thought it was because I was getting older, but then I learned about *you*, a Winter Chosen One with a Winter wand. And it all started to make sense. I mean, we're in Winter's territory, aren't we? You must feel it, too."

Ellery thought of earlier in the day, when her spell to clear the road had been so unexpectedly powerful. She grasped Iskarius more tightly in her lap. Ice crusted the top of their seats, then flared out through the bar, until the interior of Altitude Sickness was gilded and garlanded with icicles. People elbowed each other and laughed, marveling at the sudden décor change.

"I do feel it," Ellery said breathlessly. "It's like my magic is *more*."

Kester grinned. "Exactly."

Ellery decided in that instant that she believed Kester was truly a Winter magician.

She wasn't alone.

For a moment her pulse quickened with the wonder of what that might mean for her, for Alderland, for the winterghast hearts in her pocket. Then she pushed her hope aside. She couldn't get distracted.

Kester might still be Summer's traitor.

"What about all the others here?" she asked. "Are they convinced they're Winter magicians, too?"

"Most of them at least suspect it, although it's not like we can truly prove it. But that's why so many of them have come up here, some older, some more like us." Kester nodded around at the bar.

"Julian said people are also coming here because they heard about *you*."

"Yeah, that wasn't really on purpose. But after the first few magicians showed up, word got around fast. Some of them were confused. Some were really scared. And I became the person who explains why they don't have to be. Because someone has to, right? We live in a country where being a magician means dreaming of a Living Wand and a destiny to go with it, but every Living Wand except yours wields Summer magic. So even if a Winter magician makes it to the national academy, none of us would stand a chance at bonding with one. The best we can do is be hedge magicians with a little more power."

Kester's easy demeanor seemed strained now. They fiddled with their rings.

"So that's what you and your friends want to do?" Ellery asked. "Stay up here and haunt some bar?"

"There's not much point in doing anything else."

Summer's traitor surely had a motive and a goal that involved hurting Alderland. Yet Kester wasn't describing anything of the sort. If anything, Ellery admired what they were doing. They could still be lying, but Ellery was running low on reasons why they would.

"All right. I can see why you'd like it up here," Ellery pressed on. "But there's plenty of people in the fallen—in Winter's territory who aren't magicians. Why wouldn't they move south?"

"In the beginning, I think most people were like my family. There was a lot of worry going around about repeating the Thirty Years' Chill. But we didn't know for sure if that was what would happen to our home. And as it turns out, losing a bit of territory to Winter isn't the same as surviving a cataclysm. For the last seven years, we haven't been bothered by a single scurge or ghast. It's colder, but it's peaceful. And besides, it's been really good for the land."

Ellery furrowed her brow. "What do you mean, good for the land?"

"You know how we're taught in school that Living Wands handle most farming? Apparently it's because Aldrish soil is hard to work with. But since this region became Winter territory, the land's changed. Every year, more and more crops grow without needing any magic at all."

There *had* been more farms than Ellery had expected surrounding the city. But the idea that they flourished without magic was so strange, she didn't know how to feel. Kester made it all sound so idyllic. Too idyllic, maybe.

"Why haven't you tried to tell the Order about this?" Ellery asked. "Why haven't you tried to tell *me*?"

"The NDC's sent people up here, but they don't know we're Winter magicians. They just think we're Order rejects with a death wish. As though *they're* not the ones all excited to die on some battlefield." Kester snorted derisively and set down their glass, now empty. "And as for you, do you have any idea how hard it is to reach a Chosen One? All your correspondences and appearances are screened."

"Julian could've gotten through."

"He only showed up a week ago. But he didn't need much convincing about Winter magicians. He immediately wanted to talk to you, but the phone lines here are terrible and the mail is slow. So he was about to head to Gallamere to tell you in person. Julian wanted me to come, too, said that a Winter Chosen One needed to know about Winter magicians, and that he could definitely get us a meeting. But instead, well, here you are."

The timing was quite the coincidence. More than coincidence. Maybe Kester thought so, too. Their gaze bored skeptically into Ellery as they fiddled with their rings again.

Warnings raced through her mind. This could still be a trap. Kester could somehow still be the traitor.

But Ellery didn't think so. And with each passing second, she suspected—no, she was certain—that she'd been brought here for a reason. Her hand slid toward the winterghast hearts in her pocket.

"Julian was right to want to tell me about this," she said determinedly. "And I think he should come back. All three of us need to talk."

Kester went to fetch Julian. When the two of them returned, he handed Ellery a glass of red wine—her favorite—before sliding into the booth beside her. Ellery thanked him, then removed the hearts from her pocket and set them upon the drink-stained table.

Kester frowned at them. "You wanted to show us . . . enchanted seeds?"

"Not quite," Ellery began cautiously. "But before I explain, I need you to both promise me that you won't breathe a word of this to anyone. . . ."

They promised, and so Ellery explained the Dire Three as briefly and clearly as she could, fielding the necessary follow-up questions about the other Living Wands, including Valmordion and Iskarius. But rather than seeming wary, as soon as she was through, both of them reached eagerly for the seeds.

Kester grabbed the pinecone. Julian snatched the aspen pod.

Instantly, silver light radiated from Maltherius's heart, casting their dark corner booth in a cool glow.

"I can feel it," Julian gasped. "My magic suits it, somehow."

Ellery's hope flared brighter. "I think it could be your wand."

"I think so, too." He stood abruptly. "And you said all we have to do is take it to an aspen tree? We should go, now—"

"Wait," Ellery said hastily. The horror of Ravfiri's vigil was still fresh in her mind. So was the vision of Nordmere that Maltherius had shown her.

It had led her directly to its potential wielder. *That* couldn't be a coincidence, either.

Maybe it wasn't Kester she should've been worrying about, but Julian. But he couldn't be Summer's traitor. She'd known him for too long to think him capable of betraying his country. And the idea that he might somehow have colluded with the winterghast who'd hurt their former classmates, many his own friends, was unfathomable.

"If Maltherius *is* your wand, you need to understand what it was like as a ghost," she continued solemnly. "It's the Winter equivalent of Syarthis. It's no small burden to wield a wand like that."

Julian paused. He was from the half of their class who'd survived that day only out of happenstance, his schedule shielding him from tragedy. "Syarthis, huh?"

Ellery touched his arm gently. "I didn't get much say in my fate. You deserve to choose yours."

He studied the heart a moment longer. Then he shot her a grin, his dark eyes alight with familiar ambition. "I always knew I was destined for a strong corporeal wand. I'll wield it."

"Mine's not doing anything," Kester grumbled, examining the pinecone.

"I don't think Eledrium suits you," Ellery said. "I'm sorry."

Kester scowled but set the seed down. "Well, are there more?"

"That depends on if we can get this to work."

Kester rose from the booth. "Then what are we waiting for?"

They exited through the back, past the dumpsters. Trees crowded at the edges of a snowy backyard, and their trio strode quickly into the forest behind it, still cloaked, until they found the nearest aspen.

None of them spoke, but anticipation hummed palpably between them as Julian walked to the tree. He held Maltherius's heart to its trunk.

For a second, the night was still. Then, with a creak, a branch began to bend. Ellery's breath caught in her throat. Her gaze locked with Kester's, on Julian's other side. And Ellery saw her own hope reflected back at her, and beneath it, something deeper: awe.

After the horror-struck magicians at the border, Maltherius's attack, and the awful headlines, she'd assumed no one would ever look at Winter's Chosen that way again.

Then the branch stiffened. The tree stilled. And the light within the heart dimmed.

Julian muttered a curse. "My magic is reaching for its magic, but they can't touch. There's something blocking it."

Ellery's hope withered. She was in Winter territory, with the right potential wand, the right wielder. But it still wasn't enough.

"I don't get it," she whispered. "What else could be blocking the wand from being made? What else *is* there?"

Julian and Kester exchanged a glance.

"El, you should know why I wanted you to meet Kester so badly," Julian said fervently. "Because you see now, don't you? Nothing about magic is how we thought it was. Winter's territory, Winter magicians, Winter wands . . . Winter's not inherently dangerous or wrong. You know that better than anyone. So we think—we hope—that you might be able to stop Summer from destroying its potential. *Our* potential."

Ellery had seen Julian like this before, his squared shoulders, his argument seamlessly rehearsed. But Ellery struggled to share his conviction. All she'd learned tonight had only made her less certain of what part she was meant to play, her future suddenly distorted.

"I know there's more to Winter than what most people see," she said. "But that doesn't change the fact that for the past thousand years, Winter's terrorized this country. That ghasts and scurges could be killing people *right now*. I'm sworn to protect Alderland. You can't ask me to turn my back on that."

"I'm not," Julian urged. "I'm asking you not to turn your back on *us*. We're part of Alderland, too. In every interview, you and Barrow talk about how you want to reclaim Summer's territory. But do you really think that's the right thing to do? To take all of this away, when some people want to keep it?"

"I don't know! I only just learned about this. I need time to think. And I'd have to talk to the Order before I could ever make that kind of decision—"

"As if the Order would care," Kester cut in. "Let's say you *do* side with Summer. What do you think the Order will do to you after you finish? You think they'll pat you on the head and give you a reward?"

"Kester," Julian said warningly.

Kester hiked up their chin. "No. I'm done playing nice. All she's done all night is question everything we stand for. Everything she *should* stand for. But she hates Winter. She hates herself."

It clicked, suddenly. Kester's goading tone. She'd heard it before.

"It was you," Ellery breathed. "You're the one who called in on Wilder's radio show and asked me all those questions about destroying Winter."

Kester made a show of twisting toward her, the heels of their combat boots crunching through snow. "I sure did."

"Why?"

"Because I thought my questions might get through to you. But you're not just unreachable because you're a Chosen One. Even now that you're here, you're still hiding. First you show up cloaked. Then you can't believe you're stronger up North until I ask you about it. And guess what? You're hiding from people who would've embraced you as a hero. So where is your conviction? Where's your self-respect? You have a wand that could level a fucking city in your hand, but you spend your time surrounded by Summer, playing Alderland's paper-doll princess. And you just . . . take it."

A cold, unending fury swept through Ellery. An anger she'd never let herself feel before because she didn't think she was allowed it. But now, it was the only thing she *could* feel.

Frost wafted from her lips. Ellery's shadow uncoiled in the silver glow of Iskarius, then grew, engulfing the surrounding trees until it loomed above them, around them. Until the very stars dimmed behind the veil of her magic.

Julian stiffened. But Kester grinned wickedly.

"I 'take it' because I have no other choice," Ellery snarled. "I sit there and smile while the Council debates behind my back whether I'm dangerous or not. I watch every single thing I do or say or even *wear,* because for all people insist they believe in destiny, they're awfully damn willing to overlook it when it doesn't line up with what they want to be true. And the truth is . . . the truth is . . ."

"The truth is what?" Julian asked softly.

That destiny had never asked Ellery to fight against her nature. But she had. She'd punished herself her entire life. Because she'd believed, deep down, it was what she deserved. What *all* of Winter deserved.

"It'll never be enough," she whispered. "I will never be enough. And they will *never* change their minds. The Order will use me, because they need me. But they'll hate me all the same. And when we finish fulfilling the prophecy . . . when they don't need me anymore . . . I don't know what they'll do."

Julian squeezed her shoulder gently. "I know how loyal you are, and I know how much we both wanted to be part of the Order. But you don't deserve to be hated, El. You deserve to be part of an Alderland that actually respects who you are. And that Alderland could exist. Maybe you're destined to build it."

Ellery remembered Glynn's warning that Iskarius's destiny was unprecedented, uncertain.

Ellery had dismissed it—she knew she was fated to save Alderland. But what if saving it meant transforming precedent entirely?

"What would you have me do?" she asked somberly. "I want to help you. I want to get rid of the ghasts. I want to make Winter wands. But I still don't know how."

"I've got an idea," Kester said. "It might be Winter now, and we might be in Winter's territory, but it's Summer that controls this country. If that changed, I bet we could make wands of our own."

Ellery bristled. "I'm not waging war on the whole country."

"I don't think you have to," Kester said. "We also call Chosen Ones champions, don't we? A champion doesn't need to lead an army. They fight on behalf of one. Except now, for the first time, we have two champions. One Summer Chosen One who's supposed to fight Winter. And you."

Slowly, insidiously, a despicable understanding took root.

"You want me to fight *Dom*?" Ellery choked.

"You can't possibly mean that, Kester," Julian said, aghast.

"I'm not saying I like it," Kester said gravely. "But it makes sense, doesn't it?"

It did. All this time, Ellery had insisted she couldn't be Summer's traitor. But here she was, being asked to rebel against it. Being asked to fight—no, to *kill*—Summer's Chosen.

"No. No, it doesn't make sense," Ellery growled. "Maybe the rest of the Order will never support Winter magicians, but Dom will. You don't know him like I do. He might be playing a part in the news just like I am, but he's smart and passionate and he cares so much about doing the right thing, about protecting everyone. Dom's an actual hero. And he *will* listen to me."

"Shit. You're not hesitating because of Summer and Winter at all, are you?" Julian narrowed his eyes. "This is about *him*. I should've seen it earlier. But I was your best friend for five years, and I was a distraction. And it took you, what, a few weeks with Barrow to put destiny on the line for him? What the fuck, El?"

Ellery flinched. When she'd apologized to Julian about their relationship, he'd acted like he'd forgiven her. But he hadn't.

"Wait, wait, wait," Kester said. "Are Alderland's Chosen Two *sleeping together?*"

"It's not like that," Ellery protested, even though it would've been easier if it had all been some fling. But the truth was that it didn't matter that they'd broken up. That she'd lied to Domenic about giving up on Winter wands, that he'd hidden the Council's suspicions from her.

She was in love with Domenic Barrow anyway.

And if she truly was destined to become Summer's traitor, then she would fail. Because the only person she could never betray was him.

"Think whatever you want about me. I don't care." Ellery tore the aspen pod from Julian's grasp, then stormed away, leaving behind what could've been the only place she truly belonged.

XXXIII
DOMENIC
WINTER

Going on a walk. Be back soon.
—El

Domenic lay on the mangled hotel carpet, the note crumpled in his fist, counting the passing minutes until his dread felt justifiable.

Finally, he hissed, "Hanna."

No response.

"Hanna."

Scowling, Domenic shuffled toward her. She slept like a pill bug, curled up tight on her side. But as he reached for her, he froze. Her eyes shifted beneath her lids, back and forth, back and forth. Sweat gleamed across her brow.

Trembling, he slid aside the covers until he glimpsed her hands: one hugged to her chest, another wedged between her knees. Empty.

He shook her shoulder. Her eyes stilled. She groaned indignantly.

"Ellery's gone."

Hanna shot up. *"What?"*

He passed her the note, now bunched into a ball and slightly damp. She snatched Syarthis from the nightstand, unsheathed it, and squinted into its light.

"Shit. *Shit.*" Hanna sprang out of bed and scooped up her clothes from yesterday. She hoisted her trousers up beneath her nightgown. "Why are you just standing there? *Move.* Get dressed."

"You think something happened to her?"

"To a Chosen One? No, Dom. I want to know who she's with, what she's doing, who Syarthis and I can question." She sniffed the armpits of her thermal, scrunched her nose, and yanked it on anyway. "What? Don't look at me like that. I know you're suspicious, too."

He was, but he didn't want to admit it.

Nevertheless, Domenic scanned the floor for his discarded socks. "And you, you're all right?"

"Why wouldn't I be?"

"Because when you were asleep, you looked . . ." He couldn't bring himself to finish.

Hanna scoffed. "No. We're not doing this. You want to worry about something, worry about your own . . ."

They stared at each other, both haunted, both wretched.

Three minutes later, they jogged through Nordmere's nighttime streets. The near emptiness of the city that had unnerved Domenic during the day was nothing compared to the desolation of its darkness. Everywhere, buildings lay abandoned to rot.

"How much farther?" Hanna huffed.

Domenic, too, already felt run ragged, a stitch in his side, the frigid air brittle and sharp. The wire-thin thread of his tracking spell pulled tauter with every step.

"We're close."

They at last stopped along a street with more life than most. Light shined a murky halo around a nearby door, labeled Altitude Sickness. Music clashed from inside.

"The fuck?" Hanna asked, her hands braced on her knees as she panted.

"I think . . ." Domenic gasped. "It's called . . . a bar. It's where . . . normal people go . . . to have fun."

She shot him a withering look, then she threw open the door. But she only made it three steps inside before Domenic collided with her back.

Perhaps the streets of Nordmere were so dead because every person was *here,* bodies crammed together like matchsticks. The floorboards were a hazard, spiked with protruding nails and spongy with water damage. Drinks were served in every type of vessel, from pint glasses to mugs, jars, and even a vase. For a room so cold, it smelled remarkably like sweat.

And everywhere, inexplicably, was magic.

They were all flimsy spells, half-faded and fraying at the seams and glowing the harsh, artificial white of being cast by training wands. Enchanted graffiti glittered on the walls. Coats and scarves floated where their owners had last left them.

"These people are . . . magicians," Domenic said.

"Yeah, and they're all staring at us."

"I know you don't get out much, but believe it or not, I'm actually quite the celebrity."

Hanna waved dismissively. "No one will recognize you without all the makeup and gel." But she mustn't have been truly sure about it, as she squinted up the length of him and muttered, "Just . . . put away Valmordion. It's not like this place is big. We'll find her eventually. And I don't want any suspects escaping out the back door."

Domenic managed a snort, even as he grappled for a reason why Ellery would be here, of all places.

Then the back door in question slammed, and a cool draft grazed his neck.

He spun, and Ellery halted in surprise as her eyes locked onto his from across the bar. Her hair was frizzed and wild, and tears shimmered frozen on her cheeks.

He rushed toward her. "Are you all right? What's wrong?"

Before she could answer, someone called out from behind her. "Hey! You can't just—"

"Let her go," said another voice. "It's not worth it, Kester."

As the two newcomers and Hanna shoved their way toward them, Domenic realized he recognized the speaker. And he felt a clench of horror as he examined his scars, remembering the shape of him doused in flames, the sound of his scream.

Domenic schooled his face into neutrality. He refused to betray pity.

Even as he hid Valmordion behind his back.

"Norwood?" he said incredulously.

Julian Norwood scowled, as if the sight of Domenic personally offended him, though Domenic was pretty sure the only words they'd ever exchanged was when Domenic had asked to bum a training wand off him before their third-year corporeal exam.

"Barrow," Norwood grunted. "I should've known you'd show up."

"Don't," Ellery told him warningly.

Hanna examined Norwood. "You know this guy, Dom?" Hanna remembered none of her former classmates. She claimed it was because no thirteen-year-old had made much of an impression, in the tone that never offered room for other suggestions.

Domenic didn't know how to answer. He only knew Norwood as Ellery's best friend. He'd sat next to her in every class, walked with her down the academy's halls, was a fixture in every piece of gossip about whether Miss Perfect was so perfect behind closed doors.

"You know what, El?" Norwood growled. "Kester was right. They told me we shouldn't have bothered with you, and I should've listened."

"Yeah, you should've," Ellery snapped.

With a final inexplicable glare at Domenic, Norwood stalked off.

The other newcomer, meanwhile—Kester—didn't budge. They were pale and lanky, with a storm of brown curls and a stance as if they, a teenager, owned the whole establishment. Training wands jutted out from every pocket of their jacket. Several even peeked out from their boots.

"Do you mind?" Domenic asked them. "We're trying to have a conversation."

They held their hands up in mock surrender. "Oh, don't worry, Domenic. I won't interrupt."

Domenic frowned at the usage of his first name.

Hanna, however, smiled wide. "Oh good, a prime suspect. Let's start with your full name, age, and whether or not you harbor ill will against the Republic of Alderland."

Kester crossed their arms. "I'm Kester Wright. Eighteen. And the Republic? No. Although I don't appreciate Order magicians crashing my party. Especially swinging around a wand like *that*." They nodded at Syarthis in Hanna's fist.

Impatient, Domenic turned to Ellery. "What happened? Why are you here?"

Ellery vainly tried to smooth down her hair. "I'll explain everything back at the hotel."

"Oh, we're not going anywhere without some answers," Hanna said.

Kester shrugged. "I'm an open book."

"Are you?" Hanna challenged.

Kester examined Syarthis again. "I'm not afraid of you."

Hanna hesitated. Syarthis curled its tip around her pointer finger.

Domenic, too, hesitated. Hanna had to be as exhausted as he was. And light enchantments were one thing; peeling open a stranger's mind was another.

Then she mumbled, "Go, Dom. We got this."

"You don't know what you're agreeing to," Ellery told Kester warily.

"Oh, I know what wand that is," said Kester. "And while you all clearly think otherwise, I've got nothing to hide."

After they left, Ellery tugged Domenic by his shirtsleeve against a far wall, and he settled for the privacy of a cloaking enchantment. Despite his many questions, it was a relief to have found her, to let the stage of the world fade out around them.

Until she said, direly, "I have something I need to tell you."

Domenic listened to her confession of stealing the seeds and the harrowed events of that night. Yet even before she'd admitted to lying, he'd decided he didn't care. None of her secrets compared to his own. For days, it'd tortured him. He couldn't keep down food. He'd barely slept. And for all he reminded himself that every second had become precious, never had the details of his life felt so inconsequential. What did it matter if he was well? If his actions were rational? Apparently, every choice led to their demise.

"I shouldn't have lied to you," she finished. "And I know you didn't tell me the Council's suspicions because you've been trying to protect me. But I think they're right. I must be Summer's traitor. Because Kester has a theory about me, about *us,* and—"

"El, stop."

"But this is important. And after I tell you, you might not—"

"I don't care," he said fervently. "Besides, you can't be the traitor. It's your turn to hear the next prophecy piece. So now that you've accused yourself, have you?"

Ellery's throat bobbed, like whatever words she'd left unspoken had lodged there. "No."

"Then it's not you. And I don't care that you went behind my back either. All these people here, you really believe they're Winter magicians?"

"Yeah. I really do."

Domenic smiled for the first time since they'd left Gallamere. "That's amazing, El. How are you feeling right now?"

She backed away from him, stretching his cloaking enchantment tight enough to fray. "You don't have to do this."

His smile collapsed. "Do what?"

"Take care of me. It's hard enough trying to keep things between us the way you wanted, but—"

"You think *this* is what I wanted?" He gestured at the chasm of twelve inches between them.

"Isn't it?"

"Of course not!"

"Well, that's not what you said when you broke up with me. So if you're miserable, too, then why are we still doing this?"

Domenic tilted his head back, blinking as his vision blurred. "I'm just trying to do the right thing. The noble thing."

"So am I! Of course I am! But do you even know what that is? Because I sure don't."

He didn't. He never had.

"And I don't think admitting that makes me less capable," Ellery continued fiercely. "I think the idea that we'd always know what to do is yet another impossible thing that's been asked of us."

A laugh escaped him like a whimper. She had no idea what might truly be asked of them.

But for all Domenic could curse destiny for stealing their future, it bore no blame for their present. Domenic had shattered that all on his own. And he could no longer conceive of a single reason why.

He stepped closer to Ellery.

"What if I hate them for asking too much?" Domenic gestured viciously at the people around them, at everyone, at everything. "What does that make me then?"

Ellery met his gaze boldly. "Sometimes I hate them, too."

Always, always they were the same. Even if they were terrible. He could never think her terrible.

"Shit, El." He snaked his arms around her waist and drew her against him. "I'm so sorry. I never wanted to hurt you. I've been trying so hard to act the way I thought a Chosen One should. Because if I don't, people get scared. I've *seen* it. And I know what fear feels like. I can't stand everyone's fear being my fault."

Ellery cupped his cheek. "Even if we're responsible for everyone, the way we feel matters, too. You're the one who showed me that."

He leaned into her touch. If he had to die, he could choose no better place than in her arms. "I'm . . . embarrassed to admit how long I wanted this. I knew from the first time I saw you. From the first time I learned who you were. And for years, before you even glanced at me, I couldn't look anywhere but at you. And *knowing* you, seeing who you really are, you're so much more than the perfect image I'd fantasized in my head. And when I'm with you, the way I feel, what we have . . . It's terrifying. Because I should be fighting for the sake of everyone, but what I'm really fighting for—what I've *always* been fighting for—is this. You and me."

Ellery's eyes widened. "Dom, do you really mean that?"

"So what if I do?"

"Well, then maybe you were right. Maybe this *is* a mistake."

However, for all Ellery's logic, she wrapped her arms behind his neck. He nudged his forehead against hers and shuddered at the exquisite cold of her magic, the torment of it. The dancing lights of gas lamps and shimmer of graffiti brightened around them. Yet they were elsewhere. They were in a forest bathed in color and stars and impossible dreams.

But his own confession festered inside him. He couldn't kiss her and not tell her. Even he knew it wasn't right, wasn't noble.

"No, we shouldn't," he agreed.

Yet as he readied to admit the awful truth, no words came. Maybe it was his cowardice, his selfish want to survive. But ever since Hanna had told him that every Chosen One had sacrificed themselves, a desperate hope had lurked in Domenic's heart.

He and Ellery weren't like every Chosen One before them. They were the Chosen Two.

And if Domenic wasn't sure, what good was it to burden

Ellery with this same fear that'd been unraveling him? He'd already broken her heart once. He refused to do so again.

As he lowered his mouth to hers, suddenly, someone kicked him behind the knee.

He spun around deliriously. Hanna and Kester glared up at him. His heart careened to a stop.

"I knew it," Hanna snapped. "You are so fucking typical."

"Hanna," Domenic croaked. "It's not . . ."

He had no idea what he meant to say, but it didn't matter, as Hanna cut him off to bark at Ellery, "The seeds, the hearts, whatever they are. Give them back. *Now*." She held out her hand.

Ellery didn't protest. She withdrew Maltherius's and Eledrium's hearts from her pocket and relinquished them to Hanna. "Wh-what are you going to tell the Council?"

Hanna's gaze flitted furiously between Ellery, then Kester, then Domenic, as if she wanted to fight someone but couldn't decide whom. Then she grunted, defeated, "I don't know." And she stomped away.

Kester hugged their arms tight to their chest. Their brashness from earlier had dimmed, though after Syarthis excavating their mind, Domenic couldn't blame them.

"So after I just endured *that* delightful experience, you're still not gonna listen to me?" Kester spat. "Fine. Why should I matter to you? I'm just a person who has to survive whatever bad choices the two of you make."

They stomped off, too.

Ellery tugged Domenic's sleeve and muttered, "Come on. Let's just go."

He hesitated. However direly he wanted to escape with Ellery, he couldn't reconcile with one person he cared about while betraying another. He needed to make things right with them both.

"I'm so sorry, but I can't leave Hanna. Not like that." He

looked at Ellery pleadingly. "I promise I'll catch up with you. Is that all right?"

Her jaw clenched, like it wasn't. But she nodded. "Yeah. Go."

Domenic scoured the crowds for Hanna, but she was too short. He considered silencing the music, climbing atop a stool and calling for her—him, a Chosen One, at 2 a.m. in a bar. But as he squeezed Valmordion, he felt that familiar heat of Syarthis, familiar in a way that ran deeper than friendship, deeper even than blood.

He found her out in the cold.

Hanna sat against the wall with her knees to her chest, clutching Syarthis to her heart. A circle of wet pavement haloed her from the wand melting the slush.

She didn't look at him. "So did you tell her, then? How your great love story ends?"

"Not yet." He didn't tell her it was because he wasn't sure. Hanna would only call him a fool.

"She deserves to know, Dom."

"Like I did, all this time?"

Hanna glowered at the nearest trash bin.

"I'm sorry, Hanna," he snapped. "I really am. I'm sorry I'm so fucking predictable. But I'm not going to bother explaining myself if you're just gonna keep hating me anyway. And for the record, I really don't want to die with you hating me."

"I . . . I already told you. I could never hate you."

"But you're mad at me. You've been mad at me since, when? Since the night I bonded with Valmordion?"

She smeared her nose on the back of her hand. "Yup. That sounds about right."

"*Why?* Tell me, and I'll fix it."

"I'm not sure you can fix it," she murmured. "It's not your fault. It's never been your fault. I'm just . . . not very good at being a person, I think."

"Tell me anyway. Let me try."

"All right." Her voice cracked. She cried. "But you can't look at me when I tell you. You can't."

Domenic slid down beside her. He fixed his gaze on his own trash bin. "I won't."

"I really believed you back when we were kids, when you promised there was some greatness in store for us. You were so sure, you made it hard not to get my hopes up. And well, we were so powerful, weren't we? Even then." Her laugh was weak and wet. "And after it was *me* who had to save us from Syarthis that day, I was still stuck hoping for that great future you talked about. I waited for you to get better. I encouraged you. I hid everything about my job from you because I was so scared of upsetting you. And shit, I was mad at you then, too. Because I was killing myself trying to prove to everyone that I wasn't going to . . . to *explode*. And you were just . . ."

"Pathetic," he finished for her hoarsely.

She didn't disagree. "And when it was *you* who bonded with Valmordion . . . well, I thought we were all fucked. Then Peak couldn't shut up about you stopping that scurge in Oldermere. And suddenly, you've slayed one of the Dire Three. You're yelling at Sharpe, something I've sure as hell never managed to do. You're some whole new, capable person! And every time I heard a reporter call you a hero, I could've thrown up."

Domenic thought he was about to. "I'm so sorry, Hanna. I—"

"*No.* Don't apologize," she choked. "I'm not done."

Again, he obeyed, but it was getting harder not to look at her. His vision swam.

"I knew you were supposed to die, obviously. Iseul and Peak, they wanted to tell you. Glynn sure wanted to tell Ellery. But I told Sharpe you couldn't know. That you couldn't handle it."

Domenic held his breath so she wouldn't hear how hard she'd struck him.

"I meant it. But I also thought maybe, if I tried hard enough, Syarthis and I could find a way to save you. And I-I've tried *so* hard. I've watched all the past Chosen Ones burn in Syarthis's Archives so many times that sometimes when I look at you, I just see . . ." She sobbed.

He couldn't play along anymore. He grabbed her and pulled her against him. She was comically small in his arms, and feverishly warm compared to the cold press of the pavement.

"It's okay, Hanna. You don't need to save me."

"I will *always* be trying to save you."

Overhead, the icicles weeped, droplets splattering on their cheeks.

He pressed his forehead to the top of her hair. "You were right to be mad at me. I should've at least asked what it was like to wield Syarthis, no matter how ashamed I was that it was you who had to. I should've been better for you first. But do you know what kept me in the vigil chamber when Glynn told us all we could leave?"

She uttered some incomprehensible noise against his chest.

"You. The Danmere Duo. That I'd promised you I'd be someone worth hoping for." Domenic floundered for the right words. "I mean, all of Alderland needs me to play a hero. And fuck, that's not me. But from that first press conference, whenever I thought of a real hero I could pretend to be, someone who actually inspired me to be brave, I immediately thought of you."

Hanna shoved him away. "*Ugh.* You're so sentimental. It's disgusting."

Domenic laughed. "Yeah, well, you could've worn a fresher shirt."

She made a rude gesture, which only made him laugh harder. Then she scooted around to face him and leaned her head against the brick wall. "I think if I wasn't so determined to resent you, I would've seen it years ago. That you didn't bond with Syarthis because you really were destined for something else. Having now spent a thousand hours with your predecessors, I'm pretty sure you and I didn't find Valmordion thawing that night in the Vault. I think it *started* thawing that night, like it sensed you near it." Domenic blinked—he'd never considered that. "Also, you were a weird kid."

"Yeah, I was."

"Kind of a bummer to admit that my destiny is now Sy's, though. What? Don't look so creeped out. I don't get a nickname for my wand?"

Domenic remolded his expression. But he couldn't quite lift his eyes from Syarthis, still grasped in her hand. "How bad has it been?"

"Eh."

"I'm serious. Please be honest. You know I've always worried about you."

Hanna gulped and twisted Syarthis in her lap. "I might not be the *Chosen One,* but I'm a good magician."

"I never suggested otherwise."

"I know. I just . . . I don't hate Syarthis. I know I should. And part of me does. Not a day goes by when I don't wonder if I could've crawled to it sooner. But Syarthis isn't like the other Living Wands. I could wander its Archives my whole life and barely scratch its surface. Do you know what it's like to have lived the most intimate memories of people who've been dead for centuries? To see the country debate the same problems over and over? Sometimes I want to strangle Sharpe. He's the kid, not me."

As she spoke, Syarthis's tongue coiled around her pointer, and she twirled it absentmindedly, pleasantly.

"I don't pretend it *thrills* me the way people duck for cover when Sy and I walk by," she continued. "I can feel their fear, you know. I can feel their hearts quicken, their muscles tighten. And the ones who don't run away, they call themselves brave. They have no idea how corporeal emotions are. That when I focus, it's all of a nudge, and they're breathing easier. We—"

"Hanna," he said tightly. "You can't do that."

"You mean I *shouldn't*."

"Yeah. You shouldn't."

"Well, it's either that or I'm alone," she challenged. "The day Iseul retires, either one person doesn't flee from me, or it's just me and Sy."

Domenic didn't know how to answer. He couldn't tell if she wanted him to condemn her to be alone or give her permission for it.

"So our suspects," Domenic spoke instead. "Kester's clean?"

Hanna shifted out of the way of a dripping icicle. "Oh, Kester's just bitter at the Order for not accepting them as a kid. So they brave it up here and throw parties and commiserate with fellow academy rejects or dropouts. Not exactly a mastermind. And that Norwood kid. Based on Kester's memories, all he's done is show up here a week ago and blabber about Ellery. Who's his ex-girlfriend, by the way. That's why he hates you."

Domenic stifled a smirk; how ironic that the once king of the academy favorites was jealous of *him*. Then he forced himself to sober.

"But Kester and Norwood both think they're Winter magicians," Domenic said. "Everyone in that bar does. Are they right?"

"Yeah. I think they are."

He wrung out his hands. "So what do we do next, then? We still have no suspects on the traitor. We—"

"We do have a suspect, Dom. Kester wants Ellery to side with them. To make a case for Winter. To—"

He jumped to his feet. "No. Ellery already told me everything."

"Really? And you still don't think—"

"I said no, all right? It's not her. I know it's not her."

Hanna grimaced. "So it's like that?"

Domenic had never admitted it to himself, but he couldn't deny it. Of course it was like that. It had always been like that.

"I'm sorry I was such an asshole about the two of you," Hanna said. "I mean it. I see why you like her. You've always liked her. But what if you really are destined to fight? Half the Council thinks so. Kester thinks so. And if it came down to you or her, I'd take a torch to Ellery myself—"

"*Don't* say it. Fuck, I love you, and I'm sure you mean it, but—"

"Well, what else am I supposed to hope for? Tell me, Dom! Tell me what to hope for! Because I'm not giving up. Not until you're gone."

Domenic considered telling her that the past wasn't a guarantee of his future. But after poisoning Hanna with false hope for years, he couldn't bring himself to speak. Not without being sure.

Yet without a word from him, Hanna stared vacantly into the distance. When she squeezed her eyes shut, so, too, did Syarthis.

Then their eyes shifted to him.

"I'm sorry," she muttered. "If that's how you feel about her, I . . . I don't have to tell the Council about the seeds, about Kester, about any of it. I can keep looking for the traitor. There's still plenty of Order magicians we haven't questioned. And there's less than two weeks of Winter left. Some cataclysms take years. We could still have time."

Domenic managed to nod, even as his doubt warred inside him—doubt that he and Ellery would live, doubt that he and Ellery would die. But worse was his *hatred,* such hatred. Not at Hanna, but at everything. Everything except the one person he was potentially meant to hate. The true monster he'd maybe been born to slay.

Domenic paced, yet as he strayed onto trampled, snow-packed grass, his muscles automatically locked tight. His magic simmered. Like it knew he stood on Winter's land.

A horrible realization dawned on him.
If Ellery Caldwell was truly his enemy.
If he couldn't kill her.
If he loved her.
Then all along, Summer's traitor had been him.

XXXIV
Ellery
WINTER

The phone rang in the dead of night, rousing Ellery from her uneasy slumber. She fumbled for the light. After returning from Nordmere, no sooner had she changed out of her traveling clothes and curled up with a magazine than she'd promptly passed out on her living room couch. Although she'd lived in her Order-subsidized apartment for a month, it still didn't feel like home.

The three days they'd spent in Nordmere had been an utter nightmare. But even after their confrontation with Julian and Kester, Hanna had insisted they remain in the city until they'd combed through nearly every alleyway in search of Summer's traitor, of Kythion, of anything that might prevent the trip from being a failure. But multiple visits to the alban tree from Maltherius's vision had proven fruitless, and the journey back to Gallamere had been a tense, near-silent affair.

"Hello?" she answered the phone.

"Hey. It's me. We need to talk."

It was the first time Domenic had called her since before the border's fall.

Ellery reached for Iskarius on the coffee table, then hesitated. She longed to feel his closeness, but after Nordmere, she didn't know if she could bear it.

"Oh, now you want to talk? After you confessed all those feelings at the bar and then haven't even made eye contact with me in *days*? Why should I care what you have to say when you've made it impossible for me to ever believe you? So good night, and—"

"No, no, no, don't hang up! I know I've been avoiding you, but that's because I've been keeping something from you."

The direness of his tone kept her on the line. "Whatever it is, just tell me."

As he spoke, time seemed to slow. She was suddenly, acutely aware of the tiniest of sensations: her bare feet on the hardwood floors; the snow that had blown in through the open windows as she slept, clinging to her collarbones; the rustle of her silk slip against her skin.

The receiver trembled in her hand. Oblivion descended, not the quick slash of a scythe but a cruel crush of inevitability. She felt eerily, pristinely calm.

"So that's it, then," Ellery said once he finished. "We were never supposed to be heroes. We were supposed to be martyrs."

"You're sure?" Domenic whispered.

"What Hanna told you didn't leave much room for interpretation."

"I know, but you really think *this* is what we've been meant for? Something . . . something *terrible*?"

She chuckled darkly. "I think part of me always knew."

At last Ellery understood the final wall between her and Glynn. If he'd suspected all along that she was Chosen, then he'd always known that one day, destiny would ask her to die.

"If you're so sure," Domenic said weakly, "then I guess I really have just been kidding myself."

After that, neither he nor Ellery spoke for a while, instead only listening to the other breathing, still breathing, at least for now.

"I wanted it to be different," she said matter-of-factly, as though she were talking about someone else. It almost felt like it. "I wanted it so much."

"So did I. If only the cataclysm had come that first night of Winter. I would've made the sacrifice then. It would've been easy."

"I would've done it, too. It's a simple equation, isn't it? Just us, so that everyone else can be safe. Only us."

"So you're ready, then?"

The question hung dreadfully between them.

At last, Ellery reached for Iskarius. She felt Domenic instantly, a warm caress across her cheek, her neck, as though he'd joined her on the couch. The lamps throughout the room brightened. The snow-clogged fireplace sputtered to life.

It was a lovely ache to feel his presence, so familiar and comforting. But it melted her eerie calm along with the frost.

"I-I don't want to die," she admitted. "And I know how selfish it is, how pathetic, but—"

"It's not any of those things," he cut in. "It's not . . . it's not *fair*."

She wished Domenic was truly beside her, so they could touch each other, hold each other. Maybe that would be enough to ease the pain of every opportunity they'd wasted, to mourn their useless dreams of a future that would never come to pass.

"If this is all we'll ever get, then I'm done caring about being noble," she said. "Do we have to be heroes tonight?"

"No," Domenic murmured. "We don't."

Ellery brushed spare snow off her lap and fixed her hair, as if this was just another of their late-night calls, commiserating about the paparazzi sleeping outside their doors or Sharpe referring to the fifty-one-year-old Prime Minister as a "girl."

"I almost forgot how it feels to talk to you like this," he said playfully. "With your magic this close, it's like you're right here, lying next to me."

Ellery flushed. "So you're in bed, huh?"

"I might be. Where are you?"

"I fell asleep on the couch." She fiddled with her necklace. "You know, for all the time we've spent together, you've never actually visited my apartment."

"I imagine it as Gallamere's finest. A penthouse. Huge windows.

Posters of Kent Sinclair all over the walls." She was impressed—finally Domenic had remembered a movie star's name.

"So you've been imagining it, then."

"More times than I care to confess. I'm almost jealous. You, a Chosen One, living it up in the best accommodations the Order can buy. Then there's me, a Chosen One, sleeping in the same bed as when I was thirteen."

"Well, it seems only right after you gave me a grand tour that I return the favor." Ellery enchanted her phone cord until it elongated and piled on the floor. Then she wandered through the apartment, her footsteps muffled on the plush carpet. "There's a fireplace I don't use, a kitchen I don't cook in. A study filled with books I've never read. The dining room, for all the entertaining I do. And the walk-in closet."

"Your favorite part, I'm sure."

"It certainly gets the most use." Ellery strolled inside it, admiring the racks of designer clothes, the jewelry drawers, the shoes lined in neat perfect pairs along the floor. It was more than anyone could reasonably wear in a lifetime. Not that Ellery had much of a lifetime remaining.

"Now I'm thinking about you in that dress from the Solstice Gala," Domenic drawled. "I remember the color of it, that bluish-purple. You look quite striking in Valmordion's filter, you know."

Though he couldn't see her, she felt suddenly, tantalizingly exposed in her lace-trimmed slip. His warmth kissed her bare shoulders, and a heat kindled in her center that had nothing to do with Summer's magic.

"Sorry," he said, sounding anything but. "Did I fluster you?"

"How can you tell?"

"I don't feel the cold of you breathing." His words had an oddly serious weight. "Do I look different to you when you hold Iskarius?"

She pondered that while she wistfully dragged her hand down the clothing rack, relishing the softness of cashmeres and wools and satins. "You're . . . vivid."

"Oh?"

"There's pink on your cheeks, gold on your brow, red on your mouth, purple beneath your eyes. It's like you're somehow brighter than the rest of the world. And I know we crossed paths sometimes at school, but from the first time I looked at you, really looked at you, I've been unable to look away. As if my eyes are drawn to you. As if you're a . . ."

An intrusive thought needled in her mind, in Kester's voice:

A target.

"A what?" he pressed.

"A focal point," she managed.

Ellery had tried to dismiss the idea that she and Domenic might be on opposing sides of a thousand-year war. But after so long without another prophecy piece, she needed to explore every possible path, no matter how desperately she wished it to be a dead end.

"Now it's your turn," she said coyly. "How do I look to you, when you hold Valmordion?"

"Hm, fair is fair, though it'll be hard to find the words to do you justice," he said. "You look like . . . like a diamond. Every slope of you is like a cut. Some parts of you, your cheekbones, your hair, your eyes, they shine a thousand shades of silver. But your shadows, the ones across your neck, your jaw, they have layers and layers. The entire world is dull in comparison, as if I'm supposed to notice you. As if I could find you no matter where you are."

The heat in her kindled more brightly. Yet just as Ellery was ready to cast her doubts aside, Domenic added, "You know, maybe we should've realized it as soon as I found you under the alban tree. That we were . . ."

"What?" she blurted. "What were you going to say?"

The silence between them shuddered. Ellery had spent weeks learning the patterns of his breathing. Now he exhaled against her cheek—slow, deliberate, measured.

He knew what she was doing. Except rather than accuse her, he answered, his voice oddly smooth, "Smitten."

He was fishing too. Which meant he'd also considered that they were supposed to be enemies. Which meant that after weeks of playing their parts for everyone else, this entire conversation was built on a ruse.

She should call them both out; clear this bullshit aside. But even if they were wrong, merely voicing the possibility would be crossing a line. They would never be able to take it back.

"So, to resume the tour," Domenic ventured finally. "Is there anything else in your apartment to show me?"

"I suppose all that's left is the bedroom."

The warmth of his magic heightened, as if she felt the very flush flooding over his skin. Apparently even their faux flirting could have a real effect.

"Sorry," Ellery echoed him from earlier, pushing open her bedroom door. "Did I fluster you?"

"Fluster, no. Intrigue, maybe." Then he tossed out, "So what was my giveaway, dear?"

"Your heart. It's pounding."

The lamps on the nightstands flickered—he'd noticed the strain in her voice. Anxiously, she held her breath, but of course he could sense that, too.

"Lie down," Domenic commanded, and she didn't know if his intensity was from want or worry.

Ellery curled up on the bed and tucked the phone beneath her ear. Her heart hammered in more ways than one.

"Close your eyes," he instructed. "Where do you feel me?"

Her eyelids fluttered shut. His breath skimmed across her cheek, as if he lay inches away.

"You're right beside me," she answered. "You always are."

"And are you lying on your back?"

Ellery turned over.

Immediately, she understood the point of his suggestion—she'd never considered the specifics of his presence, only that it was always so close, tantalizingly close. But his magic swept down the back of her neck.

She'd never wondered why, if they were meant to fight side by side, his presence was always behind her.

Her magic chilled, crackling beneath her skin as she clutched Iskarius.

Domenic didn't acknowledge it. He didn't need to—he felt it. Just like she felt his.

"Imagine me touching you," Ellery spoke next.

The heat suddenly heightened enough to burn. "In any particular way or . . . ?"

"Imagine I'm kissing your neck." A twinge of longing escaped with her words as she remembered their kiss at the solstice. They'd felt so invincible then. "How does your magic feel?"

"It feels stronger when you touch me. But stronger's not a good enough word for it. It's like my magic flares when you're near. Like my every sense is magnified. Like a fight-or-flight response." Domenic must've caught how that sounded, because he chuckled hastily. "No, I'm not doing a good job at describing it. Because I—I love it. How couldn't I? It's electrifying. Your magic pours over me like ice water, but inside, I burn like a star."

His excuses only deepened her dread.

"Imagine that I sweep your hair aside so I can return the favor," he went on. "I trace my finger down the back of that dress. How does *your* magic feel?"

Ellery let the fantasy play out. Her body responded, so alert, so alive. She wanted to melt in his arms, but she wasn't sure she should. Suddenly the delusion shattered, and Ellery pictured herself engulfed in a brutal blaze, charring away to ash.

"D-do you hear what we're saying?" she gasped. "Are we wrong to like this? Are we really meant to be—"

"No, don't say it," Domenic choked. "Please."

"But we're both thinking it," she countered. "You've been fishing just as much as I have."

"Only because I've been looking for proof it isn't true."

"And did you find any? Because all this conversation has done for me is make it harder to deny. Maybe we've only been fooling ourselves from the start."

"I . . . I know how this looks. Believe me, the thought of it's been torturing me for weeks. But this traitor business, champion business—it's all just getting into our heads, making us consider things that don't even make sense. The original prophecy called for *peace*. So please, El. Tell me you see how wrong this is. Tell me you're still sure we're in this together."

Ellery touched the empty space across the bed, the duvet still perfectly made.

"I have a confession," she said despairingly. "I know I told you Gallamere was my home, but I think I was wrong, Dom. I think it's you."

He uttered a fragile, hopeful sound.

"I'll come over," he said urgently. "I'll leave right now. Because we're in this together. Of course we are. So say the word, and I'm there."

Yes hovered on the tip of her tongue. But she couldn't be with him like this, doubting, dreading, wondering if they would die alone, or together, or in each other's arms, or on each other's swords.

"Don't," she forced out, and hung up.

XXXV
DOMENIC
WINTER

Domenic hung up the phone with a shaking hand. Always, always he and Ellery were of one mind. But if she was that close to giving up . . .

Phantom red tinted the edges of his vision, and he braced a hand against his nightstand. He was unraveling at the same seams he'd sworn he'd sealed.

He crept out of his room. He meant to go to Iseul's, but to his surprise, a light still shined from downstairs. He descended the steps to find Iseul curled on a sofa in the parlor, her pajamas and reading glasses on, the *Gazette* in her hands, a tea tray upon the coffee table.

"You're still up," she said.

"So are you. Calling family?" Sometimes Iseul woke or retired at strange hours to place calls to the other side of the world.

"No, not tonight. I've been waiting for Hanna. I don't like that she went right to the Citadel after dropping you off. The Council is debriefing your mission to Nordmere first thing in the morning. Does she never plan to come home? She needs to rest. And so I can only assume, probably to bathe . . ."

"I tried to tell her, but, well, she insisted."

Why? There's no one at the Citadel. At least let it wait until morning. Until Syarthis and I find Summer's traitor, this never ends, Dom.

He hadn't been brave enough to tell her not to bother.

Domenic glanced at the grandfather clock—it was a quarter past three. He was exhausted. Iseul was exhausted, yawning and sinking into the throw pillows. But he still needed to be brave tonight.

"I need to talk to you," he said seriously. "Not as—as you and me. As Councilor and Chosen One."

Iseul's brow creased as she scrutinized him. "All right."

She patted the spot beside her on the sofa. Calynia's enchantment draped a blanket over the cushions, welcoming him.

He stayed standing.

"It's me," he choked. "I'm Summer's traitor."

She jolted. "What? Why would you ever think such a thing?"

"Because I'm in love with Ellery."

Iseul hitched her breath, and when she responded, she spoke slowly, carefully. Like a politician. "I need you to help me understand. A few weeks ago, you were adamant that we trust Ellery. Now—"

"I know what I said. And Ellery would never endanger Alderland, not on purpose. But lately, I can't get the question out of my head: What if Summer's champion and Winter's champion have been enemies from the start? The evidence seems split both ways. Ellery doesn't want to believe it, but she can't dismiss it, either. And I . . . I don't know what to believe. I don't trust myself to be objective."

Iseul set the *Gazette* on the coffee table. "But how does that make *you* the traitor?"

"Because if she's my enemy, if I have to kill her to save Alderland, I-I can't. I *won't*." He paced across the carpet. "When I'm with her, everything else in the world dims. My body angles toward her. My magic reaches for her. Even now, she's a mile across the city, but a mile—a mile is meaningless! When we both hold our wands, she might as well be in my bed for the way I feel her breathing down my neck. And I don't care. Her hands could be in mine or around my throat, and all I would be thinking about is that I'm touching her. So, if I'm destined to save everyone, then of course I'm the traitor. I'd die and let the whole world die with me so long as the only person I saved was her."

While Iseul fell silent, Calynia attempted to tend to them both. The poker stoked the fireplace. The kettle poured Domenic his own cup of tea.

"You're not the only one who fears your feelings get in the way of your duty," Iseul said at last. "Because I don't know how to speak to you as a Councilor right now—I really don't. I can only consider this as someone who loves you, and hearing how much pain you're in, it breaks my heart."

"Right, hence why it was easier not to tell me about the whole sacrificial lamb thing."

She paled. "Hanna told you?"

"Yeah, but don't sweat it. I'm over it. Already found myself a fate worse than death to worry about."

"Oh, Dom," she said hoarsely. "I'm so sorry I didn't tell you sooner. I wanted to, but—"

"No, it's fine! I get it! You need me to protect you, but I've had lifelong performance issues. So don't apologize. But don't give me pity either."

"Then what *do* you want? Fury? Disgust? How could that possibly be preferable to you?"

"Because I'm not a child anymore! You don't need to be gentle with me. You should—you should yell at me! Tell me to stop acting like this! Tell me what I'm supposed to do!"

Iseul barked out a laugh. "Goodness, is that all?" Then she heaved out a sigh and folded her hands neatly on her lap. "Sit, Domenic."

"I'm better standing."

"You are exhausted. *Sit.*"

And so he did.

She faced him solemnly. "I cannot tell you what to do next, because, as you said, you're not a child anymore. But if you'd like my *opinion,* I'd tell you that you're only human. No one can expect you to be more than that."

"But I *am* more than that." He swatted aside the blanket trying to wrestle him into comfort. "I know it's hard for you to understand. You've seen me at my worst. But if you saw what I really am, what I'm capable of, you wouldn't recognize me. I'm more than just a magician. Or at least, I'm supposed to be. I have to be."

Domenic waited, yearning for her to finally see.

Instead, Iseul clenched her jaw. "Did Tenney ever tell you why the two of us went our separate ways?"

"No," he answered, surprised. Iseul never brought up their divorce.

"He'd just hurt his knee, and he was lucky that was all he hurt. You've seen how he fights, the way he rushes into battle without pausing to think."

"Because he has to. The other NDC officers all look up to—"

"No. Trust me, Domenic, I've known Tenney since the academy. He can call it duty, or destiny, or survivor's guilt, but the only reason he fights recklessly is because he wants to." She shook her head as she reached for her teacup. "After he got hurt, I told him it was time he retire. It was past time, really. But he refused. Even if that meant he was going to die on the battlefield." She grimaced. "In his version of events, I made him leave, and he had no choice. But he's the one who made the choice. Because he likes being a hero."

Domenic frowned, unsure how such a word could be flung as an insult.

"What does any of that have to do with me?" he demanded. "I *don't* have a choice."

"But if you did, you'd really choose her over the whole country?"

Domenic's hands trembled, and finally, he tugged the blanket over his shoulders. "I don't know. She's one person. But everyone else I'd be saving—they don't know me. They sure like your version of me, with my talking points and suits. They literally line candles up on our sidewalk. They buy stamps with my face on it. And I don't give one shit about them!"

"You don't mean that."

"Don't I? And the Order, it's not like we're some perfect institution! There's so much we don't know. Up North, there's no scurges anymore. The land grows food, tons of food, without having to rely on magic. And all this time, there might've been two types of magicians!"

Though Domenic and Hanna had agreed not to expose Ellery's meeting with the Winter magicians, what they'd learned still mattered, could change *everything*.

Iseul blinked. "Those conditions do sound better than in our reports. And as for types of magicians, it's something to investigate, certainly. After tomorrow's debriefing—"

"But will you even listen, then? You shut Ellery down before."

"Do you realize how much you've asked us to reconsider? Until a few weeks ago, we'd never thought it possible to have one Winter magician, let alone . . . let alone many."

"Yeah, well, you didn't bother paying attention. You didn't . . ." He didn't know if that was fair. He didn't know what he was saying.

Iseul returned her empty teacup to the tray. "Dom, I'm not going to claim the Order is perfect. But I didn't join the Council to perpetuate its problems—I joined to help fix them. My parents were proud when we learned I was a magician. Even if magicians elsewhere don't use wands, being one is still celebrated, and there are many methods for casting spells. But I had to convince my parents to let me enroll in Alderland's national academy. When my father moved us here for his work when I was a toddler, my family didn't intend to stay here, to put down roots. And at the time, the country saw the national academy as prestigious, but also ruthless. And they were right to. Students went to extreme lengths to bond with Living Wands. We worked ourselves sick. And our classmates were rarely our friends—just our competition. After Smith and Hoover were found dead the week before Calynia's vigil, and I was attacked . . . No one understood why I stayed, least of all my protective family. But Alderland *was* my home, and I dedicated my whole career to helping change the Order's culture and the country's perception of it. I won't pretend that solving that problem solves our every problem, but that change once felt impossible. And whatever feels impossible next, we can change that, too."

Domenic couldn't bring himself to argue. Even if the Order had virtues worth defending, even if its flaws could improve, that wasn't enough to justify choosing it. Not for such a price.

The red bled out from the edges of his vision.

"Even if I'm destined to kill her," he whispered, "it still doesn't feel right."

She squeezed his shoulder. "Tell me—after all this agonizing you've done over being the traitor, have you heard the next words of the prophecy? Has Ellery?"

He swallowed. "No."

"Then what good is it taking yourself down such a dark path?"

He jerked out of her grasp. "Because isn't this what I have to do? Follow every piece of the prophecy? Consider everything destiny has been trying to tell me?"

"Dom, I know to be a Chosen One is to heed the words of destiny. But even if this *is* what destiny wants from you, please, don't depend on it to rationalize your choices. Because if you do this believing destiny made the choice for you, then I'm scared you won't be able to live with it afterward."

"Would that be so bad?"

Iseul stared at him despairingly, but Domenic didn't retract a single word. Ellery could tear out his heart just as he stabbed a knife into hers. Let destiny play semantics about who won or lost. What did it matter if they killed each other so long as they died together?

"You're . . . You're not in a good headspace to be making any decision right now, Dom," Iseul told him cautiously.

"Oh, so you're saying it's not healthy to keep imagining what Floyd Wilder will say if my girlfriend kills me in a great, earth-shaking duel? 'Book your one-way passages now, folks. Because the forecast today is fucking freezing with a chance of gigantic monsters, just like tomorrow, and the next day, and the next. Courtesy of Domenic Barrow, Chosen One, who we now know did actually spend his whole life thinking with his—'"

Iseul uttered an exasperated sound. "Can we not joke about this? Because I-I'm really trying to give you what you need, but I don't know how to give you that."

Her voice cracked, and a second blanket drifted over to wrap around her shoulders. Domenic cursed under his breath—now he'd lost all ability to laugh too. What a tragedy it was to love him.

He groaned and lowered his forehead against his kneecaps. "Sorry."

She hugged him. "It's all right. This isn't a choice to rush into, nor is it one you need to. There's no reason to think the cataclysm is imminent, and Summer is only one week away. Maybe once we're all breathing easier, we'll have the perspective to find the true answer to the prophecy."

"Fine."

"And you do need to sleep. You need to take care of yourself."

"Uh-huh."

"And . . . if you can't find something worth fighting for, then you should at least consider the cost of what it is you're dying for."

Domenic let those words haunt him for several more hours.

He stalked his most hated streets of Gallamere under a cloaking enchantment, watching the city slowly awaken from its slumber. He scowled invisibly at an elderly couple strolling arm-in-arm. He silently cursed at a wailing toddler in a stroller. He considered shouting at the dog yapping in his owner's arms, outrageously small, wearing a handknit sweater. He almost did. He sort of grumbled a bit.

He hated all of them.

He did.

He did.

He stormed his way to Gallamere Gardens. He lay in the snow as the pale Winter sun kissed his cheek, and he thought about how much he hated the city, how much he hated the cold, hated the way the Gardens looked in the cold, hated that he still missed the woods at home, that he somehow missed things he'd never gotten just as much as he missed things he'd never have.

Until he couldn't take it anymore, and he cast the Gardens into bloom.

He cast an entire menagerie of enchantments on the Gold Line. He made mailboxes belch and mirrors play dress-up and cobblestones squirm. He (quite artfully) landscaped around the academy's student center. He made Professor Clark's textbook swear so crudely that entire lecture halls of second years would faint. He immortalized himself in a Council-wing restroom. He restored the Hook Up Halls to all their original glory.

He waited two hours, lurking, all to watch triumphantly as a single weary traveler emerged from the subway and marveled at the bespelled lampposts brightening their route home.

There. Even if Domenic had made the hero's choice, the awful choice, it was truly their City of Magic now.

XXXVI
ELLERY
WINTER

The first day of Summer was Alderland's most joyous holiday. From the moment dawn broke, snow melted, and the entire country bloomed in instantaneous awakening. Fresh leaves budded on barren trees. Flower petals drifted through the countryside like confetti, perfuming the breeze. And in the Gallamere Gardens, an enormous picnic heralded a weeklong jubilee.

But this year, tension permeated the crowd. Although the band onstage doggedly played the national anthem, no one clapped or sang along. Vendors fruitlessly hawked balloons and hot dogs. People shivered in the dim glow of the lampposts.

Gallamere's leaders sat on risers behind the band, Summer frocks readied beneath their thick coats. Ellery sat among them, trapped in an outfit that didn't suit her in a color she didn't like. She tugged anxiously at her necklace.

Ellery glanced at Glynn amidst the rest of the Council across the stage. When she, Domenic, and Hanna had returned from Nordmere, they'd told the Councilors about Winter territory and its magicians, omitting Ellery's theft of the winterghast hearts. Only Glynn knew otherwise.

You're on the precipice of a breakthrough, Ellery, Glynn had promised her. *But the rest of the Council will be more amenable to the notion of Winter wands after Summer comes. Just be patient for one more week. Everything will feel better then.*

As much as she wanted to trust Glynn, he'd lied to her about the deaths of every previous Chosen One. And so had the rest of the Council. She hadn't told any of them she knew; she didn't want platitudes and excuses. Especially when their scrutiny had only grown after the failed mission North. Even now, they glanced at her as though she might spontaneously morph into a winterghast in heels and a designer dress.

They will never change their minds, Ellery repeated. *The Order will use me, because they need me. But they'll hate me all the same.*

No. Not all of them.

Domenic sat beside her, the heat of his magic a distracting press against her neck. He wore the garb of Summer's Chosen: a crisp collared shirt with a jaunty green vest. He fiddled with a clump of dandelions, mangling their stems. He did not look at her.

What I'm really fighting for—what I've always been fighting for—is this, he'd told her. *You and me.*

Such a future had always been impossible. Even if they saved Alderland together, they were still doomed to die. But it would be an even worse fate to betray him, and despite all her doubts, she could never do so without proof. Maybe once Summer came, with the winterghasts gone and the country safe for another year, they could finally find the traitor. Maybe the next piece of the prophecy would put their paranoia to rest.

Even the best she could hope for was still a tragedy.

The first rays of light reached above the horizon like outstretched fingers rising from a grave. The sun crested above the Gardens, and the national anthem crescendoed along with it. People clasped their hands together, waiting, wishing.

Ellery held her breath. Domenic clamped the flowers in his fist.

Seconds ticked by, then dragged. But the barren trees didn't bud.

The snowy meadow didn't melt.

The band cut off, horns and woodwinds wailing in a final, frantic cry before falling silent.

And Ellery *knew.*

It was unprecedented. It was unfathomable. But Summer wasn't coming.

Murmurs rose in an anthem of their own. People called out questions, some pulling each other close, some breaking away from the crowd. Children began to cry, their families too aghast to soothe them. For once, even the reporters didn't lift their cameras. Instead they stared at the gray sky, the frozen ground, the lifeless foliage.

Then, as one, their stares swiveled to Ellery.

She felt the collective force of their fear, a crushing, foreboding pressure. Instinctively, her defense mechanism kicked in. She reached for Iskarius. And she reached for Domenic.

As their hands brushed, they met each other's gazes.

He'd never been good at concealing his feelings. Especially not from her. And she knew what lurked in the quiver of his lips, in the haunted depths of his eyes.

Defeat.

Her heart shattered, and yet Ellery endured, as she always did. She cloaked herself, and she fled.

XXXVII
Domenic
WINTER

In the apartment lobby, the bellhop stared at the drifting snow outside and worried at his wedding band. The radio crackled a death rattle.

The bellhop didn't notice the revolving door spin. But he glanced up as the flickering chandelier brightened, and inexplicable warmth pressed against his side. Yet just as suddenly, the cold returned, the lobby dimmed, and Domenic took the private elevator to the penthouse.

He dropped his illusion. His fingers flexed around Valmordion, and even after the elevator halted, he swore the ground swayed beneath him.

A frigid draft wafted from the crack of the doors.

Warily, hopefully, he slipped Valmordion into its sheath.

Then, before he even rang the bell, the doors opened, revealing Ellery. Tear tracks glistened down her cheeks. Like him, she still wore her costume from Alderland's most disastrous holiday, and—

And she held Iskarius.

"Let me go, Dom," she warned. "You know we can't do this here."

Yet Ellery made no move to stop him as he brushed past her. Despite the flurries outside, her apartment windows were thrown open, and flakes accumulated atop the sills and dusted the floor. The phone dangled off its hook. A suitcase lay open on the carpet.

"And what would we be doing, exactly?" he murmured.

"Do you really need me to say it?"

"Well, if you're so sure we have to fight, why are you running away?"

"What else would you have me do?" She tilted her head up to look at him, blinking rapidly. "Do you think I *want* to run away from the city I love, from the people I only ever wanted to protect? Of course I don't! But I've been waiting for Summer to come, thinking maybe then, we'd find proof one way or the other. But Summer *didn't come*! That hasn't happened since the Thirty Years' Chill. So if that isn't a sign of how badly we messed up, I-I don't know what is."

"No. I know it looks bad. Believe me, Summer not coming, I'm terrified, too. But—"

"*Don't*. Do you know how many times you've gotten my hopes up just to break my heart? So just please, stop. You're only making it worse for both of us."

Domenic flinched. But rather than apologize, his response was slow and venomous, as suited the villain of her story.

"Well, I'm glad I broke your heart," he hissed, leaning down close. "Let's call it practice for when I stop it."

Ellery balked. "Really? This is how you want to talk about us killing each other?"

"What, was there another cue card I was supposed to read? Is there a fucking script?" He stalked away and threw up his arms. "Or would it be better to be classy about it? Should we shake hands beforehand? Offer a kiss of good luck?"

"Actually, yes, it's better that you be an ass about it! Maybe then it won't hurt so much when you're dead."

He barked out a laugh. "Oh, so you assume you'll kill me?"

"You assumed you'd kill *me* first. I was only returning the favor."

"If it was just a matter of you and me, I'd happily let you, dear!"

He must've finally said something unforgivable, because Ellery pointed Iskarius at him. Her shadow writhed upon the carpet, and frost glimmered from each of her seething exhales.

Domenic's mouth went dry with fear. He licked his lips. "So you'd really just ignore what's left of the prophecy? Skip everything else and go right to the finale? That is so like you."

"Oh, this ought to be good."

"You accuse me of making you hope like it's a bad thing. But of course you think that, because you'd rather believe your life was doomed from the start than admit how badly you want a happy ending."

Ellery went utterly still.

"Of course I want a happy ending," she whispered. "But that's never been our story."

Domenic glanced outside at the flurries whipping past—a scene that should've been Summer. He staggered back as the world blurred, dreamlike. Yet Ellery remained the irrevocable focal point of his vision.

He swallowed, his hand hovering near Valmordion. "I already made my choice. That if we have to do this, I'd choose duty. But even now, it doesn't feel right."

"It never will," Ellery rasped.

"No, i-it's more than that." Domenic struggled for the correct words, knowing how pathetic he sounded. There was no honor in denial. "I've always known what my magic was, even when I tried to run from it. It's instinct. But ever since that night in Mercester Square, my instinct has always been . . ."

He didn't finish. He didn't need to. Ellery's expression went stricken.

Because of course, her instinct had always been him, too.

Like an explosion of sunlight, a sudden, delirious thought burst within Domenic's mind. His hope bloomed like it never had. And he gasped at the perfect simplicity of it. The *rightness* of it. Even his magic responded, smoldering feverishly, until he burned with conviction.

"We've always been the same, haven't we?" he said. "We always know what the other is thinking. We always understand how the other feels. Because we're the only people who can truly see each other for who we are."

Ellery's lips quivered, but she didn't speak. He could glimpse his hope reflected in her gaze, but there was also pain, far too much of it.

He walked cautiously toward her.

"You think I could've slayed Eledrium and Maltherius without you? You think I could've stood up to Sharpe, smiled through any of those interviews, stopped assuming I was a failure, if you hadn't been there beside me? The other Chosen Ones might've sacrificed themselves to save Alderland. But destiny didn't just give us our wands—it gave us each other. And before I ever believed in destiny, I believed in us."

Step after step, he closed the distance between them. He wiped his own watery eyes on his sleeve.

"What if everything we've ever felt, everything we've spent so long punishing ourselves for, has always been what will save us? What if I save you, and you save me, and we save everyone else?"

He halted before her. Iskarius wobbled in Ellery's grasp as she pointed it at his throat.

"Yeah, I know how it sounds," he continued fiercely. "Here I am, getting your hopes up again! Or worse, I sound like I've lost my fucking mind. And I don't care! I think we were meant for each other—to be a team, to fall in love, all of it! Because no matter what parts we got wrong, there's no version of this story where I don't fall in love with you."

Slowly, tortuously slowly, Ellery lowered Iskarius. Domenic's chest heaved, in triumph, in relief.

"I love you, too," she breathed.

Then Ellery dropped the wand, and they broke toward each other. Their mouths met, their kiss urgent and desperate and slick with tears, and Domenic crushed her against him until not an inch separated them, until not one force could've divided them. Immediately, Winter streamed through his veins like ice water, and he shuddered as his every nerve ignited. Even with his eyes closed, he saw color, thousands and thousands of shades of it. A future so vibrantly, undeniably bright.

He couldn't fathom how he'd never seen it before.

Of course Ellery Caldwell was his destiny. For if he had been made for anything, it was her. Her magic ran in his marrow. Her thumbprint was branded into his heart. And years and years from now, when his body lay to rest in the woods somewhere and fate had had its fill, they would know him, not from the wand frozen at his side, but from her name carved into his bones. That would come closer to the truth than any movie or monument could dare aspire. And that truth would be more than enough for him.

Wind blustered through the open window and whirled around them as they twined together. Its snowflakes glittered in Ellery's lashes, melted and steamed against Domenic's skin. Her fingers fumbled over the buttons of his vest, and Domenic shrugged off his suit jacket, bending so as not, for even a morsel of a second, to part his lips from hers. She moved onto his shirt collar next, and chills swept across him as the frigid air met his bare chest. Gently, he tugged at the straps of her dress, and he watched it ripple over the crests of her shoulders and fall, lost, into the umbra of her shadow. The slip beneath was petal-thin, and as his hands skimmed over where it hugged the slopes of her hips, he marveled that, in all the scenarios he'd contemplated when he'd come here, never had he considered this one, the only one imaginable, the only one inevitable.

Then, with his face cupped in her hands, Ellery guided him down the hallway. He stumbled, but he didn't dare draw away. Not even as they laughed at their clumsiness, at their euphoria.

The lamp on the nightstand brightened as Domenic sat on the bed.

Even as he reached toward her, the pads of his fingers just barely brushing the silk of her slip, she didn't move to him. She hovered there, her gaze roaming over his face. He knew his magic must be obvious, embers aglow in his eyes no different than her bright, unnatural blue. But he lifted his chin boldly, letting her study him. It was a relief not to prove himself. It was a relief to be beheld.

He smiled, and so did she.

Finally, she lowered onto him. Her fingers slid through his hair until she grasped ahold of him and tilted back his head. Her mouth met the pulse point beneath his jaw. He squeezed her thighs at both his sides, dizzy with the sensation of how soft she was. Of his hips crushed against hers. Of her cold so near his throat. And as her lips trailed down the hollow of his neck, his hands coaxed up the hem of her slip. He relished the sound Ellery uttered as he drew a slow, sinuous pattern across every curve of her, every groove of her spine. Until his hands found her back, and, holding her close, he laid her upon the sheets. Her hair cascaded around his face. Her tongue grazed his own.

It was so easy to get lost in this, in her. But he knew how little time they could spare, that not even he had the power to draw a curtain over the sun and grant them a whole, perfect night. Besides, he didn't want to rush. Because the truth was, despite the lurid gossip surrounding Domenic Barrow, he'd only ever slept with two people. And the first time, it'd been based only on the assumption that it was *not* his first time, and he hadn't been brave enough to correct her. After that, there no longer seemed a point in being precious.

Neither of those instances felt remotely like this.

Not that Ellery knew that history. And yet, as she grasped his belt buckle, he felt her whisper against his ear, "Is this all right?"

He drew away to look at her. "Of course it is." His breath fogged in the air. "Even if we were Chosen, I choose you. I'll always choose you."

"I'll always choose you, too," she echoed, without hesitation.

As time eddied past and fate kept course, one by one, lights blackened across the skyline. But Domenic didn't notice.

It was perfect all the same.

XXXVIII

ELLERY

WINTER

"It's always been so obvious, hasn't it?" Ellery murmured, her cheek against Domenic's chest. "This. Us."

Domenic gently brushed a tendril of hair from her face. "At the risk of sounding corny, I think part of me always knew."

In the dreamy dim of Ellery's bedside lamp, Alderland's Chosen Two lay curled beneath the covers, impossibly, inevitably together. The windows were shut. The shades were drawn. A clock ticked on the nightstand, marking time's passage in the outside world even as they carved out a fraction of it for their own.

"I do recall a confession of you fantasizing about me for five years." Ellery tilted her head back and smirked. "Come on. You can't expect to admit that and have me never tease you about it."

"I never said you couldn't tease me," he drawled.

Ellery laughed. She wished they could linger the way they deserved, reclaiming every moment they had so foolishly denied themselves. But the rest of the country could only wait so long.

"If we're going to be the first Chosen Ones to survive our cataclysm, then I think we're meant to do more than just save Alderland," she said, sobering. "I think we're meant to change it."

"So do I. *This* is what the prophecy meant by peace. No more ghosts. No more scurges. And Summer and Winter wands serving Alderland side by side."

"That's what I want, too. But even with the right wielder paired with a winterghast heart, in Winter territory, we still couldn't make a Winter wand."

Domenic's fingers traced up and down her arm thoughtfully. "So what do you think would need to be different?"

Ellery hesitated. For all they'd promised each other, she didn't know if he could promise her this.

"I think Summer would have to cede territory permanently. An Alderland that's split between the two seasons, I guess. Is that a compromise you can make?"

"Of course I can," he said immediately, fervently. "For people to stop living in terror of the day Winter arrives? For magicians and civilians both to stop dying in a pointless war? That's worth sacrifice. That's worth anything."

The only acceptable response was to kiss him again. After how close she'd come to surrendering all hope of their shared future, the truth burned deliriously within her. Domenic Barrow was as much a part of her as her magic, and she could no sooner uproot him from her heart than she could purge Winter from her veins. Of course loving him was her destiny. It could be nothing else.

Abruptly, the bedside lamp cut out. The room darkened, but the darkness bore a heaviness, as if the air Ellery breathed crushed her from the inside out.

"What was that?" Domenic gasped against her lips.

"I-I don't know."

Simultaneously, they bolted from the bed. Ellery yanked open the window shades and uttered a horrified noise.

It was midday, and yet a false, sunless twilight was suspended across the firmament. No lights shined in any neighboring windows, no lampposts glowed on the streets, no billboards glared from atop the buildings. Gallamere, the City of Magic, had gone dark.

And above it, descending in a terrible oblivion, was a storm.

It was a winterscurge at its beginning: frost just sharp enough to grate against the window glass, winds that whined rather than wailed. But it wasn't the storm's power that horrified Ellery—it was its size. It smothered the skyline, vaster than anything she'd ever lived through, even heard of. Yet as she searched for a heartbeat, she couldn't feel Kythion's, nor any other winterghasts as its source. It didn't have one. It was nothing but Winter magic—unbridled, ravenous magic—threatening to devour the city she loved.

"This is it, isn't it?" she rasped. "This is the cataclysm."

Domenic staggered back from the window, the ember gleam of his eyes the only hint of him in the darkness. "You're right," he choked. "This is it. I feel it. I feel this . . ."

"Dread," she finished gravely.

"All right. W-we don't need to panic. Even if we can't thwart the cataclysm before it begins, we can still stop it before it gets worse." Domenic riffled through his discarded clothes until he wrenched Valmordion from his pants pocket. Its core ignited, and he stumbled as he held it and dressed. "But what do we do? Do we fight this thing like a scurge?"

"I don't know if that'll be enough," Ellery said. "Chosen Ones can't defeat the cataclysm until they finish the prophecy. And we haven't."

"Then we finish it. Right now. I know we've been going in circles about the traitor for weeks, but things are different now. We have each other."

His words steadied the more he spoke. And they steadied Ellery, too.

"You're right," she said. "Where's Iskarius?"

He cocked a brow. "I believe it's where—"

Ellery flushed. "I remember now." She darted into the living room, then snatched her wand from the carpet and cast a light. It illuminated the slivers of ice creeping like ivy across the floorboards. A vase swept off her mantel in a gust of wind, then shattered.

She hurried to the closet and yanked hanger after hanger aside, overwhelmed with the suddenness of so many decisions, both significant and trivial. For all Ellery knew of fashion, she wasn't quite prepared to choose an outfit for the potential end of her world. She pulled on a pair of thick woolen trousers and a random sweater, then shoved her feet into combat boots.

"If Summer's traitor isn't me, or you, then who *is* it?" Ellery called.

Domenic appeared at the closet entrance, still buttoning his shirt. "I've got no clue. I really don't. We've interrogated every last member of the Order."

"Is it possible it could be someone outside the Order?"

"What, like a hedge magician?" he asked skeptically.

"No, that doesn't seem right. And we know it's not the Winter magicians, either. It has to be someone with real power. Someone important."

He barked out a stressed, high-pitched laugh. "'Ms. Prime Minister, ma'am. Sorry to disturb you in your hyper-insulated bunker, but are you actually working to dismantle the current magical order?'"

Ellery laughed direly in return. "There must be something we haven't thought of, something we missed. Someone Hanna didn't . . ."

She froze.

"What?" Domenic asked uneasily.

"Hanna," she breathed.

He snorted. "You're suggesting *Hanna* is the traitor? I don't know . . . If Hanna wanted to destroy the country, believe me, it'd already be ash."

It did seem preposterous. Hanna had given more to the Order than almost anyone. But as Ellery searched for another suspect, she struggled to let the thought go.

"She's the *only* magician with a Living Wand who hasn't been questioned."

Domenic paused tucking in his shirt to study her incredulously. "Well, no shit. She's the one doing the questioning."

"And yet after all this time, we've made no progress. She could tell us anything, and we'd believe her. Everyone trusts her word. She knows all about the Order's plans, its defenses, its weaknesses . . ."

"You can't tell me you're really considering this," he hissed. "Hanna would never betray the Order."

"We have to consider everyone—"

"Hanna would never betray *me*."

Ellery reflected on her conversation with Hanna in Nordmere. How Hanna had seemed not just suspicious of Ellery, but deeply bitter. How much the burdens of Hanna's own duty clearly weighed on her. How, like Ellery, so much seemed buried below her surface.

"I know it's a horrible thought." Ellery rested a hand gently on Domenic's chest, right above his heart. "But she's our only lead. And we're running out of time—"

"Exactly. And this would only be a waste of it."

"Do you have a better idea?" she demanded, drawing away. "Because we can't just do nothing. The cataclysm is *here*. And it's only going to get worse."

Domenic stared, haunted, out the window at the oncoming storm. Then he dragged a hand down his face, smoke leaking from his nostrils.

"Fine," he surrendered. "We'll find her. We ought to, anyway. Because once we prove it isn't her, we could really use her help."

XXXIX
Domenic
WINTER

By the time Domenic and Ellery arrived at the Citadel, the scurge had worsened. Frost hurled through the wind in whole, dagger-edged shards, and blackness choked the city like a dense smog. The figures who sprinted throughout the Citadel's atrium resembled specters, their shapes blurs, their fluorescent-orange NDC gear rendered sepia within the gloom. Nature magicians positioned themselves at every entrance. Enchantment magicians cast extra protection atop armor, extra fortifications across the Citadel's grounds. Corporeal magicians readied healing stations, while battlefield medics bundled to follow soldiers into the storm.

Domenic and Ellery bolted past them all, cloaked from sight. They couldn't afford to slow down, not for morale, not even for aid. The Order's only true hope of surviving the cataclysm was the Chosen Two obtaining the next prophecy piece and learning how to defeat it.

They ducked inside an empty elevator. But as Ellery reached to press the top button, Domenic immediately slammed the lowest.

"Wouldn't Hanna be with the Council?" Ellery asked.

"She isn't," Domenic said. "I can feel her."

He fixed his gaze on the closing doors to avoid the suspicion in Ellery's eyes. Whatever reason Hanna had to be in the subterranean levels while the rest of the Order prepared for war, it was a legitimate one. Hanna would help them find who the real traitor was. Then they'd stop this nightmare. They'd save everyone.

As they descended ever deeper, Domenic glanced at his hands. He was trembling.

He reached for Ellery's own. They locked their fingers tight.

The doors opened into the damp tunnels of the Citadel's underground. They ran past the vigil chamber until Domenic slowed at the Vault's entrance. Even amidst all the magic within it, he could sense Syarthis's suffocating, feverish heat.

"Hanna!" he shouted. "Hanna!"

Silence.

"Dom," Ellery said warningly. "Why is she here? What could she possibly be doing?"

Domenic had no answer. He stalked across the aisles, his thudding footsteps disturbing the Vault's reverent quiet. Then he halted at the final one. In the distance, a small figure slumped upon the floor.

"Hanna!"

Every candle flared as he ran past. But as he neared her, something slowed his pace. Hanna was not collapsed but rather sitting cross-legged, utterly still. He cringed as Valmordion's light flooded over her. At the celebration this morning, Hanna's hair had been swept back. Now it hung stringy around her face. Tracks of dried blood streaked down her cheeks. And her eyes gleamed with a glossy sheen, rolled back so far they were nothing but white.

As he approached, her irises slid down like slots. Until they froze, locked directly on *him*.

Hanna rose, swaying, and a sudden pressure crushed against Domenic's muscles, his bones, his windpipe. He knew he was only imagining it, no different than the red he blinked from his vision. But his body couldn't be sure.

"Wh-what is it, Hanna?" he stammered. "What are you doing down here?"

Ellery slowed to a stop beside him. She pointed Iskarius.

Domenic seized Ellery's forearm and wrenched it down. "*Don't* hurt her."

"I'm not trying to," she hissed. "I'm trying to disarm her. Look at her wand."

Domenic whipped back toward Hanna. Her grip on Syarthis was so tight that her knuckles had paled to match the aspen wood. And as he peered closer, he realized Hanna wasn't simply holding Syarthis—her skin had fused to it, the tips of her fingers crusted with bark.

"*Hanna,*" he said desperately. "Why won't you say anything? What's wrong with you?"

Still, Hanna gave no answer, made no expression at all.

Then, with a jerky hand, she raised Syarthis.

This time, when Ellery lifted her wand, Domenic didn't stop her. Yet when he tried to do the same, he couldn't. He was paralyzed, aching, petrified.

"That's not her," Ellery murmured.

Domenic already knew that, yet he still struggled to piece what was happening together. He'd never heard of a wand possessing its wielder before. But even if Hanna had insisted otherwise, she'd been pushing herself to the limit for years. Still, however much Hanna unnerved people, her perpetual scowl, her crassness, her unkempt appearance, Hanna was unmistakably *good*. She'd never hurt anyone on purpose, let alone Alderland, let alone him.

It couldn't be her. It wasn't. It *wasn't*.

Then, as Syarthis's gaze bore at him and only him, the full awful truth clicked into place.

"It's not Hanna who's the traitor," Domenic rasped. "It's Syarthis."

Ellery hitched her breath. "Could a wand really be capable of that?"

"Syarthis isn't like the other wands," he answered, and shame throbbed in his chest when he thought of how terrible Hanna had looked all Winter, how exhausted. How she seemed to snap in and out of focus. How often she'd hovered silently in the corner of the room, holding Syarthis, always holding Syarthis.

It had been possessing her on and off for *months*.

She was his best friend. How couldn't he have seen it?

A glow gathered at Syarthis's tip, and immediately, Ellery conjured a shield between them, glimmering with prisms of light. But before Syarthis cast anything, Hanna's left hand shot toward its hilt. Her arms shook as she tried to wrest it down, fighting against her own body. One of her eyes thrashed, like a prisoner trapped.

Domenic's exhales stuttered out in spurts. Syarthis's corporeal magic might've been unparalleled, but it still was a Living Wand. And like all the Living Wands in this room, it answered to Summer. To *him*.

"Tell me what you've done," Domenic commanded. "What treason did you commit?"

Suddenly, Hanna's free hand slackened, falling subdued to her side. Her other rose higher, until the tip of Syarthis pressed against her throat.

"Don't . . ." Domenic croaked. "Don't hurt her."

"I don't think it will," Ellery said.

"We don't know that. It could—"

"Look at its eyes. Look at it trembling."

She was right. The hand gripping Syarthis quivered, and sap trickled like tears from several of its eyes.

"I don't think it *wants* to hurt her," Ellery said.

A sound escaped Hanna, a quiet hiss, *"Take . . . risk?"*

At first, Domenic was certain he'd misheard. But of course Syarthis had to be capable of speech. It knew humans, had bonded with dozens of wielders and devoured countless memories from countless minds.

He couldn't risk it hurting Hanna, but he also couldn't waste time deliberating. Every second he squandered brought them closer to Alderland's doom.

Yet before either he or Ellery reacted, another glow shined from Syarthis, searing Hanna's throat.

Immediately, Domenic raised Valmordion.

Invading Syarthis bore no resemblance to invading Maltherius. Despite the two entities being counterparts, Syarthis had spent a millennium as a wand. It was more human. It knew how to defend itself from another's mind.

It knew how to fight back.

At once, a terrible pressure pulsed within Domenic's skull. Memories he hadn't dwelled on in years were suddenly pried open: thirteen-year-old Hanna dragging Domenic along for an abominable Saturday at the Aldrish History Museum; Domenic lying that her first train ticket to Gallamere had been paid for by the Order when really it was his parents who did; the week Domenic had lurked alone and unsure in Iseul's home, after he'd been discharged—and she hadn't.

Domenic whimpered at the pain of it—his skull pounding, his heart breaking. He wrenched open his eyes, and the memories faded. But so, too, did his tether to Syarthis.

"Dom, are you all right?" Ellery asked.

"I-I . . ." he sputtered, but he was too ashamed to answer.

He couldn't do this. He couldn't save her like she'd once saved him.

"How can I help you?" Ellery urged.

Domenic swallowed. It felt like a betrayal to need her to.

But as he closed his eyes to try again, another memory shuddered through him: the spit on his and Hanna's hands as they shook them, a solemn vow.

You and me, twelve-year-old Domenic had declared. *We're going to be great together.*

"I-I need you to hold back Syarthis's power," Domenic gasped. "*Please.* I'm Summer. I'm connected to Syarthis, just like all the wands here. But I can't focus enough to subdue it if all I'm thinking about is . . . is how much this feels like that day."

"I'll block the worst of it," Ellery said. And though Domenic didn't see her cast her spell, at once, he felt the relief of it. The pain drilling into his temples eased to a subtle pinch.

Domenic pushed against the pressure of Syarthis's magic with all the force he had. And, like sediment collapsing, the pressure caved in. Suddenly, though his eyes were closed, he *saw* things. Roots that extended in all directions, thousands and thousands of them—like the entire vastness of the alban network contained in a single wand. Countless spider-thin hairs sprouted from the roots, twitching, and the longer he stared at any particular one, the more it unraveled. As he touched a finger to one in his mind, he saw images. He saw memories.

He was in Syarthis's Archives.

It was so different than the pilfered hoard Domenic had always imagined. It was wilder, more primordial. But of course it resembled a tree, when Syarthis itself was crafted from—

Distantly, he heard a thump. With effort, Domenic opened a single eye to see Hanna lying limp in Ellery's arms. Hanna's skin had gone flushed. Blisters peeled across the hand that held Syarthis, just as the invasion of Valmordion's power had burned Tej Kumar. But no sooner did terror seize Domenic than Hanna's wounds receded.

"Syarthis is healing her," Ellery said, her relief a mirror to his own.

"How did you betray Summer?" Domenic asked Syarthis again, fiercer this time.

In his mind's eye, the Archives' roots rustled. One of the closest tendrils began to glow gold, and the moment Domenic touched it, the light brightened, and its memory unfurled.

"I'm in one of Hanna's memories," Domenic breathed. "In it, she's here. In the Vault. And it's . . ."

It was the very night Hanna had dragged Domenic here for his intervention. He could tell because of her muddied boots and the humidity of Summer still clinging to the air. Yet Domenic was no longer with her, and despite the scene happening from Hanna's vantage point, he realized instinctively this wasn't her memory at all—it was Syarthis's. It had been controlling her, even then.

Anguished, Domenic continued. "It's walking her to the door in the Vault's corner. I hadn't even noticed it when I was here. I think it . . ."

"What? What is it?" Ellery whispered.

"Remember how I told you after we bonded with Val and Izzy, the Council gave me the first piece of the prophecy on a leaf? They told me that it'd grown in the same place where all the past prophecies had first grown. Somewhere sacred beneath the Citadel. Well, I think *that's* where I'm watching Syarthis take Hanna. And it's the same night Hanna brought me to the Vault. The same night Valmordion thawed. The same night the words of the prophecy first appeared."

Indeed, in the memory, Syarthis opened the door into a cavern. Roots tangled over its ceiling and walls, iron-thick and starkly white.

The roots of Gallamere's alban tree.

"I see it," Domenic continued. "The leaf they showed me—it's the only one left. And Hanna's plucking it. But I-I can't read the words on it, for some reason."

Even as Hanna stared down at the leaf in her hand, its image blackened, as if an ember had ignited in its center and was spreading, seeping over the entire memory.

Syarthis had tampered with it, somehow. Maybe to hide it from Domenic. Maybe to hide it from Hanna herself.

"And now Hanna . . ." Domenic clutched his stomach. He tasted bile. "She's *tearing* it. The leaf with the words of the prophecy—Syarthis destroyed it before anyone else ever saw it. A-and now Hanna's pointing Syarthis at the alban roots, and there's a new leaf sprouting. And the words on it, 'an ancient peace must be restored' . . . El, that's *our* prophecy. The first piece, the one the Council showed me, Syarthis wrote it. It's *fake*."

Domenic fell to his knees beside Ellery and Hanna. The very shape of the world felt changed beneath him.

"What did the true prophecy say?" he demanded, seething.

Syarthis stared at him but gave no answer.

"Why would you do that?" he shouted. It was disorienting to yell at Hanna when it was Syarthis he was truly yelling at. But he was so furious he couldn't be sure that was true. Even if he should've noticed something was wrong with Hanna a long time ago, shouldn't she have noticed, too? If Syarthis had been controlling her for months, certainly her memories had holes, inconsistencies. Why hadn't she told anyone? Why had she always, *always* insisted she was all right when she clearly wasn't? *"Why?"*

This time, the Archives responded freely. The roots coiled around him, and Domenic squinted into the flashes of millions of memories. Even Domenic, so often overwhelmed with emotion, had never felt a deluge of it like this. Though none of these memories belonged to him, he *felt* their pain; he *felt* their sorrow. And so did Syarthis.

In the deepest chasm of the Archives, ancient memories shined. Glimpses of untouched forest. Of mountains and rivers whose names he knew but had yet to ever be spoken.

"Syarthis wants . . . release," Domenic said, and though he wished to feel no sympathy for this monster, despite himself, he did. "Not from any magician, but from *all* magicians. From humanity. It wants to return to what it was before it became a wand. A ghost, I guess. Or something like it."

"So Syarthis sabotaged the true prophecy because it wanted us to fail. It *wants* this cataclysm—the final cataclysm—to come to pass. Because it thinks that if it does, the Living Wands will fall." Ellery gazed around the Vault with horror. "Th-that must be why it came here. To wait. For itself to change. For all the others to join it."

"Then how do we learn what the prophecy truly said?" Domenic choked. "Not even Syarthis knows anymore. The memory is destroyed."

"Maybe we never will," Ellery whispered. "But we *can* get the next piece. We know the traitor, so now, according to destiny, we have to—"

"Condemn it," Domenic finished. He swallowed.

On Ellery's lap, Hanna shuddered. Syarthis's healing magic had begun to falter. Her blisters spread, blooming bloody around her collar, her chin. Her chapped lips darkened as if with char. Smoke wafted from her breath.

Panicked, Domenic reached toward Hanna. Then he froze, his fingers hovering inches from her shoulder. For years, he'd buried thoughts too despicable to confess, yet no matter how deep they lay or how much he hated himself for them, they were still there.

All this time, it had not just been Syarthis that terrified him, Syarthis that disturbed him.

Finally, he grasped Hanna and tried to prop her against him, gentle even as he cringed. Her hair smelled greasy and burnt, yet he pressed his forehead to it. He held her tight. "Hanna, if you can hear me, I need you to last a little longer. I need you to survive this."

With one hand squeezing Valmordion, Domenic rested his other over Hanna's eyes. He envisioned his magic as Hanna had always described her own—like a needle. As soon as it touched her, she thrashed—or Syarthis thrashed, it didn't matter. He felt her heart accelerate, felt the fragile skin around her sockets begin to burn. Yet he didn't stop. Not until the heat of Valmordion's power surged through her bloodstream. Not until he scorched every trace of Syarthis out.

At last, Hanna stilled. Her hand went limp, and Syarthis clattered onto the stone floor, its eyes closed in slumber. Still condemned to be a wand, but bonded to a wielder no longer.

In the terrible silence that then fell, even so deep underground, Domenic could hear the dim raging of the storm outside. The storm that was coming for them all.

And in the storm, he heard words.

from where the magic of Summer and man
united, and the land was forged anew,
restore dominion to a dying throne
through your sacrifice you shall build your own

Ellery also stiffened—she'd heard it, too.

"It has four lines," Ellery breathed. "This is the last piece."

After everything Syarthis had done, Domenic couldn't call it a victory.

An immediate scan of corporeal magic told Domenic that Hanna was still alive, that her pulse was, inexplicably, strong. But still he couldn't bear to let her go. He'd broken so many promises to her, yet he had a horrible suspicion that when she woke, she would never forgive him for this.

XL
Ellery
WINTER

Ellery watched, stricken, as Domenic lowered Hanna gently to the Vault floor. He'd healed the worst of her burns and injuries, but a few remained—Syarthis's bark had separated from her hand, peeling off strips of skin along with it. But they did not wake her. The mind was a fragile organ; to rouse Hanna so soon after an unbonding might risk irreparable damage.

"Dom, we have to go," Ellery rasped. "The storm's only getting worse. I know you feel it, too."

Domenic rose, his gaze feverishly focused even as he swayed. "I do, but we have the final piece now. And once we fulfill it, we can stop the cataclysm. We still have an hour, maybe two, until the storm goes full—"

"But we have no idea what the first lines of the prophecy even said!" Ellery's panicked words echoed through the Vault's deserted aisles. She, too, stood. "Everything could be different—we know Syarthis wanted us to fail, so if it told us to believe in an ancient *peace*—"

Domenic grasped her shoulder. "We believe in peace because we know it to be true. We *feel* it. So we're not gonna let this distract us. We keep moving. The last piece of the prophecy told us to go where Summer and man's magic were united."

"Summer? But the piece didn't . . ." Ellery swallowed. "What exactly did you hear?"

Shock flickered across his face. "What did *you* hear?"

Ellery spoke:

where devastation left the land a grave
revive the past and claim a new future
bring Winter glory on a silver throne
the whispers of the trees will guide you home

Domenic staggered back, knocking into a wand case. The nearest candle flickered wildly, as though disturbed by an invisible gust of wind. "Destiny told us different things."

He recited his own piece.

With each mismatched word, Ellery's dread deepened. Frost wafted from her mouth, and Iskarius's core pulsed in time with her ratcheting heartbeat.

"So we split up," she managed. "I have to go to the Barren. That must be what destiny wants."

"And I need to go to the room where the prophecies grow. The room I saw in Syarthis's memory."

His throat bobbed, and Ellery braced for him to retract his adamance that they were still meant to save each other. Instead, he sheathed Valmordion and pulled her into his arms. He crushed his lips against her forehead. Ellery buried her head in his shoulder and clutched him tightly, so tightly.

"Go to the Barren," he told her. "I'll take Hanna somewhere safe before I finish my own piece. We'll find each other after. And we'll calm the storm together."

Ellery wasn't sure she believed him, but as she released him and left, she tried to.

She tried.

She tried.

XLI

DOMENIC

WINTER

Domenic carried Hanna down the winding corridor to the Citadel's elevator, and he did so without magic. Magic had always defined their friendship, their effortless talent, their unrivaled strength, but now he felt he owed her his strength, his effort.

As he suspected, the Council's floor was in disarray. Frosty wind whirled through shattered windows across vacant cubicles. Yet the few magicians who sprinted past didn't bother to mend them. Some wore NDC gear over their office clothes, preparing to join the teams fending off the storm. Others raced to gather irreplaceable documents and artworks.

As Domenic emerged, several skidded to a halt. One saluted. The others only gaped at him, at Hanna.

"Where is Councilor Seong?" he demanded.

"Sh-she's with the president, sir. They're down the—"

Domenic didn't wait to hear the rest. With his hands too full to draw Valmordion, he kicked open the door to Sharpe's office.

Sharpe shouted a curse in surprise, and his eyes bulged as he took in the sight of Domenic and Hanna. Then he spoke back into the telephone, "Yes—sorry, Prime Minister. I'm . . . Well, what the fuck do you want me to say?! Of course the situation isn't under control. . . ."

While he continued his conversation, Iseul lunged toward Domenic, who knelt and rested Hanna on the emerald carpet. "Oh my . . ." Iseul's mouth quivered as she took in Hanna. "What happened?"

"I don't have time to explain," he told her. "But you need to get her out of the city—"

"But the Order needs Syarthis, Dom. If not to fight beside Tenney, then to heal the magicians who—"

"I severed Hanna's bond with Syarthis."

Iseul uttered a quiet sound of horror. Even Sharpe balked, dropping the phone so that it clattered atop his desk.

"You . . ." His face reddened. "You did *what?*"

"I had to. Syarthis was the traitor. But it's going to be all right. Ellery and I—we have the last prophecy piece. We're gonna fulfill it. We're gonna stop the storm. But . . ."

He cut off. It was one thing to feel the storm worsen; it was another to gaze out the window, at what should've been Gallamere's skyline, and see nothing but whorls of darkness. Even through the reinforced glass, frost had begun to invade, creeping up the wall and ceiling like skeletal fingers. Some of it had clawed across Sharpe's portrait, shriveling his already shriveled glower.

"*Please,* Iseul. Take Hanna and get out of Gallamere. I'd feel better knowing you're both safe."

"Oh, Dom. I'm so sorry. I-I don't even know what to say." Tears brimmed in Iseul's eyes, and she threw her arms around him. "I know you'll stop this, though. The way you've risen to your destiny . . . It takes real strength to do all that's been asked of you and still have such a kind heart."

Domenic tensed. For all he'd sworn confidence to Ellery, he did not feel strong.

But he didn't confess his doubts to Iseul. He only allowed himself the small relief of letting her hold him, if just for a moment.

"Th-thank you," he managed.

"I love you. I love the two of you, so, so much."

"I love you, too."

After their goodbyes, Domenic tried hard to banish his dread.

It didn't matter how dire the odds. If his heart was truly what made him strong, he knew what his heart was telling him, same as it had always told him.

Domenic Barrow would always fight for a happy ending.

Ellery

WINTER

Ellery emerged from the back of the Citadel to an assault of blaring alarms and furious winds. Debris whipped past her, withered leaves and trash and snow, so much snow, slicing into her with serrated teeth. It resembled a category three scurge, yet it was like none Ellery had ever faced. It churned in a colossal tempest across the horizon, seething with terrible power and terrible promise. Ellery didn't know when the storm would reach the ceiling of its strength, if it even had one. The lone undefeated cataclysm in Aldrish history had obliterated the country's western regions. But whatever her and Domenic's prophecy truly predicted, it *was* the final one, the ultimate cataclysm. If they didn't stop it, it could wreak extinction.

Ellery ached to fight it, if not to stop it than at least to shield everyone she could, to defend her home.

But until she and Domenic finished the prophecy, it was a fight she couldn't win.

NDC vehicles were parked haphazardly in a nearby lot. Ellery found one with the keys left on the dashboard and scrambled inside. She started the engine, jammed her foot down upon the gas pedal, and sped down the block, dodging non-magical cars left abandoned in the road. She drove past parents carrying children and yapping, panicked pets, past dark windows and doors hanging open on their hinges, as though people had fled in too much of a hurry to shut them. The radio stations all blared static.

The storm worsened as Ellery drove toward the Barren. Ice crusted on her windshield and dimmed her headlights; snow flurried through her vents, collecting in her hair. She gripped Iskarius with one hand and the steering wheel with the other, casting frantic spell after spell to clear the glass and keep light beaming upon the treacherous road. Once, she nearly hit a ghast as it stampeded across the pavement, wheels skidding frantically as she swerved at the last second.

Ellery's chest heaved as its blue eyes disappeared from her rearview mirror. If she'd seen one, there had to be more.

The Barren was even worse than she remembered. As she ran through the desolate forest, Ellery's light spell illuminated the carnage of her and Domenic's battle with Eledrium: some trees were gone, obliterated by their magic, while others lay like bodies frozen to the ground. Although snow crusted the dirt, scarring still peeked through like rotted veins in the land.

At last, she found the clearing with the dead alban tree: the trunk cracked in two, its leafless branches clawing at the sky as though frozen in perpetual agony.

Ellery was positive the prophecy piece had led her here—*where devastation left the land a grave*. But now she contended with the rest, all of it maddening.

revive the past and claim a new future—maybe she was supposed to heal the tree. But she and Domenic had failed to heal this tree before.

bring Winter glory on a silver throne—Ellery had no idea what that meant.

But the final line did hold significance: *the whispers of the trees will guide you home.*

"The alban network," she said aloud. When she and Domenic had fortified the network at Winter's beginning, the alban trees whose roots connected across Alderland had felt so alive, had seemed to whisper with every rustle. Maybe, if she could reconnect this tree to its brethren, she could revive it.

She didn't know how doing so would stop the storm. But she didn't have time to question it.

Ellery pressed her palm to its mutilated trunk. Immediately, silver glowed around her hand.

Previously, she'd felt the power of the alban trees intrinsically, her own magic melding to their tangled roots as though extensions of each other. But this time, she felt no such power. She grasped Iskarius and shut her eyes, trying to block out the barrage of wind and snow. Then she reached out beyond the tree's ossified roots, searching for any sign of life with which to forge a connection.

Until, at the very edge of her awareness, she felt Winter's territory.

Ellery hadn't been able to sense Winter's trees when she'd fortified the network. But at the time, she'd yet to visit Winter's territory, yet to feel how much stronger she was there. Now that strength flooded through her, pouring into every groove and crack in the dead wood beneath her hand.

A great, heaving groan sounded overhead. Ellery's eyes shot open, then widened as the two halves of the tree knitted back together. Gray bark flaked away, revealing fresh ivory wood beneath. Buds sprang open across the branches, then bloomed into delicate flowers. Silver plums grew from them until the branches lowered, creaking, weighed down by the sudden bounty.

But it was not just the alban tree that resurrected. The terrible scars throughout the forest faded, and saplings burst through the ground. Bushes sprouted between them, some dense and adorned with red berries, some thinned and coated in ice.

The Barren was barren no more.

It was Winter territory. And it was beautiful.

Ellery tipped her head back, wishing, hoping. But the storm didn't wane. The cataclysm hadn't been defeated. Maybe Domenic hadn't fulfilled his own prophecy piece yet. But no, that didn't make sense—if she'd truly fulfilled the final piece of the prophecy, she should have what she needed to defeat the scurge.

"What else am I supposed to do?" she called into the wind.

Frustrated tears pooled in her eyes, and she felt so powerless despite being surrounded by evidence of her strength. "How do I s-stop this? I've always done everything you've asked of me, and here I am, regrowing this random fucking forest when the entire country's about to get annihilated, and if I fail, if I can't save everyone—"

Ellery cried out as pain burst through her palm. She tried to wrench it from the tree, but something tethered it there. Her veins bulged as roots wound beneath her flesh, then burrowed deeper, and deeper, as though infusing themselves into every inch of her muscle and marrow.

This time, it was not her reaching out to the alban network—it was the network reaching into *her*.

Impressions and images of Alderland coursed through her mind: woods striating across the country; mountain peaks marbled with snow; waves roiling upon rocky cliffs. Suddenly, the Nordmere alban loomed before her, the same tree where she'd first discovered her magic. Its leaves rustled in ominous greeting.

Although Ellery hadn't touched it since she was a child, it bore her silver handprint.

The agony continued until Ellery swore the roots had wound all the way into her heart. She scarcely recognized the sound of her own whimpers; they felt so distant, so human.

She returned to herself, panting. Iskarius glowed searingly bright in her grasp. When she at last yanked her hand from the trunk, its print had indented deeply into the bark.

But although Ellery no longer touched the tree, her connection to the alban network remained, anchored to her grip on her wand. Iskarius had always felt like an extension of her own magic, but now that magic was far vaster and wilder than ever before. She had been broken, then remade. She *felt* the whole of Winter's power across Alderland. Somewhere far away, a pine forest swayed as she shuddered. A lake rippled with her sigh.

Ellery understood now why the prophecy had led her here.

She no longer simply wielded Winter—she *was* Winter. But there was a price to so much power; if she died trying to defeat the cataclysm, Winter's hope of ever becoming more than monstrous would die with her.

She was truly Winter's champion now.

But along with that thought came a terrible dread. A branch lowered before her, just as when she'd made her wand. A fresh leaf budded on it, then grew. Faded words were webbed through its veins.

Ellery reached for it.

 XLIII

Domenic
WINTER

Within the cavern where all prophecies had first grown, Summer's champion gasped for breath upon his knees. Alban roots threaded across every crook and crevice of the stone around him, entirely white except for the golden handprints beneath his palms.

A lone leaf sprouted beside him.

Fearful yet still hopeful, always hopeful, Domenic reached for it.

XLIV
Destiny

as Summer wilts and Winter lays its siege
an ancient battle shall be waged anew
and from the ruins only one endure
or see the land destroyed forevermore

XLV
Ellery
Winter

Snow lashed against Ellery as she knelt in the once-Barren's clearing, sobbing. The leaf that had borne the true beginning of the prophecy was crumpled in her trembling hand.

One line replayed in her mind. Again. Again.

and from the ruins only one endure

For all that Domenic had stoked Ellery's hopes, it was only now that any chance of peace had been ripped away that she realized she, too, shared the blame for their grand delusion. She'd wanted a happy ending just as desperately as he had; she'd convinced herself just as wholly as he'd convinced her.

But she and Domenic had never been destined to fall in love.

Around her, the storm's darkness had encroached ever closer, so stifling that she couldn't see beyond the bounds of the clearing. She cast a light, squinting into the violent wind. Freshly grown trees bowed and bent. Plums tore from the alban as it lurched back and forth.

So this was to be their great feat of magic that would stop the cataclysm, their so-called heroic sacrifice.

A duel.

Summer or Winter. His life, or hers.

Maybe she should forfeit. When Ellery had drawn her wand on Domenic this morning, she'd been driven by panic more than logic. To fight him now felt like a different choice; if it were just a matter of her life for his then she would choose Domenic's without hesitation. She didn't want to be in a world without him in it.

Maybe the world would be better without her anyway. Winter had been Alderland's greatest enemy for a millennium; if its champion died, it wouldn't be eradicated completely—it was too much a part of the land to be fully destroyed. It would merely be subdued again.

But no. *No.* Even if she died, the winterghasts would return year after year. This senseless, awful war would forever continue.

Yet if she won . . .

Ellery stood, surveying the land she had resurrected: every ruby fruit, every evergreen bough. For all Winter's terror, it contained beauty, too.

With her victory, it would be Winter that ruled Alderland. Surely then she could create new Living Wands. And though Summer might be weakened, it would never be the enemy Winter had been. Its own wands would remain. After all, Syarthis had sought to revert to what it had been before. If it had believed Ellery's victory alone could accomplish that, it would've tipped the scales in her favor, not sabotaged both her and Domenic in hopes that they would never duel, and the cataclysm would go unthwarted.

Six weeks of Summer wasn't balance. But Ellery could double the size of the Order while freeing the country from ghasts and scurges in the process. It was as close to peace as Alderland could hope for.

And so, Ellery made her choice. She'd fight for Winter.

But that choice didn't change her heart. She would still love Domenic Barrow until the day she died, even if she was the one to kill him.

XLVI
Domenic
WINTER

Domenic held his head in his hands. Since the alban network had burrowed within him, *changed* him, he had the surreal notion that as he trembled, so, too, did the earth around him. He felt every root of the alban rattle throughout the mountain. He felt all the roots woven throughout Alderland shudder with a seismic grief. He felt so much.

Too much.

Until his grief faded; his despair ebbed. Yet he did not feel peace.

He felt nothing at all.

Domenic staggered out of the cavern and through the Vault. In the minutes he'd spent fulfilling the final piece of the prophecy, the elevator had lost its function. So he stumbled up the stairwell. Each time he braced his hand against the wall to steady himself, its imprint scorched the stone.

The Citadel's central floor was in disarray. Even indoors, the winds whirled with broken glass as well as frost, the debris grating across the marble floor. Domenic shielded his face with his arm and pressed dazedly through the grand doors to the steps outside.

The city of Gallamere was gone.

Despite looking out from the mountain's zenith, Domenic could not see it, its skyline obscured by the storm. What nearby shapes he could make out were blurs: the slivers of blackened lampposts, the tangled masses of overturned trees, the silhouettes of other magicians. Up and down the Citadel steps, they rushed past, their heads bent low against the freezing, lashing gusts, their faces indistinguishable beneath their gear. Wands gleamed as he approached, Summer's supposedly great champion. And their magicians turned, baffled until they saw him, squinting at his radiance. A shadow of golden light shimmered beneath him. Several cheered at his presence, their hope so desperately bright.

Domenic didn't acknowledge them. Then a figure suddenly seized his shoulder—only to release him, cursing violently. Domenic spun to face Sharpe hunched over, bundled in a down coat and cradling his burnt hand.

"Y-you're here," Sharpe sputtered, gawking at Domenic's antithetical shadow. "Finally. I've got the entire Order out here and in the city, but it doesn't matter how many ghasts we slay. There's no slowing this storm."

Domenic didn't respond.

"*Well?*" Sharpe demanded. "Seong said you were leaving to finish the prophecy. So have you? Do you know how to stop this? And where's Caldwell?"

In the darkness beyond, a chorus of winterghasts screeched—hundreds and hundreds of them. An invasion.

Sharpe's mouth quivered. "What the hell is wrong with you? Didn't you hear that? Aren't you going to do anything? *Say* anything?"

The nothingness throbbed in Domenic's chest. He couldn't answer.

Yet Sharpe seemed to understand enough. He grimly surveyed their surroundings, then, with his jaw locked tight, he pointed Ballathim toward the dim outline of the Citadel. With a deafening groan, its exterior shifted, ancient bricks huddling closer together, fresh mortar weeping from their cracks, crumbled cornerstones hardening and sealing tight. It was astounding. It was incredible. And while Sharpe hacked out coughs of exertion, while the very wand that had first constructed the Citadel fortified it once more,

Domenic turned and wandered down the steps, without a destination, without any purpose at all.

As he neared the front lines, the panic around him descended into chaos. Winterghasts advanced toward the Citadel as if in siege. At first, the magicians who battled them attempted to keep formation, but any semblance of order quickly shattered. There were too many monsters, in all manners of grotesque shapes and sizes, and in the ever worsening scurge, they had the advantage. Domenic passed bodies splayed on cobblestones, already half-buried in snow. In their limp, frostmauled hands, he glimpsed wands he recognized. They belonged to students who'd once walked the halls beside him, magicians whose hands he'd once shaken, once promised he would save.

It wasn't their fault Domenic couldn't bear his destiny. Nor was it fair they should bear the consequences. But if Domenic could speak, he would tell them the world wasn't fair.

Then something caught in the corner of his vision—an orange light.

As Domenic moved toward it, he realized it was no simple beacon. Targath's power had carved a sanctuary out of the storm, light and heat cascading in a shield that covered the mountain's entire eastern slope. Over a thousand people crammed within it, battle-weary magicians and city personnel and civilians all together on the slushy pavement. Up the hillside, Peak stood within a cluster of parked and toppled cars, several of them smoldering with flame. Winterghasts drawn to Targath's heat swarmed toward him, and no sooner did he slay one than another took its place.

Yet he never stopped fighting, not even to catch his breath.

Something stirred like bile in Domenic's chest. Peak was an even greater fool than he was.

As Domenic watched him, his sight flickered. Its edges broke like fractals, yet he couldn't focus enough to know if he was hallucinating. For the first time since he'd entered the storm, a chill shuddered through him.

Thirty yards uphill, Peak froze, then he craned his head back. Domenic realized he, too, sensed something. But if the other magicians had noticed it, they made no move to act—they only stared at Peak with desperation, with awe.

Then above Peak, something glinted, like a spark of electricity.

Domenic sucked in his breath, but even when he tried, he couldn't force it out in any shape, not Peak's name, not a warning, not even a scream. He could only watch as lightning crackled across the oblivion, the tempest so loud that whatever thunder followed was drowned out. Two tremendous eyes beamed open overhead, monstrously blue.

Peak's eyes widened in alarm, and his bad knee faltered as he spun around.

In a bolt of lightning, Kythion's claw shot from the sky and speared through Peak's abdomen.

Domenic's lodged breath escaped him in a gasp. He clutched at his own stomach as Targath's magic blasted outward in a fiery shockwave, making a nearby car explode and several members of Peak's audience fling themselves aside.

As Kythion wrenched its arm away in a burst of crimson, the sanctuary collapsed, and darkness fell like a guillotine. Yet the ghost still loomed above, still peering at Domenic through the black.

Domenic froze. The nothing he felt splintered, cracked.

Then, as if dismissing him, Kythion turned instead to another magician, who clambered frantically away. Electricity sizzled in the wake of Kythion's movements as its icy hand stretched toward its prey.

Until Domenic hurled a barrage of magic toward it.

He fought furiously, deliriously, one enchantment immediately following the next. Like grenades, they detonated across

Kythion's gargantuan frame. Gouges of ice shattered across it, re-forming mere seconds before Domenic destroyed them again. Until a mass the size of a train car collapsed upon the steps, and Domenic's spell lanced straight through the monster's exposed heart.

Kythion shrieked, a sound like a meteor strike. A network of explosions ruptured across it, so bright the surrounding, cowering magicians ducked so as not to be blinded. Then the stone of its heart smashed onto the concrete, and Domenic stared at the blackness where the beast had just been, and, finally, he screamed.

He didn't know what made him tread toward Peak, as it couldn't have been hope. Yet after Domenic cast a scan of corporeal magic over the body, he still flinched from a fresh blow of despair.

It wasn't fair.

But Domenic didn't allow himself one more moment to grieve—he didn't deserve it. Lifting Valmordion, he let his magic roam beyond to where he felt her, the true enemy he needed to slay.

She was close, and growing closer.

She was on her way.

Domenic couldn't bring himself to look at Peak again, but he did gaze out at the people around him, left to shiver in the dark.

They needed a hero.

And although the legacy Summer had built wasn't perfect, it was a nation, a people, a home.

"Thank you, sir," someone gasped, making Domenic startle. It was the magician he'd saved from Kythion, his gear shredded and askew. "But is Peak . . . is he . . . ?" He glanced down at the body, and Domenic didn't answer—he didn't need to. Sure enough, hopelessness caved in across the man's face.

Domenic's grip tightened on Valmordion, with purpose. Then he pointed it at the sky. Gold beamed through the scurge, carving a new sanctuary within it over the whole of Gallamere.

He couldn't fend off the cataclysm forever, but he would buy time for Ellery to arrive.

For their duel to begin.

"Go find Sharpe and tell him to shelter everyone underground," he commanded the magician.

"B-but the storm—"

"*Everyone,*" Domenic repeated. "I will face the cataclysm alone."

XLVII
Ellery
Winter

As Ellery entered the Citadel's grove, she barely recognized it amidst the storm's destruction. Leafless trees wailed and shuddered as the winds contorted them and stripped away their bark. The cobblestoned path was slicked with ice, and the cataclysm seethed around her with palpable fury. But as she neared the alban tree in the grove's heart, the storm shifted. Its gales retreated from her. Directly above, its clouds thinned, just barely, so that a frail light broke through. Until an eye opened within the scurge across the grove, a small stretch of solace.

And as soon as Ellery sighted the tree, she knew why.

Domenic awaited her beneath it.

The storm had not given them solace. It'd given them an arena.

Domenic was unmistakably remade, just like her. His shadow shined golden. Heat wafted around him, blurring the air like a mirage. Valmordion remained sheathed at his side, and so Ellery sheathed Iskarius, too.

But she didn't lower her defenses.

His gaze raked over her as she stepped closer. "Hi."

"Hi," she echoed. Then, softly: "You know the true prophecy now, don't you?"

He inclined his head. "I do."

"And you chose Summer."

"Just like you chose Winter."

Yet again, they were the same. But the reality of the task ahead still nauseated her. Ellery pushed it down. She would swallow this even if it poisoned her.

"I should've known it would end here, in the grove," she murmured. "The first place Valmordion and Iskarius met."

Domenic's voice cracked. "So were we just fools, then?"

Instinctively she stepped closer, wanting to comfort him, to comfort herself. Then she halted, grimacing. Domenic was dangerous. Not just because he was Summer's champion. But because she still couldn't see him as her enemy.

"Maybe we *were* fools," she said. "But Syarthis still hid the truth from us."

He scoffed. "Oh, come on. The only reason Syarthis got away with so much was because I refused to accept Valmordion at first. Because you already had a prophecy piece, and I didn't. But as soon as I bonded with it properly, I got mine. The one I should've had from the start."

Painful realization fissured through her. If he'd had a prophecy piece from the beginning, he never would've gone looking for her, and their story would've been entirely different.

Except the ending.

"We thought we were fulfilling each other's prophecy pieces, but we weren't," she choked. "They've always been two separate prophecies. They were never meant to be combined." The vortex of the storm seemed to press in tighter around them. "We thought we were meant to do this together, but we've been on different paths all along, haven't we?"

XLVIII

DOMENIC

WINTER

Domenic couldn't bring himself to respond. It ached enough to speak at all, to gaze at her looking so monumentally beautiful. Silver glinted wherever her skin was thinnest—around her eyes, above her collarbones, along her throat—as if her very bones were diamond-made.

Ellery had chosen Winter, and he understood her reasons, even if he didn't agree with them. But he wouldn't beg her to change her mind, just as he knew she wouldn't ask such a thing of him. This was the truth of who they were, the destinies that had stalked both of them their entire lives. They wouldn't demean each other by suggesting this be a willing execution.

Still, even with the knowledge that Ellery was his enemy, had always been his enemy, Domenic couldn't see her as a monster.

Between them, the splintered bough of a tree broke through the eye and whipped across the cobblestones. At once, Domenic reeled in his thoughts. His task was already unspeakable; it did no good to make it harder for himself.

A tear trickled down Ellery's cheek like a bead of glass. "D-do you wish you could take it all back?"

At once, his composure tore like the flimsy thing that it was. A sob racked through him.

"I don't know," he answered, because he felt he owed her his honesty. "It'd sure be easier if the answer was yes. Because the way I feel right now . . . this is agony."

Now Ellery, too, broke into a sob. "You still understand. And you're the only one who ever will."

For a time, they stood there, staring at each other as if pretending this brought either of them any comfort. Because all Domenic could think was that this was it—this was the final time he'd get to talk to her, to look at her.

But with each additional second that crept past, more and more Domenic felt his mind stray into a ruthless part of himself, a part he didn't even know existed. They were stalling. But he didn't know how to begin what happened next. He still had so much he wished to say to her. That he loved her. Or at least goodbye.

But none of the last words he conjured felt enough to suffice. And all the ones that came close were too painful. Despite resigning himself to kill her, he couldn't possibly hurt her.

Domenic wasn't sure who moved first. But suddenly, he was breaking toward her, and so was she. And in an act of what could've been either self-preservation or destruction, he took Ellery Caldwell in his arms, and he pressed his lips to hers.

XLIX
Ellery
Winter

The kiss brimmed with longing. Every breath that passed between them was another wish wasted. No goodbye could express what had been ripped from them, what had never been theirs to begin with.

Still, they tried.

Ellery attempted to numb herself, but she couldn't staunch her emotions. With Domenic, she never could.

The kiss became annihilation, her defenses stripped away, her heart bared and bloodied between them. He had excavated every piece of herself she'd buried, and this was her reward: to feel each moment of the battle to come, to bear the full grief and guilt of his demise. It would hurt until she followed him to the grave. It would be agony.

At least she could spare him suffering. She could make it painless. Quick.

Slowly, she reached for Iskarius. Until a searing heat flared against her, and she jolted away from Domenic as he, too, drew Valmordion.

They backed away from each other, wands raised.

They fired their first shots at the same time.

L

DOMENIC
WINTER

Like two stars colliding, the end began.

Magic exploded across the grove, and wherever the ice devoured, there was fire to melt it, then water to douse it. Back and forth, their battle waged. The trees leaned in close as if to watch, even as the leaves were wrenched from their canopies, as the weight of icicles snapped their branches from their boughs and flames scorched their bark until they warped and crumbled into cinders. Uncontained, their duel could make a wasteland of the world.

Domenic had always known his power to be great. Yet to feel it and to witness it were two separate things entirely. With a single moment of distraction, he could carve a gorge across the continent. He could shatter the very sky.

I will shield Gallamere, he promised.

Her death will be painless, he promised.

I will save everyone, he promised.

Yet as the storm beyond the eye worsened, as spell after spell was thrown, still neither he nor Ellery had come close to achieving a killing blow. It was too much to manage all three.

Anguished, Domenic let the sanctuary he'd cast over the city fade. He apologized to Ellery in his heart. For all his vast, devastating power, he was still making promises he was doomed to break.

He could keep one.

LI

ELLERY

WINTER

Ellery bled. A gouge oozed from her left palm from when she'd fallen and braced herself. Her shoulder throbbed where she'd slammed it, so much her arm quivered as she aimed Iskarius. For all the power at her command, she was still human. Her bones could still break. Her muscles could still give out. Her body could only take so much.

And yet each time the debris settled, the smoke cleared, she frantically searched for him.

It was a terror each time she spotted him. For all Domenic also bled and heaved and staggered, he still lived, still fought, his power as formidable as her own.

It was a relief, too.

DOMENIC
WINTER

Across Gallamere, Domenic felt the effect of his enchantment's end.

The streets were deserted, cars left abandoned with frost splayed over windshields and water frozen in exhaust pipes. The power citywide had long since gone out. People crowded in makeshift fortresses of apartment buildings, schools, and hospitals, bundled in layers and carrying what little they could afford to deem precious. With today's promise of the dawn of Summer, firewood supplies had all been freshly, measuredly depleted—and so they burned all manner of flammable refuse scavenged in the storm's early hours: books and newspapers, furniture and fence posts. Victims of frostmaul already lay curled upon sidewalks, in subway stations, even in homes where the cold had crept through the subtle cracks of thresholds and windowpanes. And despite Domenic's command that Sharpe shelter the Order magicians, there were too many ghasts to truly abandon their defenses, all converging on the Citadel.

In the storm, no one could see the battle unfolding upon the summit. Even the magicians nearby could only glimpse a dim flash of light, hear the whisper of explosions.

Until, with a deafening *boom,* a crack cleaved through the earth and split the mountain apart.

LIII
Ellery
WINTER

They wrought ruin around them.

A nearby hillside collapsed, dragging down the historic building upon it and exposing a cliff at the edge of the grove—if it could still be called a grove. Only the alban tree remained, the others fallen, charred or splintered down to mangled stumps. Whatever structures once stood in their vicinity had crumbled. Several burned.

It seemed today Ellery Caldwell would destroy every home she'd ever had.

Domenic, too, swayed with horror as he took in the decimation around them. He panted, his shirt stained with soot, the embers of his eyes aglow as—

Something snapped around her wrists and wrenched her backward. Ellery shrieked as white branches seized her, tethering around her ankles, her stomach, her mouth, so forceful that Iskarius slipped from her grip. The alban tree dragged her backward, and she slammed into it, gasping as the air was knocked from her lungs.

She thrashed, whimpering. But she couldn't free herself. Iskarius lay close, so close. But she couldn't reach it.

The earth tremored as footsteps strode toward her.

The storm shuddered as Ellery hitched her breath.

Slowly, fearfully, she looked up to the boy she loved, aiming Valmordion at her heart.

LIV
DOMENIC
WINTER

Domenic nearly retched at the sight of her: her countless wounds, her limbs pinned down in the tree's rigid embrace, her eyes wide with terror as they met his own.

He had never felt less like a hero.

Yet as Domenic tried to steady his trembling hand, an idea bloomed in his chest. He couldn't tell if it was real or only a stupid, desperate want.

You know better than to trust yourself, he scolded.

But it was too late. The idea took root before he could prune it, and suddenly it was sprouting, blossoming, the very thing that had always cursed him, that he inflicted on everyone around him.

Hope.

From the start, their love had been wrong, yet it had never once felt that way. And even if their story hadn't followed the original route destiny intended, Domenic could not fathom any path that could've brought him here, to the very act he was meant for, had Ellery not walked beside him on it.

So what power did fate truly hold if any path could diverge from it at all?

And thus, as their perfect tragedy came to its awful end, Domenic Barrow hesitated.

 LV

Ellery

Winter

Ellery Caldwell didn't.

While she and Domenic stared at each other, subtly, Ellery flattened her palm against the alban that held her prisoner. Within it, Summer's magic pulsed, fervent and warm, but she thought of what she'd done at the Barren, and she poured her magic into the wood, and she claimed the tree for Winter.

The golden leaves above withered.

The branches binding Ellery released their hold.

The roots ruptured from the broken earth, and while Domenic flailed back, Ellery lunged forward.

She snatched Iskarius. She raised it to his heart.

Domenic's expression went stricken, and as he righted himself, he sputtered, "El—"

She cast her spell.

Ice burst across his chest, radiating outward, and immediately, whatever words he meant to say broke into a scream. It clawed a violent path across his skin. Its shards punctured through his shirt, making crimson seep and spread through the white fabric. It encased his hands, his face. Until the lips that had once pressed against hers turned purple. Until the light of his shadow vanished. Until her sense of him dimmed, dimmed, to the barest flicker of a flame.

Ellery sobbed through every moment of it. No matter how much she'd longed to believe otherwise, there was no love stronger than destiny. There was no fate colder than this.

At last, the warmth of his magic extinguished, and he was gone.

She'd won.

Yet although it was Domenic's life that had ended, not her own, Ellery still felt as if she'd taken her dying breath alongside his.

LVI

DOMENIC

WINTER

He suffered.

Merciless, agonizing cold seared across his skin and clotted the blood in his veins, and the ice entombing him tightened its grasp while his insides froze and bulged, and the scream he'd cried out crystallized into a sheath across his lips, and the frost stabbed needles into his eyes and his broken heart battered his ribs like an ice pick and the terror, the *failure,* lashed through him, a storm of its own, until the heat within him sputtered, then waned, then finally, hopelessly snuffed out. For all that he'd sacrificed, for all that he'd agonized twisting himself into someone greater than he was, he'd ignored a simple possibility.

His destiny was a terrible one.

LVII

ELLERY
WINTER

The instant Domenic's heart stopped, Valmordion ignited.

Flames erupted across the wand's shaft, and as its core flared, so too did the center of Domenic's chest. Golden light radiated outward, brighter and brighter, until he was a molten silhouette.

Then they both shattered in a blaze of magic.

Ellery had no time to react. Shrapnel thorns and jagged ice stabbed into her skin, and her flesh burned from the explosion's searing, roaring heat.

She careened back, her wails scarcely audible over the debris thudding atop the pulverized cobblestones and the ground rumbling beneath her. Blisters swelled upon her cheeks. Her neck. Her shoulders. Ellery frantically cast a healing spell, but although the burns stopped spreading, they didn't mend.

Sunspots spun dizzily in her vision as she blinked at the scorch marks where his body had stood seconds ago. But Domenic and Valmordion were gone.

Gradually, the vortex surrounding the eye began to slow. The darkness dissolved like smoke, and true pristine sunlight poured into the grove, beaming through the alban's branches. Above, the foreboding clouds thinned, then dissipated, revealing a cerulean sky. The barrage of winds diminished into a gentle breeze. And the temperature rose, brutal, frigid cold lifting into a crisp chill.

The scurge was gone.

She'd defeated the cataclysm.

Ellery stared at the leaves on the alban. They had turned to silver. To Winter. She felt the rustle of every root throughout

Alderland, from coast to coast, and knew that she had not just transformed Gallamere into Winter's territory—she'd transformed the entire country.

But she felt no pride at her victory, only a distant relief.

Then a tide of grief swept through her, overwhelming, unbearable. She doubled over, whimpering. Her burns throbbed in agony. But after the brutality of Domenic's demise, it was an agony she deserved.

In the absence of the storm, sound infiltrated: the roars and shrieks of winterghasts, the wailing of sirens, and human screams, a horrifying cacophony.

Ellery jolted upright. The cataclysm was gone, but the battle for the city was far from over. Which meant she couldn't break, not yet.

She ran through the ruins of the grove, then inside the Citadel and down familiar corridors, all deserted. Pain lanced through her with every breath, alongside the stench of scorched flesh and singed hair. Finally, she burst outside again and skidded to a halt atop the entranceway stairs.

Ellery scarcely recognized the Gallamere sprawled before her. Skyscrapers decapitated by the storm's winds. Rooftops torn off and scattered. Smoke pouring from gouges in the buildings. Ice floes drifting in a dead man's float across the river. City streets crusted in dirty snow.

She took in the nearby carnage in grisly detail. Frostmaul-riddled bodies slumped across the steps where she and Domenic had given their first press conference. Exhausted magicians dueled with winterghasts down the length of Main Street, the trees that had once lined it snapped in two, the great gates at the end wrenched violently open by claws.

Ellery picked out familiar magicians in the fray; Tej Kumar speared a ghost with a ray of sunlight conjured from his training wand, fighting back-to-back with Demelza, who blocked a monster's blows with a luminescent shield.

"Ellery!" Glynn rushed to her, clutching Aetherium. His glasses were cracked, one sleeve of his jacket torn and bloodied. She struggled to process careful, measured Glynn wounded in battle. "The scurge is gone! Does that mean you and Barrow—" He cut off, eyes widening as he took her in. "You need a healer. You look . . ."

"N-no," Ellery rasped. It hurt to talk. "I already tried."

"What could possibly. . . ." Glynn sucked in a horrified breath. "Did *Valmordion* do this? And you've survived, but Barrow's not here. Oh, Ellery . . ." He surveyed the city, as though noticing for the first time that despite the lack of a scurge, it was still cold.

Then his expression hardened, and he leaned in, voice low. "We can't let anyone see your burns. They can't guess at how you got them. Do you understand?"

Tears blurred Ellery's vision, and with a sick lurch, she realized her performance was not over.

"I understand," she whispered wretchedly. She cast a hasty illusion over herself. A mask to hide her injuries, her terror, her all-consuming guilt. And not a moment too soon, because Sharpe limped up the stairs. Crimson wept down one of his legs, but he still held himself upright.

"There you are," he said urgently. He clasped Ballathim with both hands. There was something terribly wrong with it. Strips of its blackthorn wood peeled away and crumbled into dust.

"Wh-what's happening to it?" she stammered.

"It's *dying*," Sharpe snarled. "Just like all the others. You have to fix this. *You have to fix this.*"

Ellery took in the battle before her with a new, terrified focus. Gold magic sputtered out as the Living Wands disintegrated in their wielders' hands. Ghasts advanced upon newly defenseless magicians. Cries of horror rang out across Main Street.

No. This doesn't make sense.

But for however well Syarthis knew the past, it couldn't predict the future. It had been wrong about Living Wands enduring unless the cataclysm came to pass. With Winter in control of Alderland, the Summer wands couldn't survive.

The Order was destroyed. And it was all Ellery's fault.

But the magicians didn't know that. Gaze after gaze turned to her. Beseeching. Begging. Clinging to hope that she would save them even though she was the one who'd condemned them.

Ellery couldn't bring back what was lost, but she alone could protect what remained.

And now that Winter ruled, its champion could finally end this war for good.

She staggered to the center of the steps. Then she pointed Iskarius down at Gallamere and listened for the winterghasts' heartbeats. First she heard several, then a dozen, then too many to count, thumping within her rib cage in a massive, erratic rhythm.

Her shadow undulated like a train around her, then spilled across the city she loved, seeping in rivulets down every alleyway, every sidewalk, every bridge. It engulfed Mercester Square and the Crystalline Pavilion. It swept across Gallamere Gardens. And within its tenebrous embrace, one by one, the winterghasts began to glow. Silver pinpricks shone across the streets, each creature gleaming as they succumbed to her power.

"Surrender," she commanded.

In a great ripple of refracting light and shining ice, the winterghasts bowed.

Then they disappeared, evanescing into clouds of frost. The seeds of their hearts clattered to the ground in their wake.

Ellery heaved out breath after breath as her shadow shrank. Unbearable pain coursed through her burns as she lowered Iskarius.

Then she turned from her awestruck audience, and she crumpled.

LVIII
Ellery
WINTER

Ellery dreamed of burning. Flames crashed against her in excruciating waves, then yanked her down in an undertow of memory. And yet she didn't wish to resurface, even as her flesh blistered and charred and peeled away, leaving nothing behind.

At last she bolted upright, the name on her lips crumbling to ash before she could speak it. Her hands were clenched in starchy, unfamiliar sheets. Iskarius sat on her bedside nightstand. She stared blankly at the rest of her surroundings: neutral, impersonal furniture, a window with the curtains pulled shut, bland canvases hanging on beige walls. She was in a private infirmary room at the Citadel.

"You're awake." A person sitting at her left stirred, then rubbed his face.

"Julian?" Her throat felt raw and crusted over.

"So you know who I am now. That's good."

But before he could say anything else, she coughed, and a clump of blood and wet soot splattered into her lap. An echo of Summer's magic seared through her chest. Sweat beaded at her temples.

"I should be dead," she rasped.

Domenic's face flashed in her mind, frozen, agonized; she whimpered; she thought she might faint, *wished* it even—

"Hey," Julian said. "It's okay. You're okay."

Her vision blurred as he kept speaking, and reality blurred

along with it. She clutched frantically at the sheets, trying to ground herself. It was several minutes before her sobs slowed and her breathing steadied.

Julian handed her a glass of water. As she drank, her gaze caught on the hilt at his waist. Cold, clammy magic pressed against her.

"Is that *Maltherius*?" she gasped.

"Yes," Julian said somberly, and drew his wand. His *Living Wand*. Maltherius wasn't identical to Syarthis, but the resemblance still unnerved her. Its aspen eyes were clustered closer to its hilt, and there was a symmetry to the grain in its bark and the precise triangle of its point that reminded her of Julian.

Its eyes turned toward her, then blinked all at once, as though curious.

"A Winter wand," she murmured, scarcely able to believe it. She had fought so hard for this moment, this victory. "Are there more?"

Julian smiled. "Yeah, El. There are more."

Fresh tears welled in her eyes. "How many?"

"Forty-one, as of this morning. Although the number increases every day. The Order's still trying to hunt down all the seeds the ghasts left throughout the city, but—"

"Wait. How long has it been?"

"Since the cataclysm? Ten days."

"Ten days," she echoed, trying to process it. "I was unconscious for a week and a half?"

"Well, the Order was using training wands to keep you alive at first. It was all they had left."

"So the Summer wands are really gone. Every single one."

A haunted expression stole across his face. "Yeah."

Somber silence stretched between them, and Ellery wondered if he too was thinking of that morning not so long ago when they'd sat in the student lounge and dreamed of their bright futures. Before they'd known Valmordion had thawed, before any of it.

She could scarcely recall who she'd been. She could scarcely fathom who she'd become.

Julian cracked his knuckles. "Anyway, that's, um, that's part of why healing you was so rough. By the time I got down here, it was a struggle just to stabilize you, so I've pretty much been sleeping here to stay on top of it. Honestly, I was starting to worry you wouldn't . . ."

As he trailed off, Ellery took him in more closely. His usually crisp collar was rumpled, his dark coils disheveled. His sharpness seemed blunted by exhaustion.

"You saved my life, didn't you?" She reached for his hand. "Thank you." Julian blinked in surprise as she squeezed it. Then, cautiously, he squeezed back.

"You're welcome. But it was the least I could do after you saved Alderland. After you saved *everyone*."

Words echoed in her mind, once so comforting, now accusatory:

What if you save me, and I save you, and we save everyone else?

Ellery tugged her hand back. "Y-you don't know what I had to do."

"I do, actually," he said gravely. "And I know I was harsh with you about Barrow back in Nordmere, but . . . I'm so, so sorry, El. I know it must've been a terrible choice to make."

But he didn't. He couldn't. The only person who possibly could understand was gone.

"But you did what destiny asked of you," Julian continued. "You shouldn't blame yourself for that. And if those wounds are any indication, he almost killed you, too."

Yet Domenic hadn't killed her. He could've. He could've been the one to walk away as Alderland's savior. It should've been *him* waking up beside people he loved.

Instead, he'd hesitated. Maybe he hadn't been able to go through with it.

And Ellery had.

Even if destiny did bear the blame, it'd been her hands that had held Iskarius. Her magic that had cast the killing blow.

"Who else is gone?" she asked.

Julian grimaced and rubbed the scar on his brow. "They're still working on the final count, but several hundred civilians at least, including some hedge magicians. A few . . . a few students. And around fifty from the Order, including Councilor Peak."

Ellery stiffened, stricken. All those people she'd failed to protect. And Peak—she hadn't known him the way Domenic had, but the man had been kind to her.

"But you saved countless more lives than the ones that were lost. If you hadn't stopped the cataclysm, it would have destroyed the country. Not to mention, you single-handedly tamed an army of winterghasts. And ended a thousand years of war."

"Still, savior or not, Alderland must despise me," she said wretchedly. "I destroyed Summer's wands."

Julian shook his head. "No one hates you. No one blames you for that."

"But how? Why?"

He hesitated. Then he shuffled through some odds and ends on a nearby table before pulling out a copy of the *Gallamere Gazette*. Ellery snatched the paper from him and gazed at the headline.

A CHOSEN ONE MOURNED

Domenic's obituary was peppered with photographs of his funeral, which had taken place the week prior in Danmere, organized by his family—how he would've hated that. His body hadn't yet been recovered, but Ellery knew there was no body left to find.

She skimmed the article, growing more distressed with every word. The spin was clear: he and Ellery had faced the cataclysm together, yet where she'd triumphed, he'd perished, and thus the

Summer wands had perished with him. The scales of Alderland had tipped in the aftermath, leaving it suspended in a new, peaceful Winter.

As far as the obituary was concerned, he hadn't died a hero. He'd died a martyr at best, a failure at worst.

"None of this is true," Ellery choked. "This is awful. Why would the Order let this happen?"

"The Council will explain, as soon as you're able to meet with—"

"Oh, fuck that. I'm going to meet with them right now."

"You can barely sit up."

In response, Ellery reached for Iskarius. As soon as she touched it, strength surged through her. The aches in her body didn't vanish, but they eased. She exhaled, frost twinkling into the air, and pushed aside the bedcovers.

"Is there anything better to wear around here than my hospital gown?" she asked.

"Yeah, in the wardrobe. Although you should probably shower first."

Ellery glared at him, then touched a strand of greasy hair. He was right. But no sooner had she stomped to the adjoining bathroom and shut the door than he called, "I should warn you—"

"What else could you possibly have to warn me about?"

She heard his sigh through the door. "I couldn't heal everything. Even Maltherius has its limits."

Slowly, Ellery opened her hospital gown. Bandages crisscrossed her torso. She peeled back one on her chest, above her heart. The skin was blistered and raw, just like in her dreams.

"They'll scar," Julian continued. "But aside from that, you should make a full recovery."

Ellery bit back a terrible laugh. "Right."

As she pressed the bandage back down, her fingers grazed the edge of the wound. Instantly, an image of roots veined within her eyelids. She saw a flash of a familiar alban tree. Her handprint gleamed upon its white bark.

Nordmere.

She blinked, and it was gone.

* * *

Ellery walked with Julian across the Citadel's campus, through winding pathways dusted gently with snow. Someone had brought clothes from her apartment to the Citadel, so Ellery wore a familiar wool dress that covered her wounds. She didn't bother with a jacket.

She gazed down at Gallamere's skyline, no longer familiar. Several iconic buildings were gone. Others were partial rubble. But much of it, most of it, hummed with life. Smoke puffed from chimneys; lights glowed in apartment windows. The pond at the center of Valley Park gleamed like a hand mirror. Flurries drifted peacefully through the air. And a crystalline layer of ice glistened across the rooftops.

The City of Magic sparkled like a diamond beneath it.

But for however beautiful Gallamere looked dressed in Winter, the Citadel was less so. In the absence of Summer wands, the enchantments that had maintained the compound had faded, although Julian assured her that Winter magicians were already at work replacing them. Yet some things could never be replaced. Every holiday was changed. All the works of Glynn's favorite magical philosophers, every wand that had made Alderland special, wondrous, great, rendered obsolete. A thousand years of tradition, overturned. By *her*.

"I know it's still a bit rough around the edges, but we're rebuilding," he said. "Soon enough, the Citadel will be the pride of Alderland again. Winter magicians can run the country just as well as Summer magicians. Plenty of us were already academy students, anyway."

Ellery supposed that was true. She glimpsed several new Living Wands as she and Julian walked past, clutched in the hands of some former classmates. The cold of each wand's magic needled at her skin.

"Have any adults been able to bond with a Winter wand?" she asked.

"No, not yet. I'm pretty sure the window rule still applies."

People gaped at Ellery as she passed. Their gazes darted from Iskarius in her hand to her bright blue eyes and the shadow that feathered behind her, moving of its own accord. They whispered. They murmured. They stared at her with awe.

At last, they'd decided she was a hero. But Ellery knew better. She was a monster after all.

They reached the door of a familiar conference room.

"You should have some privacy with them, I think," Julian said seriously. He stepped aside, and Ellery entered.

Sharpe and Glynn were inside, engaged in an intense discussion. At the sound of the door opening, they both glanced up. Glynn rose from his seat and rushed to her, then wrapped her in a hug. Abruptly, he jolted away, gasping. Frost coalesced on his hand where it had brushed her arm.

Ellery knew that after fulfilling the final prophecy piece, she'd changed. But she hadn't realized how much. She swallowed and sheathed Iskarius, severing her connection to Winter's power. Then, surprising herself, she hugged *him*.

This time, she wasn't too cold to be touched.

"You're truly awake. You're here," Glynn said incredulously, drawing away. "When I visited yesterday, Norwood said . . . Well, we weren't expecting you back so soon. How are you feeling?"

"Alive," Ellery answered hoarsely. "Mostly."

"Caldwell. You pulled through." Sharpe's voice was unreadable. He looked different without Ballathim, less imposing—his smoldering cigarette a paltry substitute. Glynn, meanwhile, appeared almost identical without Aetherium.

"Where are Seong and Hanna?" Ellery asked, sitting. It was

them she dreaded seeing most. She didn't know how she could look either of them in the eyes.

"Mayes is gone." Glynn sounded pained. "Seong evacuated her during the cataclysm, and they spoke. But apparently Mayes fled soon after, and we haven't tracked her down. We believe that she ran to avoid the repercussions of her and Syarthis's crimes."

"So you know about Syarthis?" asked Ellery cautiously.

"Yes. A wand as Summer's traitor. It's no surprise we didn't see it coming," Sharpe muttered. "Seong claims Mayes wasn't fully aware of what Syarthis was doing to her, that she hadn't a clue Syarthis tampered with the prophecy until you and Barrow confronted her in the Vault. Seong feels we should've caught how badly the girl was managing—felt guilty enough to resign, apparently. Between that and Barrow's . . ." He took a drag of his cigarette. "I don't buy it, though. If Mayes believes herself blameless, why would she run?"

"I don't know." Ellery didn't believe that Hanna herself had truly wanted to hurt Alderland. And she understood what it was like to live with the constant pressure of being judged for what she wielded, rather than who she was. But Syarthis had almost destroyed the country. It had threatened everything Ellery had sworn to protect. And it had put her and Domenic through unimaginable anguish.

"Given what Seong told us, it didn't take a genius to figure that the true prophecy must've compelled you both to duel," Sharpe continued. "Not to mention the state of you. Guess Barrow put up a fight on his way out."

Ellery flinched.

"Sharpe," Glynn said warningly. "Surely even *you* should know to be more sensitive."

"What? It's not like tiptoeing around what happened will make it any better. The only reason the public hasn't gotten wind that we were wrong about the prophecy is because of how quickly we've been salvaging the situation."

"This is what you call salvaging?" Ellery demanded. "Insisting Domenic was a failure? Blaming the Summer wands on him?"

"I assure you, we didn't relish it," Sharpe grunted. "But we had no other choice."

"No other choice?" Ellery had always been so careful with the Council. She was through with being careful. "He died fighting for you! You and your wands, and your magic, and *this* is how you want the country to remember him? This is his reward?"

"Ellery," Glynn cut in, "we know how much you cared about him, but—"

"No! He's a hero. You know he is. He deserves to be treated like one."

"Our opinion of him doesn't matter," Sharpe said grimly. "If we tell Alderland the truth, well, he still lost, didn't he? And you go from the country's hero to its villain. It's not pretty. It's not nice. But the Order still has a duty to this nation, to rebuild from the brink of disaster." He sighed, exhaling smoke. "And it's not as though the boy's around to cry over what they're saying about him now."

"So you used him when he was alive, and now you'll use him for whatever story you need to spin after he's dead?" Distress seethed in her. "That's how it's always been, hasn't it? Every single Chosen One who's died for Summer. How convenient that they never made it past their cataclysms."

Glynn recoiled.

"You knew?" Sharpe asked.

"Oh, yeah, we figured that part out weeks ago! That everyone else who had our shitty job died! That you lied to us!"

"I wanted to tell you from the start," Glynn said vehemently. "But you *did* make it out, Ellery. You survived your cataclysm. You—"

The door banged open, and a familiar figure stalked in. Immediately, Ellery felt a shocking, brutal chill.

"Hey, Ellery," Kester said coolly. They looked just as at home in the Council's conference room as they had in a Nordmere dive bar. In their hand was a wand wreathed in crackling blue veins, like lightning.

Kythion.

"K-Kester?" Ellery stammered. "What are you doing here?"

"Well, where else would I be? It's a Council meeting. I'm kind of obligated to attend." Ellery watched, astounded, as they pulled out a seat and lounged in it. She half-expected them to kick their feet up on the table.

"*You're* on the Council?" she asked.

"We've had to make some changes," Sharpe grumbled.

Julian hurried into the room a moment later, Demelza a step behind him. The magician starlet sank into the seat beside Julian, her eyes glassy, her blond hair limp. She stared at her lap as though she would rather be anywhere else. A staticky cold flared from the hilt at her hip. Although she did not draw her wand, Ellery recognized it, too: Eledrium.

Of course these three had been recruited for the Council. They might've been young, but they wielded the most powerful Winter wands aside from her own. The Dire Three.

"We were about to explain," Glynn said. "We've re-formed the Council with the entire country's best interest in mind. Sharpe and I will train each of our new members to take up their predecessor's positions. Norwood will replace Mayes as our historian. Turner, as befits her background, will take on Seong's responsibilities as head of Public Relations. And although the NDC is now defunct, Wright will oversee the other nature magicians as they transition into a more peaceful role. And perhaps prepare for the slim possibility that whatever resided within our Summer wands are not dead, but . . . changed."

The room fell silent for a moment. Ellery considered the word none of them seemed willing to speak aloud.

Summerghasts.

Maybe Syarthis had gotten its way, after all.

"That makes sense," Ellery said. "But what about me?"

"When you're ready, we hope you'll join us on the Council," Glynn said. "Whatever it is you wish to do, we'll find a position. Perhaps you could be in charge of student outreach like you once wanted. But we understand that you need some time to heal."

"In the meantime, we've got a new role for you," Sharpe said brusquely. "Alderland needs a happy, pretty face to reassure them that everything will be fine. A few interviews here, a few photo shoots there. Whatever the country needs to sleep soundly at night and know that our new magicians still have destiny watching over them. All we need you to do is show up and smile."

Ellery's stomach roiled, and she stood abruptly, grasping for Iskarius.

"I won't play your bullshit parts anymore," she spat. "I did my duty. I'm done."

She turned on her heel and left.

As soon as the door shut behind her, she cloaked herself, then ducked into the stall of a nearby bathroom. One hand clutched the most powerful wand in the world while the other dabbed at her face with toilet paper.

Her blurry gaze focused on a piece of crude graffiti, scrawled in painfully familiar handwriting. Its enchantment had begun to fade:

D. B.—even better than advertised

She let out a sudden, incredulous laugh. It echoed off the tile walls as Ellery trembled, aching for him, his voice, his smile, his touch. It was selfish to crave what she'd so cruelly ripped from the world, yet she did it anyway. Her treacherous heart still loved him. She always would.

She fortified his enchantment so that no magic could eradicate it. Even if the Citadel crumbled to dust, his vandalism would still be there, glinting amidst the rubble.

And as Ellery stared at his words, she knew she would never escape Domenic Barrow. In truth, she didn't want to.

* * *

After months of obligation, Ellery had nowhere to be and nowhere to go. Returning to her apartment was unthinkable. Another version of her remained there, the version who dreamed of an impossible future in Domenic's arms.

As she invisibly wandered the Citadel, something pulled at her, urgent and insistent. Her body seemed to move of its own accord, down abandoned paths that led deep into the bowels of the Citadel. Until she crossed beneath the archway, into the Vault.

Someone had cleared out the cases that had once held Living Wands. In their places, glowing like tiny fallen stars, were hundreds of seeds. They stretched down the aisles, encased in glass, waiting for a wielder to transform them into a Winter wand.

On the wall behind them was a door. It opened without her touching it.

Inside, roots coiled over soil and stone, so numerous they nearly covered the entire expanse of the cavern. As she walked inside, Iskarius's silver core illuminated the ivory: they were alban roots. Two golden handprints glinted on the floor.

In the cavern's center, despite the lack of sunlight, a dozen leaves had grown in a neat circle, like a wreath. Each was blank.

But Ellery knew what would appear on them one day.

Prophecies.

She thought of the Chosen Ones who'd died before her. The ones who'd follow after her. Of Iskarius dormant in the Vault one day, awaiting its next wielder.

Ellery whispered the words destiny had once whispered to her. Now that she understood that she and Domenic had fulfilled two separate prophecies, not one, she puzzled out the pieces that had been meant for her and her alone.

the unveiled truth of everything you are
is power that will rise from your own ruin

Domenic had believed he'd fulfilled this piece during the winterscurge in Oldermere. But as Ellery recalled the fight with Eledrium—how terrified she'd been, how she had almost frozen to death—she felt the significance of that final word: her *ruin*. How she'd overcome it only by admitting that she had always been Winter's Chosen, no matter how long she'd tried to hide from it. It was her power. Her truth.

join an old legacy to a new fate
uncover the tangled roots of the past

Ellery had fulfilled this piece at the solstice ceremony, alongside Domenic. She'd thought it was their joined magic that had triggered it somehow. But that was the night she'd confessed the deepest depths of her past. After a lifetime tangled in her parents' cruelty, she had finally let it go. And she'd looked toward the future.

in treacherous land an enemy lies
but what was lost invasion can reclaim

And of course, Syarthis. For Ellery, treacherous land was Summer's territory, not Winter's. It was the first piece of the prophecy that had been lost. And invasion hadn't meant Summer *or* Winter. It had meant invading the wand itself.

where devastation left the land a grave
revive the past and claim a new future
bring Winter glory on a silver throne
the whispers of the trees will guide you home

Ellery could decipher the first two lines; she'd healed the Barren, then claimed it as Winter's territory. And she'd brought Winter glory after giving herself over to the alban trees. But she still didn't understand the mention of a throne.

And of course, the first piece and yet the last one. This, at least, required no explanation.

> *as Summer wilts and Winter lays its siege*
> *an ancient battle shall be waged anew*
> *and from the ruins only one endure*
> *or see the land destroyed forevermore*

She'd fulfilled it to the letter. She'd nearly followed it to the grave.

Ellery stared at the wand in her hand. She wielded the ancient, primordial magic of an entire season. Yet even she was not as powerful as the force that truly controlled this land: destiny.

But destiny could be tampered with. And for all superstition claimed that destiny knew the future, its words came piece by piece. It was responsive. Reactive.

Maybe it wasn't all-powerful.

Maybe it could be changed.

Maybe it could even be thwarted.

EPILOGUE

Amidst the peace of Winter's reign, one alban tree had failed to flourish. Its branches were bare. Its trunk had shriveled into a husk, the gray roots splayed around it as brittle as straw. It was a grave wherever they touched.

It had once been a meadow.

For several months, the land where the tree stood remained undisturbed, regarded as a haunted place, a lifeless place.

Until the first day of Summer came.

As sunrise blazed molten across the horizon, a scorching wind tore from the east, tinged with smoke and warning of storm.

The barren alban rustled with it. And though no leaves sprouted, no flowers bloomed, a magic kindled within the roots. The arid earth shifted. The dead grass whipped flat, revealing a shape that hadn't been there before—the corpse of a boy.

His eyes were closed. His face was long and pale, dusted with freckles like specks of ash. A silver scar rippled across his chest in a jagged crater.

As a ray of sunlight seared against him, his lashes twitched.

His fingers curled in the dirt, as if reaching for something he no longer held.

Then his last breath burst back into his lungs with a gasp, and, alive and fearful and shivering, Domenic Barrow realized that destiny dared have more to ask of him.

ACKNOWLEDGMENTS

Eight years ago, the two of us began our All of Us Villains co-writing journey with a shared love for a famous trope: the death tournament.

A Fate So Cold began with such a love for an even more famous trope: the Chosen One. Inherently, it came prepackaged with many themes: heroism and duty, choice and sacrifice—to name a few. And we decided from the start that *A Fate So Cold* would be a love story—and a tragedy. But as captivated with it as we were, we had no idea of the magnitude of the task we'd assigned ourselves.

There have been four truly unique versions of *A Fate So Cold*, not counting several extensive revisions made in between. Over and over, we rewrote the book in order to find the right iteration of our story. To do Domenic and Ellery's heartbreaking tale justice. And though we're tremendously proud of finally accomplishing that task, we never would have succeeded without the help and support of the following people.

First, our entire, fantastic team at Tor Teen, thank you for your faith in us as storytellers and for granting us the time we needed. That team includes our wonderful editor, Ali Fisher, as well as Dianna Vega, Giselle Gonzalez, Anthony Parisi, Lesley Worrell, Heather Saunders, Jeff LaSala, Steven Bucsok, William Hinton, and Devi Pillai. Thank you to our authenticity readers for their thoughtful advice regarding our cast. And thank you to our team at Gollancz for their hard work bringing our book to UK readers.

Our next thanks is to our agents: Kelly Sonnack and Whitney Ross. You have been beside us for every step of this journey with such endless guidance, dedication, and friendship. *A Fate So Cold* simply would not exist without you. Thank you as well to our foreign agent, Taryn Fagerness, who has worked so ardently to see Domenic and Ellery's tale shared across the world.

To our talented, trusted friends: Allison Saft, Rory Power, and Katy Rose Pool—your feedback on our early drafts of *A Fate So Cold* was invaluable. And to the whole of our writing group—Mara Fitzgerald, Janella Angeles, Kat Cho, Amanda Haas, Axie Oh, Meg Kohlmann, Erin Bay, Akshaya Raman, Melody Simpson, Tara Sim, Ashley Burdin, Claribel A. Ortega, Maddy Colis, and Alexis Castellanos—thank you for the retreats, the event and post-event meet-ups, the laughs, the weddings, the years of friendship. We are unfathomably lucky to know each and every one of you.

To Devon and Jo, thank you for your insights and your willingness to read a book we very much emphasized was *not done*.

To Trevor and Ben, who put up with our bullshit—namely, us oscillating between grand soliloquies regarding the literary wonder of tragedies to the depths of despair (and absolute gremlin behavior) as we questioned whether we would ever manage to finish this book—thank you. We love you.

Lastly, and perhaps most importantly, thank you to our All of Us Villains readers. For a book that began on a whim of two best friends, we were both blown away and truly, truly touched by the love that our villainous story received. We hope you loved our heroic tale just as much, even if there was some heartbreak along the way.

In our defense, we warned you Domenic and Ellery were never destined for a happy ending.

ABOUT THE AUTHORS

AMANDA FOODY has always considered imagination to be our best attempt at magic. She is a *New York Times, USA Today,* and indie bestselling author of fantasy novels, including the All of Us Villains duology, the Wilderlore series, the Shadow Game series, and more. Foody lives in Philadelphia, and you can find her on Instagram @amandafoody or at amandafoody.com.

C. L. HERMAN is the *New York Times, USA Today,* and indie bestselling author of atmospheric, magical novels, including the All of Us Villains duology, the Devouring Gray duology, and *The Drowning Summer*. Currently, they reside in Massachusetts with their partner and cat. To learn more, follow them on Instagram @cl_herman or visit clherman.com.